THE LIAR'S BONES

MORAG PRINGLE

Storm
PUBLISHING

Ebook ISBN: 978-1-80508-312-2
Paperback ISBN: 978-1-80508-314-6

Cover design: Lisa Horton
Cover images: Shutterstock

Published by Storm Publishing.
For further information, visit:
www.stormpublishing.co

To the Campbell Family

ONE

The last few hours of Ellen Hargreaves' life were happy.

The day started well. In the morning she spotted the elusive corncrake on her dawn walk on Balranald nature reserve then, a short while later, above the cliffs lacing Hosta beach, two golden eagles. The birds circled for ten minutes, allowing plenty of time for Ellen to record the details in her notebook. The only blight in an otherwise perfect morning was her failure to spot the snow eagle rumoured to have taken up temporary residence near Scolpaig. Maybe tomorrow.

On her way home she stopped off at the Co-op for bread to go with the mussels she planned to have for lunch. A chance conversation with one of the girls on the checkout had given her an important lead. Duncan Mór from Grimsay had once lived on the Monach Islands and knew more about their history than any living soul.

It was all coming together.

If only she knew for sure that the bone she'd found was human. Unfortunately, rib bones were the hardest to identify.

Maybe she'd get a reply from her friend at GUARD Archaeology later today? Ellen didn't have email, her cottage didn't have a telephone, and although she had a mobile it almost never got a signal. All it was good for was taking snaps.

She had to get back out to the Monachs and do some more digging. But she needed someone to take her. Preferably in the next couple of days. Today, with the sun shining and the sea a perfect mirror, would have been perfect.

Her unscheduled visit with Duncan Mór meant she was much later arriving home than she'd anticipated. The tide wasn't at its highest yet, so she still had time to make a quick trip down to the shore to pick the mussels from the rocks near her house. It wouldn't take long to shuck the shells and fry the shell-fish in butter and garlic. Her stomach growled. It had been a long time since breakfast.

She checked the cobbled-together postbox at the end of the track leading to her cottage. Only a couple of flyers from the Co-op advertising bottles of gin and whisky and other essentials at reduced but still grossly inflated prices. Nothing from Glasgow. She hadn't really expected Kevin to have time to study the bone she'd sent him, but nevertheless she was disappointed. Now she knew she might really be on to something she would put some pressure on him to get back to her. She would phone him from a call box later. She couldn't get reception on her mobile out here.

She left her car by the gate and completed the last mile to her cottage on foot. Walking never bothered her even if she was, like today, laden with plastic bags of shopping. As she trudged down the track, Ellen sniffed the air appreciatively. The distinctive smell of peat lingered on the breeze. It was a promising sign. The fire she had lit in the old and temperamental stove this morning must still be burning. Good. She wouldn't have to fiddle around with it before she could cook her meal.

It amused her to live in the same rudimentary conditions as the original owners of the cottage. Well maybe not *exactly*. She didn't really fancy having to use an outside loo, so was pleased that a small shower room had been added, but was more than happy to use Tilley lamps for light and the stove for cooking and hot water. Her needs were simple.

Before she knew it she was at her cottage door. As she was about to step inside, her attention was caught by a boat moored down by the rocks. No one had ever tied up there before – it wasn't safe. The shore was too far away to see who it was, so she fished her binoculars out of her backpack and twirled the knobs until the blurred image of a figure swam into focus. She wasn't sure, but she thought she recognised him. If it was who she thought it was, it was more good luck on a day that had already been auspicious. She left her bag and shopping on the doorstep and hurried off towards the boat.

In the last few moments of her life, Ellen was happy.

TWO

SIX DAYS LATER

Katherine Mowbury ground the toes of her trainers into the wet grass and glared at her mother's back. Katherine's feet were soaking, her fringe had started to frizz, her stomach making unattractive gurgling noises. Fishing a crumpled pack of Benson & Hedges out of her jacket pocket, she struggled with her lighter. Eventually, after turning her back to the wind, she managed to spark the cigarette alight. A few paces ahead, her mother whirled round and glared at her.

'For God's sake, Kat, get a move on. And put that bloody cigarette out.'

Katherine ignored her. What more could Mum do to punish her? She'd already done everything she could to ruin her life. Dragging her to this godforsaken place, taking her away from her friends and her computer, even confiscating her mobile. All because she'd found a couple of Es and a spliff in her room. Everyone did a few drugs. Where was the harm?

Katherine pulled on the cigarette, drawing the smoke spite-fully into her lungs. She had to swallow hard to suppress a cough. In fact, she rarely smoked tobacco, but she wanted to make sure Mum knew what she was driving her to. Happily,

Katherine had managed to source something better to keep her going for the next few days. It was easy when you knew how.

At least it had stopped raining. It seemed to have rained ever since they had stepped off the ferry four days earlier. Who took their holidays at this time of year? In the Outer Hebrides of all places! Outer Fucking Mongolia was more like it. As if the relentless drizzle wasn't bad enough, it was so windy that Katherine was sometimes blown around like a leaf, surprising gusts slapping into her face, or forcing mini rivers down her jacket collar. Not that wind or rain stopped Olivia. Not for a moment. She insisted they had a walk every day regardless of the weather. *You might even lose some weight*, she'd said. It was enough to make Katherine want to vomit. She tossed the half-smoked cigarette onto the beach and chewed at her lip piercing. She was beginning to get fed up with it. Food was forever getting trapped in the hole and she was constantly having to suck it back out. She'd remove it if she didn't know how much its disappearance would delight her mother.

Olivia waited for her to catch up.

'Come on, darling, you must admit it's beautiful here.'

Katherine didn't get it. All she could see were miles of sandy beach, acres of boring fields and stretches of never-ending sea.

But, she had to admit, it was more interesting on this side of the island, the waves crashing over lumps of black rocks, spewing foam like an agitated washing machine. For a moment Katherine was tempted to remove her socks and shoes and clamber onto the rocks, then remembered she was way past the age for childish games.

At last, they found what her mother had been searching for – an enormous hole in the ground. It was as if a giant had punched his fist into the moor to make it. The land surrounding the chasm was wrinkled like the skin on the porridge Mum had tried to force on her that morning. More evidence of Oli's hypocrisy. One minute telling her she needed to lose weight, the next trying to make her eat even when she wasn't hungry. Telling her to wash her hair, polish her boots – who even did that? Pointing out her jeans were too tight. Was there any part of her life Mum didn't want to control?

Katherine edged towards the hole to get a better look. Despite herself, she was curious. She peered in. It was deep, maybe the height of a double-decker bus.

'Don't go too close,' her mother fretted. 'The ground could give way. You can see where it's being eroded.' She stood in front of Katherine, stretching out a protective arm.

I could push her. One tiny shove and she'd be a goner. No one would ever know.

Katherine savoured the image for a moment. No overbearing parent telling her what to do. She'd be able to live on her own – Dad wouldn't want her – and do as she pleased when she pleased. But just as quickly she dismissed the image. She didn't really want the old bitch dead.

At the bottom of the chasm was a narrow gap that allowed the sea to enter. The pressure of the incoming tide forced the waves to crash against the cliff sides, eating away at the earth bit by bit. Katherine's pulse quickened as the waves receded for a moment exposing something a few feet long caught on the rocks. It looked like a seal. Was it trapped? Had it got stuck? If so, she had to try and help it.

'Can I have the binoculars?' she shouted above the sound of the crashing waves. Her mother frowned but passed them over, for once without feeling the need to say anything.

Pushing her wet hair out of her face, Katherine focused on the rocks. It wasn't a seal. Not unless seals wore patterned Wellington boots. Perhaps it was rubbish?

She dropped to her knees, then lay flat on her stomach, ignoring her mother's cries of alarm, only vaguely conscious of her mother tugging on the waistband of her jeans in a vain attempt to pull her away.

Katherine shuffled closer to the ledge, once more training the binoculars on the rocks. The extra couple of inches were enough. A wave rolling in lifted the object and turned it on its side. Katherine's heart stopped. What she'd initially thought was seaweed was hair fanning out from a pale globe of a face.

'I think we should phone the police, Mum,' she said.

THREE

Mondays in the Death Unit were always hellish. Not as hellish as it was for the families and friends of the dead – or the dead themselves, come to that – but hellish enough, particularly if you were still suffering from the queen of hangovers and phones were ringing off the hook.

They weren't supposed to call it the Death Unit, not even amongst themselves.

Officially they – four lawyers and two admin assistants – made up the Scottish Fatalities Investigation Unit North.

Their official title more or less said it all. As part of the Crown Office Procurator and Fiscal Service they had responsibility for receiving reports of deaths occurring throughout the Highlands and Islands which were sudden, suspicious, accidental or unexplained; in essence the suspected murders, the suicides, the overdoses and the medical mishaps. It was the Unit's responsibility to decide which deaths required further investigation and which could be filed away, the relatives given permission to bury their loved ones.

The deaths that were clearly the result of murder – like last week's where the accused had dismembered his victim with a machete and, unbelievably, stuffed the torso in the wheelie bin outside the front door of his flat – only skimmed their desks before bouncing off again, back to the police, who would liaise with the homicide fiscals next door. It was those fiscals' job to prepare a case to prosecute in court.

Rachel McKenzie took a swig of her coffee and glanced around. She barely had to move her head. In a building that housed over a hundred, the Death Unit had the smallest office, the six of them squashed into a space meant for half that number.

Buff-coloured files festooned with Post-it notes covered what little workspace the computers left on the economy-sized desks crammed up against each other. What didn't fit on the desks was piled up on the floor. Although reports had been digitised years ago, Douglas Mainwaring, the principal procurator fiscal depute, was old-fashioned and liked paper copies printed. Rachel's boss was the only person who had space to call his own. From somewhere he'd found the resources to erect three stud walls in a corner to create a small office for himself. A man and a woman sat opposite him.

Suruthi was on the phone, twirling her pen between her fingers as she spoke. It was hard to believe the immaculately groomed, bright-eyed, and bushy-tailed lawyer had been clubbing with Rachel until three that morning. Neither would anyone at the club have suspected the beautiful woman dancing with complete abandon was a ruthlessly efficient prosecutor.

Alastair, the third fiscal in their team, was currently away from his desk. Most likely in the loo playing with his mobile phone.

The office staff – Linda (short grey hair, a stare that could stop you in your tracks, who'd been there so long she probably knew more than Mainwaring) and Clive (pecs like Dwayne Johnson, similar number of tattoos, ferociously bright – currently studying forensic science part-time at university) scribbled away, simultaneously answering phones while taking notes, jotting down names and details, filling in forms before passing them in stacks to the fiscal deputes.

For the most part, they got on. No one asked too many questions or shared too many details of their social life – except for Alastair Fuckwit Turnbull. Everyone knew he had only taken a job with the Fiscal's office as a step towards making pots of money as an advocate for the defence.

Rachel rummaged in her bag for paracetamol, discarding two Polo mints attached to a used tissue before she found them. Her coffee was still too hot to wash them down so she attempted to massage her headache away with her fingertips. Waste of time. Her pile of reports was already nine-high and it was only mid-morning. She flicked through them, making notes as she went along. Two stabbings – one in Dundee, one in Inverness down at the harbour – and two drug overdoses. All four would be referred to the pathologist for a two-doctor post mortem. The next report on her pile was a poor sod who no one had seen for weeks before anyone had thought of checking he was OK. Turned out he wasn't. The awful smell everyone had blamed on a dead rat was the stench of a decomposing body. A two-doctor post mortem for sure. She jotted down the details.

Rachel stood and stretched. She needed water to wash down the painkillers.

Passing Alastair's empty desk, she noticed he'd dealt with most of his cases already and the reports were all neatly stacked, apart from one placed to the side with a Post-it on which he'd scrawled *No Pro*. No further proceedings. Part of their job was to decide when it wouldn't be in the public interest to investigate a death further. The forensic pathologists would never be able to carry out post mortems on everyone who died suddenly so, according to Douglas, *a line had to be drawn*. This year had been the worst in Scotland's history as far as overdoses were concerned – over a hundred in November alone – and two-doctor post mortems were expensive and time consuming. An unfortunate consequence was that some murders were bound to slip through, as the Wickers case almost had.

Rachel's eye was drawn to the address on the top of the police report – North Uist. For a moment she couldn't breathe as images of summer holidays flooded back: the brilliantly coloured flowers covering the machair, the smell of peat, enormous blindingly white beaches, swimming in the sea, her mother. Happiness.

She'd never been able to bring herself to return.

She did a quick recce of her colleagues. Alastair was still AWOL, Suruthi's head was down, Linda and Clive on the phone, her boss still with the visitors.

She read quickly.

The victim was 61-year-old Ellen Hargreaves, a retired librarian from Glasgow whose body had washed up near Scolpaig, North Uist. Her body had been retrieved by local divers. Dr Logan, a GP on North Uist who also acted as the police surgeon, had attended the locus and pronounced death. She had also identified the deceased. Miss Hargreaves had no living relatives – no partner, male or female – in Glasgow, no one had come to stay with her at her holiday home on the island, and there was no one she was particularly friendly with locally. Her hire car had been parked at its usual spot, at the end of a track leading to her cottage.

Her next of kin was noted in her medical notes as a Lisa Cartwright – current address Brisbane in Australia. Local police had notified her by telephone. Ms Hargreaves had been Mrs Cartwright's godmother.

Ms Hargreaves' body had been found at the bottom of a blowhole by an Olivia Mowbury (46) and her daughter Katherine (16) when they were out walking. When Ellen's body had been recovered it had been clothed in bra and panties, a vest, a thick fisherman's sweater, light trousers and heavy socks. She was also wearing one brightly coloured wellington boot, the partner of which was nowhere to be found.

Ellen hadn't been reported missing so no one could be sure how long her body had been in the water.

Ms Hargreaves was last seen at the Co-op supermarket in Sollas on the Friday – six days before her body washed up. It was Dr Logan's opinion that she had been in the water for most, if not all, that time.

The body had been examined by Dr Logan. She had determined that the deceased had suffered trauma to the back of her head as well as contusions to her torso, legs and arms, most likely the result of her body being tossed amongst the rocks. Although Dr Logan couldn't be certain whether the blunt force trauma to the dead woman's scalp had been caused pre or post mortem, she'd stated that in her opinion the cause of death was accidental drowning. A search of her home had turned up nothing exceptional – no illegal substances or stash of empty bottles – so Dr Logan had ruled out intoxication as a contributing factor. The body had been sent to the pathologist in Glasgow for a full PM and his report was attached.

Police Scotland were satisfied that there were no suspicious circumstances surrounding the death. Under additional information completed by Police Sergeant MacVicar, Miss Hargreaves was a frequent visitor to the Uists, coming every year, had done so for the last seven, and was therefore a familiar figure on the islands. Ms Hargreaves had recently purchased a cottage on North Uist and until her retirement had worked in the library at Glasgow University. According her work colleagues, Ellen had been an enthusiastic amateur archaeologist and a keen birdwatcher.

The victim's handbag, or more precisely a small waterproof backpack of the type day hikers used, a pair of Zeiss binoculars and the remnants of plastic shopping bags had been recovered from outside the unlocked front door of her cottage, roughly ten miles away from where the body had been found.

Rachel frowned. Now that was odd. Who left shopping and their valuables – Zeiss binoculars were eye-wateringly expensive – outside their front door?

The report listed the contents of the backpack: a comb, a purse containing £130 in notes plus a receipt from the Co-op dated the Friday before and time-stamped 12.15, a senior rail-card, a packet of tissues and a black biro.

In what remained of the shredded carrier bag – animals or birds, possibly both, had been at it – were bread, eggs, milk, and toilet cleaner. The mince and salmon detailed on the receipt were missing, most likely scavenged by animals.

Sergeant MacVicar was certainly thorough.

Rachel turned to the pathologist's report.

Once the body had been received in Glasgow a one-doctor post mortem had been carried out. The pathologist noted the contusions and the trauma to the head – likely caused pre-mortem as she had some water in her lungs. Otherwise, the sixty-one-year-old had been fit and healthy. Toxicology had shown no evidence of alcohol or drugs. The pathologist had agreed it could have happened the way the local police surgeon had postulated. The woman had fallen, banged her head, knocked herself out and drowned. He listed the cause of death as unascertained and, as Rachel had suspected, was unwilling to say how long she'd been dead, only that it could be as much as a week and as little as two days. All that could be said with any certainty was that she'd died sometime between the date on the receipt and the date her body was discovered.

Rachel jumped as she felt a hand on her shoulder.

'What, may I ask, are you doing?' Alastair's accent had the well-bred tones of his Fettes college education. Just in case people didn't recognise it, he dropped the fact he had attended the same public school as Britain's ex-prime minister into the conversation whenever he could.

Rachel held out the file. 'This case should be investigated further. Why did you PO it?'

'If you read it you'll see there's nothing to suggest it was anything but an accident.'

'And nothing to say definitively it wasn't.'

'Oh, come on. You have to be kidding. Haven't we all got enough to do?'

'Aren't you worried we'll mess up again? We don't need another Wickers.'

Alastair had passed on that one too.

Everyone had assumed that Susan Wickers had killed herself. All the evidence had pointed to an accidental overdose and the Unit had signed off on the death on that basis. Until the boyfriend had come forward and admitted to murdering Susan in a fit of jealousy. False confessions weren't unheard of, but the boyfriend had coughed up enough facts that he couldn't have known unless he'd been the one to administer the fatal dose.

Douglas had been like a bear with a sore head ever since. It had impacted on all of them. The boyfriend had almost got off with murder. No one liked making mistakes.

All the same, mentioning Wickers was a low blow.

'This is nothing like that case,' Alastair retorted.

'Ms Hargreaves left her shopping and her valuables on her doorstep and then apparently went for a walk. Who does that? Why not take a few moments to stick your bags inside the front door away from animals or birds?'

'How the fuck should I know? Perhaps something caught her attention and she went to have a closer look.'

It was possible. So why was her gut telling her otherwise? She picked up the file. 'I'm going to take it to the boss. Suggest another look. Everyone deserves someone to speak up for them.'

She was cringingly aware of how pious she sounded. Apparently, so was Alastair.

'What do you think the rest of us do? Get off whatever white fucking steed you think you rode up on.' He ripped the sticky note from the cover. 'Please yourself. Go speak to the boss. I doubt he'll see it your way.'

If things hadn't been great between Rachel and her colleague before, they were now going to be so much worse. Tough. It couldn't be helped. She had every right to question his decision-making. Besides, she didn't give a toss if he liked her or not.

After the visitors left, Rachel gave her boss a few minutes before tapping on the partition that passed for a door. It juddered and swayed under her knuckles.

'A word?' she asked.

'I was just about to call you in. Please, sit down, Ruth.' Douglas gestured at a rickety chair opposite him and Rachel sat down gingerly.

'It's Rachel,' she corrected.

He snapped his bushy brows together. 'That's what I said, isn't it?'

It was pointless to argue. Douglas treated all the procurators fiscal working under him like an amorphous pack of irritating puppies.

She watched nervously as Douglas eased himself into his chair. He rocked from side to side until his large frame was more or less contained within its arms.

'Did you notice those two in my office earlier?' Douglas continued in his mournful voice. When Rachel had first met him she'd assumed he had been recently bereaved. She'd soon realised that he always looked – and, when he wasn't in a rage,

sounded – like a St Bernard on Prozac. No wonder he was
called Deputy Dawg behind his back.

'You mean the relatives?'

Mainwaring widened his eyes in an exaggerated pretence of
being impressed. Obviously that's who they'd been. Criminals
weren't welcome in the office and these two, despite making an
effort – the man in a suit that had been worn so many times it
had a sheen to it, the woman in a dress of a length that hadn't
been in fashion for a decade – were definitely not lawyers.

'Their father died recently in the medical ward of Inverness
General.'

She waited for him to continue. She knew from past experience Douglas would not be hurried.

'Buggers have made a complaint against the doctor.'

'What sort of complaint?'

'Said their father died seconds after being given pain relief
by the doctor. They want it looked into.' Mainwaring's lips
drew back from his teeth in a snarl.

'Why?'

'They want the doctor charged with murder! What is the
world coming to? The sooner I retire the better.' Couldn't be
long. He had to be at least sixty.

He took several deep, rattling breaths before continuing. He
was more animated now – so animated Rachel worried he'd
clutch his chest and pass out. That was the thing with Douglas.
You never knew for certain what he was thinking or what he'd
say or do next. It was like dealing with a rabid dog. Linda said
he hadn't always been like this. Lockerbie had changed him.

Lockerbie had happened only days after Douglas had taken
up the post as the fiscal in charge of the Death Unit in Glasgow.
He'd been one of the first to arrive at the scene. He'd attended
the post mortems of every body – or in many cases, body part –
and had spent time with every single relative. He had slept,
eaten and breathed Lockerbie right up to the moment when

Abdelbaset al-Megrahi was convicted. No doubt the reason everyone endured his irascibility. And perhaps why Rachel thought she saw in him an echo of the darkness that was in her.

She slid the report on Ellen Hargreaves across the desk.

'I think this needs to be looked into a little further.'

Mainwaring picked up the report and scrutinised it. 'Why? It's been assigned to Turnbull.' Every report was assigned to the fiscal who received it.

'Some things don't quite add up. Her backpack and expensive binoculars, along with the groceries, were left outside the door, for example.'

'Shopping at the door! A reason for opening a murder inquiry if I ever heard one.' Mainwaring's small eyes almost disappeared in the folds of his cheeks, although Rachel had no doubt he was not amused. 'What do the police think?'

'The local police and the police surgeon both think that she slipped on the rocks near her home, knocked herself out from a bang on her head, and was swept out to sea. The pathologist finds no reason to disagree with that theory. But he did say that the trauma to the head could be non-accidental. He couldn't rule it out.'

When Douglas continued to survey her in silence, his eyes pinned on her like two miniature headlights, Rachel stumbled on. 'The thing is, she has no one. She was in the water for almost a week and no one reported her missing. No friend, no child, partner or colleague wondering where she was and why they hadn't heard from her. Someone should ask questions on her behalf.'

'And you think that person should be you?' He couldn't have looked more incredulous had she told him she'd taken up belly dancing.

'At the very least we should request a two-doctor post mortem.'

'I don't have an endless budget and our pathologists have

enough to do. I don't see how it's in the public interest to pursue this.'

'I don't think we should release the body until we know more,' Rachel persisted.

'What exactly do you think we should be doing?' He made no attempt to hide his irritation.

'Ask the police up there to make further enquiries.'

'The local police are satisfied. Everyone is satisfied. Apart from you.'

Rachel leaned forward. 'What if her death wasn't an accident?' She saw Ellen in her mind's eye. Solitary, lonely, soon forgotten. 'Everyone has the right for *someone* to know what happened to them, for someone to at least try and find out. No one's death should be recorded as accidental unless we are absolutely, one hundred per cent sure it is. My instinct's telling me there's more to this than meets the eye.' Bugger. She should never have mentioned instinct. 'I don't think we have enough evidence to rule her death accidental. We wouldn't want another Wickers...' She left the words hanging in the air, trusting Deputy Dawg to take the bait.

Mainwaring kept his eyes locked on hers. 'Is this personal? I understand your family originally came from the Western Isles?'

So he *did* know. Of course, he did. Every lawyer in Scotland probably knew. It wasn't something people forgot about, no matter how many years had passed. After it happened she'd thought of changing her name but decided against it. She'd lost everything and she was damned if she was also going to lose her name and all the positive things that went with it.

Rachel nodded. 'My mother did. My grandfather lives on South Uist.'

Douglas leant as far across the desk as his considerable stomach would let him. He was close enough for her to smell the garlic on his breath and it took every ounce of her willpower not to cover her nose with her hand.

'Very well. Look into it. Go to Uist. Ask more questions.'

'You want me to actually physically go there?' she asked. It hadn't crossed her mind that he'd want her to ask her questions in person. 'Can't I make my enquiries over the phone?'

'No, you can't make your enquiries by phone and yes, I want you to actually, physically, go there. If you're so damn sure something's fishy, there's no substitute for an actual visit to the locus.'

Go to Uist. After all these years. Her stomach clenched.

'I'm going to go along with your instinct,' Douglas continued, the last word said with a sneer. 'I'll request a two-person post mortem. But after the recent cock-up with the Advocate Depute's Office, which you have been at pains to point out, this needs to be done by the book. I'm damned if this office will be the laughing stock of those arseholes in gowns and wigs.'

Advocate's Depute Office, she corrected him silently.

'Go to Uist, but I want you back in the office by Monday – Alastair is being seconded to a Fatal Accident Inquiry and I need you back by then – at the LATEST.' He'd bellowed the last word at her.

Six days. Hopefully less. Maybe only a couple of days. She could manage that. She would ask her questions, make sure the police had been thorough, and get the hell off Uist.

'Linda has too much to do without running after you,' he continued, 'so you'll have to make your own travel arrangements. Economy, of course.' Douglas heaved himself out of his too-small chair, wiping the sheen of sweat from his forehead with a handkerchief. Rachel watched, fascinated, as a button strained against the expanse of his stomach. She prayed it wouldn't pop and embarrass them both.

Douglas slid the slim manila file back across his desk.

'Could you stay with your grandfather? Save the office a few quid?'

Was he kidding?

She shook her head. 'No way. Forget it. I'm not going to ask my grandfather if I can stay with him. I'd rather pay for the hotel myself.' She clamped her lips together.

Rachel thought the corner of his mouth twitched. Whether with amusement or irritation was anyone's guess. She said nothing, just held his gaze.

'Bit more fire in your belly than you'd like people to know,' he said, lurching to his feet. 'Find out what this Ms Hargreaves was doing in the days before she died, who the last person was to see her alive – anything that might confirm that this was an accident. I'll get in touch with the local police, but if you have any questions speak directly to me. Before you do anything. Understood?'

Then, with a final wave of his podgy hand, he shooed her out the door.

FOUR

TUESDAY

The plane dipped and tilted in the turbulence as it flew towards Benbecula. When Rachel had come to Uist as a child – every summer for as long as she could remember – it had been by car and ferry, the journey part of the adventure; the beginning of endless days of sunshine and happiness. Until that last summer when there had been an odd, angry atmosphere. They'd never returned to Uist and Rachel had never seen either grandparent again.

What happened that holiday? What had caused her grandparents to turn from their only child and consequently their only grandchild too? Mum had never said and Rachel had never asked.

The captain's voice came over the speakers announcing that they had started their descent and they'd be landing in Benbecula in twenty minutes. Rachel looked out of the window. Beneath her as far as she could see was water, splattered with land linked by causeways. The west coast was fringed with powder white beaches, the east coast more rocky, the interior sprinkled with numerous lochs that glittered in the April sunshine. The plane continued to descend until it was low enough for her to make out the cars on the narrow roads stitching the pieces of land together.

The wind hit Rachel the minute she stepped off the plane, whipping her curly black hair across her face and obscuring her vision. The airport terminal was little more than a large garage plonked down on a vast field. Apart from the building there was nothing else to see except sea, land, and sheep. She paused for a moment, taking in deep breaths of air. She'd forgotten how pure it was here, like liquid oxygen.

Rachel followed the last straggling passengers as a small truck towed the baggage past her.

Inside, the prefabricated terminal looked more like a real airport than it had from the outside. There were a number of chairs and tables, a kiosk selling snacks and, on the far side, a door with a conveyor belt terminating in an X-ray machine. The disembarked passengers greeted friends and relatives, the sound of Gaelic and melodic island accents at once alien and familiar. An ache blossomed in Rachel's chest. She could almost hear her mother's voice.

A tall, statuesque woman with wild, greying hair and fierce, intelligent eyes hurried over to her.

'Miss McKenzie?'

'That's me,' Rachel acknowledged.

The woman held out her hand. 'I'm Sophie McKinnon. Welcome to Uist.'

Rachel shook the proffered hand and almost cried out as her fingers were crushed by the woman's grip. Was it her Viking heritage? An image of Sophie striding across the moors wielding a sword flashed in front of Rachel's eyes. A giggle bubbled in her throat. She thrust the image away.

'Your car is all ready and waiting for you outside. If you could just fill in some paperwork?' Sophie was saying. Rachel had found the car hire company on the internet. Apparently the only one on the island.

The documentation only took a couple of minutes to complete. 'How long are you wanting the car for?' Sophie said when Rachel was done.

'No longer than a week.'

'I should warn you there's a nasty storm on the way – maybe as big as the one we had in 2005. Be here by the weekend, they reckon. If it hits the way we expect it to, then no one will get off the island – or on, for that matter!'

Rachel intended to be long gone by then. 'I hope to have finished my business in a day or two, but could I let you know?'

'Oh, and what sort of business is that?' Sophie asked.

Rachel answered with a question of her own. 'Any chance of having a chat with the owner of the car rental company?' Whoever had hired Ellen the car might know more about her.

'Well now. You're in luck. As it happens, you're talking to her!'

Good start. Maybe Rachel would be off the island sooner than she'd hoped. 'Do you have a few minutes?'

Sophie peeled off a copy of the rental agreement and handed it to Rachel to sign. 'What is it you want to talk about?'

'I'm here in connection with the death of Ellen Hargreaves. Did you hear about it?'

Sophie gave a bark of laughter. 'You'll soon find out that nothing happens on this island that everybody doesn't know about within minutes.' She eyed Rachel with blatant curiosity. 'Are you a reporter?'

'A lawyer. More specifically, a fiscal with the Sudden Death Unit in Inverness.'

Sophie looked thoughtful for a moment and Rachel suspected she was being sized up.

'Aye, I knew Ellen,' Sophie said. Rachel must have passed muster. Sophie nodded in the direction of a black-suited man who kept glancing at his watch. Most of the other passengers had drifted away. 'Look, I have another customer to attend to.

Why don't you get us some coffee?' She indicated the kiosk at the faraway end of the building with a nod. 'Then I'll be with you and you can tell me what it is you want to know.'

By the time Rachel returned with the drinks, Sophie was seated at a table laughing with a weather-beaten man wearing a threadbare sweater and jeans that had seen better days, tucked into a pair of wellington boots. Rachel caught enough of the conversation, even though it was in Gaelic, to gather it was about some man whose cow had escaped from its field. Why they found this so amusing, Rachel had no idea.

'Oh, Hector,' Sophie said, still smiling. 'This is Rachel McKenzie, a lawyer from Inverness. Rachel, this is Hector Ruadh.'

Red Hector, Rachel translated inwardly, taking in the sprinkle of remaining hair on his scalp and his bushy red beard. How appropriate.

'Hector likes to come down for a wee cup of tea when the plane lands and departs so he can keep track of everyone. Isn't that right, Hector?' Sophie continued.

'I'm pleased to meet you,' Hector said to Rachel. 'We were very shocked when we heard about Ellen. We'd got used to seeing her walking the hills and crofts. It's a terrible shame.' He rolled his Rs and elongated his vowels the same way her mother had. It was going to be a tough few days.

'Did you know her? I mean, to talk to. Anything either of you can tell me about her would be helpful.'

Sophie took a slurp of coffee. 'Ellen's been a regular visitor to the islands during the summer these last few years – renting a house for a month at a time. She bought a place here when she retired, oh, about two months ago now. I don't think anyone even knew that cottage was for sale until Ellen moved in. It needed a bit of work. No one had lived there for many years – not since Donalda, and she was very old when she died so there wasn't even electricity to the house. But Ellen didn't seem to care. Mind you, she'd only moved in a couple of weeks ago. She might have felt differently after a couple of winters.' She grinned at Hector, who was listening with a lively interest. 'The winters here are not for the faint-hearted.'

'You knew her pretty well then?' Rachel asked.

'I wouldn't say that exactly,' Sophie replied, seeming to choose her words with care. 'I don't think anyone knew her well. We chatted sometimes, that's all. Every year since she started visiting the islands she's hired a car from us. Anyway, she still wanted to hire a car rather than buy one. We give – gave – her a good deal. Sometimes she'd stop for a wee chat. Mostly she'd collect her car without so much as a word. Depended on what mood she was in. She wasn't rude – I wouldn't want you to get that impression. Just reserved.'

'What did she chat about?' Rachel asked. 'When she was in the mood?'

'She liked talking about birds and old ruins. And bones. Aye, she loved bones.' Hector joined in, his doleful smile revealing a wide gap where his two front teeth used to be. 'That's why she's known as Skeleton Ellen around here.'

Sophie gave Hector an admonishing shake of the head before turning back to Rachel. 'Almost everyone on the island has a nickname,' she said, a note of apology in her voice. 'It helps differentiate people. So we know which Tommy MacDonald is being referred to, for example. Or Hector, for that matter.'

Rachel smiled to let them know she understood and, deciding that there was little else to be achieved for the time being, drained the last of her coffee and stood.

'Is there anyone else I could speak to about Ellen?' she asked. 'Friends? People she spent time with. A walking companion?'

Sophie's eyebrows shot up. 'Why are you asking? Is there some doubt about Ellen's death?'

'We just have a couple of questions. Nothing to cause

concern. We'd like to know a little more about Ms Hargreaves
and her movements in the days before her death. That's why I'd
like to speak to people she might have been friendly with.'

Sophie looked less than convinced. She shrugged her large
shoulders. 'Oh, I don't think she was *friends* with anyone. Kept
herself to herself. One of those women who like their own
company. But I can ask if anyone spoke to her recently or saw
her around. Most people, tourists and locals, use us if they need
a vehicle. People will have spotted Ellen going about. Might
have passed the time of day with her or seen her talking to
someone.'

'I'd appreciate that.'

'Do you have a map? We don't bother fitting the cars with
GPS. It's not helpful. You can hardly put in Wee Johnny's
house and expect it to direct you!' Her smile was wide.

'I have Google Maps on my phone.'

'What network are you with?'

When Rachel told her, Sophie shook her head. 'They're one
of the worst for getting a signal and they don't have 4G, so your
chances of getting an internet connection are slim to none.
You'll be lucky to get a good enough signal to even make a call
most of the time.'

Bugger. Not much she could do about it though.

'Where are you staying?' Sophie continued.

'Tioran Lodge, I think it's called.' Rachel retrieved the piece
of paper with the name of the hotel she'd booked from the zip
pocket of her handbag. Hector had closed his eyes and folded
his arms across his chest.

'Yes, that's it, Tioran Lodge. In North Uist. Could you tell
me how to get there?'

Sophie pointed to a map on the wall. 'I can show you on
here.'

It wouldn't be hard for Rachel to find her way about, Sophie
explained. Uist was basically made up of three main islands:

South Uist in the south, Benbecula in the middle and North Uist in the north. There were other islands, some inhabited, many not – except by sheep. One road linked the main islands by a series of causeways. The difficulty was finding places once you left the main road. The houses weren't signposted – most didn't even have a number. All the locals knew who stayed where, so for them it wasn't an issue. Rachel would just have to ask.

The hotel was more or less halfway between Lochmaddy, where the ferries came into North Uist, and the airport. Although it was off the main road, because it had a bar, Tioran Lodge was signposted. Rachel thought it wouldn't be too difficult to find, even for someone with her hopeless sense of direction.

'What about Ms Hargreaves' cottage?' She consulted her notebook. 'The address I have is Crow's Cottage, Grimsay.'

Sophie tutted. 'Known as Blackpoint when I was a child. Incomers like to give their houses these daft names.' Her mouth tightened with contempt. 'Up to them, I suppose. Anyway, where was I? Grimsay is part of North Uist, but Ellen's house isn't on the main road – or any road for that matter – so I can't show you on this map. You need one with a smaller scale. Best you buy one like the walkers use. There's a shop near here that sells them – MacMillans. Turn left at the end of the road, drive about a mile and you'll find it on the right. Catriona will sort you out with anything else you might need.' She glanced down at Rachel's feet. 'If you're planning to go to Ellen's house – or anywhere off the beaten track, for that matter – the ground and the sands can be boggy, so make sure you wear wellingtons.'

Rachel had dressed in her usual working outfit of black trousers and jacket with a white blouse. Her shoes had a heel but were nowhere near as high as the ones she wore clubbing. She'd brought her walking boots but it hadn't occurred to her to bring wellingtons too.

'And don't go there after the sun goes down. We've lost many a tourist on the moors in the dark.' Sophie brought her heavy eyebrows together and wiggled the right one at Rachel.

Rachel was taken aback. Had there been other mysterious disappearances no one knew about?

'Och, I'm only kidding,' Sophie said with a grin, clearly enjoying her joke. 'We haven't lost anyone apart from Skelly Elly, sorry, Ellen, for a few years now. You'll be all right, as long as you're careful.'

Rachel picked up her suitcase.

'She wrote everything down, that woman,' Hector said, surprising Rachel. She'd thought he'd fallen asleep. 'In a note-book. Skelly Elly showed it to me once. She was asking me about some bird or another, where the best place to find it was, and she wrote down what I said. In that notebook.' He sucked his lip through his missing front teeth. 'Oh yes, she liked her birds as well as her bones. And she wrote it all down.' He took a satisfied swig of his tea. 'Aye, that was Skelly Elly for you. Poor woman.'

FIVE

Thirty minutes later Rachel emerged from MacMillans General Store the owner of a pair of wellington boots at least one size too big (they were expecting more in but when, Catriona the owner, couldn't say with any certainty), a hat with a very large bobble, and a 1 in 25000 Landranger map with the police station in Lochmaddy, Tioran Lodge (apparently Catriona's daughter Rhoda worked there part-time so Rachel had to be sure to say hello) and the site of Ellen's cottage circled in pen.

The road leading from Benbecula to North Uist started as a fairly decent two-lane, but soon narrowed to a single track which threaded its way past sea lochs and moor.

As Rachel waited in a passing place to let an oncoming car go by, she surveyed her surroundings. When she'd been here as a child she remembered endless hot, clear days, or so it had felt. No doubt the landscape had been coloured by happiness. Now, despite the sunshine, it struck Rachel as bleak. There were no trees, and the mud-coloured moor hadn't recovered after the long, cold winter.

A crofter trundled his tractor up and down a field, furrowing the soil ready for planting. On the other side of the road peat bogs were open wounds. Rachel switched on the radio.

As the familiar notes of Runrig's 'The Mighty Atlantic' filled the car, Rachel was transported back in time to that last holiday. She'd been twelve. It had been just her and Mum. Dad couldn't make it because of work. They'd driven in her mother's second-hand Astra – windows down, belting out Runrig's version of 'Loch Lomond' at the top of their voices as they'd negotiated the narrow, winding roads that curved around the loch of the same name.

Every moment of that journey had been gilded with happiness.

Rachel snapped the radio off. She'd give anything to go back in time. To make it up to Mum – to say sorry.

She bit her lip so hard she tasted blood. She couldn't make it up to her mother, only do her best for other dead women. It was Ellen who mattered now. Ellen she had to concentrate on. What kind of person had she been? What had made her tick? What secrets did *she* have? One thing Rachel was sure of – everyone had something they preferred others not to know.

Realising she was still in the passing place although the oncoming car had long since receded in her rear-view mirror, Rachel pulled back onto the road. No fixed time had been agreed for her to present herself at the police station, and Ellen's cottage was on the way, so why not go there now? The sooner she discovered what had happened to Ellen, the sooner she'd be able to satisfy herself that Ellen's death had been an accident and the sooner she'd be able to get off the island.

She followed Catriona's instructions, driving along the untarred road, which was as full of potholes as the shopkeeper had promised until she could go no further. She stopped beside the gate, noting the narrow track stamped into existence by sheep. To her left, half covered by the tide, were the sands as described by Catriona. There was no sign of a house, only a small hill. Crow's Cottage had to be on the other side. Rachel pulled on her new wellingtons and set off along the track. She wouldn't chance walking across the sands until she knew the rhythms of the tides.

Ten minutes later she crested the hill. Below, around two hundred yards away was a single-storey house built on a small, thumb-shaped peninsula. There was nothing else in sight apart from moor and water. Ellen had clearly liked living off-grid. Rachel could see the attraction. There had been a time when she'd have given anything to get away to a place where no one knew her. Could Ellen have been hiding from something or someone? Fuck. She was at it again – seeing sinister motives for perfectly normal behaviour. More likely it was the view and the bargain price that had sold the cottage to Ellen.

As she squelched over the moor Rachel had reason to thank Catriona for the wellingtons, even if they were too big. More than once she sank up to her calves in the marshy ground and had to haul a trapped foot from its boggy prison.

As she approached the squat, stone-built house set on its own small peninsula she felt as if she was being watched. Perched on the spine of the roof, staring at her with malevolent eyes, was a long, almost regimental, line of crows, dark as coal, bigger than any she'd ever seen in the city, all perfectly still, all looking in her direction as if guarding the house. As Rachel drew closer the crows flapped their wings and took off with harsh, chiding cries. They flew in a circle before three broke away from the rest and swept down, heading straight at her. She covered her head with her hands and ducked, almost losing her balance. The birds passed so close she could feel the air pulse from their beating wings. They circled again before settling on the roof once more. Was this what had happened to Ellen? Had they attacked the older woman, causing her to fall?

To the left and right, the land dropped away to the sea. Rachel walked along the shoreline, passing a disused well

covered by a grid on the way, until she came to the edge. The
drop wasn't steep – no more than a couple of feet. White foam
licked the edges of black, seaweed-coated rocks, occasionally
sending a spew of water in Rachel's direction. The tide was still
coming in, not quite covering the sand of a natural inlet on the
far side of the peninsula.

Squatting down, she reached out a hand to touch the
seaweed clinging to the rocks. As she'd anticipated, it was slimy.
If Ellen stepped carelessly or if those bloody crows had dive-
bombed her the way they'd dive-bombed Rachel, it was entirely
possible that she'd slipped, knocked her head on a rock, lost
consciousness, fallen into the water and drowned. Exactly as
everyone believed. Rachel was simply making an idiot of herself
by suggesting there was any other possibility. Yet she couldn't
get that shopping, binoculars and rucksack out of her head.
Something must have caught Ellen's attention before she had a
chance to go inside her home. A sheep in difficulty perhaps? A
rare bird?

Hunkering back on her heels, Rachel looked out to the horizon. In the distance a shaft of sunshine lit up a circle of sea,
hinting at a different life elsewhere. It was beautiful, but desolate. She shivered, resisting the temptation to look behind her.
For what? A ghost? Ridiculous.

Nevertheless, she quickened her pace as she headed back
towards the cottage. She was going too fast for the marshy
ground, not watching where she stepped. She caught the toe of
her boot in a rabbit hole and stumbled, falling to all fours, her
hands sinking in the mud.

Just as she was about to scramble to her feet, something, lit
by a sudden ray of sun, glinted in the long grass to Rachel's left.
Curious, she rummaged until her fingers closed on a hard, flat
object around the size of her palm. She stood and examined it.
Encased in a rigid silver waterproof case was a mobile phone.
Had it belonged to Ellen? In which case, why hadn't the police

found it? The report they'd sent had been nicely detailed, implying the small force was dutifully run. It occurred to her that neither a phone nor a notebook had been included in the list of the contents of Ellen's backpack. Nor, now she came to think of it, had a set of car keys. The local force hadn't been as thorough as she'd first thought.

She pressed the start button but the screen remained blank. Either it was broken from being left outside in the rain, or the battery was flat. She slipped it into her pocket.

Back at the cottage the crows watched her return in silence but made no move towards her. Outside the front door a collection of bleached bones was piled against the walls. Rachel thought she recognised a whale vertebra, but the rest were a mystery to her. The wind picked up, whipping Rachel's hair into her eyes. She tucked her wayward locks back under her bobble hat. Her father had once said her curls looked as if she'd stuck a thumb into a live socket and electrocuted herself. He'd always been able to make her laugh when he chose.

She hated that sometimes she missed him.

Keeping one eye on the crows, Rachel slipped on a pair of disposable gloves and tried the door, expecting it to be locked. To her surprise it opened easily.

Inside, the tiny windows prevented much of the remaining daylight from coming in, making it difficult to see. She scrabbled around for a light switch but failed to find one. Rachel remembered then what Sophie had told her about there being no electricity. How could anyone live without it? Where would you charge your phone, your laptop, your hairdryer?

She took a few steps further into the room and noticed a lamp, like the one her parents had used when they had taken her camping, on the kitchen table. Using the torchlight of her phone, she searched the mantelpiece and found a large box of extra-long matches. As she lit the lamp a greasy spiral of smoke reached for the ceiling. At least now she could see.

The interior of the cottage was one large room. On her left was the kitchen-cum-sitting room with an ancient, soot-stained Rayburn to one side. To the right, cordoned off with a makeshift screen, was the sleeping area. A table, with a few rickety chairs and a small sofa covered with a throw, completed the furnishings.

Covering every surface, in between dishes, jars of coffee and jam were more bones. Around the edges of the room, set against the walls, were stacked cardboard boxes.

Rachel squinted at the labels. Although her knowledge of Latin was limited to a term in her first year at university she understood enough to work out that the boxes contained more bones. Now she understood why the locals referred to Ellen as Skelly Elly.

Rachel jumped as a gust of wind slammed the door shut behind her. The Tilley lamp flickered, making her oversized shadow do a macabre dance on the wall.

Books took up any remaining space on the kitchen work-tops. Rachel picked one up. *Archaeological Sites of the Western Isles*. It had been borrowed from the local library with a return date for a week hence. The others were either about Scottish history, archaeology or birds. Next to the sink was the tattered remains of a supermarket plastic carrier bag with a bottle of toilet cleaner pinning it to the counter. Beside it was a small camping stove. A frying pan, a plate and a knife and fork sat in a plastic bowl in the sink. There was no sign of Ellen's day ruck-sack. That too was probably still with the police.

Rachel continued to open cupboard doors, uncertain of what she was looking for. Apart from a few tins of beans and tomatoes, there was nothing of interest. No bottles of wine or gin. No half-eaten packets of crisps or biscuits. Only a mug with a rather beautiful painting of a dolphin.

Rachel stepped over to the right and peered around the room divider. A neatly made single steel-framed cot bed was tucked into a corner. Next to it was a chair with an alarm clock and, against the wall, a clothes rack with a couple of flannel shirts and waterproofs draped over the spine.

Fairly sure there was little else the house could tell her, Rachel made her way back outside, closing the door behind her. As the sky continued to darken, she realised it was about to pour. It would make her journey back to the car even trickier than her trip out. She should hurry, maybe come back for another look after she'd spoken to the police and handed over the phone. Then, unless anything else jumped out at her, she would get the next available flight back to Inverness and put Uist and its associated memories behind her.

At least she could in all conscience say she'd done everything she could for Ellen.

SIX

Lochmaddy, the township where the police station was situated, was little more than a cluster of houses by the ferry port for the north side of the island. There was a community centre, a post office, a tourist information centre and a hotel, all vaguely familiar. It didn't appear to have changed much over the decades.

The police station was a converted croft house in the centre of the village adjacent to the courthouse. If it weren't for the simple blue sign marked 'Police' and the presence of a white SUV with a blue and yellow chequered stripe outside, Rachel would never have guessed the building's function.

Inside, the on-duty constable stood behind a small counter.

'What can I do for you, miss?' he asked politely.

'I'm here to see Sergeant MacVicar. I believe he's expecting me. I'm Rachel McKenzie. From the Fiscal's office in Inverness.'

A look of alarm crossed the constable's face. He shook his head. 'No one said anything about a girl coming from Inverness. From the Fiscal's office, you say? Well, well. Who would have thought a wee thing like you would be a lawyer? You couldn't be much older than my daughter and she's only just started at university. Are you sure you're not pulling my leg now?'

Very funny, very original. Rachel smiled briefly, suppressing her irritation.

Surely Sergeant MacVicar had let his team know she was coming?

Rachel took out her ID. The constable scrutinised the photo for a few minutes before handing it back.

'Well then, right enough, Miss McKenzie. But we still didn't know you were coming. Unless it slipped the sergeant's mind. Wait now 'til I ring his house. Just you take a seat over there while I do that.' He pointed to one of two chairs in the hall.

As Rachel sat down, a slight woman with shoulder-length hair dashed into the hall, peeling off her coat as she went. Underneath she was wearing a police officer's uniform, her shirt halfway out of her black trousers.

'Bloody well went and forgot that I was on the back shift, didn't I, Fergus?' she called out. She noticed Rachel and caught her lower lip between her teeth. 'Oh, I'm sorry. I didn't see you there. Is Constable Campbell attending to you?' She tucked in her blouse with one hand and stuck the other out towards Rachel. 'Constable Selena MacDonald.'

For someone who looked as if the slightest breeze might blow her off her feet, Selena had a surprisingly strong grip.

'Rachel McKenzie from the Fiscal's office in Inverness. Apparently no one knew I was coming. The constable has gone to phone the sergeant to let him know I'm here.'

Constable MacDonald flung her handbag down on the counter. 'Bloody typical. Never mind. I'm guessing you're here because of Skel— oops, I mean Ellen Hargreaves? Would you like a cup of tea while you're waiting? I could murder one myself. Come on into the office.' The police officer barely paused to draw breath.

Suppressing a smile, Rachel did as she was asked.

The office, as Selena called it, must once have been the

kitchen of the house. It still had what looked like the original cabinets along the length of one wall as well as a sink, an old-fashioned cream-and-white Rayburn, similar to the one that had been in Rachel's grandparents' house, with a worn armchair to one side. A black and white cat slept in front of the stove. The only indication that the space was used for work was the couple of desks littered with paperwork and empty crisp packets. The constable from reception was sitting behind one of the desks speaking on the landline.

Selena followed Rachel's gaze, clicked her tongue and scurried around picking up rubbish. 'Who would work with men?' she said. 'Especially Highland men. They think all a woman is fit for is to tidy up after them.' She tapped her colleague on the leg. He lifted his feet obediently, allowing Selena to grab the overflowing rubbish bin from under his desk.

'Aye, but you love us anyway,' the male police officer said, replacing the receiver. 'You know you'd just get bored if you didn't have us to look after.' He turned to Rachel. 'Sergeant MacVicar's no answering his phone, so for the time being you're stuck with us and Selena Doigheil over there.'

Selena Doigheil. *Wise Selena*. Rachel hoped to hell the nickname wasn't ironic.

The kettle on the stove rattled.

'Coffee? Tea?' Selena asked.

'Coffee would be great. Black no sugar.'

'Then why are you here?' Selena said, once she'd made coffee for everyone and had settled herself in the armchair. 'I thought everyone had agreed Miss Hargreaves' death was an accident?' Selena looked at Rachel over the rim of her oversized mug. 'Wasn't our report detailed enough?' Her wide eyes were anxious. 'Did I – I mean we – leave anything out?'

'You wrote it?' Rachel couldn't hide her surprise. She would have thought that duty belonged to the sergeant.

'Aye. First one I've done. But the sergeant checked it.'

'I was impressed,' Rachel said, reassessing the police officer.

Selena grinned. 'Cheers! I like to make sure it's all done by the book.'

'However, the Fiscal's office isn't ready to conclude that Miss Hargreaves' death was an accident.' Rachel didn't say that when she referred to the Fiscal's office she meant herself. 'There are a couple of loose ends we'd like to clear up. I'm perplexed about the valuables and shopping left on the doorstep. And now I'm here I realise there were a couple of things missing from the report.' Rachel said, 'I didn't see any mention of a notebook or a phone listed among her possessions, for example. Nor mention of car keys.'

Selena placed her mug down on the stovetop and frowned. 'That's because we didn't find a phone or a notebook, and the car keys were left in the ignition.'

'Didn't you think that odd?'

'The phone yes – now I come to think of it. But the car keys, not at all. Most of the people who live on the island leave their keys in the ignition, as did Ellen. We've a very low, almost non-existent, crime rate here, always have. Old habits die hard, although we're trying to get folk to stop doing it. It's not that cars get stolen, at least not permanently; a thief couldn't get them off the island without booking them on the ferry, and people would notice someone driving a different car. But we do get the occasional youth who likes to do a bit of joyriding when he or she has had too much to drink or is high.'

'Why wasn't the door to her cottage locked? Surely it should have been secured? At the very least until the procurator fiscal signed off on the death. Anyone could walk in and help themselves to whatever they like.' God, she sounded like such a prig. She smiled, hoping to take some of the sting from her words.

'You've been to her house already! That was fast work.' Selena shot her a look. 'Shouldn't one of us have been with you?'

She had a point. Not one Rachel wished to respond to.

'Islanders don't bother locking the doors of their house either,' Selena continued when Rachel didn't reply. 'I'm not even sure there is a key to her cottage.' Selena stood and put her empty mug in the sink. 'The sergeant didn't think the cottage needed securing.'

Unlocked doors, keys left in ignitions. It was a world stuck not unpleasantly in the past. In which case, perhaps valuables left at the door wasn't so odd after all. Rachel was beginning to realise she was in danger of making a bit of an idiot of herself. However, the police had missed the phone so they might have missed something else.

'I found this on Ellen's croft.' Rachel took the phone she'd found from her pocket and handed it to Selena. 'I think it might be hers.'

Selena narrowed her eyes, looked as if she were about to say something, but instead pulled on a pair of disposable gloves and took the phone from Rachel. 'We assumed her phone got washed away when she fell in.'

'If it *is* her phone, it might be useful to have a look at what's on it. There might be contact information, texts, emails – I don't know – something of interest. Maybe she was on the phone to someone when she fell? We might even be able to track where she was on the day she died.'

Selena pressed the power button. 'The battery is either dead or the whole phone is knackered.' She frowned and tipped back in her chair. 'Hey, Fergus,' she called over her shoulder, 'I thought you searched Ellen's croft?'

Fergus stood and crossed over to them. 'I did. As best as I could.' A red flush spread up his neck. He turned to Rachel. 'Where did you find it?'

The constable looked so aghast to have missed it, she decided to come clean. 'It was under a rock. If I hadn't caught my foot in a rabbit hole and ended up on my hands and knees, I probably wouldn't have spotted it. It might not even belong to Ellen.'

Selena passed the phone to her colleague, who slipped on gloves before taking it.

'I'll see if I can find a charger for it,' he said. 'If I can't, the shop in Benbecula might have one. Or Stornoway. Quicker than ordering one from Amazon.'

'Amazon delivers here?' Rachel asked as Fergus returned to his desk.

Selena looked at her with mild exasperation. 'Aye. We have internet and telephones and electricity too. Amazing, isn't it?'

'Ouch,' Rachel said. 'I deserved that, didn't I?'

Selena gave a terse smile. 'It gets on my nerves a bit. The way visitors seem to think that just because the island is remote, it's backward in some way.'

'I'm sorry. I didn't mean to sound like a twat.'

'A small amount of twatiness is permitted,' a mollified Selena replied. 'To be honest, I'm not sure why you came in person. You could have phoned if there was anything you needed to ask.'

Another good point, given Rachel wasn't sure either why Douglas had insisted she make the trip. 'I thought it might be helpful to see for myself where Ellen lived and how her death might have happened.'

Selena continued to look puzzled. 'Why do we need to know who she's been messaging or emailing?' Her eyes lit up and she leaned forward. 'Bloody hell. You think she might have been murdered!' There was no mistaking the relish in her voice. 'How extraordinary.' The spark left her eyes. 'And I have to say, unlikely. No one has ever been murdered here. Any deaths we do come across are accidents, suicides, or natural.' She smiled ruefully. 'Nothing quite as exciting as murder! Anyway, I thought everyone had agreed it was an accident. Sergeant MacVicar certainly thinks so.'

'Don't you?' Rachel asked, clocking she hadn't said we.

Selena shifted uneasily in her seat, flicking a glance at Constable Campbell, who had turned his back and was rummaging in a drawer, one ear cocked to their conversation. 'It's not really for me to say, but yes, I think there are one or two things that need to be clarified.'

'Such as?'

'I don't care what anyone says but there is no way – even on Uist – that a woman goes for a walk, leaving her shopping by the door. Why not just pop it inside? Especially when there's meat and fish amongst the shopping. The birds and the beasts would be at it – *were* at it – in a flash. Ellen would have known that.'

'Maybe she saw something down by the shore? A piece of rubbish she wanted to pick up before it blew away, for example. Perhaps those crows attacked her, and she tripped. They went for me.'

Selena stared into the middle distance as if visualising Ellen's last movements. 'Possibly. Mum's always getting set upon by the bloody seagulls when she puts her washing out. She takes a floor brush with her and waves it above her head so the seagulls will go for that and not her.' Selena waved her arms, mimicking her mother. 'Makes her look like a mad woman!' Selena stood. 'If the crows did go for Ellen, she might have lost her balance.' She held her arms out to the side, balancing on one foot. 'She stumbles, her phone goes flying, she falls, hits her head on the rock and knocked out, gets dragged out to sea.' She was quiet for a moment. 'Except...'

'Go on,' Rachel prompted.

Selena frowned. 'Where did you say you found the phone?'

'About halfway between her house and shore.' Rachel realised immediately what Selena was getting at. 'Roughly a hundred yards from the sea.'

'Mmm. OK, so let's imagine she had her phone in her hand

and she was attacked by the crows. She's using her hands and arms to fight them off and her phone goes flying. Could it really travel that distance only to wedge itself under a rock? I very much doubt it,' Selena answered her own question. 'Unless she fell where you found the phone, and, dizzy and disoriented gets up, but instead of heading towards the house ends up down by the shore where she loses consciousness and falls into the water.'

'That seems equally unlikely,' Rachel said.

'I agree. I'm no expert,' Selena continued, 'but wouldn't there have been something to indicate she'd fallen in? Like a piece of clothing? Evidence of a boot or shoe sliding in the mud? I don't know – something. Was there anything like that near where you found the phone?'

'No, but I wasn't looking that closely. It might not be obvious. The ground was pretty boggy. I gather there's been days of rain.'

'There was a bad storm, but that was over a fortnight ago. It's rained most days since. Enough to have made the rocks slippy and probably enough to wash any marks away.'

'I assume it was still checked out by you guys.'

'Well, Sergeant MacSticker – I mean MacVicar – and Constable Campbell did. They said they found nothing of interest. *Nothing to suggest a fall or a scuffle* were the sergeant's exact words, isn't that right Fergus?'

'That's right,' Fergus agreed from the other side of the room. 'No reason to believe it was anything but an accident.'

Rachel hadn't thought he'd been listening. Neither was she reassured. Given she'd found the phone, their examination of the croft surrounding Ellen's cottage couldn't have been that thorough. 'Unless of course it isn't Ellen's phone,' she said. 'We should try to establish that before we jump to any more conclusions.'

Selena leaned back on her chair. 'Hey, Fergus. Any luck with finding a charger that fits?'

'Nope. Sorry. I'll need to hunt one down.'

Selena turned back to Rachel. 'You don't think she might have gone in deliberately?' She dropped her voice to a whisper. 'You know – suicide?'

'Who goes shopping before they kill themselves?'

Selena chewed on her lower lip. 'Maybe I want it to be more than an accident.' She flushed. 'I know that makes me a terrible person, but I always fancied myself as a detective with the CID. Just finished the exams, as it happens. We've had suspicious deaths here before, but they've always turned out to be accidental. I'm guessing this one will turn out the same. You know, Occam's razor.'

'Occam's what?'

'Razor. It's a principle from philosophy. Imagine there are two explanations for something. Occam's razor says that the one that requires the least number of assumptions is usually correct. In other words, the more assumptions you have to make, the more unlikely the explanation. On that basis, I'm pretty sure Ellen's death will turn out to be exactly what we thought all along – an unfortunate accident.'

'Probably,' Rachel agreed, although her gut was still telling her otherwise. 'However, I'd like to be sure. What do you know about her last movements?'

'Not much. The last definite sighting of her was at the Co-op on Friday. We found the receipt with the date and time.'

'Did anyone talk to her? Notice anything unusual?'

'Apparently not.'

'Anything on CCTV?'

Selena laughed. 'CCTV? Here? What do we need CCTV for? God, you can hardly nip out for a sly fag without it being reported on the jungle drums. No one would dream of paying for CCTV, although I understand that some crofters in Orkney are using it in their sheds to keep an eye on their ewes when they go into labour. Saves them having to go outside to check on them through the night. So, unless Ellen visited one such byre there is no chance of finding her on CCTV.'

Hearing the loud thumping of boots followed by a mumbled swear word in Gaelic the two women turned towards the door. A stocky man, wearing the stripes of a sergeant on the shoulder of his uniform, burst into the room. Furious eyes, bulging from a florid face, scanned the occupants, landing on Selena.

'How many times have I told you not to let the general public in here? This is not the local tea shop.' He hunched his thick neck inside his jacket like a turtle. He had the red-veined cheeks of a man who liked his drink.

Selena held his gaze and raised her eyebrows. 'Miss McKenzie is not the general public, Sarge. She's the lawyer from the Fiscal's office that's been sent to look into Ellen Hargreaves' death. Rachel, this is Sergeant MacVicar.'

The head bobbed out again. Rachel held out her hand only to find it ignored.

'I sent my report and Dr Logan's to Inverness,' the sergeant ground out. 'Did they not tell you it was our view that Miss Hargreaves' death was nothing but an unfortunate accident? We might be a small force but I know what I'm doing.'

Ah. So that was it. He resented his professional competence being challenged. Not totally unexpected or surprising. All the same, his reaction was a little over the top.

Rachel sighed inwardly. It was unusual, but not unheard of, for the Fisc's office to visit a crime scene. Douglas must have rattled his cage when he called to let him know Rachel was coming. She could imagine the conversation. Short and to the point would pretty much cover it. Rachel tried a smile.

'Sergeant, I'm not convinced, not yet, that Ellen's death *was* an accident, and neither is the pathologist who did the PM.' The latter was stretching the truth slightly but MacVicar didn't need to know that. 'I think there's a good chance Ellen's death was accidental but there are one or two loose ends I'd like to tie up before I sign off on it.'

His head bobbed a few more times. 'What loose ends?'

The bag and shopping left outside the door, the keys in the ignition, had been covered earlier with Selena. It all seemed so flimsy now – even to Rachel.

'As far as I'm aware you've found no evidence she did slip.'

Sergeant MacVicar pinched the bridge of his nose between his thumb and forefinger. 'Not finding evidence doesn't mean she didn't! What else could have happened?'

'I found a phone that I believe belonged to Ms Hargreaves near her house. If she fell in down by the shore it doesn't make sense that she dropped her mobile where I found it. If it is hers,' she conceded grudgingly. 'But if it isn't, we should try and find out who it belongs to. Do you have a mobile number for Ms Hargreaves?'

MacVicar gave another annoyed shake of his head. 'What the hell were you doing, wandering around without checking in with me first? Good God, what was Mainwaring thinking sending you out here?'

'I don't have to check in with you,' Rachel said, keeping her voice level. 'And I brought the phone here as soon as I found it. Furthermore, I should point out that Ellen's home and cottage should have been secured until my office said it could be released.'

'Selena, get me a couple of painkillers,' MacVicar ordered in Gaelic. 'My headache's getting worse.'

Selena mumbled something Rachel didn't quite catch, before heading out of the door.

'What else do you intend to do?' MacVicar asked.

'I'd like to speak to anyone who might have spoken to Ellen in the days leading up to her death.'

'We've made those enquiries. They revealed nothing of interest.'

'Yes, Constable MacDonald did say. Nevertheless, we may yet find someone who hasn't come forward. I'd also like to have a look at Ellen's car. It wasn't at the cottage. I assume you have it here?'

His head almost disappeared as he scrunched his shoulders. 'The car hire company took it back. I didn't see any reason why they shouldn't. We checked it out. There was nothing in it.'

MacVicar ran a finger around the inside of his collar. He must know he had no right to make those decisions before the Fiscal's office had signed off on the death. However, there was little to be gained by pointing it out again. It would only antagonise him more.

'I assume you still have Ms Hargreaves' rucksack?' Rachel asked instead.

'Now why would you want to look at that?'

Rachel's patience was wearing thin. If matters continued at this pace she'd be here forever.

'To begin with I'd like to see if there is anything in it that might be of interest. She kept a notebook. I didn't see it in her cottage. It wasn't listed among the contents, but perhaps it was missed. There might be something helpful in it.'

'If we'd found a notebook it would have been listed,' Sergeant MacVicar snapped. 'As was everything of relevance. There was no need to go through every drawer and box, if that's what you're implying.'

Rachel refused to rise to the bait. 'At some point, I'd like to see where her body was recovered. I'd also like to speak to the women who found her. Do you have their contact details?' Surely to God he did?

MacVicar screwed up his eyes as if the light pained him. Selena handed him two tablets along with a glass of water.

'They're still here,' Selena replied for him. 'Mrs Mowbury

told us that despite being involved in *a horrible discovery'* –
Selena held up her forefingers and used them to indicate quota-
tion marks – 'she had no intention of cutting her holiday short
and that she fully intended to stay another week as planned.
They're staying at the Polochar Inn on South Uist. I'll text you
the numbers.'

Rachel stiffened at the mention of South Uist. For a while
she'd forgotten where she was.

'I'd also like to know more about Ellen's movements in the
days leading up to the discovery of her body. If we can access
her phone records, its GPS might be able to give us more
information.'

MacVicar puffed out his cheeks. 'Look, Miss McKenzie. I
can't stop you doing whatever your office has asked you to do,
but I can't see the point of your requests. We've looked at and
around Ms Hargreaves' house, talked to people who might have
seen her, put out an appeal on the local radio station and found
nothing untoward. There is nothing that suggests that anyone
else had any part to play in her disappearance. She was a
woman who kept herself pretty much to herself. She liked walking, poking around ruins and recording birds. For Christ's sake,
she was a librarian!'

'I didn't realise working in a library precluded you from
being murdered,' Rachel said before she could help herself. But,
damn it, she wasn't going to let him treat her like an unwelcome
guest at a party.

'Murder! Who the hell is talking about murder?' the
sergeant spluttered. If anything, his already puce face turned
redder. 'People don't get murdered here. Certainly not people
like Miss Hargreaves.'

Constable Campbell suddenly chimed in. 'Well, there was
that one in South Uist. Remember? The one brother shot the
other...'

MacVicar glared at him. 'That wasn't a murder. That was

sheer stupidity. A hunting accident. The idiots had been drinking. What fool takes a gun and goes shooting when they've been drinking?'

'I'd also like to speak to the police surgeon who examined Ellen's body after it was pulled from the water. Where can I find...' Rachel consulted her notepad, 'Dr Logan?'

'Why?'

Rachel was near the end of her tether. 'Sergeant,' she continued evenly, 'Please understand I have a job to do – one I intend to carry out to the best of my ability. And that job involves deciding on behalf of the Crown whether a crime has been committed. Now, I expect you're right and Ellen's death was an accident, but as yet, I'm not convinced. So, until I am, I would appreciate your cooperation. Otherwise, I'm afraid I'm going to have to speak to your superior officer.'

MacVicar stared at her, the veins in his forehead throbbing as if they had a life of their own. Rachel refused to look away.

'Och, do whatever you have to,' he conceded. 'But make sure you keep me informed or I'll be speaking to *your* boss. Selena here will take you to see Dr Logan.' He turned on his heel and left the room.

'Just give me a tick – need the loo,' Selena said, looked disproportionately delighted to be tasked with accompanying her.

Rachel waited for Selena outside the police station. MacVicar was probably correct and there was little point going to see the police surgeon. She would only tell them the same thing she had said in her report. However, MacVicar's unhelpful attitude made Rachel all the more determined to be thorough. *She* wouldn't be the one to embarrass the Fiscal's office.

As she breathed in the salty, briny smell of the sea underlaid with the tantalising whiff of peat, her chest constricted. How could a place make a person feel happy and sad, peaceful and anxious all at the same time?

The arrival of Selena, her slight frame almost submerged in her fluorescent jacket, was a relief.

'Is Sergeant MacVicar always so—' Rachel bit back the rest of the sentence. She didn't know Selena well enough to criticise her boss.

'Och, he's not that bad once you get to know him.' Selena squinted up at the sky. The clouds had moved away and the sun warmed Rachel's face. 'I suspect he thinks you've been sent to check on him.' She gave Rachel a small smile. 'His father and grandfather were police officers here before him. I doubt he would have even become a police officer if they hadn't been. So he doesn't want to come out looking inferior to them in any way. According to my aunt, who was at school with him, he had his chance to take exams, possibly get a promoted post on the mainland, but he chose not to. I think he believes he knows everything. Somehow learned it by osmosis. Mam says he'd do anything for an easy life.' She clamped a hand over her mouth. 'Oh bot-ach, I shouldn't have said any of that. I don't think he likes it that I plan to go to the mainland and become a detective. As soon as I hear I've passed the exams I'm applying to Inverness CID.'

For the first time since she'd set foot on the island, the tension in Rachel's gut eased. 'So where do we find this Dr Logan?' she asked.

'At the practice just round the corner. It's not far. We can walk. I could do with the fresh air.'

The surgery – a modern, single-storey, red-brick new build – was a five-minute walk along a single-track road which skirted a loch.

'It's new,' Selena said. 'Before this was built the doctors consulted from a converted croft house, a bit like the police station. I wish they'd build us a new police station.' Her voice was wistful.

The receptionist at the surgery told them that the doctor was expecting them, that Constable Campbell had telephoned to let them know, and they should take a seat while they waited. Rachel sat next to a man whose entire body shook whenever he coughed, which was every couple of seconds. The only other patient was a young, tired-looking woman accompanied by a fractious toddler. Selena seemed to know her and they struck up a conversation about a forthcoming dance, speaking English for Rachel's benefit.

They waited as the woman and the coughing man were called in. Just when Rachel was wondering whether Dr Logan was deliberately ignoring them, the receptionist showed them into her consulting room.

Dr Logan was in her late fifties, dark-haired and sombre-featured. She wore a trouser suit and a striped blouse. She smiled and waved them into a couple of chairs opposite her desk. Once they were settled, she studied them over steepled fingers. 'Sergeant MacVicar warned me you were on your way.'

Rachel thought 'warned' was an odd choice of word. She explained why she was there and asked if the doctor minded if she recorded their meeting on her phone.

The doctor nodded her agreement. 'I really don't know what else I can tell you.'

'Let's just start at the beginning, shall we? I understand you act as the police surgeon for the whole of the island?'

'Yes. In addition to my general practitioner duties. I'm on call twenty-four seven – except, of course, when I'm on holiday. Not that that happens as often as I'd like.'

'Can you explain what the role of police surgeon involves?'

'At the most basic level I can be called to review the mental or physical health of anyone the police have arrested or detained. It is my responsibility to ensure that they are looked after appropriately as far as their health is concerned. We also have the odd reported rape and I carry out, with the complainant's consent, the forensic exam. In addition we have our share of suicides, accidents and unexpected deaths here. When that happens I'm called to view the body in locus and to pronounce death. I may be asked to supply a report on my findings, as I did with Ms Hargreaves. Occasionally I'm asked to appear in court and give evidence for any of the former.'

'Do you carry out the post mortems?' Rachel asked.

'No. I'm not qualified. That has to be done by a pathologist. And that's up to the PF to request. If he does, then the body is sent to Inverness or Glasgow for the PM.'

'But you didn't think there was anything suspicious about her death?'

'No.' She shook her head slightly. 'To be frank, I'm surprised that anyone considers it could be anything but an accident. I wasn't aware that the results of the post mortem indicated otherwise.'

'It didn't,' Rachel admitted. 'But neither did the pathologist rule it out. He listed the cause of death as unascertained.'

'Which is exactly what I would have expected.' Dr Logan rifled through a wad of papers piled haphazardly on her desk until she found the one she was looking for. 'Ellen Hargreaves. Here it is. The copy of the report I sent.' Dr Logan scrutinised the sheet of paper before passing it to Rachel. 'Evidence of blunt force trauma to her head. Lacerations to her legs and torso. All compatible with being tossed around on the rocks. As I said in my report, I believe she slipped, knocked herself out on a rock or boulder, fell into the sea and drowned. I've seen similar cases. We have one drowning every couple of years on average. Sometimes tourists, sometimes fishermen, most of whom refuse to wear life jackets or learn how to swim. They say they'd rather go quickly if they fall in.' She smiled briefly. 'To be fair, there might be something in that view. The sea here is so cold it could kill you in minutes.'

'What about suicide? Could Ellen have drowned herself deliberately?'

Although, as she'd said to Selena, she didn't believe it for one moment, she was interested to hear what the doctor had to say. Had Dr Logan considered every possibility?

A look of irritation crossed the doctor's face.

'Naturally as soon as I got back to the surgery after pronouncing death, I checked her notes. The last time I saw Ellen she displayed no sign of a low mood.'

'Does that mean Ellen visited the surgery recently?' Selena asked.

Dr Logan seemed pleased to be asked a question she had an easy answer for. 'Actually, she did. She consulted me last month for a mild chest infection. I gave her a thorough going-over. I was impressed. She was fit for someone of her age. I'm pretty certain she hadn't had a heart attack just prior to falling in.'

'Could one or more of the injuries have been caused by a deliberate blow to the head?' Rachel asked. 'Can you definitely rule that out?'

The GP looked at her, incredulous. 'Hardly likely though, is it? The islands aren't exactly a hotbed of murder and Ellen isn't your typical victim. Just a harmless middle-aged woman who tragically was alone when she got into trouble.'

Dr Logan stood. 'I wish I could be of more help. I have a number of home visits waiting for me. I don't mean to be rude, but if there's nothing else?' She opened the door and stepped aside.

'Thank you for your time, Dr Logan,' Selena said politely. 'Miss McKenzie and I will get back to you if there's anything else.' She took hold of Rachel's elbow and ushered her out of the room before Rachel could protest.

Outside, the wind had whipped up and Rachel huddled into her jacket. 'Dr Logan and Sergeant MacVicar are clearly of the same mind. She hid it better, but I don't think she cared to be questioned either.' She jammed her hands deep into her trouser pockets. Day one and she'd managed to upset two key people.

'I guess they are both used to calling the shots here, not used to having their judgement questioned. They're friends, have been for years. According to my aunt, they went to school together.'

'They aren't having a thing, are they?'

Selena shrugged. 'Some people think so.'

'It must be difficult for you?' Rachel said. 'Policing an island when you're part of the community?'

Selena grimaced. 'Let's say it has its challenges. Sometimes you have to turn a blind eye. Pretend you haven't seen or don't know someone's deepest, darkest secret. Cos we all have 'em.'

Rachel suppressed a shiver of unease. How long would it take Selena, or MacVicar or even Dr Logan, to discover who she was? Minutes, if they were interested. She pushed the thought away. There wasn't much she could do about it.

'But back to Dr Logan,' Selena continued. 'She is lovely once you get to know her. She really does care about her patients. I shouldn't have passed on the gossip about her. I don't know what's got into me today. I'm usually better at censoring what comes out of my mouth. I blame a bloody awful hangover. Should never have gone on the piss last night.'

Rachel knew how that felt too. She didn't go out clubbing often but when she did she almost always drank too much.

'Is Dr Logan your GP?'

'She would be if I ever needed to see one. But I'm as strong as a horse, me.' Selena flexed her biceps and grinned at Rachel. 'There's a small gym at the school in Benbecula. I try to work out at least twice a week and in between times go for a run with my cousin.'

This was the point when Rachel might have suggested they run together. It was what most people would do when they came across someone they clicked with. But she wasn't most people.

'What now?' Selena continued when Rachel didn't respond.

'I'm going to go to my hotel check-in.'

'Where are you staying?'

'Tioran Lodge.'

'Why there? You could have stayed in one of the hotels here in Lochmaddy. We have two. It would have been handier.'

'I'm on a budget and Tioran Lodge was offering a great deal.'

Selena's brow puckered. 'Offering more deals? Doesn't sound good. My cousin Rhoda works there. She's worried that she might lose her job if this summer turns out to be as quiet as the last.' Selena nodded in the direction of the police station. 'I should get back.' She hesitated. 'Perhaps the sergeant and the doctor are correct? There's not enough to suggest it was anything but an accident. Just a feeling you and I have that something's not quite right.'

'Instinct. Womanly intuition,' Rachel replied, recalling Douglas's derision when they'd had a similar conversation. 'Whatever we want to call it. Right now, despite the evidence to the contrary, that's what I'm going with. I'm ninety-nine per cent confident we can rule out suicide but I'm not leaving here until I'm convinced Ellen's death was accidental.' Rachel smiled at Selena. 'Although I might need your help to prove it.'

Selena grinned back. 'You're kidding! I hoped you'd say that! It's the most exciting thing that's happened here in years. So whatever help you need, you've got it.'

. . .

Selena watched Rachel's retreating back. She was pleased someone was taking an interest in the Ellen Hargreaves' case.

She stepped back inside the office. Fergus had hold of Ellen's phone and was stabbing the screen with his finger.

'It's working then?' Selena asked.

'Aye. Got a charger for it, but it's locked. Do you have any idea how many combinations of four numbers there are?' he asked.

Selena shrugged. 'Thousands? Hundreds of thousands?'

'Ten thousand, to be precise.'

Fergus had been a police officer far longer than Selena, yet somewhere along the line they'd silently agreed she was the boss of the two of them. It was up to him if he wanted to spend his time on a hopeless task. There was little else to do. She swung the screen of her computer around to face her and typed Rachel McKenzie into the Google search engine. There was no need to google anyone on the island. All a person had to do was to ask someone of the right generation and a full history was immediately available – much more than could ever be found on Google for most ordinary people. But something told Selena that Rachel McKenzie with her dazzling smile and haunted eyes was different.

As always, the computer took its time – the internet wasn't much better now than it had been in the days of dial-up, or so her mother said. Selena couldn't remember those days.

Eventually the search engine spewed up some answers.

At first she thought she was reading about the wrong Rachel McKenzie.

She glanced behind her. Fergus was still absorbed with the phone. She focused on the screen and re-read the article.

She leaned back in her chair and gave a low whistle. Bloody hell! Who would have guessed? Poor lass. She closed the screen. God help Rachel if and when Sergeant MacVicar found out. As for the rest of the islanders? She'd give it until tomorrow.

SEVEN

Tioran Lodge was at the end of another road to nowhere. Nestled in a small dip between hills, the double-storey building looked as if it had been constructed in the early part of the twentieth century, possibly as a hunting lodge. But it had been added to recently; the square cement extension with its tin roof, abutting uncomfortably with the original sandstone, the older and newer part of the building joined by a roof creating a sort of outdoor foyer, the walls and ceiling of which were covered with etchings of fish, each one with a weight and a name inscribed next to it.

Inside, the reception area was deserted. Rachel pressed the bell on the counter and, while she waited, studied the notices lining the wall. There were dances advertised as well as tea rooms, concerts and talks. There was more going on in Uist than she'd imagined.

Someone cleared their throat and Rachel turned to find a milk-skinned woman with wind-tousled black hair and a practised smile standing behind her. In her late thirties or early forties, she was pretty in a way that wouldn't last into middle age. Her shoulder-length hair was kept out of her eyes with a narrow scarf tied at the top with a bow.

The woman held out her hand. 'Miss McKenzie? Welcome to the island. I'm Michelle Howard, one of the owners.' Rachel identified an Edinburgh accent. 'I've given you a room in the new extension,' Michelle continued after they'd shaken hands. 'We just finished it a few months ago and your room has one of the best views. The dining room, bar and the conservatory are on the other side of the hotel. All are open to locals as well as guests.'

Rachel followed Michelle along a corridor. Michelle opened the door of the third room on the right with a flourish and stood aside to let Rachel go in front of her. The room was a pleasant surprise. If Michelle had styled the room herself, she had done a good job. It was welcoming and cosy, steering away from the blandness too many hotels seemed to think essential. A large double bed faced the floor-to-ceiling windows and a bright red throw hung over the back of a comfortable-looking armchair. There were the usual tea and coffee facilities, a TV and an en suite. Patio doors led directly onto a small garden. A few steps away from Rachel's room was a bench where trees and shrubs offered shelter from the wind. But it was the view that made the room special. The clouds had cleared as suddenly as they'd arrived and late afternoon sunshine bathed the hills in lilac and gold.

'That's Eaval you can see in the distance,' Michelle said, coming to stand next to her. She opened the door out onto the garden. 'If you like hillwalking it's the highest in Uist, although that's not saying much.'

'Unfortunately, I don't think I'll have much time for hiking while I'm here,' Rachel replied. 'But I think I could find time for that titchy one over there.' She pointed to a hill a short distance from the bedroom window.

Michelle smiled. 'I'm sure you could – it would take you

about ten minutes at a push. It's worth a look. It has some interesting standing stones halfway up and a burial chamber on the top that's almost five thousand years old. At least, that's what the sign says. At one time you could crawl inside and look at where the folk who lived back then used to put the bodies. Not anymore. They've blocked the entrance. Health and safety, you see. I gather it's not very stable.'

In the ensuing pause, Rachel became conscious of a scratching sound. Faint at first and then more persistent, it seemed to be coming from directly above her – as if there were rats scurrying across the roof of her bedroom.

'What on earth is that?' she asked Michelle.

Michelle followed her gaze to the ceiling. 'It's the crows, I'm afraid. They roost on the roof. It's made of corrugated iron so unfortunately their claws make a bit of a racket. I hope they won't keep you awake. If we'd known they'd choose there to roost, we would have made the roof from something else. It's too late now. It would cost a fortune to replace it.' Her grey eyes were anxious. 'I can give you another room if you prefer. You're our only guest so you can have your pick.'

'No, this one is perfect. I don't mind the noise as long as I know what's making it. Although some crows tried to attack me earlier. They flew straight at me – gave me a bit of a fright. I felt as if I was in that Hitchcock film...' The moment the words were out of her mouth Rachel regretted them. They didn't really fit with the professional image she was going for.

To her relief, Michelle gave a small hiccup of laughter. 'The locals hate them. Especially at this time of year with the lambs. If the lambs are weak when they're born, the crows peck out their eyes. But as for attacking people?' She gave a slight shake of her head. 'That's more unusual. Crows *have* been known to attack humans when they feel threatened, but it's usually when they're protecting their chicks. And who can blame them? They're not so different to us, really. To be honest I find them quite fascinating. They're actually far more intelligent than people give them credit for.'

'In what way?' Rachel asked, intrigued.

'Apparently they have very long memories. There are studies where it's been shown that they can pass on information about people they feel threatened by to young crows and these crows are subsequently able to recognise that person as an enemy too.'

Rachel smiled. 'I've never harmed a crow. Or any other bird, for that matter. At least not intentionally.'

'Have you heard of a crow's parliament?' Michelle asked.

Rachel raised a questioning eyebrow. 'Can't say I have.'

'Apparently sometimes crows get together to judge another crow. According to legend they surround the accused crow in a circle. Then they seem to confer or something, because after a while they either fly away with the accused or' – she grimaced – 'they decide that the bird is guilty and peck it to death.'

'Seriously?' Rachel said, unable to disguise her cynicism.

'Many here believe that sort of thing. This island is full of similar stories, as you'll no doubt discover.' Michelle pushed a lock of hair behind her ear. 'If you don't mind me asking, how long do you think you'll be staying? When you made the reservation you said a couple of nights, but possibly more? I'm sorry to press you. It's not that we're particularly busy right now, at least not in the hotel, but I have to plan staff-wise. We only have one permanent housekeeper. The rest come in on an as-needed basis. It helps keep costs down.' She chewed her lip. 'Oh, bugger. There I go again. Mike always says I talk too much. I'm sure you're not the least bit interested in any of this.'

Rachel opened her mouth to make a polite protest, but Michelle cut her off. 'And why should you be? I can think of nothing more boring myself.'

When she grinned it transformed her face. She really was quite beautiful.

'Can I let you know tomorrow? I should have a better idea by then.'

'Sure.' Michelle hesitated. 'You're here because of Ellen, aren't you? The woman they found in the blowhole out at Scolpaig.'

'What makes you say that?'

Michelle gave a rueful smile. 'You'll find there's precious little that goes on here that the islanders don't know or make it their business to find out. Particularly when it comes to strangers. We've already heard about the lawyer who's come to investigate Ellen Hargreaves' death.'

A cold finger pressed Rachel's spine. Sooner or later they would find out who she was – her link to the islands – the skeleton that lay in *her* past. All the more reason to do what she needed to as quickly as possible – particularly if there was the smallest chance of being stranded here by the predicted storm.

'In which case, the locals will be able to tell me all about Ellen.' Rachel lifted her carry-on bag onto the bed and unzipped it, hoping Michelle would take the hint.

'They'll be *able* to tell you, all right. Whether they will or not is another matter,' Michelle said flatly. 'Sharing gossip with each other is one thing; talking to outsiders quite another. I should know. I've been here for eight years and they still regard me as an incomer.' Michelle turned away, but not before Rachel saw the flash of hurt in her grey eyes.

Rachel felt another pang of sympathy. She knew only too well what it was like to be an outsider.

'Anyway,' Michelle added, her shoulders silhouetted against the dying sun, stiff and unyielding. 'I thought Ellen's death was an accident. We heard she slipped on the rocks and fell into the sea. Although...' Again she hesitated before turning round to face Rachel, her expression once more the polite mask of the professional hostess. 'Oh, never mind. I need to get on. I've a group coming in for a bar supper and it's only me and Rhoda in the dining room. Will you be eating here tonight?'

'Yes, please. But what were you going to say? If there's anything you can tell me about Ms Hargreaves, I'd really like to hear it.'

'It was nothing, really.' Michelle edged towards the door. 'Except Mike, my husband, says Ellen couldn't have washed up where she did. Not if she fell outside her house at any rate. And he's not usually wrong about things like that.'

Rachel's skin prickled. Had she been right all along?

'Why is he so sure?'

'He owns the diving company that helped retrieve Ellen's body. He knows about tides and currents. His livelihood depends on it.'

Why on earth had Selena not said?

'Is Mike here? Could I speak to him about it?'

'He's in the kitchen right now. It'll have to be after we finish serving dinner.'

Rachel was confused. 'I thought he owned the diving company?'

Michelle sighed. 'He does. But you'll find there's no such thing as having one job on these islands – especially if you own a business or, as in our case, two. I help him with the diving company, the books at least, and he helps me in the hotel. That's how we survive. As I mentioned earlier, we try to keep staffing to the minimum – as a consequence there is no slack in the system.' Her shoulders slumped. The bandana had slipped, the bow now just above her ear. 'We're more short-staffed than usual at the moment. The cook left at the end of last season and we haven't found a replacement yet. Not everyone likes how remote it is here.'

Rachel could believe it. 'Would you let Mike know I'd like to speak to him?'

'Will do.'

A final smile from Michelle and Rachel was alone. She sat on the bed thinking about what she should do next.

So, she and Selena weren't the only ones to have doubts about Ellen's death. She needed to speak to Mike as a matter of urgency. But, as he wouldn't be available until later, questioning him would have to wait. Douglas would have left for the day so there was no point phoning him. She had nothing new to tell him anyway, although she should make a record of the day's events while they were still fresh in her mind.

She'd almost completed writing up her notes when her mobile rang. She didn't recognise the number and when she answered all she could hear was crackle. She checked the reception. A single bar was fading in and out. She went outside and, holding her phone in front of her, started up the small hill that led to the standing stones. Her phone pinged. It was a text from Selena. *Soz. Forgot how lousy the signal can be. I've attached the number for Polochar Inn as well as Olivia Mowbury's mobile no.*

Back in her room Rachel tried to log in to Google Maps on her phone but couldn't connect to the internet. She made a mental note to ask Michelle about the hotel Wi-Fi. Frustrated, she resorted to technology that did work and spread out her paper map. Polochar Inn was situated on the southernmost tip of South Uist – past the turn-off for Lochboisdale where her grandfather still lived, but not much further. And very close to the cemetery where Rachel's grandmother had been buried.

Tossing the map aside, Rachel changed into trainers, a T-shirt, and leggings. She needed a run to get rid of some of the pent-up energy from the day and there was just enough time before dinner.

The hotel bar was tiny, the half-dozen occupants filling it to capacity. As she entered there was a moment's silence as everyone stopped talking and turned to give her a curious look before turning away and continuing with their conversation.

Rachel perched at the bar and ordered a vodka and Diet Coke from Michelle, who appeared to be on double duty as barmaid.

'Did you have a good run?' Michelle asked as she passed Rachel her drink.

Christ, Rachel might as well be a contestant on *Big Brother*!

'Yes, thanks. I don't suppose your husband's available yet?'

Michelle nodded towards the restaurant. 'He's still in the kitchen. I expect he'll be out in a sec to help behind the bar.' She attempted a smile but it came out more like a grimace. She blew a stray lock of hair away from her face.

'It must be a long day for him. For both of you,' Rachel said sympathetically.

'You could say that. A long, long day.'

There was more than a trace of bitterness in her voice. As if realising she had revealed more than she wanted to, the practised smile slid back into place. 'Sorry. There I go again. I did say I talk too much. I blame the lack of female company. Mike isn't the most talkative of men.' She looked over Rachel's shoulder. 'Speak of the devil. Here he is!'

'Who wants to know?' Michelle's husband was stockily built with short, thick hair, piercing blue eyes and beak of a nose. Despite the grey in his hair, he looked to be in his mid-forties. He struck her as a man who didn't miss much.

'This is Miss McKenzie – I told you about her? She's looking into that poor woman's death.'

Mike accepted the drink Michelle poured for him and smiled at Rachel. 'Welcome. It's a shame you're here on police business.'

'I'm not with the police, as a matter of fact. I'm a lawyer with the Procurator Fiscal's office.'

He gave her a sharp look. 'I didn't know lawyers got

involved in accidental deaths. Is someone looking for someone to blame?'

'Why would you think that?'

'Because in my experience folk always look to hold someone else responsible for their misfortune.'

Rachel was struck by the venom in his voice.

'No. Or not to my knowledge.' She explained again about the procurator fiscal's role in Scotland. 'In England the coroner performs that duty. Think of my being here as being similar – a sort of roaming inquiry.'

Although no one actually stared, Rachel was conscious of the interest in the room.

Mike took a long pull on his pint of lager, wiping his mouth with the back of his hand. 'To be frank, I'm glad someone is taking it seriously enough to look into it further. Look, I have a few minutes before dinner service starts. There's only you and another four and they aren't booked in until eight. Let's have a seat and you can ask me anything you want to know.'

Pint in one hand, he took her by the elbow with the other and steered her into a conservatory that opened off from the bar.

There were landscapes on the wall, a row of books on a shelf and a telescope directed towards Eaval, the hill Michelle had pointed out earlier. They took a seat at an empty table in the corner.

'OK. Shoot,' he said, when they were seated.

'I understand you were part of the diving team that helped recover Miss Hargreaves' body?'

Mike took another long sip of his drink and relaxed into his chair.

'Terrible business. I wasn't there personally but I sent my divers, yes. The islands are tidal. A high tide must have pushed her body in, the retreating tide exposing it to view. By the time the emergency services were alerted, the tide was on its way back in. Divers are the best people to retrieve bodies in these conditions. It isn't work we take pleasure in, but there's no one else that can do it. The nearest police divers are based in Glasgow and it would take time for them to get here. No one likes to leave a body in the water while waiting for them to come.'

Rachel detected a flicker of revulsion in his eyes.

'I gather you're a commercial diving company. What exactly do you do?'

'Anything and everything. We dive for scallops, help repair nets at the fish farms, untangle nets and lines that get stuck in propellers, repair the piers. We'll consider any work that requires a diving team.'

'And you're the only commercial diving company on the island?'

'Yes. The next nearest is on Lewis. After that you'd need to go to Oban or Inverness.'

'Michelle said you weren't convinced about where the body washed up.'

Mike glanced across at his wife, his expression unreadable. 'Look, this is only my opinion, nothing more. Except, I happen to think I'm right. The f— sorry, frigging coastguard is always telling us that they know the tides, but they're talking through a hole in their arses.'

Rachel raised a brow in encouragement.

Mike shook his head. 'There's no way that woman's body would have washed up where it did if she fell outside her cottage – or from anywhere else nearby, for that matter.'

Rachel's pulse upped a notch. 'Why do you say that?'

'You have to understand some things about this island. The coastguard here is made up of volunteers – not like other places – and half of them are incomers who are used to farting around in yachts. The other half is made up of retired folk who should know better. If the coastguard had the faintest idea about tides and currents they would realise that the only way she could have got into that bloody blowhole would be if she'd fallen in there, or...' He dropped his voice so that Rachel was forced to lean towards him to hear him above the piped accordion music. 'Or if she went into the water somewhere further out to sea and the current, along with an ebbing tide, brought her in.'

'Are you sure?' Rachel asked.

'I can show you. Wait here. I'll just get a map from the guest lounge.'

On his return he spread the map on the table.

'OK, so this is the blowhole in Scolpaig where Ellen was found.' He used his finger to stab a spot on the north-west of North Uist. 'Here is where she supposedly fell in.' He pointed to the tiny inlet where Ellen had her cottage. He traced the coastline between the two points with his finger. 'See all the nooks and crannies around the coastline. Even as the crow flies it's a good twenty miles from her cottage, further if you follow the coastline. And then there's all the bays and inlets, the rocks where her body could have snagged.' He leaned back in his chair. 'Anyone with half a brain should have been able to see that her body ending up in that blowhole was very unlikely to begin with, and even less likely if she fell in near her house.'

'But not impossible?'

Mike puffed out his cheeks. 'One thing I do know about is the sea. Believe me, there is no way her body could have been dragged in there all the way from the shore near her house in Grimsay.'

An electric charge swept across Rachel's skin. He seemed so certain.

'Did you tell the police this?'

'Who? Sergeant MacVicar and that load of half-wits that pass for a police force on the island?' He sighed. 'Actually, I did try to tell them, but they weren't interested. Claimed the coastguard said it was perfectly possible and that was good enough for them.'

'What do *you* think happened?'

'Haven't a clue – all I know is what *didn't* happen.' He stood abruptly. 'I'm sorry, I need to get back to the kitchen. I've told you everything I know. If you don't believe I'm right, speak to someone who is an expert on tides and currents for these parts.'

As he strode off, Rachel sat back in her chair and let out a slow breath. Her office was bound to have access to experts on tides and currents. Would Douglas sanction the expense of speaking to one at this stage? Probably not. Therefore, before approaching him, she should hear what the coastguard had to say. Someone at the police station should have a name and number.

She studied the map again. She knew a little about tide and currents, but it did look an incredibly long way.

A dark-eyed, black-haired woman with a notepad came over to Rachel's table. She smiled shyly. 'Hello. I'm Rhoda, Catriona from the shop's daughter. Mam said to be sure to say hello.'

Rachel smiled back and held out her hand. 'Pleased to meet you, Rhoda, Catriona from the shop's daughter. I'm Rachel from the Fiscal's office in Inverness.'

'I can recommend the ham pie,' Rhoda said, her cheeks pinking, making Rachel feel bad for teasing her.

'Then I'll have the ham pie. No chips, just salad. And a glass of Chenin Blanc.'

Rhoda jotted the order down on her pad and scurried off.

As Rachel waited for her food to arrive she reviewed what she knew so far.

If Mike was right and there was no way Ellen's body could have been carried by the tide as far as Scolpaig then she must have fallen in there or somewhere nearby. What if the last person to drive Ellen's rental hadn't been Ellen? What if Ellen had been at the blowhole with someone and she'd fallen in and the person she'd been with had been too scared – why? – to call for help and had driven Ellen's car back to the cottage, leaving the keys in the ignition and her bag and shopping at the door? No. That made no sense.

Alternatively, could Ellen have fallen from a boat out at sea? In which case, why hadn't whoever she'd been with reported it? Unless Ellen had been sailing alone? Again no one had mentioned Ellen being a sailor or having access to a boat. It also still begged the question why she'd left her shopping and rucksack at the door before sailing away. Furthermore, an empty boat would have eventually attracted notice – washed up some-where. Worth checking though.

Rachel stared out at the darkness, her reflection a ghostly twin in the window. Whatever had happened to Ellen, it was still too soon to rule out murder. She needed to find out more.

EIGHT

WEDNESDAY

After a breakfast of scrambled egg and toast washed down with several cups of strong coffee, Rachel phoned the police station using the landline in her room. The phone was answered by Selena.

'Hey, Selena. Rachel here. Any luck with the phone?'

'Not yet. Sorry! It's charged but Fergus hasn't been able to unlock it.'

'Bugger. In that case can I speak to Sergeant MacVicar?' Rachel asked.

'He's not usually in until later. Is there anything I can help you with?'

'I need to speak to someone from the coastguard. Do you have a name I could contact?'

'That would be Calum Stuart. He's the head honcho. At least on Uist, he is. The full-timers are all in Stornoway.'

'And where will I find Mr Stuart? Does the coastguard have a base here?'

'Nope. Not unless you count the Portakabin near Hosta. Hey, if you hang on, I'm sure I have Calum's mobile number somewhere. I don't think the coastguard would thank me for using the emergency number to track him down. Might be a bit of a laugh though.'

There was a clunk as Selena put down the receiver. She was back after a couple of seconds. 'Sorry, can't find it right now but I'll get it for you. Why do you want to speak to him?'

'I'd like to hear what he has to say about the tide and currents the day Ellen was last seen alive. Which reminds me, why didn't you tell me it was Mike's company that had pulled Ellen from the water?'

'It didn't occur to me. I didn't think it mattered. Mike wasn't actually there when his team recovered the body. Why are you asking? Is it important?'

'It could be. Mike told me he doesn't believe Ellen could have washed up where she did if she fell in near her house. He said he told the police that.'

'So I understand. But Constable Campbell loves to sail and both he and Sergeant MacVicar say Mike is just plain wrong.'

'Nevertheless. It would have been helpful to know that someone disagrees with the coastguard's opinion.'

'I suggest you take that up with the sergeant,' Selena replied, her normally soft vowels clipped. 'Good luck with that. I'll find a number for Calum and get that meeting set up.'

After finishing the call, Rachel reviewed her notes. The mother and daughter who had found Ellen hadn't been able to tell the police much. They'd found the body by chance, called the police, and waited while it was recovered. It was probably a waste of time, but Rachel decided she should speak to them, if only for the sake of completeness.

She tried Olivia's mobile number but couldn't get a connection. She dialled the number of the inn only to be told by the receptionist that the Mowburys were out for the morning. Rachel left a message saying that she would call back later.

Apart from speaking to the Mowburys, she wanted to confirm that the phone she'd found did belong to Ellen. She had no faith in Sergeant MacVicar making it a priority. The easiest way would be to get hold of Ellen's number. Sophie was bound to have it somewhere on record.

The address of the hire car company was on the business card Sophie had given her along with the paperwork.

Rachel found it easily, situated as it was just off the main road. A number of vehicles were parked outside and a familiar black-haired figure, this time wearing jeans tucked into boots instead of a white shirt and black skirt, was spraying one with a high-pressure hose. Rachel waved to Rhoda, who waved back. She found Sophie inside a small office running her finger down entries in a ledger. Sophie glanced up and gave Rachel a surprised smile.

'Oh, hello. I didn't expect to see you so soon. How're you getting on?'

'I wanted to ask about the car Ellen hired. I gather it was returned to you?'

Sophie switched her attention to an ancient computer on the counter. She pressed a few keys and a printer whirred into life.

'Sergeant MacVicar said it was OK for us to fetch it. Ellen had left the keys in the ignition, so it was easy enough.'

'Is the car here?'

Sophie laughed. 'You're kidding. All our vehicles are out almost all of the time.'

'I assume it was valeted when it came back. Did you find anything in it?'

Sophie tipped her head to the side. 'Funny you should ask. This morning, the client who has it out on hire at the moment brought in a book he found in the glove compartment. I was going to drop it off at the police station later – but seeing as you're here I could give it to you, if you like? Maybe you could give it to the police for me?'

Rachel followed Sophie into a small room at the back of the

reception. 'I'm forever telling the girls who clean the vehicles to check the cars thoroughly. People are always leaving their belongings. You'd be amazed. We've found knickers and money and other stuff you wouldn't believe. Now where did I put the damn thing?' Sophie raised her voice. 'Rhoda! Where's that book we found in Ellen's car?'

Rhoda appeared in the doorway drying her hands on an old tea towel.

'Hello again. I didn't realise you worked here too,' Rachel said.

'Lots of locals have more than one job. Rhoda has three, if you count her helping her father on the croft,' Sophie said.

'I put the book on the shelf in the waiting room.' Rhoda said, giving Rachel a smile. 'Give me a sec and I'll get it for you.' She returned a few moments later holding a book with a picture of an eagle on its glossy cover. Sophie nodded for her to give it to Rachel.

'It's not very interesting, I'm afraid,' Sophie said. 'Just a bird book. But someone might want it.'

Rachel took it from her. It was an illustrated bird guide, of the type that could be acquired in any bookshop. Disappointed it wasn't Ellen's notebook – it might have given them clues as to what Ellen had been up to in the days prior to her death – Rachel shoved it in her bag.

'Do you have a mobile number for Ellen? I noticed there was no landline at the house.'

'Sure do. Give me a minute. It's on my phone.' She pressed a couple of buttons. 'What's your number? I'll send it to you.'

Having the number would make it easier to get hold of Ellen's phone records. That would give them a better picture of Ellen. They might even be able to track her movements in the days before she died.

'I don't suppose you know anything about what Ellen was doing in the days leading up to her body being found?'

Sophie grinned. 'As a matter of fact I do have something to tell you. I've been asking around. The last time anyone remembers seeing her was about a week before her body was found. Her car was seen at Balranald nature reserve near Hougharry on the Friday morning – it's one of the best places to spot birds – and someone said they saw her heading up the cliffs at Hosta a little while later. Apparently there was a report of some rare bird being seen up there. Then her car was spotted outside Sollas Co-op at lunchtime.'

That all fitted with what Selena had told Rachel. She was disappointed. She'd hoped to learn something new.

'Did you get hold of a map at the shop?' Sophie continued.

Rachel nodded.

'If you have it with you, I can show you.'

Rachel took the map from her handbag and they spread it out on the counter.

'That's Hosta, that's Balranald and Sollas is on the other side,' Sophie said, pointing to the different locations on the map.

'To get to the Co-op from Hosta, Ellen would have taken the road around the tip and that would have taken her past Scolpaig. You can only get to the blowhole on foot by the way, or boat. Now, my niece works at the Co-op in Sollas, so I phoned her. She said that while Ellen was in for her shopping she was asking about Na h-Eileanan Monach – the Monach Islands.'

Islands of the Monks. 'Do they actually exist?'

'Sure do. They're islands just off the coast of North Uist.' Sophie tapped the map with her pen. 'You can see them from Balranald. They used to be inhabited but nobody has lived there for decades. The fishermen from North Uist used to use it as a place to kip overnight in the old days when they went out fishing for a week at a time. That stopped when they got bigger boats. Anyway, my niece Sheena said Ellen was excited about something.' She paused for dramatic effect. 'Ellen asked Sheena

if she knew anything about the Monachs. Sheena told her she
didn't but knew someone who did.'

When she didn't continue, Rachel prompted her with a
'Go on.'

'Sheena remembered that her husband's grandmother had
told her that Duncan Mór's family lived there back in the fifties,
so she told Ellen that if she wanted to know more about the
place she should ask him. Sheena offered to look up his telephone number for her, but Ellen said it was all right – she
would call in on him on the off-chance she'd find him in. His
house was on her way home, so she wouldn't have had to go out
of her way.'

'Any idea why Ellen was so interested in the Monach
Islands?'

'Not a clue! You'd have to ask Duncan Mór that. He lives
on Grimsay – fifteen minutes back the way you came.' She
circled a dot on the map. 'That's his house if you want to go and
talk to him yourself. As you can see, it's not far from Ellen's
cottage as the crow flies, although quite a hike on foot, especially if the tide's in.'

Rachel did want to talk to him. He might have been the last
person to see Ellen alive. 'What about later?' she asked. 'Anyone
see Ellen after she left the shop?'

Sophie shrugged. 'She was seen turning off towards her
house about four in the afternoon we reckon. That's the last
anyone saw of her.'

Jesus, Sophie knew more than the police did.

'Did Sheena tell the police this?'

The door tinkled as a customer walked in. Sophie's eyes
were puzzled as she looked over Rachel's shoulder. 'Apparently
they never asked.'

NINE

Back in her car, Rachel tapped her pen against her teeth. Where was Ellen between 12.30 and 4pm? Had she gone to see Duncan Mór? Ellen's interest in the Monach Islands probably had nothing to do with her death, but if Ellen had called to see him and he'd been in, she might have mentioned if she had plans, or even if she was meeting someone. It was a long shot, but right now Rachel felt as if she were driving around in the dark without headlights.

She found Duncan Mór's house easily enough. Like Ellen's cottage, it was built on a peninsula. Unlike Ellen's cottage though, there was no need for Rachel to get out and walk as the house was linked to the main road by a number of short causeways that brought the road right up to the front door. Rachel climbed out of her car, revelling in the warmth of the sun on her shoulders. In another mercurial shift in the weather, the sky was a dome of blue smeared with white and the sea lapping the edges of the land was calm, a light turquoise close to the house, navy blue further out and every possible gradation of blues and green in between. Rachel loved how different the light was here; how it made colours clearer, more vivid.

The smell of peat drifted on the breeze and once more something shifted behind Rachel's ribs. These islands were where her mother had spent her childhood. She imagined her as a girl, skirt bunched to her waist as she paddled, skinny knees pumping as she ran wild across the moors exactly as Rachel had every summer she'd come here on holiday. It was a wonderful place to be a child. Why had it taken her so long to come back when some of her happiest memories of Mum were here? Because it hurt too much. That part of her life was an angry boil buried below her skin, to be picked and prodded only in her darkest moments.

An elderly man answered the door to her – a welcome distraction from the turn her thoughts were taking. He was dressed in a pair of faded jeans and a jumper with several holes, his bony arm peeping from a particularly large one on his elbow. What was left of the hair on his balding head was white and his skin heavily lined but he had sharp eyes and the upright stature of a much younger man.

An expression Rachel couldn't identify flitted across his face when she told him who she was and that she was there to talk to him about Ellen.

'Come away in,' he invited her. She followed him into a small sitting room piled high with books, newspapers and the detritus of a long life, leaving barely enough room for an armchair and a sofa.

He cleared a space for her to sit on the sofa while he took the armchair. He'd rigged a makeshift reading light over the left side of his chair and Rachel guessed that this was where he spent most of his time.

'Well, then,' he said, lifting a poker and prodding the open fire until it flared. 'What can I do for you?'

Rachel explained why she was on the island. She finished up by saying that she understood Ellen had intended to visit him.

'She came here, right enough,' he said after a long pause which he used to rummage in his pocket for his pipe. 'A few days before they found the poor woman's body. I think it was on the Thursday – my memory isn't as good as it once was.'

'Could it have been Friday?' The day Ellen had been in the Co-op.

'Yes, it could. Actual days don't mean much to me anymore. They're all the same.'

'Can you remember what time she arrived?'

He tapped the upside-down bowl of his pipe against a metal bucket filled with peats, waiting until he'd finished before replying. 'I think it was in the afternoon. Yes, I'm sure that's right. We'd not long had our lunch.'

'How long did she stay?'

'An hour, maybe more. You'd have to check with my sister Chrissie.'

'Why did Miss Hargreaves come to see you?'

He was silent while he concentrated on filling his pipe.

'The same reason they all come – the visitors and incomers. They want to know things. They're always asking questions.' He shifted in his seat. 'They want to know about the old days. What life was like here in the past.'

'I understand she wanted to know more about the Monach Islands in particular. Is that correct? Do you know why?'

Something flickered in his eyes – anxiety? irritation? impatience? Rachel couldn't be sure.

'She said she'd heard that my family lived there a long time ago.'

'Why was she so interested? Did she say?'

Duncan removed his spectacles and rubbed the lens with a threadbare handkerchief he pulled from his sleeve. Rachel had no choice but to wait until the glasses were cleaned to his satisfaction and placed back on his face.

'Someone had told her Chrissie and I were the last people

to have lived there. She wanted to know what life was like for us in those days – especially living in such isolated circumstances.' He spoke around the stem of his pipe. 'A lot of people come to this door asking the same thing. As if Chrissie and I are museum pieces.' There was no mistaking his irritation now.

'And you get fed up answering their questions?'

'I'm seventy-two, you know. I have better things to do with whatever time God has left for me.'

'What else did she ask?'

He fiddled with his pipe again. 'She wanted to know if I knew someone who might take her back to the Monachs.'

'Back? So she had been there?'

He relit his pipe and puffed on it before squinting at her through the smoke. 'I believe so.'

'Did she say who took her?'

'No. Only that they'd said they wouldn't be able to take her again.'

As they were talking Rachel heard the door of the kitchen open and the heavy tread of someone moving about. Moments later, a man wearing turned-down waders and a thick, hand-knitted fisherman's sweater entered the room. He was in his mid to late thirties, Rachel guessed, with the weather-beaten complexion of a man who'd spent his working life outdoors. Ignoring Rachel, he spoke in Gaelic to Duncan. Rachel understood enough to know he was asking who she was and what she was doing there. He didn't seem very happy with Duncan's reply.

'This is my nephew, Roddy,' Duncan introduced him. 'Roddy, this is Miss McKenzie.'

Roddy held out a calloused hand and smiled tightly.

'I must ask you not to stay too long. My uncle doesn't keep well and needs a rest in the afternoon.' His soft voice had a definite edge.

'I won't take up any more of his time than I have to,' Rachel replied.

'Roddy, this is not the way we treat guests in this house and especially not *this* guest,' Duncan remonstrated in Gaelic.

Rachel kept her expression neutral, not wanting to let on she'd understood what had been said, lest it led to questions about her background she'd prefer not to answer. Mum had spoken Gaelic to her when she'd been a child. It had been their secret way of talking to each other.

'I apologise if I sounded rude,' Roddy said to Rachel. He turned back to his uncle. 'I'll be on the croft if you need me.'

Duncan shook his head at his nephew's retreating back. The grandfather clock ticked into the silence.

'Anyway, back to your lady. I told her what I could, which is what I tell everyone. We left the Monach Islands, let me see... around fifty years ago. In the winter of '69. We had some good times while we lived there but life was often hard. Especially as we were the only family. In the end we couldn't make it on our own, so we left. Came back here. And that's that. People don't stay there anymore. Not even the Grimsay fishermen, unless they're caught out by the tide or weather. There's nothing left now except a few ruins and the old schoolhouse, and that's what I told Ellen. I suggested if she wanted to know more then she should speak to Chrissie. She'd tell her what it was like for the women.'

'Do you know why it's called the island of Monks?'

Duncan shrugged. 'Monks must have lived there at one time.'

A clam would be more forthcoming than Duncan Mór.

'Was there anything specific Ellen wanted to know?' Rachel persisted.

Duncan hesitated. Once again, there was something odd in his expression that made Rachel wonder whether he was holding back on her.

'Just about its history. Who lived there and when. But she

seemed interested in all sorts of things,' he went on quickly. 'She also wanted to know about the *Politician*. You've heard about the boat that was wrecked off Eriskay? The one they made the film about. You know it's a real story? Well now, there's a rumour that there's another wreck off the west coast of North Uist.'

He moved to the edge of his chair and placed his hands on the armrests. 'I am very sorry to seem rude, but will you excuse me? I like to have a nap in the afternoon.'

Rachel stood. 'Of course. One more thing. How did Ms Hargreaves seem to you? Did she appear happy? Worried? Distressed in any way?'

'What sort of question is that? I'd never met the woman before. How could I possibly know what sort of mood she was in!' He seemed to collect himself. 'She seemed normal to me.'

'You said your sister might be able to confirm the day Ellen came and what time she left. Where might I find her?'

Duncan eased himself out of his chair. 'I'll show you. Come with me.'

Rachel followed him outside. Duncan pointed an arthritic finger to a piece of land in the distance. 'She's up there. On that hill straight ahead. Just hop over a couple of stiles. You can't miss her.'

Rachel was surprised to find Chrissie stacking peats into miniature pyramids. She worked with steady rhythmic movements, handling the clods of earth as if they weighed nothing.

Chrissie looked up when Rachel's shadow fell across the peat bog she was working on. Her hair was covered with a scarf tied in a knot beneath her chin, and she wore a wool skirt, an oversized cardigan rolled up at the sleeves and heavy brogues. Her eyes were the same intense blue as her brother's, and

Roddy had inherited her beak-like nose. Rachel felt herself equally scrutinised.

'Hello,' Chrissie said softly. 'You must be Rachel. And you want to ask me about Ellen.'

Rachel was taken aback. How did Chrissie know who she was? Surely the jungle drums hadn't reached this far, so soon? She remembered her mother telling her that the Islanders were psychic. She had laughed back then, but perhaps Mum hadn't been joking.

Chrissie grinned, then dug around in the pocket of her cardigan, eventually pulling out a mobile phone. 'Duncan called me to tell me you were on your way up. Good thing this stack is on a hill and I have a reception. Most of the time the damn thing is no good to man or beast.'

Rachel laughed.

'Now then,' Chrissie said, in her gentle island accent, 'If you want to talk you'll have to carry on while I finish what I'm doing here. The summer won't be long in coming and these peats need to be sorted before then.'

'Can I help?' Rachel asked. There was no way she could stand idly by and watch as the older woman worked.

Chrissie looked at her critically. 'You're a wee slip of a thing. You don't look as if you've much strength in those arms of yours. And it will ruin your nails.'

'I'm stronger than I appear,' Rachel protested with a smile.

'Very well then. If you really want to help, watch what I do.'

She showed Rachel how to take the peats from the rows beside the deep cut in the earth and stack them so that air could reach to dry them. Although at first the work didn't seem too onerous, after ten minutes Rachel was sweating and down to her T-shirt. All the while Chrissie worked methodically as if she had all the energy in the world, even though Rachel was the one who worked out – thank God she did – and had youth on her side.

'Now, you wanted to know about Ellen,' Chrissie said eventually. 'Well, there's not a lot I can tell you. She wanted to know about the Monachs and who had lived there over the years. I told her about the families who lived on the island before us and a little bit about our time there.'

'So it was just general questions about its history – nothing specific?'

'She said she was an amateur archaeologist, although her main job – before she retired – was in a library. She said she loved coming to the Outer Hebrides because of the birds and the number of ancient sites. Said she was always looking for new places to explore – places that might lead to sites for her to dig.'

Chrissie stopped what she was doing for a minute and looked at Rachel. 'There's a wheelhouse on the common grazing, about half a mile from Ellen's cottage.'

'Common grazing?'

'Land that belongs to the estate – that anyone can use for grazing their sheep. Ellen found evidence of an ancient ruin a couple of years ago and started excavating it on her own. She spent almost every hour of the last two summers working down there. You can go and see it if you wish. They say it's pretty interesting if you like that sort of thing.'

'Was she allowed to do that? Excavate on her own? Aren't there rules against it?' Rachel placed her palms in the small of her back to ease aching muscles.

Chrissie chuckled. 'We don't go much for rules here and it seems Ellen didn't either. A couple of the incomers were annoyed right enough. They said she should have waited for the proper authorities instead of messing about by herself. But as for the locals...' She shrugged. 'We didn't care. As long as she didn't disturb the sheep or the cattle she could do what she liked. We're not too concerned with the past.' She looked over Rachel's shoulder and into the distance. 'At least, not the ancient past.' The downward grooves of her mouth deepened as she frowned. She gave herself a little shake, as if coming back to the present.

'I'm not sure Roddy was too pleased though. The place where this wheelhouse is, it borders his croft. If the government, or whoever it is that's in charge of these things, wanted to, they could probably stop him from using the land for his sheep if they thought they could make the wheelhouse into a tourist attraction. Some of the best grazing is up there.'

'Does that mean you'd met her before she came to see you?' For someone who claimed not to know Ellen very well, Chrissie seemed to know quite a lot about her.

'I knew who she was. I'd seen her around and asked about her, but I never spoke to her before that day.'

'Your brother said she wanted to find someone to take her back out to the Monachs? Who might that have been?'

'I don't know why you keep going on about the Monachs,' Chrissie snapped, taking Rachel aback. 'I told her that there was nothing to see there. Why are some people so obsessed with matters that happened long ago? Especially when it has nothing to do with them!'

Because, Rachel thought, whatever happened in the present usually had its roots in the past.

'What sort of mood did she seem to be in?' Rachel asked. Perhaps Chrissie would have a better idea than Duncan.

Chrissie thought for a moment. 'Excited, I would say. Certainly very pleased with herself.'

'Did she say anything about where she was going next? If she was meeting anyone?' Rachel asked

'No. She didn't say and I didn't ask. It was no concern of mine.'

'Can you remember what time she left?'

'It was about a quarter to four. Almost time for our cup of tea. We always have it at four.'

They carried on working in silence. Rachel's attempt at the peats had only resulted in a small pile so far whereas Chrissie had completed the whole of one side. Rachel knew she should really be making a move; there was nothing more to be learned from Chrissie or Duncan. But Rachel found the slow, methodical work comforting in a strange way. Maybe it was some hidden memory in her genes. No doubt her female island ancestors had done the same thing in the decades they lived here. How different it was from her life. When she wasn't running, she used weights and apps to keep in shape.

'If you are going, you need to go soon,' Chrissie straightened and nodded in the direction of Rachel's car. 'The tide's coming in and it's going to be a high one. High enough to cover the causeway and your access to the main road. If you wait much longer you won't be able to get away until it's on the way out again. It's going to be even higher in a day or two – especially with the storm we're expecting.' She stared Rachel directly in the eye. 'So you'll need to be on your guard.'

It almost sounded like a warning. Sure enough, the water was already lapping at the sides of the causeway. The last time Rachel had looked it had been halfway out.

'If I need to, would it be OK to come again?' she asked.

Chrissie narrowed her eyes, her expression unreadable. 'I'm not sure there's anything more I can tell you. It's a busy time of year for us.'

Rachel wiped her peat-stained hands on her jeans. 'Thanks for talking to me, I appreciate it.'

'By the way,' Chrissie said. 'That storm that's coming – they say it's going to be a bad one. Maybe as bad as the one we had ten years ago. The planes and ferries will probably go off. You might get stuck on the island.'

'I'll bear that in mind.'

Chrissie pointed to the rising tide. 'Go on, then. Before it's too late.'

As Rachel turned to leave, she saw something flicker in Chrissie's eyes. If Rachel had to put a bet on it, she would have said it was fear.

TEN

Rachel made it over the causeway just before the tide covered it. Once on the other side she pulled into a passing place to check her phone. No messages or missed calls from the local force. She clicked her tongue in frustration. The visit to Duncan Mór and Chrissie had revealed little that helped – except that Ellen had been on the Monach Islands and had been excited about something. Could be something or nothing. However, no matter how much she felt as if she were going around in circles, she wouldn't give Douglas any reason to say she hadn't been thorough. She drummed her nails on the steering wheel thinking about her next steps. Her mobile rang. Suruthi.

'Hey, where the heck are you?' her colleague asked. 'I asked Douglas and he almost bit my head off. I was worried you were ill or something.'

Rachel explained the reason behind her sudden trip to the island.

'Cripes. Haven't heard of a fisc attending a scene in ages – although I gather Deputy Dawg used to. You're not planning to be away too long, are you? We're snowed under here.' She lowered her voice. 'Alastair's up to something. He's walking around like the cat that's got the cream. Clive and I asked him to come for a drink to try and get it out of him, but he refused. Said he had an important dinner appointment. I think he might be interviewing with a private firm.'

'You'd care if he left?' Rachel asked.

Suruthi sighed. 'Better the devil you know than no devil at all. We need the extra pair of hands and when he puts his mind to it, he's not half bad.'

Rachel wasn't convinced.

'Hey, got to go,' Suruthi said. 'Boss is looking this way. Glad all's OK. Keep in touch.'

Rachel was about to start the car when the skin on the back of her neck prickled with the uneasy sensation someone was watching her. Slowly she scanned the horizon. It had clouded over in the time she'd been speaking to Duncan and Chrissie and all she could see was land. She turned around and pretended to reach into the back seat while taking a good look behind her. Not even a single sheep. She was simply giving in to the paranoia that had become part of her everyday life.

She thought what to do next. The Polochar Inn, where the Mowburys were staying, was at the other end of the island, 30 miles away. It would take a good hour to get there on the narrow, winding roads, but she decided to take a chance on finding the Mowburys at the hotel.

Rachel had to concentrate on driving. Sometimes the road widened then reverted without warning to a single track, often catching her unawares. More than once, she was forced to reverse into a parking space when faced with an oncoming vehicle whose driver refused to get out of her way – like a tank facing a smaller enemy.

When she eventually made it to Polochar and stepped out of the car, the view took her breath away. That and the wind, which in the time she'd been driving, had whipped up again, massaging the sea into white-capped waves that lashed the shore, spewing water onto the road. She decided she liked the way the weather kept changing.

To her right, the tide hadn't quite covered the sands of a sheltered bay, and a number of black-and-white birds with orange beaks pecked along the shore. A large bird used the wind and currents to circle overhead. This side of the island was where her mother was from: these rocks, this sea, the sand, part of her mother's world as a child, as familiar to Mum as Inverness-shire was to Rachel. The ache in her chest blossomed again as something stirred deep inside: a tug of recognition, of belonging, of coming home even.

Quite, quite absurd.

And with that thought it started to pour in heavy, sight-obscuring sheets. Rachel pulled the hood of her waterproof tighter and turned towards the low-slung, whitewashed inn.

Inside, a pot-bellied stove blasted heat into the bar. The place had been modernised. Judging by the hammered copper tables and tartan dining chairs which matched the rug covering the floor, the inn was unsurprisingly trying to appeal to tourists. With the strict drink-driving laws, no bar could afford to rely on local trade. A fresh memory surfaced, another that had remained suppressed for years, of her parents spilling out of a pub, her father's arm around her mother's shoulder. They'd both been laughing. It hadn't always been bad between them.

'What can I get you?' the barmaid, a woman in her forties with short cropped hair asked Rachel.

'An orange juice. Oh, and a packet of cheese and onion crisps, please.'

While the barmaid organised her drink Rachel studied the occupants of the room. It didn't take long: two middle-aged women, an elderly couple sitting in a strained silence, and three younger men at the other end of the bar, who had stopped talking and were now studying her with open curiosity. The tallest made no secret of the fact he was eyeing her up and liked what he saw. His companions tugged at his sleeve and whispered. The staring man laughed before turning his attention back to his mates.

'That'll be two pounds fifty,' the barmaid said, sliding the orange juice towards Rachel. She'd forgotten the crisps. Rachel couldn't be bothered to remind her.

'Do you know if Olivia Mowbury and her daughter are around?' Rachel handed the money across.

'I don't think so.' The barmaid's glance swept around the room as if making sure that they weren't hiding in a corner. 'I haven't seen them. They could be in their room or the resident's lounge, I suppose. Why do you want to know?'

'No particular reason,' Rachel replied. She could be as tight-lipped as anyone. God knew she had plenty of practice.

For a long moment she and the barmaid stared each other out. The barmaid broke first. 'I was only asking in case there was something I could help with,' she said, pursing her lips. 'They went out earlier. Said they planned to be back for lunch.' She looked at her phone. 'They'd better hurry, the kitchen closes soon. So, if *you* plan on having something to eat...'

She might as well. It was almost two and she hadn't eaten since breakfast. The crisps would only have held her hunger at bay for an hour or so. Taking the proffered menu from the barmaid, Rachel drifted over to a table next to the window.

The men standing at the bar said something in Gaelic she couldn't quite catch and laughed. Rachel used her best *oh please* stare on them and took her time contemplating the menu. Returning to the bar, she ordered the hand-dived scallops.

While she waited for her food to arrive, she stared out of the window. The rain hurled itself at the panes of glass as if the drops were sacrificing themselves, clinging to each other in desperation before losing the battle and sliding away.

When the scallops arrived they were enormous, and at least

half a dozen had been heaped on her plate. Not bad for under a tenner.

'Are they local? The scallops?' she asked the barmaid.

'Delivered not thirty minutes ago. Local and fresh. Better than any you'd get in the city.'

She was right. They were plump, sautéed to perfection, and absolutely delicious.

Rachel was finishing her last scallop when the door swung open and two women entered as if blown in on a gust of air. One was older, with the resigned look of someone who'd been pushed beyond her limits. The other was a teenager with a pierced lip and, when she removed her hood, hair gelled into jaunty spikes. It didn't take a rocket scientist to work out this was the mother and daughter Rachel was looking for.

'I'm going, whether you like it or not,' the younger woman spat. Spotting the men at the bar, she stopped. A sly smile lit her sullen features and she moved towards them, shaking off her mother's restraining hand.

Rachel approached the woman, who was looking at her daughter with something close to dislike.

'Mrs Mowbury?'

Hazel eyes met hers.

'Yes?' Her accent was this side of the border. Edinburgh? Possibly. East coast at any rate.

'My name is Rachel McKenzie. I'm from the Procurator Fiscal's office in Inverness. Could I have a word?'

There was a rumble of male laughter from the bar followed by a high-pitched giggle. The girl had eased herself onto a stool beside the men. She cast a triumphant glance in her mother's direction.

Olivia sighed with weary resignation before dragging her attention away from her daughter and back to Rachel.

'Is it about the dead woman we found? If it is, I don't know what else I can tell you. We've already told the police everything.'

'It won't take long, I promise. Why don't I get us something to drink and we can have a chat about it?'

When Olivia's face relaxed into a smile, the stress and strain left her and years fell away. 'A cup of tea would be perfect.'

Rachel gave their order to the barmaid and ushered Olivia over to a clean table where there was no one close enough to eavesdrop.

While they waited for their tea, Olivia kept glancing at her daughter and Rachel couldn't help but look too. Katherine was leaning towards the eldest of the three men, whispering in his ear. There was something urgent, almost desperate, about the way the girl was speaking. The man held his hands out in a keep it down gesture while looking over Katherine's shoulder, directly at Rachel.

Olivia looked at her daughter with something like longing before turning back to Rachel. 'Forgive me, Miss McKenzie, feel free to go ahead and ask your questions. I'd like to change my clothes. We got soaked – again.'

A tea tray was placed on their table.

'This won't take long. Could you tell me about finding Ellen's body?'

Another bray of laughter drew Rachel's eyes back to Katherine. She appeared to be pleading with the older man, but he was shaking his head. Katherine shot an anxious glance in her mother's direction. Rachel looked at Olivia. Concentrating on pouring her tea, Katherine's mother hadn't noticed.

'We were out for a walk. I wanted to see the blowhole out at Scolpaig. I'd heard about the legend and wanted to see it for myself.' She shrugged. 'It was somewhere to aim for, if nothing else.'

'The legend?'

'There's a strip of land that remained after the blowhole was formed. The legend has it that a newly married couple will cross it and fall to their deaths. A bit creepy, but this place is full of stories like it.'

'Did you see anyone on your way?'

'Not a soul.'

'Who spotted the body?'

'Kat. She thought at first it was a seal that needed rescuing. But when she took a closer look she realised what it was.' She half smiled. 'Underneath that grim exterior, Kat is still such a child. She wants everyone to believe she's tough as nails. But she's not. Not really.'

'What did you do?'

'There was no way we could get down to it. No way anyone could. So we called 999. They sent an ambulance and a couple of police officers. Without a way to reach her, there was nothing they could do. Anyway, it was clear the woman was dead.' She shuddered. 'The waves kept rolling her out of the water. Turning her on her side, so we could see her face.'

Rachel laid her hand on top of the older woman's and left it there for a moment. 'It must have been awful.'

'The police called the local diving company out to help them retrieve the body.' Olivia nodded towards the group of men in the corner. 'That's two of them at the bar. There was a third diver with them, but I haven't seen him since.'

Rachel studied the men more closely. The one who had been eyeing her up and on whom all Katherine's attention was focused was good looking, with a Roman nose and a wide mouth. She estimated him to be in his early thirties. He wore a leather jacket over a blue T-shirt and faded jeans. Next to him was a smaller man, a little older, with features like a ferret who was wearing what looked like a boiler suit. The third was a bit younger than the other two, closer to his early twenties. He seemed a little in awe of his companions and unsure of what to make of Katherine.

'Is that how Katherine met them? At the blowhole?'

Olivia frowned. 'Odd you should ask. The first time I saw any of them was when they came to help lift the body out of the water.' She shivered. 'But I got the distinct impression Katherine had met them before, although I can't say for sure and she wouldn't tell me. Teenage girls are so secretive. Anyway, they had one of those inflatable boats with an engine. They managed somehow to get it into the blowhole, then they got in the water and dragged the woman into the boat. It was awful. I wanted to go back to the hotel, but Kat insisted on staying to watch and I couldn't exactly leave her there by herself could I? To be honest, I didn't have the energy to argue with her.

'After they'd removed the body, we were taken to the police station. Once Sergeant MacVicar took our statements we came back to the hotel.' She rubbed her arms as if trying to get heat into her body. 'It was a horrible experience. I have no idea how long the poor woman had been in the sea. She looked almost inhuman; bloated, white. Quite, quite ghastly.'

Rachel searched for something else to ask but came up blank. It all seemed straightforward enough. Nevertheless, she wanted to talk to Katherine.

'Could I talk to your daughter? I promise I'll be as quick as I can.'

'I'm not sure what else she can tell you. She'll deny it, but she was pretty shaken by the whole thing. We both were.'

'Yet you continued with your holiday. Didn't you want to go straight home?'

Olivia shifted in her chair and looked at her daughter again.

'It was better that we stayed.'

'Better? In what way?'

'Oh, nothing to do with what happened. Family business.'

Curious, Rachel raised an encouraging eyebrow.

'Oh, you might as well know,' Olivia said, lifting her hands and letting them fall. 'Katherine's father and I divorced recently. Katherine hasn't taken it well. I'm the disciplinarian, he's the one who thinks money fixes everything. There's been a spot of trouble at school. Nothing serious, but I thought some time away might help. Happily, Katherine's father agreed. It's his money that's paying for the trip.'

Katherine was no different to how Rachel had been as a teenager. Better behaved, most likely.

'Is there anything you want to add?' Rachel asked. 'Anything at all?'

Olivia shook her head quickly.

'Let me get Kat for you.' Her smile was strained.

Katherine Mowbury detached herself from her companions with a great show of reluctance. She sat down huffily and crossed her arms. Despite the surly expression and cultivated look of boredom, her green-brown eyes were alert. And wary.

'What do you want to know?' Her voice was educated and accent free. Rachel hid a smile. It gave her away. No matter how much make-up she trowelled on, no matter how many piercings, she was obviously someone's well-brought-up daughter.

'If you could just tell me in your own words what happened that day.'

'Nothing to tell really. I saw this thing caught on the rocks. I thought it was rubbish at first, then I thought it was a seal or something that had got trapped. Mum gave me her binoculars so I could see better, and that's when I realised it was a body. Her face was all milky looking, so I knew she was dead.'

'It couldn't have been very pleasant for you.'

Katherine shrugged.

Rachel tipped her head in the direction of the men. 'Which two were at the blowhole and helped recover the body?'

Katherine clamped her lips together and looked at the floor. She mumbled something Rachel couldn't catch.

'Speak up, darling,' Olivia said. 'No one can hear you when you talk to the floor.'

Katherine sneered at her mother, her top lip curling with practised ease.

'Not Johnny – the skinny one. The other two. Dunno their names. At least, not their proper names.' Her eyes followed the departing men. 'The big one's called Seal. The other one's called Shark because he was attacked by a shark once. He has amazing scars on his arm, Mum. You should ask him to show you. You can actually see the teeth marks.' She sucked on the ring inserted in her lower lip.

Rachel made a note to find out the real names of the divers. In the meantime, she should grab a word with them while she could.

'Your mother says she thought you'd already met two of the divers who came to help get the body out. Is that right?'

'Yeah. They were in the bar one night when I came down for an orange juice.' She flashed a defiant look at her mother. 'You were asleep!'

'You mean to say you sneaked down to the bar, on your own, when I was asleep!? Oh Kat, what am I going to do with you?'

The three men finished their drinks, stood, and shrugged into oilskins. The young girl's eyes glinted. 'Take me home for a start, so I can go to a proper club. S'boring here. Except for finding that body.'

ELEVEN

Rachel gave Olivia her business card in case she thought of anything she wanted to add, paid for her meal, and hurried outside. It was just after three and although the rain had stopped the glowering sky and swollen clouds hinted at more to come.

In the car park, leaning against her car, smoking cigarettes, were the divers from the inn. The one Katherine had called Seal let his eyes linger on Rachel with undisguised interest while the other two sniggered. As she approached they straightened but made no attempt to move away.

'Seeing as you're here and I was planning to come and speak to you, could we have a chat?' Rachel asked.

Seal released a plume of smoke through his nostrils. 'Sure,' he said. 'What about?'

'There's a dance on tomorrow night if you're interested?' Shark interrupted. Despite his unfortunate, ferret-like features, he had beautiful green eyes. 'We could take you.' He looked at his companions and said something in Gaelic that Rachel didn't catch but that made them laugh.

'I'm not here to go to dances.' God, she sounded just like a headmistress.

'Then why are you here?' Seal asked. He ground out his cigarette under his foot. It was clear he was the alpha male and the leader of the little group.

'I'm here because of the death of the woman whose body you helped recover the other day. I'm from the PF's office in Inverness.'

'PF? What's that stand for? Prize fart?' Shark said, looking at his friends, hoping for a laugh.

Seal shook his head at him. 'Ach, Shark, don't be rude to our visitor. Let her ask her questions.' He smiled at Rachel. 'Ignore him. He's from Lewis – a Leodhsach – so has no manners. What is it you'd like to know?'

'Who asked you to recover the body? And why you? Why not wait for police divers?' Although she knew the answer, she wanted to hear what these men would say.

'It would have taken the police a day or two to fly divers up from the mainland and nobody wanted to leave the woman in the water,' Seal said. 'The local police know us well. They've used us before.'

'Before?' Rachel queried. More dark clouds were moving in and the temperature had dropped. She shivered. The second man – could he really be nicknamed Shark? – took off his oilskin and passed it across to Rachel. 'Put this on,' he said. 'It might be a bit fishy smelling, right enough.'

Surprised at his unexpected offer, Rachel accepted the jacket, laying it across her shoulders. He was right. It did smell of fish and the sea, but these weren't smells she minded. Her own fishing jacket, which she'd flung into her suitcase, probably smelled the same. Furthermore, Shark's jacket was warm.

'Aye,' Seal said. 'Once a year or so, sometimes more, we help the police and the coastguard search for people who have gone missing or have fallen from the cliffs. We know the lochs, tides and the sea around here better than anyone – except perhaps the fishermen, but their boats don't have the speed needed for a search. Our vessels have sonar radar too. Often we're the ones who find the poor sods.' There was a note of pride in his voice. 'They asked us to help recover the woman. It was tricky, given where it was, but we managed all right.'

'Had you ever seen her before? Met her, even? Everyone seems to know everyone else on this island.'

'No!' Shark's laugh was shrill. 'She was old. Even if we'd walked right by her, she wasn't the kind of woman we'd notice. Now you, on the other hand...'

Rachel cut him off. 'Was her body where you'd expect it to be?'

'What makes you ask that?' Seal asked, shooting a glance at Shark.

'Your boss doesn't think it's possible.'

Shark cleared his throat and spat on the ground. 'He owns the company, if that's what you mean. Doesn't mean he gets to boss anyone.'

Rachel decided to let that ride.

'He's got it wrong. I don't know why he thinks there's any mystery,' Seal went on. 'There's no one who can tell for sure how she got there. She probably just fell in and drowned. If you've seen where she was found you'd see how easy it would be to do that. Likely she was having a look, went too close to the edge and lost her footing. The same thing happened to a tourist a few years ago. Not there, but somewhere nearby. He was also killed.' He shrugged broad shoulders. 'It happens. Cliffs and weather can be a bad combination.'

It was possible. Rachel couldn't rule it out. Not yet. But it didn't explain the shopping, binoculars and bag left at the door. Or the timings. Ellen's car had been seen turning off towards her house around four, which fitted in with the time she'd left Duncan and Chrissie. Unless she'd gone back out later with someone? In *their* car. Perhaps Ellen had been so excited by something she'd simply forgotten to put her valuables and shopping away? Maybe someone had called to tell her about a rare bird that had been spotted. Rachel had read somewhere that twitchers happily dropped everything to chase after a particular bird. In which case why hadn't that person come forward? And why hadn't Ellen taken her binoculars instead of leaving them on the doorstep?

'What if she fell in somewhere else?' Rachel asked.

'Like where?' Seal demanded, pushing away from his slouched position against the car.

'Near the cottage where she was staying for example? It's on the north side of Grimsay. I'm assuming you know where it is?'

The three men exchanged looks without saying anything.

'Well, do you or don't you?' Rachel demanded.

'I know roughly where it is,' Seal conceded reluctantly.

'Why would you think she fell in near her house?' Johnny spoke for the first time. He looked much paler outside than he had under the artificial light of the bar.

'Because she left her shopping and valuables on her doorstep.'

'It's rocky around her house. Maybe she was picking mussels or something and slipped on the rocks,' Johnny suggested. He, at least, appeared eager to help.

'Then you *do* know where she lived?' Rachel said.

Seal shot Johnny a look. 'We have no fucking idea where she was or what she was doing, and we don't fucking care.' If he was like a sleepy cat before, he was like a panther now. 'We did what we were asked – recovered her body – and as far as we're concerned that's the end of it. Come on, guys, we need to get going.'

Rachel shrugged out of the borrowed oilskin and returned it to Shark. 'One more thing, before you leave. Could I take a note of your real names? In case I need to get in touch again?'

The divers looked at one another. Shark folded his arms over the oilskin.

'I'm Charlie Ferguson,' Seal pointed a thumb at Shark, 'He's Hamish MacLean, and the kid is Johnny Holland. Why would you need to talk to us again? We've told you everything we know.'

'Hopefully I won't have to. It's mainly for my records.'

Johnny had gone back to studying the tips of his boots. He looked up at Rachel with a frown.

'Are you here because you think it wasn't an accident? That's stupid. Everyone knows it was. What else could it be?'

'That's what I'm here to find out. Are you certain you don't have any doubts?'

'I wasn't there, was I?' His eyes flickered between Seal and Shark.

Rachel pulled more business cards out of her handbag and held them out. 'If you think of anything, could you give me a call? I'll be here for a day or two yet.'

Johnny glanced at Seal. When the older man dipped his head, Johnny took the card and slipped it into his trouser pocket. The other two grudgingly accepted one as well.

Shark grabbed Johnny by the elbow and nodded in the direction of their jeep. 'C'mon, mate, we've got work to do.'

As the divers pulled away in their battered jeep, Rachel stared after them. She had the distinct feeling the divers knew more than they were letting on. They had to know as much as Mike about tides and currents. What were they not telling her?

The wind swirled around her, pushing her hair into her eyes and making her shiver. Missing the warmth of Shark's jacket, she got back in her car, switched the ignition on and turned the heat up to full.

Her thoughts drifted to Katherine and Olivia. Their relationship reminded her painfully of that between her and her own mother when she was the same age. She leaned her head

against the seat rest and closed her eyes, recalling the day eleven
years ago when her life had been blown apart.

Rachel let herself into her house and dropped her rucksack and
coat on the floor, her pack of Regal King Size shoved to the
bottom of her bag under last night's clothes. She'd stayed over at
Gabby's house and they'd snuck out to a party. Hopefully,
chewing gum and deodorant would have taken care of any
lingering smell of smoke. Not that it mattered. Mum had a good
idea she smoked. Not that she approved. Not that she approved
of anything Rachel did. And that was only going to get worse.

Mr Tulloch, head of year, wanted a meeting with both her
parents. He was unhappy with the deterioration in Rachel's
marks. Said if they didn't improve, there wouldn't be a university in Scotland that would take her.

It was all a load of bollocks. Gabby was the one who cared
about going to uni. Not Rachel.

God, her mouth was dry. She needed a drink of something.
Diet Irn Bru if there was any. She became aware of a shift in the
atmosphere of the house. It felt strangely empty. Wait, wasn't it
Saturday? In which case, where were the parentals? Dad was
probably at the office. That was where he spent most of his
time. Apparently he needed to be on call for the North of Scotland's criminals twenty-four seven.

But Mum never went into her office on a Saturday. Not
since she got the manager job at the Social Work Department.
Said it was the one day that she and Rachel could do stuff
together. Mostly that involved Rachel on her phone in her room
and Mum downstairs cooking.

Perhaps she'd gone to the shops? To buy whatever she
needed for tonight's dinner. Or perhaps she was having a nap. It
wasn't like Mum, but maybe she wasn't feeling well. Rachel
tried to ignore the pang of guilt. They'd had a row – another one

– about Rachel wanting to stay over at Gabby's after she'd been grounded.

She ran up the stairs. She would make Mum a cup of tea as a peace offering. Maybe even dinner. It was exhausting to be at loggerheads all the time.

She tapped lightly on the door of her parents' bedroom. When she got no reply, she opened it. It looked as if a tornado had ripped through the room. Drawers were pulled out, clothes spilling from them, the bed unmade. Mum wasn't particularly tidy but she'd never leave her room in such a mess. Rachel was seriously spooked, every instinct telling her that something wasn't right.

Had they been burgled? If so, where was Mum? Rachel took a deep breath. This wasn't America. This was Moy. The telly was still in the sitting room. Mum's car hadn't been in the driveway. She must have been called out to a work emergency. It didn't happen often but it had happened. Didn't explain the tornado in her parents' bedroom though. Dad might know. Rachel would call him.

She went downstairs and put on the kettle, before looking up Dad's office number in her contacts. She couldn't remember ever calling him at the office. She was about to press the call button on her phone when something on the kitchen table caught her attention. Mum's wedding ring. A shiver ran up her spine. Mum never took it off. Dad didn't like it when she did.

She had a leaden, sick feeling in her chest. Something was definitely off. But she never imagined she wouldn't see her mother again.

Rachel snapped her eyes open, nausea churning her stomach. Putting the car in gear, she drove back in the direction of North Uist. When she neared the junction at Daliburgh, she hesitated. A right turn would take her to Lochboisdale and her mother's family home, where her grandfather still lived, a sharp left to the cemetery where her grandmother was buried. She'd loved her grandparents when she was a child, particularly her grandmother. Gran had always found time to walk the moors with her, or to take her to the beach to show her how to dig for cockles and look for crabs under rocks.

None of that excused the fact that in the years since that last holiday on Uist, neither of them had phoned or written to Rachel, not even when Mum had left. Over the years, the only time her grandfather had been in touch was to send her a brief letter to let her know Gran had died. She'd heard nothing from him since.

Fuck him. Rachel pressed down on the accelerator and took the road straight ahead. She couldn't blame her grandparents for not attending the funeral or the trial. She couldn't even bring herself to care that they hadn't kept in touch with her over the years. What she couldn't forgive them for was not being there for Rachel's mother when she'd needed them most. If they had, she might still be alive.

TWELVE

Back at her hotel, Rachel changed into her running gear. Normally when she wanted to let off steam she'd find a mountain to climb. That wasn't an option here. Instead, she ran the seven miles to Lochmaddy and all the way back again. She ran until she was streaming with sweat and it was painful to breathe. She ran until all she could think of was putting one foot in front of the other.

It was getting dark by the time she got back to her room. The crows were roosting on the roof again.

While she cooled down, she pulled out the book of birds that Sophie had given her and idly flipped through the pages. Why people were interested in birds defeated her. As she was about to close the book, something slipped out and fluttered to the ground. It was a folded page torn from a notebook. Rachel opened it and smoothed it out.

At first she couldn't work out what she was looking at. A drawing, certainly, possibly of a whale's backbone. She examined it more closely. They weren't bones. It looked like a group of four islands, the largest of which was labelled Ceann Ear. Where the hell was that?

She booted up her laptop and attempted to log on to the internet. Even after several attempts, it wouldn't connect.

Rachel rang the police station's landline but there was no reply, so she tried Selena's mobile. To her intense frustration, her phone wouldn't connect either. Remembering what Michelle had said about getting a signal on the hill she opened her bedroom's patio doors and stepped into inky darkness. The night sky was studded with thousands of stars, the air as pure as liquid gold. From the bar the sound of country music trickled across the still air.

Eventually, after a few abortive attempts, she managed to get through to Selena.

'Rachel!' Selena's chirpy voice answered. 'What can I do for you?'

'Hi, Selena. Any luck getting hold of the coastguard?'

'Yep. I tried to call your mobile but you must have been out of range. He says he can see you tomorrow morning. Down at the harbour in Griminish at nine, if that suits? The place where Ellen's body washed up is near there so he could show you that at the same time.'

'I had hoped to see him tonight.' Rachel suppressed her impatience. 'I guess it'll have to wait until tomorrow.'

'Did the Mowburys have anything to add?' Selena asked.

'No, but I met a couple of the divers in the bar who helped retrieve Ellen's body. Can you believe it – one was called Seal, the other Shark.'

Selena laughed. 'Everyone has nicknames. You'll get your head around it eventually.'

'Something else. I found a drawing on a page torn from a notebook in a book about birds that belonged to Ellen. She left it in the cubbyhole of her hire car. I think it might be a drawing of the Monach Islands. She was asking about them at the Co-op the day she was last seen. Something about them intrigued her.' She paused. There was no delicate way to put this. 'I thought you said that she hadn't spoken to anyone when she was at the Co-op?'

'Who said she did?'

'Sophie's niece, Sheena.'

There was silence on the other end of the phone. 'I'll ask Fergus when he comes back inside,' Selena said eventually. 'He was the one who went to the Co-op. He's outside having a smoke.' She sounded subdued, embarrassed for her colleagues. 'What did Sheena say?'

'Just that she was asking about the Monach Islands. Sheena gave her the name of someone to speak to – a Duncan Mór from Grimsay. I went to see him. He confirmed that she visited that day. She asked about the islands' history, said she'd been there and was hoping to find someone to take her back out. She arrived at his house in the afternoon and left just before four.'

'Do you think all that's relevant?' Selena asked.

'I don't know. Maybe, maybe not, but it's always helpful to know what a deceased person was doing in the hours before they died.' Rachel tried to keep the exasperation from her voice.

'I'll pass your comments on to my colleagues,' Selena said stiffly.

Clearly Rachel had failed to keep the censure from her tone. 'I'm happy to pass them on myself. Could we chase up Ellen's phone records? Here's her number.' She reeled it off. 'It might be worth dialling first – just to check if the phone we found is hers.'

'We're not all totally incapable of doing basic police work,' Selena snapped. 'I'm sorry,' she said before Rachel could respond. 'I didn't mean to growl, but no one likes it when people think their team doesn't know their arse from their elbow. I'll get on to it. See you tomorrow.'

After Rachel disconnected, she checked her phone for missed calls. None. She glanced at her watch. Michelle had told her that they stopped serving evening meals at eight, so she had plenty of time for a shower. She turned to go back into her room and almost bumped into Roddy, Chrissie's son. She hadn't heard him approach. She took a step back.

'What are you doing here?' she asked.

'What am I doing here?' he repeated, rocking back on his heels. 'Having a drink in the bar. I just came out for a smoke.'

'Outside my room? This area is private.' Rachel pointed to the low-slung rope that separated her bit of garden from the rest.

'I heard you on the phone just now – asking about the Monach Isles. Mother and Duncan said you were asking them too.'

Rachel hesitated, then reached into her pocket. She unfolded the map she'd found tucked in Ellen's book and handed it to him. 'Is this them?'

He tossed his finished cigarette on the grass, took the paper from her, walked over to the pool of light spilling out from the conservatory and studied it. It was a few long minutes before he walked back.

'Aye. It's the Monachs.' He gave the map back to her. 'Where did you get it?'

'Does it matter?'

'Why are you so interested?'

'No particular reason.' At least, none she was prepared to share.

He was close enough for her to smell his smoky breath. When she stepped to the side, he grabbed her elbow.

She looked pointedly at his hand on her arm. 'Do you mind?'

'Too good for the likes of me?' Roddy bent his head towards hers and for a second she thought he was going to kiss her. She ripped her arm from his grip and pushed past him.

'Aye well,' Roddy said in Gaelic to her retreating back. 'A

person tries to be civil but some folk are so full of airs and graces it's surprising they still need to walk on earth.'

Rachel continued walking, pretending she hadn't heard, or understood. She stepped into her room and closed the patio doors with a sigh. She was making a lousy job of keeping on the right side of the locals – both police and civilians.

By the time Rachel had showered and dressed and made her way downstairs, Roddy was back in the bar, a pint of beer in front of him. When Rhoda came to take Rachel's order, she asked for a chicken salad and a large glass of white wine. Rachel nodded in the direction of Roddy.

'Does he come here often?'

'Who? Oh, Roddy?' Rhoda shrugged. 'About once or twice a month.'

'He was hanging about my room earlier,' Rachel said. 'Does he make a habit of doing that?'

Rhoda glanced over at Roddy, who was staring morosely into his pint. 'He's harmless. Quite sweet, actually.'

'You know him well, then?'

'Not really. I've seen him in here and sometimes in the pub in Benbecula. My mother was great pals with his mother when they were at school.'

'Catriona was at school with Chrissie?' That couldn't be right. There was no way the two women were close enough in age.

'No, not Chrissie! Chrissie's younger sister, Peggy.' Rhoda leant closer to Rachel, glanced over at Roddy and lowered her voice. 'Chrissie isn't his birth mother – she's his aunt. Roddy's mother died when he was a baby.'

'But he calls Chrissie his mother.'

'Apparently Peggy, Roddy's mother, was quite a bit younger than Chrissie and Duncan, and very young to be having a baby,

In cases like that it's very common for the child to be brought up by a sibling and for the child to call the woman who is really his aunt or his grandmother, mother. Especially if the real mother is dead.'

Rachel felt herself soften toward Roddy. She knew how awful it was to lose a mother.

Rachel ate quickly and decided to take her wine to her room. It had been a long and frustrating day. She'd start early tomorrow.

Back in her room she finished her wine, brushed her teeth, changed into her pyjamas and got into bed. Hoping a film would help her relax, she propped her laptop on her knees. Frustratingly, despite several attempts, she still couldn't log onto the internet and without a connection she couldn't watch Netflix. She got up again and fetched her book from her bag, but not before locking both her bedroom and patio doors. Nothing Rachel had learned so far had convinced her there wasn't a murderer on the island.

THIRTEEN
THURSDAY

Rachel was wrenched from sleep by the strident ring of the telephone beside her bed. It was so dark in her room she couldn't see a thing. Fumbling for the receiver, she sent the glass of water on her bedside table flying.

'What the hell have you been up to?' her boss shouted down the line when she picked up. 'The local force have been complaining to their powers-that-be that you've been blundering around up there like a pig in shit, interfering with their investigation, tampering with evidence, interviewing all and sundry. Who do you think you are? Miss bloody Marple?'

'The local force have not been as thorough as they might have been,' Rachel replied stiffly. She explained about the unlocked house, the phone she'd found and Mike's view that Ellen could not have been carried by the tide and currents from her house to the blowhole where her body had been found.

'Which is why I am meeting the coastguard,' she checked the time on her phone – God, it was after eight – 'later this morning.'

It was enough to pacify him. 'Very well. Let me know what

he has to say. If he has nothing new to add, then I want you on the next plane. Is that understood?'

'Perfectly,' she said, mentally crossing her fingers. Storm or no storm, there was no way she was leaving until she had the answers she'd come for.

The directions Selena had given Rachel to where she was to meet the coastguard were easy to follow. Straight along the main road, passing the turn-off to Balranald on her left until she came to a medieval tower built on a loch near the road. After that she was to take the first turn on the right and first right again until she came to Griminish Harbour.

Rachel knew she had found the correct place from the number of creels stacked several rows high next to a pier. There had to be over a hundred of them. Apart from the creels, there were coiled ropes and nets. A number of boats ranging in size from small yachts to large commercial fishing vessels were berthed in the harbour.

As she drew up, a fair-haired man in his mid to late thirties jumped out of one of the larger, newer-looking boats. He was tall, well over six foot, and wearing jeans shoved into green wellingtons. No hat. A roan and chocolate-coloured spaniel danced at his heels. Even at a distance, energy radiated from him.

'Miss McKenzie?' he asked, opening her car door for her. 'I'm Calum Stuart and this is Loach,' he continued when she nodded. Although there were traces of an island accent in his voice, it was overlaid with the educated tones of a well-heeled southerner. Loach wagged her docked tail in welcome.

Calum's eyes were a disconcerting shade of green. When he smiled, twin brackets formed at either side of his mouth. His nose was long and straight, almost aristocratic.

Inevitably, it started to drizzle. Rachel pulled the hood of her fishing jacket over her head, thankful she'd thought to wear it.

She took his proffered hand. 'Please, call me Rachel. Thanks for meeting me. I know you must be busy.'

Her hand practically disappeared in his. 'Not a problem. As I said on the phone, I was due to walk this part of the estate anyway. This way I have company.'

'How far is it?'

'To the blowhole? No more than an hour's walk. If that.'

Rachel retrieved her wellingtons from the boot of her car and, resting her bottom on the open lip, changed out of her shoes.

They set off, with Loach running ahead, looking back every now and again to check that they were following. The wind spat nuggets of rain into their faces and the sea had darkened to a gunmetal grey topped with spots of white, as if an artist had flicked a paintbrush across the water.

They followed the path that hugged the coastline, passing a large house on the right. It was perched on top of a slight rise with full-height windows facing out to sea.

'That's the Grand House where the current Lord Buckley lives – when he's here, which isn't very often,' Calum said. 'He owns most of North Uist. I'm his estate manager.'

Loach sped after a black-and-white bird that dipped its wing to the ground, seemingly enjoying the game of catch.

'It's a lapwing,' Calum told Rachel. 'It's trying to keep Loach away from her nest by making him chase her.'

'How come you have two jobs?' Rachel asked. 'Or is that a daft question? Everyone I've met so far on the islands seems to have more than one.'

When Calum grinned, Rachel's heart missed a beat. It had been a long time since she'd found a man attractive.

'Managing the North Uist estate is my paid job. I keep the deer numbers down, take shooting and fishing parties out, issue fishing permits, make sure fences are kept in good repair. Like everyone on the coastguard team here, I'm a part-time volunteer. We're not busy enough to warrant a full-time team. Luckily, managing the estate isn't a nine-to-five job either. Sometimes I leave the house before it's light and don't get home until midnight, but I can have long periods off during the day, and the winter is quiet. The busiest times tend to be during the shooting and fishing seasons. On the whole it's easier for me to leave work at a moment's notice if I'm needed than it would be for a fireman or a doctor, for example.'

They were following the coastline, which was to their right. Rachel tried to get a picture in her head where they were, relative to Ellen's house. Bloody miles away, anyway.

'Do you know Mike? The owner of the Uist Diving Company?' she asked.

'Yes.' He shot her a look from the corner of his eye. 'He's an interesting guy.'

'In what way?'

Calum looked as if he were thinking about it. 'He's pretty well thought of on Uist. If the police or coastguard need help looking for missing fishermen or other accidents at sea, they tend to call him. He has boats and the right equipment as well as access to divers. He's never refused to help. Even when it means putting his work on hold.'

'You like him then?' Rachel was surprised. Mike clearly didn't think much of the coastguard, and she'd imagined the feeling would be mutual.

Once again Calum took his time answering. 'Like's not exactly the word I would use. Respect would be more precise. He can be difficult and bloody-minded. He tends to think he knows the sea better than anyone else.'

'He certainly seems to think the coastguard got it wrong when they – and I guess by they, he means you – said Ellen's body could have ended up in the blowhole if she fell in close to her house.'

Calum stopped and turned to face Rachel. Irritation flashed across his face. 'As I said, Mike tends to believe he knows best. But in this case, it's him who is mistaken. There was a full moon around the time she was last seen – meaning the tides were higher than usual. If the tide was going out when she fell in, she could have been dragged out to sea and a very high tide would have lessened the chances of her body snagging on the rocks. Then when the tide turned again she could have been dragged back inland. It's entirely possible her body ended up in the blowhole through a combination of tides and currents. Mike's talking through a hole in his arse when he says it isn't.'

Put that way, it seemed feasible. Yet it was a hell of a long way. Either Mike was wrong or everyone else was. Time to get another, independent, opinion.

As quickly as the rain had started, it stopped. The sun eased out from behind a cloud bathing the land and sea in bright, clear light.

'Is this your first time here on the islands?' Calum asked.

Rachel's breath caught. This time it was she who took her time to answer.

'No. I was here once before.'

'On business?'

'In a way.' She didn't want to answer questions about her personal life. It was possible, even likely, that sooner or later someone on the island would make the connection between her and the murder of an islander's daughter, but she had no intention of making it easy for them. Time for a change of subject. 'What about you? Do you come from here?'

'I was born and brought up on North Uist. My father, and his father before him, managed the estate before I did. I went away to school when I was sixteen. Back then you had to go to the mainland if you wanted to continue to higher education.

After school I went to Cambridge to study economics. From there I went to London where I worked in banking for a bit.'

That explained the accent that was more south of England than local.

'I came back about two years ago,' he continued, 'and have been here ever since.'

'Quite a contrast to London,' Rachel said, curious. 'Why did you come back?'

The light in his eyes dimmed. 'To look after my mother. She has end-stage cancer.'

'I'm sorry. That must be tough. For you both.'

'It's an honour to look after her. After my father died, she raised me on her own while working full-time as a doctor. She was – is – an amazing woman.' He half smiled. 'What about your folks?'

Damn – she'd walked into that one. 'My mother died when I was in my teens. I don't see much of my father. We don't get along.'

'It's my turn to say sorry. You must miss her your mother?'

Rachel nodded, turning her head away as tears pricked behind her eyes. What the fuck was wrong with her? She was normally so good at hiding her feelings. It must be being here, surrounded by memories of her mother.

'Don't you miss London?' she asked. Better to keep the conversation on him.

'Less than I thought I would. When I first came back I was certain I'd find it impossible to live outside London – let alone here. But I discovered I enjoy being outside all year round. I like working with the coastguard and the people here. Now I can't see myself doing a desk job again.'

'Don't you get bored? I mean, what do people do for fun around here?'

Calum laughed. 'You've got to be kidding! There's tons to do. Dances and concerts, talks as well. And if you like the outdoors, there's walking, shooting, and fishing. If you like fly fishing, and I do, there's no better place in the world.'

'I fish too,' she said. She didn't tell him it was something she'd done with her father. Her chest tightened. Her father had taught her when she was six and had taken her fishing at least once a month – more, when he could spare the time. Sometimes with her godfather and his son, sometimes just the two of them. Even though they'd hardly spoken on those trips, she'd treasured those hours when she'd had him all to herself. Despite everything, being thigh-deep in water was still one of her happy places.

'Anyway,' Calum continued, bringing her back to the present. 'I'm not here all the time. If I need a city fix, I jump on a plane to London or Cambridge to stay with friends. Dr Logan is always happy to keep an eye on Mother for a few days. Occasionally my mates drag themselves up here to visit me.' He looked her directly in the eyes. 'Inverness is pretty cool too.' He smiled. 'Speaking of my limited social life, I don't suppose you'd like to have dinner with me one evening? If you're free?' He gave the last two words extra emphasis. He knew he wasn't just asking about her diary.

He was a quick worker, she'd give him that.

'I'm not sure how long I'll be here. I could be going back to Inverness tomorrow.' Her mouth had dried.

'What about tonight then? I'll even cook.'

She hesitated. Why not? She couldn't remember the last time she'd hooked up with anyone. Sometimes in the middle of the night when her panicked heart wouldn't let her sleep, she longed for the comfort of another presence. She was unlikely to see him again and that's the way she liked it. Besides, he intrigued her.

'OK. Unless anything comes up, you're on.'

His mouth curved into a smile. 'You're staying at Tioran

Lodge, right? I'll pick you up. About seven? Unless I hear from you that you can't make it.'

He knew where she was staying! Rachel felt a flash of irritation. She should be getting used to the island telegraph by now – didn't mean she had to like it though. It was worse than living in Moy. How on earth did Calum put up with it after the anonymity of London?

'Don't worry about picking me up. I'll drive.'

'You sure? It's a bit of a hike to the house from where you'll need to leave the car.'

'I'm sure.' She didn't want to rely on him to get back to her hotel.

He gave her a speculative look, then smiled. 'Up to you.'

As they walked they chatted about bars and restaurants they both liked on the mainland and compared notes on fishing.

'That's the place Ellen was found, over there.' Calum came to a stop and pointed.

Rachel couldn't see anything resembling a hole. Seeing her puzzlement, he added. 'We have to get a little nearer to actually see it.'

As they got closer the ground fell away, revealing a large circular gap, several metres across.

'Don't get too close,' Calum warned. 'Although you can't see it from this perspective, the sea's eroding the land from underneath and the ground around the rim of the hole could crumble at any time.'

He called Loach and, grabbing the dog by the collar, lifted her into his arms.

Keeping a safe distance from the edge, Rachel peered into the hole. It was much deeper than she'd imagined. The sea, funnelled through a narrow gap in the rock, shot white flames of water upwards like an erupting volcano. If anyone did slip and fall in, they'd almost certainly be killed – at the very least too badly injured to help themselves. It must have been a hell of a job retrieving the body.

'You really think Ellen's body could have washed in here after being carried all the way from Grimsay? Even with a particularly high tide? Now I see it for myself, it doesn't strike me as at all likely. A bit like the proverbial camel and needle.'

'As I said, a lot depends on the currents and the tide the day she died.' He turned to look directly at her, his eyes puzzled. 'How else could she have got in here?'

Good question. She wished she knew the answer. 'Maybe she came here, got too close to the edge and slipped? Or, as you suggested, a piece of ground gave way underfoot? I can see how easily *that* might have happened. Mike's divers think it's the most likely scenario.' One that Rachel still hadn't completely ruled out. It was too far for Ellen to have walked from her house, so someone must have given her a lift, or taken her here by boat. In which case, why hadn't that person come forward? Rachel couldn't think of an innocent reason. Unless whoever had brought her had been a visitor to the islands and not heard about her death? Or Ellen hadn't come here willingly? In which case, she'd have to have been carried or dragged across the moor before being flung into the blowhole. Rachel shivered. It was a terrible image. Without more to go on, that kind of thinking was like going down a rabbit hole. Besides, a fall or drop from this height would have resulted in broken bones. And, according to the PM, that hadn't been the case.

Calum was staring at her in surprise. 'You've spoken to the divers?'

'Briefly. They didn't agree with Mike's view. To be honest, they weren't particularly interested in what happened to Ellen.'

She dug around in her handbag and pulled out the map she had found in Ellen's book and smoothed out the creases before passing it to Calum. Free once more, Loach sped off after a rabbit.

'Do you recognise this?' Rachel asked.

He took the sheet of paper from her and studied it for a moment before handing it back. 'Nah. No idea.'

'Apparently it's a map of the Monachs.'

He squinted at it again, taking his time this time. 'Of course. So it is.' He looked out to sea, shielding his eyes from the sun. 'They're a wee group of islands out to the west. On a clear day you can see them from here.' He pointed into the distance.

'I understand no one lives there now?'

'Haven't for years. There's no electricity, no running water, nothing between the islands and North America except ocean. No one would put up with that level of discomfort or remoteness now. The St Kildans couldn't do it in the thirties. You've heard of St Kilda?' He moved his pointing finger to the right. 'See that blob on the horizon? That's it.'

Rachel had heard of St Kilda. She knew it was famous for the islanders all deciding to leave together in the mid 1930s after life had simply become too difficult. However, interesting as St Kilda and its history was, she needed to get him back on track.

'What else do you know about the Monachs?'

'I believe they were inhabited up until the late 1930s – but those families either died or left – and it remained uninhabited until a family from North Uist tried to resettle it. But it didn't work out. They came back to Uist after a few years.'

'And that was Duncan Mór's family?'

He cocked an eyebrow. 'You've done your homework. Why so interested?'

'Because Ellen visited shortly before she died. Any idea how she might have got there?'

Calum picked up a stick and threw it for Loach, who raced after it. 'None at all. I didn't know she'd been. Perhaps one of the fishermen took her? It would have to be someone who knows the channels well. It can get very shallow on the way to the Monachs, so the tide has to be high enough. You can't land there very easily – the weather and tide have to be just right – and even if you do manage to land you run the risk of getting stuck, particularly in winter if the weather changes.' He narrowed his eyes. 'Why are you asking? You can't think it has anything to do with the woman's death? I thought everyone agreed it was an accident.'

'We haven't decided yet.' Aware of how terse she sounded, she softened her tone. 'Have you been to the Monach Islands?'

'Once – maybe twice. There really is nothing to see there. No reason to go.'

A gust of wind blew Rachel's hair across her face. Calum reached for a lock, tucked it behind her ear and smiled.

Her skin goose-bumped under his fingers. How long was it since she'd been touched?

'Let's get back. The weather's about to take a turn for the worse,' Calum said.

'How do you know?'

He pointed out to sea. It had turned malachite. 'That's what is known as a wolf sea,' he said. 'It always turns that colour when a storm is coming. Just like the starlings perch on the telephone lines when rain is on the way.'

'You are kidding, aren't you?'

'Not at all. There's always a way to read portents here if you know how.'

At that precise moment the sky opened up. The rain fell in sheets, obscuring Rachel's vision: it seemed he had been right.

FOURTEEN

Rachel had just changed into dry clothes when the phone beside her bed rang.

'Why the dickens have you not been answering your mobile? I've being trying to get hold of you!' As usual, Douglas didn't bother with the niceties of polite conversation.

'I'm sorry. The reception here is intermittent – at least on my network. I have to be standing on a hill to get a decent signal. Is the result of the PM in?'

'No, it's bloody well not. Apparently there's a backlog because of some ruddy coach crash in Argyll.' Typically, no expression of sympathy for the victims from her boss. 'The pathologist's office has promised me the report by lunchtime tomorrow. That's not why I was phoning.' He took a deep, phlegmy breath. 'Apparently your victim,' *her* victim? 'sent a rib bone to a pal who works at GUARD Archaeology for testing. It's a company that knows everything you'd ever want to know about bones. She wanted him to verify whether the rib was human and, if so, how old it was. He knew pretty much at once that the bone was human – probably from an older adult, most likely male, although possibly from a big woman. He immediately notified the police, who notified us. This pal tried to get in touch with Ellen but of course that was a bit of a problem. He only discovered she was dead when the police told him.' He coughed wetly. 'This colleague knew that the rib couldn't have separated from the skeleton naturally or even through foraging animals, but that something very sharp had caused almost a clean break. A blade of some description.' Douglas barely drew another wheezy breath before plunging on. 'Now, what does that sound like to you?' Before Rachel had a chance to reply, he continued. 'Because it sounds like murder to me.'

The fine hair all over Rachel's body stood on end.

'The question is whether it has anything to with Miss Hargreaves's death. It's been sent for carbon dating – that'll give us a clue how old it is. Meanwhile, I'll phone the forensic pathologist and put a firecracker up her arse.'

Rachel smiled. She knew the pathologist he was talking about. It was debatable who would be putting a firecracker up whose arse.

'It seems you might have been right about Ms Hargreaves's death not being an accident.' He sounded as if he'd been personally bereaved. He cleared his throat. 'However, I'd like something more before I get MIT involved. I'm not ready to send them on a wild goose chase. I need more proof. I want you to find it.'

Rachel paced her room, trying to quell her excitement. Had she been right all along? Had Ellen been murdered? Because she'd found evidence of another murder?

The air went out of her. What was she thinking? It was almost as if she wanted Ellen to have been murdered. What sort of person did that make her? Well, someone who wanted justice for Ellen, that's who. Douglas was right, though, they needed more. *Think, woman, think!* If Ellen had been murdered it was almost certainly connected to the bone she'd found. Where had Ellen found the rib? Who knew that she had? And who knew it belonged to someone who had been murdered? If she could locate where Ellen had found the bone it might lead to the identity of their John Doe and what had happened to him – or her. That in turn might lead to whoever might have harmed Ellen.

It all came down to that bone.

Using the landline, she dialled Clive's extension. The office administrator picked up straight away. 'Scottish Fatalities Investigation Unit North. How can I help?'

'Hey, Clive. It's me.'

'Oh, the roaming sleuth. What's up?'

'I need a number.'

'Fire away.'

'It's for the person at GUARD who Douglas spoke to about the bone.' Clive knew better than to ask why she hadn't asked their boss herself.

'Give me a minute.'

He was back in two. 'It was a Kevin Wallace.' He reeled off the number.

The phones had been ringing constantly while Rachel had been holding. 'How's it going there?' she asked.

'Like a fair. Three overdoses, a stabbing and a woman found dead in bed by her husband. And that's just this morning. Suruthi is meeting with relatives from the coach crash.'

Rachel felt a pang of sympathy for her colleague. Speaking to bereaved relatives was one of the toughest parts of the job.

'I'll be back to help as soon as I can,' she promised, before ending the call.

She dialled the number Clive had given her and was put straight through to Kevin Wallace. She explained who she was and that she was calling about Ellen Hargreaves.

'Oh, Ellen! It was such a shock to hear she'd died! I'm still in shock, to be honest. I tried to get her on the phone a few times, but it just kept going to voicemail. I knew the reception was pretty rubbish where she was, so I didn't think too much about it. I certainly didn't think she could be dead! She was so fit, so full of energy. So happy to have moved to the Western Isles.' His shock and sorrow were evident in his voice.

'How well did you know her?'

'Well now. Let me think. I met her about five years ago on a dig on Orkney. She was just a volunteer of course, but a very keen one. It wasn't too long before she found out where I worked. She was fascinated. She loved collecting bones, I discovered. We were both avid twitchers too, so we saw each other fairly often. Although Ellen was quite a bit older than me, we became friends. Don't worry, my wife knew and approved; birdwatching bores the hell out of her. Besides, I think Ellen might have been gay, although she never said.'

Over the phone Rachel heard the squeak of a chair as if Kevin was settling in for a long chat, making the most of the opportunity to talk about a woman he'd clearly admired and liked.

'What else can you tell me about her?'

'Her parents are both dead and have been for some time. She'd no siblings and no close friends although she has a god-daughter in Australia, I believe. When we first met, I thought she seemed on the lonely side – but as I got to know her better, I realised she wasn't. She was simply one of those people content in her own skin and with her own company. She might not have been overly sociable, but she was kind, intelligent, and her passion for history and ornithology was all-absorbing. Her hobbies kept her engaged with life. She'd worked as a customs officer for years, but the hours didn't suit her, so when a position came up in archives at the Mitchell Library she jumped at the opportunity. Although I know she enjoyed her time there, I think she was ready to retire so she could spend more time on her hobbies. I believe she used part of her pension to buy the cottage in Uist.' He sighed. 'The wife and I talked about going to visit her there.'

'Was she in the habit of sending you human bones?'

There was a pause on the line. 'No!' he said eventually. 'That was the first and only one. She said in the accompanying note that she wasn't sure if it was human or animal. It's easy not to be certain if you're an amateur. She probably didn't want to embarrass herself by bringing a cow's rib to the police.' He sighed again. 'Nevertheless, she should really have done so.'

He was clearly reluctant to criticise his dead friend. If Ellen was so knowledgeable about skeletons, she must have had a fair idea the bone she'd found had been human. Naughty Ellen. Between that and excavating the wheelhouse without due process, this was a woman who knew her own mind and had no compunction breaking the rules. Rachel couldn't help but admire her for it. But what did any of it have to do with her murder?

'Why do you think she sent it?'

'She must have been hoping she'd found something of importance – like an ancient burial site – and the bone would prove it. It's what archaeologists, even amateur ones, live for.'

'Would there have been a financial reward for such a find?'

Kevin chuckled. 'No! Not at all. But archaeologists don't do it for the money. It's the fame, the kudos associated with making a major find. In the archaeological world that is everything.'

'Anything else you can tell me about the bone?'

'Only that it was separated from the rest of the ribcage by a sharp instrument. A small axe, a large knife, something of that order – the forensic anthropologist might be able to be more specific. I can't tell you much more until it's carbon-dated. I can't even say for certain if it's male or female at this stage.'

'Can DNA be extracted? Wouldn't that help confirm sex?'

'Yes. The forensic anthropologist will no doubt have plans to do that.'

Now for the most important question. 'Did Ellen say where she found it?'

'No. But it doesn't take rocket science to know she found it somewhere on the Western Isles. That's where it was posted from.'

'She wasn't more precise?'

'No. Unfortunately not.'

'Why do you think she didn't tell you where she found it?'

'I can't say for sure. Ellen was naturally secretive. I suspect she wanted confirmation that it was human and ancient before she told me more. Once I confirmed it was human, she would have known I'd have to get the police involved.'

'Can you tell what sort of soil it was buried in? Sandy versus clay? Peat?'

'Sandy. Consistent with an island.'

Rachel couldn't think of anything else to ask.

'Do you know who is organising her funeral?' Kevin asked as she was about to wind up the call.

'The god-daughter is next of kin, but she's in Australia. She's going to ask Ellen's solicitors to make the arrangements.'

'Do solicitors even do that? No. Absolutely not! That's simply not good enough. I'll speak to the god-daughter and suggest I take care of everything. Give Ellen the kind of low-key, dignified send-off she would have wanted.'

Rachel liked Kevin Wallace.

'Her body might not be released for some time, I'm afraid.'

There was a long pause on the other end of the line. 'I have to ask,' Kevin said eventually. 'It's not just about the bone, is it? This is about her death. You're not certain it was an accident, are you?'

There was no reason not to be honest. 'No, Kevin. I think there's a reasonable chance it wasn't. But I promise you...' To her embarrassment, her voice caught. 'We will find out one way or another. If Ellen *was* murdered we'll do everything in our power to make sure whoever did it goes to jail for a very long time.'

After hanging up, Rachel reviewed what Kevin had told her. When Ellen found the bones she'd hoped they were ancient. Had she found them at the Wheelhouse? Or the Monach Islands? Or somewhere else? Her gut told her the Monachs. Ellen had just been there; she'd been excited when she'd come back, and she'd been keen to speak to Duncan and Chrissie about its history. Rachel needed to find out who had taken Ellen there. Perhaps go herself. If there was one bone, wouldn't there be others? Could she persuade Calum to take her? She glanced at her watch. Four thirty. She was due at his place for dinner at seven. There was only a couple of hours or so of daylight left so it was pointless asking him to take her tonight. But tomorrow morning might be a possibility.

In the meantime, there was just enough time to have a look at the wheelhouse. It was possible Ellen had found the bone there.

FIFTEEN

As the rising breeze threatened to blow the map away, Rachel smacked it flat on the bonnet of her car. This was as far as she could get with her vehicle; the rest of the journey to the wheel-house would have to be on foot. She scrutinised the map until she found what she was looking for: a tiny symbol marking a site of interest. She had two options. She could stay on land, which would add at least a kilometre in either direction, or she could go across the sands and access the route from there.

It was an easy choice. As long as she didn't spend too long looking for it and the tide stayed out. She shoved the map into her jacket pocket and yanked on her wellingtons. She'd have to hurry if she were to make dinner with Calum in time. The sand was boggy underfoot and she had to wade through a couple of narrow streams left by the ebbing tide before reaching land again. A sheep track led up a small hill in the general direction Rachel wanted to go. The sun, which had shown its face for a brief spell, disappeared behind the clouds. Bracken was beginning to grow, making the track increasingly difficult to follow, but when she deviated from it she ended up ankle-deep in bog.

At this rate it would be dark before she found what she was looking for.

She crested the hill and started down the other side towards the coastline, scanning the desolate moor for anything that might look like the remains of an excavated wheelhouse. She was no longer sure if she was heading in the right direction. She'd had to re-route to avoid the bogs so many times, she'd become disorientated.

Although the road was only a short distance away when the wind dropped, the silence was profound. She could be the only person alive.

The back of her neck prickled. Once again she had an uneasy feeling she was being watched. She looked behind her. No one in sight. On the map the wheelhouse had seemed so close to the road she hadn't thought twice about coming on her own. If Ellen had been murdered, her killer could be watching Rachel, following her. Had she been nuts coming here solo? Perhaps she should leave investigating the wheelhouse until she had company? She was about to turn around and head back to the car when she thought she saw something in the distance that looked like it might be what she was looking for. In which case she was not turning back now.

She couldn't resist another glance over her shoulder before hurrying down the hill as quickly as the marshy ground would allow.

Nestled in the dip between two hills was a structure shaped like a large stone wheel divided by partitions.

Although the wheelhouse hadn't been fully excavated, it was easy to see how it would have looked centuries before: a large circular room with walls like spokes separating the smaller rooms from the main living space. Even the hearth was still evident.

Rachel scrutinised the ground for any sign the earth had been disturbed and could find none – only the droppings of sheep and rabbits and the tiny skull of some creature that would have been of no interest to anyone except Ellen if she were alive to see it. And if Ellen had been murdered, and her killer – thinking he'd got away with it – was still on the island, it was foolish to linger any longer.

She looked up and nearly jumped out of her skin when she found Roddy looming over her, as still as a standing stone, a shotgun in the crook of his elbow.

'Jesus!' she yelped. 'Where did you come from?'

He frowned. 'I was on my croft checking on my sheep when I saw you heading in this direction.'

And? He thought he'd follow her. See what she was doing? Because he was worried about what she'd find? Rachel was painfully aware that the pair of them could be in Timbuktu and that she'd told no one where she was going.

His eyes narrowed as his gaze shifted above her head. He whirled in an arc, while raising his shotgun to his shoulder and firing off a round. Rachel ducked, although the shot was in the opposite direction to where she was standing. Something crashed to the ground. Roddy loped off towards it.

Should she make a run for it? She was limited by the terrain and her too large wellingtons. She thrust her hands into her jacket pockets and felt the cold steel of her gutting knife. It was still there from the last time she'd gone fishing. It wasn't much use against a gun, but her time on the streets as a teenager had taught her surprise often gave the advantage.

Roddy came back holding a large black bird.

'A crow,' he said in response to Rachel's shocked face. 'Don't mind them most of the time, but not when there's newborn lambs.' He indicated the wheelhouse with a jerk of his chin. 'You found what you were looking for?'

Rachel's heartbeat was slowly returning to normal. 'No. It looks as if no one has been here for a while. When did Ellen excavate it?'

'She did it over a couple of summers. She stopped about two years ago.'

'And she's not been back recently?'

'Not that I know of.'

Out at sea a boat puttered past, and Roddy squinted at it. 'It's the McKinnons' boat from Kallin,' he said, as if Rachel had asked.

'Is Kallin harbour near here?'

'Aye. Not far at all. If you continue on the Grimsay road you'll come to it soon enough.'

Rachel tried to visualise where it was relative to Ellen's house.

'Did Ellen excavate anywhere else that you know of?'

'No, but that's not to say she didn't. There's hundreds of places all over this island where she could dig and find something. There's even a village on the west side of North Uist that nobody realised was there until a storm blew the sand away.'

Rachel couldn't visit hundreds of sites looking for the right one. She'd stick with the likely.

'Did you take Ellen out to the Monachs?' she asked.

'No indeed, I did not. But she was there. I saw her.'

'You did?' Her heart rate went back up. 'When was this?'

'Dunno,' he mumbled. 'Maybe a week before they found her body washed up.'

'Any idea who might have taken her?'

He looked distinctly uncomfortable. 'You should ask Mike.'

'Ask Mike? Why?' Getting information from Roddy was like sucking porridge through a straw.

'Because he took her there. I saw his boat anchored offshore and she was on it.'

'Are you sure?'

'Course I'm sure. Everyone who has a boat here knows all the other boats.'

'And you're certain the woman was Ellen?'

'I didn't know who it was at the time. Only that it was a woman. But when she came to see my uncle, I recognised her.'

Why hadn't Mike said? Had he been misdirecting her – everyone – all along?

'Did she see you?'

'I doubt it.'

She was tempted to ask him where on the Monachs Ellen might have found the bone but decided that was a question best left for another time. When there were other people around. Whatever Roddy said, he'd just admitted being on, or near, the island the same time as Ellen. Perhaps he'd even seen her find the bone. Rachel glanced around, feeling her unease deepen. If it had been Roddy who killed Ellen, she was alone with a murderer carrying a gun.

'Did you tell the police about seeing Ellen and Mike's boat?'

'No, I did not.'

'May I ask why?'

The sigh seemed to come from the bottom of his boots. 'Because they never asked. And why should they? The woman fell. She drowned. It was an accident. What has any of it to do with her being to the Monachs?'

That was precisely what Rachel wanted to know.

'If I took you to those islands, you'd be able to see for yourself that there is nothing there.'

No way was she going there alone with anyone until she was sure they weren't a killer.

'The coastguard said it's difficult to land on the Monachs. Especially when the weather's bad,' she said.

Roddy gave a dismissive shake of his head. 'If a man's afraid of the sea then he has no business being in the coastguard. Anyway, I already told you there's no one who knows these waters like me. There's a storm forecast but not for another couple of days. We could go tomorrow.'

He was beginning to truly freak her out.

'Thank you for the offer. I'll let you know. I know you have sheep to see to, so I'll find my own way back to my car.'

She wanted to put as much distance between her and Roddy as quickly as she could.

'No indeed. I'll take you.' He gave her a small smile. 'If anything happened to a visitor in my company, I'd never forgive myself.'

SIXTEEN

Escorted by a silent Roddy, Rachel made it back to her car without event. Before she drove off, she phoned the police station. When Fergus answered she told him what Roddy had said about seeing Ellen on Mike's boat out at the Monachs. He promised to follow it up.

Following Calum's directions to his home, Rachel took the road towards Hosta. After a short distance a sandy track veered away to the left and Rachel drove along it until it came to an end. There was nothing to see in the fading light apart from a double-storey house at the top of an exposed and inhospitable clifftop. It had to be Calum's as there were no other houses in sight. She was glad she'd remembered to take the torch from her room. The one in her phone would never be up to the job once it got completely dark.

Although the rain had died away, the wind almost wrenched the car door from her hand when she stepped out of the vehicle.

As she walked up the hill the land fell away on one side, revealing a sugar-white, empty beach that stretched away into the distance. The sea close to the shore was jade, graduating to cobalt blue near the horizon, and the setting sun smeared the sky with gold. In the near distance the sand dunes gave way to black, jagged rocks. Waves crashed against the cliffs, spewing flumes of spray into the air. It was hard not to feel part of the elements. No wonder weather was so important to the islanders when they lived cheek by jowl with nature.

Calum's house, built almost entirely of chrome and steel, surprised her. She'd assumed he'd live in something more traditional. As elsewhere on the island there were no trees to obstruct the view. Calum must be able to see for miles. Why, then, did he have CCTV cameras attached to either side of the house? Selena had said no one, not even the shop owners, had bothered to install it. Perhaps, having lived much of his life in London, Calum was more crime aware than the locals.

She pressed the doorbell to the right of the solid oak front door. As she waited, she glanced up at the CCTV camera and gave a small smile and awkward wave. She was bound to be nervous. It had been a long time since she'd been on anything remotely resembling a date.

Calum answered the door, Loach at his feet. The dog gave a happy yelp when she saw Rachel, who bent to tickle her behind her ears. Loach rolled onto her back in complete surrender.

'You've made another fan,' Calum grinned. He was wearing a white T-shirt that accentuated his sun-darkened skin and a pair of black jeans. His smile was lazy, his eyes approving.

'*Feasgar math* – good evening,' he translated automatically. 'Welcome to my humble home.' He opened his arms in a theatrical gesture and Rachel relaxed. Perhaps she wasn't the only one who was feeling nervous?

'It's an amazing spot you have here. Is this really all yours?'

He grinned. 'All mine. Come on in.' He helped her out of her jacket and hung it up. 'Would you like to have a look around?'

'I'd love to.'

On the ground floor there were four bedrooms and a bathroom, all minimalist and immaculately tidy. If it wasn't for the paperback on the bedside table and the massive TV on the wall opposite the bed, Rachel would have been hard-pressed to guess which one Calum used.

He led the way back to the spacious hall and the chrome-and-glass staircase positioned in the centre.

'The main rooms are on the upper floor,' Calum told her. 'To make the most of the views.'

Loach followed them up the stairs, claws pattering on the wood. As they emerged onto the upper floor, Rachel gave a gasp of delight. Calum had left most of this floor open plan. A modern kitchen was tucked away to one side with the rest of the room taken up by two large sofas covered in holly green Harris tweed. The floor was polished oak, the walls painted in a light chalk colour. An expensive-looking stereo and a massive flat-screen TV were set along one wall and a modern wood burner against another. Abstract oil landscapes hung wherever there was an expanse of wall. Next to the windows, pointing out to sea, was a telescope mounted on a stand, like the one in the conservatory at Tioran Lodge, only bigger. Much bigger.

But it was the view that drew her to the wall of floor-to-ceiling glass windows. They framed the sea, which stretched as far as the eye could see, empty, apart from a red-and-white fishing boat on the horizon. Below her, the ocean crashed on to rocks, sending the occasional spatter of seawater against the window.

'Did you build it or did you buy it like this?' Rachel asked.

'My mother's parents' croft house was here originally. I demolished it and built this. There's too much harking after the past here for my liking. Why not do something different?'

'And the interior?' Rachel waved her hand. 'Did you do this too?'

'*Mhic an diabhal*, no! A previous girlfriend did it for me.'

No surprise he'd had girlfriends. The surprise was that he wasn't married. At least, not as far as she knew.

'Do you like it?' He was like a little boy waiting for a pat on the head.

'I love it,' she replied, meaning it. 'Who wouldn't?'

She bent to peer through the telescope and chunks of land came into view.

He came to stand behind her. He smelled of aftershave and, more enticingly, of the sea.

'Is that St Kilda over there?' she asked, her heart beating ridiculously fast.

'Let me see.'

Relieved to put some distance between them, Rachel stood aside to let him take her place at the telescope.

'Yep, that's them. St Kilda is a group of islands, not just one, contrary to popular belief. That big flat one is the main island where people used to live. The small round one is Boreray and that pillar next to it is one of the famous stacks.'

'Where are the Monach Islands?'

Calum swivelled the telescope to the left. 'There,' he said. 'It's the group with the lighthouse on the smaller island.'

He stood back to let her look. The telescope was so powerful she could make out the ruins of the houses which dotted the land.

'I know you said it's difficult to land, but would you take me there? Tomorrow?'

When he didn't answer she turned back to face him. He had a weird expression on his face, one she couldn't decipher.

'Why the urgency?' he asked. 'Has something happened?'

How much should she tell him about her suspicions regarding Ellen? Her godfather was always reminding her that not everyone had a dark soul, that most people were decent. Rachel wasn't so sure, but at some point she had to start trusting people. Besides, the news about Ellen's find would come out sooner rather than later.

'We now know that Ellen found a human bone shortly before she died.'

He crossed the room to a side table on top of which were several bottles. 'Drink?'

'A single vodka, if you have it, with tonic, please. Lots of tonic. I think she found the bone on the Monach Islands.'

'Why do you think she found it there?' he asked as he poured the drinks. 'There are literally hundreds of ancient sites on these islands – brochs, duns, Viking graves, Temple ruins...'

'So I believe. Given the map I found in her possession, the fact she was recently out there and asking about it, my bet is on the Monachs. I'd like to go out there before I leave. So will you take me?'

He handed her a tumbler with her drink poured over ice. 'Why don't we see what the weather's like in the morning? If the storm that's forecast is here by then it won't be safe.' He smiled. 'I don't want to take any risks with you.'

When he touched her cheek, she felt a flutter of panic. It was too much, too soon. She gave herself a mental shake. It was called flirting, Suruthi's voice inside her head said. Nevertheless, she stepped back, putting distance between them, walked over to one of the paintings and pretended to study it. She could almost feel his puzzlement across the room.

To her relief he said nothing. He threw a couple of logs into the wood burner and put on some music. The strains of Capercaillie filled the room, the haunting voice of the lead singer singing in Gaelic.

'She's telling a story of loss and longing, of how it feels to be away from the islands,' Calum said as he stoked the fire.

It was on the tip of Rachel's tongue to tell him that she understood the words, but she held back. She wasn't ready to share that part of her life with him. Not yet. If ever.

'Can I do anything?' she asked when Calum started taking ingredients out of the fridge.

'Pour us some wine if you like? There's red and white. I prefer red. White's in the fridge.'

Rachel hadn't finished her vodka and tonic. She couldn't drink more until she'd decided whether she was going to stay. She opened the red to breathe while her host chopped garlic and onions with the assurance of a man who was used to cooking. Loach lay at Calum's feet, looking up at him with hopeful eyes. Rachel bent down and rubbed the dog's silky head and was rewarded with a lick. She perched on a bar stool and took a sip of her drink.

'Where does your mother live?'

'Here. With me,' he replied, to her surprise. There had been no sign of another occupant. 'She's not able to manage on her own anymore. She's in a lot of pain but she won't take the tablets Dr Logan prescribed for her.' When he looked up she saw the distress in his eyes. 'I converted my upstairs office into a bedroom for her. She spends most of her time reading and looking out to sea.' His voice was hollow, his eyes bleak.

'I'd like to meet her, if you think she's up for visitors?'

'Now? She'd like that.'

He dried his hands before leading her along a short corridor and into a room where two walls made entirely of glass faced out to sea. A neatly made bed with a dressing table was set against one of the non-glass walls and in front of the windows, in a recliner almost buried under blankets, was an elderly woman with a shock of white hair. A velvet sofa was the only other piece of furniture in the room.

'Mother, I have brought a guest to meet you,' Calum spoke to her in Gaelic. He beckoned Rachel closer. 'This is Rachel McKenzie,' he said, reverting to English. 'She's a lawyer from Inverness.'

Calum's mother smiled as if Rachel was the person she most

wanted to see in the world. 'I am so very pleased to meet you, dear. Won't you sit for a while?' She indicated the sofa with a sweep of her hand.

'I'll leave you two ladies to talk,' Calum said, dropping a kiss on top of his mother's head. 'Dinner shouldn't be long.'

'You're very pretty,' Dr Stuart said, searching Rachel's face. 'You remind me of someone.'

'Do I?' Rachel smiled.

'Didn't we go to school together?'

'I don't think so,' Rachel said gently. 'I went to school in Inverness.'

'Were you a patient then?' Dr Stuart's eyes creased in distress. 'I used to remember everyone, but I get a bit muddled now.' She grimaced. 'The pain makes it difficult to concentrate...'

'I don't believe I was ever one of your patients,' Rachel said.

It struck her then that the elderly woman might know something about their John Doe. 'When did you work as a doctor?'

'Let me see. I qualified as a GP when I was twenty-three. That was in 1969. I returned here to work immediately after.' She smiled at Rachel. 'I was the only doctor for the whole of North Uist at that time. I worked until I was seventy, you know.'

'Do you remember anyone going missing when you were a doctor?' she asked.

Dr Stuart's smile vanished and she glared at Rachel. 'Missing? In what way missing?' She plucked at a loose thread on her blanket. 'I don't know why you would ask me that! You're not the police, are you?'

'I'm sorry, I didn't mean to upset you,' Rachel said quickly. 'I just thought you might remember if something like that had happened.'

'No, I don't. Because it didn't. I'm tired now. I'd like you to go.' Dr Stuart gripped Rachel's wrist. 'Don't tell Calum,' she said. 'He mustn't know.'

'Mustn't know what?'

But Dr Stuart's eyes closed and her breathing deepened. She had either fallen asleep or was doing a very good job of pretending she had.

By the time Rachel returned to the kitchen Calum had finished gutting the salmon. Rachel stood in the doorway, watching as he wiped gobbets of dead fish and clotted blood from his fingers. What did his mother not want him to know?

'Why doesn't your mother get her meds increased?' Rachel asked. 'She's clearly in a lot of pain.'

Calum took a heavy saucepan from the rack above the cooker and set it on the heat. 'She takes half a dose of what Dr Logan prescribes. I keep trying to get her to take the full amount, but she says when she does it makes her confused, and she wants to stay as lucid as she can for as long as possible. It doesn't stop her from getting muddled though. Sometimes she thinks my father is still alive.'

'Do you remember him?'

Calum laid the salmon, skin down, on the heated pan. 'He left my mother before I was born. She heard he'd died a short time later. I can't even say I missed having a father. My mother never remarried. It was always just me and her.'

Rachel perched on a stool at the breakfast bar. 'She told me she was the only doctor on North Uist at one time.'

'She's very proud of it. Her family didn't have much growing up. My great-grandmother had ten kids, three of whom died before they reached their teens. They lived in one of those black houses the incomers are so fond of renovating as holiday homes. It used to be on this site, but further down in a sheltered dip. I have no idea how they all fitted in. You could have put that house into this one five or six times over.' He inspected a pan on the stove and, seemingly satisfied, took it off the heat.

'Mother was always very bright. She excelled at school. All she ever wanted was to be a doctor and to come back here to serve the community. After my father died we had to leave the Estate house, so we moved into the small cottage my mother's family had lived in. Although Mum worked all hours she spent as much of her free time with me as she could, making sure I did well enough at school to go to university.'

He flipped the salmon onto two plates and added some broccoli from the pan. He handed one of the plates to Rachel. 'I don't know about you,' he said, 'but I'm ready to eat. Mother had her supper earlier.'

They chatted easily until, when they were finished eating, Calum turned the conversation back to Ellen.

'I don't think there has ever been a murder on this island,' he said. 'Do you really think someone would have killed her over some bone?'

'I never said she'd been killed!' Rachel searched her memory, going over their previous conversations. No, she'd definitely kept her suspicions to herself.

'Clearly you don't think her death was an accident. You wouldn't be on the island otherwise, asking all these questions.'

'As yet there is no proof Ellen was murdered. However, I can't help but feel that the bone she found is connected in some way to her death. If we can locate where she found it, hopefully we'll find more bones or other evidence that might tell us who the bone belonged to. That's why I'm keen to go to the Monachs.'

Rachel helped Calum carry their plates to the sink.

'Tell her to go, Calum.' A shaky voice came from the door.

Rachel swung round. Dr Stuart was leaning against the doorframe, looking as if she was ready to collapse.

'There's a darkness in and all about her,' the old woman added in Gaelic.

Calum strode over to his mother and put his arm around her.

The blood rose in Rachel's cheeks. 'I'm afraid I upset your mother earlier when I asked if she remembered anyone going missing. I'm so sorry. I'll get my jacket.' She'd underestimated how distressed the older woman had been.

'Wait! Give me a few minutes. Just until I help mother back to her room.'

'No, really. I should go.'

'At least let me walk you to your car.'

'I'll manage fine. Take care of your mother.'

Dr Stuart clung on to her son's arm. Even with his support, she looked ready to collapse.

'Goodnight, Dr Stuart, Calum. Thank you for dinner.'

Rachel walked down the stairs, picked up her jacket, and stepped into the night.

Outside it was almost pitch black, the moon hidden behind the clouds. Rachel shivered and huddled deeper into her jacket. Could Dr Stuart really see darkness inside Rachel? The part she'd worked so hard on keeping hidden from everyone? To be seen as normal. The wind sighed around her. She fumbled in her pocket for her torch. Was her darkness any worse than anyone else's? It was bound to be. Her past had to have affected her. Or had the doctor sensed something darker, yet to happen?

Switching on the torch to light her path, she was dismayed to see its battery was running low, its light weak. She hurried towards her car, increasingly aware of the vastness all around her. It would be easy to get lost in the darkness with little in the way of landmarks to guide her.

A strange cry hovered above the waves, the silence that followed it, for some reason more chilling. Rachel tightened her grip on her failing torch, her eyes straining to penetrate the darkness. A sound startled her, and a shape moved in the darkness. Rachel suppressed a scream, then laughed out loud as a stag, his magnificent antlers just visible in the light from her torch, looked her way before continuing past her.

She reached her car without further incident and clambered in, locking the doors before inserting the key in the ignition. No one could say she wasn't having an interesting day.

However, if she was going to find the truth behind Ellen's death, she was going to have to pull on her big girl pants.

SEVENTEEN

FRIDAY

Rachel was once more yanked from sleep by the ringing of the phone beside her bed. The thick, impenetrable darkness told her that the sun hadn't yet risen.

'Miss Hargreaves was murdered,' Douglas said without preamble. 'Just got the results of the post mortem. Strangled to death.'

Rachel felt a jolt of adrenaline. 'How did the first pathologist miss that?' she asked.

'Easily done. Or so I'm told. Especially when the perpetrator uses something soft like a scarf, for example. It doesn't leave the same clear marks as a rope or hands even. Moreover, she'd been in the water for several days, which made it even less obvious.' He cleared his throat. 'Seems you saved this office from another embarrassment. Good work.' His voice was softer than she'd heard before. But if she thought he was going to add some more praise, she was mistaken.

'I've also heard from the forensic anthropologist. They've carbon dated the bone. It belonged to someone who was alive in the fifties.'

'Are they sure?'

'Absolutely positive. They can tell because of the nuclear tests in the fifties. Anyone alive after that time absorbed some radioactivity. It appears Ms Hargreaves stumbled upon a murder victim – and that might well have led to her own death. The CID have been notified and the MIT in Inverness will be taking over,' he said, before continuing in another one of his bewildering changes of tone. 'It's back in the hands of the police now. Your break is over. It's time to get your backside back here. ASAP.'

Before she had time to protest, he disconnected.

Rachel sank down on her bed. She'd thought she'd be pleased to have her suspicions about Ellen confirmed, but instead she felt sick. She took deep, steadying breaths and waited for the nausea to pass.

She didn't feel pleased or excited, or vindicated even: she felt fucking furious. Another innocent woman's life had been snuffed out as if she were of no consequence. Someone, perhaps a person Ellen knew and trusted, had wrapped a scarf around her neck and tightened it until all the breath had left her body. It took roughly five minutes for someone to die from strangulation – each moment agonising and terrifying. Rachel knew, because she'd made it her business to find out.

Like hell was she going back to the mainland. Not until they knew who had done that to Ellen.

Rachel flung her duvet aside. They now knew how Ellen had died. If they could discover why, it might lead to the who.

And discovering where might help too.

By the time she'd showered and dressed it was getting light.

The wind had dropped overnight and it was a perfectly still morning, a layer of thick mist hanging between the sky and the ground, the silence as profound as the earlier darkness had been. Beneath the carpet of mist, a flock of birds swooped in formation almost as if they were showing off – as welcoming and as pretty as the crows at Ellen's cottage had been sinister.

She was doing her teeth when she heard a loud thump against her bedroom window.

She opened the patio doors to have a look and almost stood in a black, glistening lump lying in a dribble of red immediately in front of the glass doors. On closer inspection, the lump revealed itself to be a large crow with blood trickling from its hooded head. The poor thing must have flown into her glass doors by mistake and killed itself. She would find Michelle or Mike and ask them to get rid of it.

There was no one having breakfast in the restaurant when she went down but there was an appetising smell of fresh coffee coming from the kitchen. Rachel followed her nose and found Michelle sitting at the kitchen table, sipping out of an outsize mug. Hearing Rachel approach, she looked up.

'Someone phoned for you while you were out last night,' Michelle said, getting to her feet and handing Rachel a slip of paper. 'He left his number. The code is Lochboisdale.'

The only person Rachel knew who lived in Lochboisdale was her grandfather. She glanced at the number, recognising it immediately. Yup, it was him. He must have learned she was on the island. But why reach out to her now? Bollocks to that.

Michelle paused expectantly but when Rachel just accepted the note and pocketed it without comment, she continued. 'Ready for your breakfast? Are you looking for the full works? I've porridge too if you fancy.'

'Just toast please,' Rachel said. 'And some strong coffee. But before that could you help me dispose of a dead bird I found outside my patio door?'

Michelle pulled a face. 'Oh, God, I'm sorry. Those bloody birds!'

'Not your fault.'

They took the outside route, going through the conservatory doors and up the small hill to the small garden in front of Rachel's room.

When Michelle saw the crow she frowned.

'I think it flew into the window,' Rachel said.

'You must have got a fright. It had to have made a hell of a racket.'

'I heard it over the sound of my electric toothbrush.'

Michelle was still frowning. 'There's no mark on the window. If it flew into the glass there would be a smear of blood or something.' Kneeling down, she inspected the bird. She became very still. 'Christ, it's been shot. Look, you can see a hole here in its head.'

Rachel crouched beside Michelle. 'Who would be out shooting birds at this time? And so close to the hotel. I could have been standing outside. Whoever it was could have hit me. And clearly he, or she, wasn't planning to eat it.'

Michelle got to her feet. 'I'll get a shovel and a bin bag.' She frowned again. 'It doesn't altogether surprise me that someone shot it, but what I do find strange is how it got here. You're quite right, no one would risk firing off a shot so close to the hotel. It's too dangerous.'

'Perhaps they only wounded the bird and it managed to fly a bit before it died?' Rachel suggested.

Michelle shook her head. 'Apart from the fact no one would wander onto the hotel grounds simply to fire at a crow, this one's been shot right between its eyes. It would have dropped like a stone.' She scanned the sky. 'You know ravens and crows are believed to be foretellers of death?'

Michelle had to be kidding. 'They don't get much positive press, do they?' Rachel said lightly.

Michelle turned back to her. There was no answering amusement in her eyes. Instead Rachel thought she saw regret – and pity. And maybe, just maybe, a glint of warning.

'Just promise me you'll be careful,' Michelle said.

Rachel held her gaze. If this was a pathetic attempt by someone – Roddy? – to scare her away, they'd made a mistake.

She was going nowhere until she knew who had murdered Ellen Hargreaves.

Rachel arrived at the police station to find all three officers present. Selena's eyes were bright with excitement. MacVicar, on the other hand, looked like a bear with a sore head. Constable Campbell was at his desk on the computer, apparently completely unaware of the electric atmosphere in the room.

'I'm assuming you heard the result of the PM?' Selena said. 'Seems you were right all along.'

'Yes. My boss phoned me this morning. He also told me the bone Ellen found was from someone who was killed after the Second World War. I assume you know about that too?'

Selena nodded. 'The sergeant briefed us when we came in.' She kept her gaze on Rachel. 'What happens now?'

MacVicar gave Selena a withering look. 'The matter is back in Police Scotland's hands. Miss McKenzie is free to return to Inverness.' He turned back to Rachel. 'Inverness is sending a detective inspector on this afternoon's plane. Whatever you might think, we haven't been twiddling our thumbs. I've requested her phone records and asked Stornoway coastguard to get us an expert opinion on tides and currents the day Ellen went into the water.'

It was as if someone had lit a fire under the sergeant. No doubt the looming arrival of a detective inspector.

'You can leave everything to us,' he finished, with another dour look in Rachel's direction.

'Miss McKenzie is going nowhere in the immediate future,' Rachel said firmly. 'My boss has asked me to meet with the inspector before I leave and make sure he's up to speed.' No need for the sergeant to know she was being economical with the truth. She turned to Fergus. 'By the way, what did Mike have to say about taking Ellen out to the Monachs?'

Sergeant MacVicar frowned and spun around to glare at Fergus, who was looking at his feet. 'I didn't manage to get hold of him,' he said with a sheepish smile. 'He was busy.'

Doing her best to hide her irritation, Rachel repeated what Roddy had told her about seeing Ellen out at the Monachs on Mike's boat.

Sergeant MacVicar's head bobbed furiously. 'After we're done here, Fergus, get yourself out to Tioran Lodge and find out what Mike Howard has to say.'

'In the meantime, there's other things we should be doing,' Rachel said.

'Such as?' Sergeant MacVicar spluttered.

'Our priority should be to find out who the bone belonged to. The likelihood is, if we find out who he – or she – was, we find who murdered Ellen. It has to be linked. It's too much of a coincidence that she digs up a bone – potentially evidence of another murder – and is found dead shortly afterwards.'

'No one has been reported missing in all the years I've been a policeman here,' Sergeant MacVicar continued, almost as if Rachel had accused him. 'Or in my father's day, for that matter. I spoke to him as soon as I heard. He is quite certain that during his time as police sergeant on Uist no one reported any missing tourists – or locals.'

Rachel remembered Selena telling her MacVicar's father had been a police sergeant on the island. 'Yet it has to be one or the other. We should search the missing persons database.'

Every year in the UK over a quarter of a million people went missing, and even with all the technology they had these days, despite all the electronic footprints people left behind, many thousands of those who disappeared from home were never reunited with their loved ones. Most didn't want to be found.

'Maybe the bone belongs to someone who was a visitor here but everyone assumed returned to the mainland? I think we should put pressure on the anthropologist to get DNA from the bone,' Rachel said. Sometimes bodies or body parts turned up that couldn't be traced to a missing person. They were logged on a national database. It would be worth checking out.

'Our Jay Doe could have been killed before your father's time,' Rachel continued, speaking directly to the sergeant. 'Is there anyone else from back then who might remember?' She thought back to Dr Stuart. Pity Calum's mother was confused.

'We'll certainly ask,' he replied.

MacVicar, apparently resigned to Rachel's ongoing presence, instructed Selena to search the missing person's database and Fergus to chase up the DNA with the lab. The phone records too, while he was at it. After that he could go and see Mike.

'While we're waiting for people to get back to us, we should try to find the burial site. There might be more bones there, more clues,' Rachel continued.

Sergeant MacVicar's mouth tightened. 'How do you suggest we do that?'

'She was wrong, but Ellen believed that the bone she found might belong to a person who lived hundreds, if not thousands, of years in the past.'

'There are hundreds of historical sites on this island where she might have found that bone. Are you suggesting we search them all?' MacVicar made no attempt to hide his sarcasm.

'I believe we can narrow it down. Start on the Islands of the Monks.'

'Why not Balivanich? Its name means Town of Monks,' Fergus piped up from his desk. 'Couldn't she have found the bone there?'

Balivanich was the main town on Benbecula.

'There used to be a nunnery on Benbecula,' Fergus continued. 'Legend has it that protestant zealots tied the nuns to the rocks to try and make them recant their faith. Apparently, you can still see the scratches on the rocks if you look carefully. There must be hundreds of bones in the ground there!'

The things people did to each other. Cruelty was no modern invention.

'I still think it's worth starting our search on the Monach Islands,' Rachel persisted. How many times did she have to bang on about them? 'Ellen had a map of the islands, it used to have a settlement of monks, she had no idea the bone she found wasn't ancient, she asked Duncan and his sister about the islands, and she'd been there recently.'

Selena placed a mug of tea in front of her sergeant. 'If we are going to the Monachs it needs to be soon. That storm's going to be here the day after tomorrow at the latest.' She looked over her shoulder. 'Couldn't you take us on your boat, Fergus?'

'There is no way I'm risking my boat on police business,' Fergus retorted from behind his desk.

'The coastguard will take us,' Sergeant MacVicar said with a reproachful look in Fergus's direction.

'He wasn't too keen when I asked him last night,' Rachel said.

Rachel caught the quick sideways glance Fergus and Selena shared. Bugger, she'd slipped up.

Fergus leaned forward and squinted at his screen. 'Hang on. The forensic anthropologist has just sent an email. She'll forward a full report later, but she wanted us to know that she managed to extract DNA from the bone. Our Jay Doe is male – a John Doe. No doubt about it.' He scanned the room. 'That should simplify our enquiries.'

'Shouldn't we interview Roddy officially?' Selena asked. 'At least take a statement from him. I mean, don't you think it's odd that he didn't tell us about seeing Ellen and Mike before? Unless of course he's lying.'

Sergeant MacVicar tugged at his bottom lip. 'I'll have a chat with him. You get on with what I asked. Then meet the inspector off the plane.'

'Shouldn't you meet the inspector, sir?' Selena asked.

MacVicar did that bobbing thing with his head. 'No indeed. I've got more important things to do.'

EIGHTEEN

'I don't think it's a load of bollocks, to be honest,' Selena said, as they drove towards the airport, when Rachel told her about the dead bird and Michelle's reaction. Rachel had left her car in a lay-by at the end of the road leading to her hotel. Selena had picked her up from there.

'Not bollocks I think that Roddy left it as a warning? Or not bollocks that it's a harbinger of death?' Rachel said the last three words as if she was doing a voice-over for a horror film.

Selena grinned at Rachel. 'Roddy could have left it, I suppose. In which case, I suspect he wasted his time. I can't see much scaring you.'

'Then you'd be wrong.' Quite a lot scared her. Mice. Failure. Relationships. Not that she was going to tell Selena. It felt too... she struggled to find the right word. *Exposing.*

But Selena either hadn't picked up on her admission or thought nothing of it. 'A lot of people here do believe in stuff like that. Portents, ghosts, second sight... My grandfather used to believe in elves.' She shot Rachel a glance. 'To be honest I think he still does.'

Rachel looked out of the window at the passing landscape. What did *her* grandfather believe?

'I wonder what the detective inspector will be like,' Selena mused.

Happy to be distracted from her thoughts, Rachel grinned at her. 'Guess we don't have long to wait before we find out.'

Detective Inspector Kirk Du Toit – his surname pronounced do toy – was a tall, solidly built man whose skin looked as if he'd suffered badly from acne as a teenager. He had round spaniel eyes like Loach's, only sadder. He wore a suit that hung on his frame as if he'd lost weight recently and hadn't got around to buying a new one. Yet, there was something undeniably attractive about him. Perhaps because he struck Rachel as a man who was comfortable in his own skin.

Du Toit looked none too pleased that the sergeant hadn't come to meet him but smiled when Rachel introduced herself. 'Miss McKenzie.' His voice was deep and heavily accented. 'Mr Mainwaring – Douglas – rang me and explained you were here. He said you'd be happy to bring me up to speed. Let's do that in the car where it's more private.'

He got into the front passenger seat next to Selena. Rachel climbed into the back. He swivelled round and asked Rachel and Selena what they'd learned so far.

'Tell me about Uist, Constable,' Du Toit asked Selena when they'd finished.

Selena waited until she'd negotiated the narrowest part of the causeway between Benbecula and North Uist. 'What would you like to know, sir?'

'Whatever you think is important.'

'Well sir, probably the most important thing is that most people have lived here all their lives, as have their parents and grandparents, so everyone knows each other. Most folk –

except for incomers obviously – are related or connected in some way. With a population of around five thousand across the whole of the Uists it would be difficult not to be. Take the school in Bayhead, for example. There are around seventy pupils in total spread across the five years. Even if they aren't friends, those pupils will know each other and about each other. They will know their fellow pupils' parents and grandparents – who probably also went to school together. By the same token the parents will all know each other too. For example, Sergeant MacVicar went to school with Dr Logan and my aunt Catriona. And Dr Stuart – Calum the coastguard's mother – went to school with Sergeant MacVicar's father – Sergeant Peter, as he was known. Some even say they had an affair. But I wouldn't give too much credence to that,' she added quickly. 'Folk here enjoy a gossip. You never know for certain what's true and what isn't. Probably just like any other small community, sir.'

'You mentioned incomers,' Du Toit said. 'What did you mean by that?'

'It's what we locals call people who weren't born here, like Michelle, Mike Howard's wife. Or even Constable Campbell, although he's lived here for a few years now and, coming from Thurso, he's a highlander, which helps.'

In the back seat, Rachel was thinking about what Selena had said about Calum's mother and Sergeant MacVicar's father. Was there any truth in it? Was that the secret she didn't want Calum to know? More importantly, was it relevant?

Dark clouds had sucked the light from the sky by the time they pulled in at the end of the road leading to Ellen's cottage.

They picked their way down the track, Du Toit in the lead and Selena bringing up the rear. When they reached Ellen's cottage the crows were still in a military line on the roof, but they made no move to attack. Perhaps they'd told each other Rachel and her companions were the good guys?

Outside, the bones gleamed in the dull light.

'*Dhia, Dhia, Dhia,*' Selena cursed under her breath when she saw the neat rows of bones. 'I'd heard she was a collector, but I didn't expect this.'

'You haven't been here?' Inspector Du Toit asked her.

'No, it was Sergeant MacVicar and Constable Campbell who assessed the scene.'

Rachel showed the police officers where she'd found the phone.

Du Toit frowned. 'The phone should really have been left in situ, or at the very least photographed before it was moved.'

Rachel felt the heat rise in her cheeks. Crap. She'd made a rookie error. She'd make sure she didn't make another one.

'Now we know she didn't drown accidentally, but we don't know where she was killed,' Du Toit continued. 'What if she was strangled in her cottage? Carried to the shore – the phone fell out of her pocket on the way – put in a boat and dumped out at sea?'

His theory made perfect sense – the only sense. A high tide would make it easier to tie up a boat close to shore and make it easier to transfer a body.

'Let's finish checking outside before we have a look inside her cottage,' Du Toit said.

They inspected the shoreline and walked all around Ellen's house without finding anything else of interest. At Ellen's front door, Selena pulled latex gloves out of her pocket and passed a pair each to Rachel and the inspector, who slipped them on in silence.

Du Toit turned to Selena.

'The key please, Constable.'

'As far as we know, there isn't one,' Selena said, the first sign of unease slipping into her demeanour. 'Constable Campbell did check with the solicitors who sold the property and asked around in general but no luck. The woman who lived here before the victim bought it died a long time ago. As far as anyone knew there hadn't been a key for years.' Tiny beads of perspiration formed on her forehead. 'Most people here don't bother locking their doors, sir.' She cast Rachel a pained glance. 'I did wonder whether the house should have been secured, but Sergeant MacVicar said it wasn't a crime scene so it wasn't necessary.' From the reluctance in her voice, it was clear that while Selena had little time or respect for her sergeant she was loath to drop him in it. 'I keep a PDF of the *Investigation of Death* standard operating procedures on my phone, sir, and I checked but there was nothing definitive about securing the scene after a drowning.'

Judging by the look on Du Toit's face Sergeant MacVicar was going to be in hot water. With a shake of his head, the inspector pushed the door open. Rachel and a subdued Selena followed him inside. It took their eyes a moment or two to adjust. The cottage was already beginning to smell musty and damp.

'What are we looking for?' Selena asked.

'Anything that might give us a clue what she was up to,' Du Toit said.

The beam of Selena's torch swept the room, illuminating the stacks of cardboard boxes and piles of books.

Rachel sucked in a breath. If the room had been cluttered before it was a mess now. Boxes had been ripped apart, bones scattered, books upended or tossed on the ground, their spines splayed open.

'It wasn't like this when I was here,' Rachel said. 'Someone else has been here. Looks like they were searching for something.'

Du Toit's frown deepened. 'You came inside?'

'I didn't touch anything, apart from the phone, without gloves,' Rachel said, annoyed she'd made another rookie error.

Du Toit shook his head in disgust. 'I'm going to have to get forensics out here to go through every box and bone in case there are human bones amongst them.'

Just then, Rachel realised she'd seen something on the grass next to the doorstep that had jarred. 'There's a cigarette stub near the front door that I'm certain wasn't there before.'

'Bag it please, Constable,' Du Toit said.

Selena left them and returned moments later, handing the plastic bag to the inspector so he could add his signature. The younger police officer pointed her torch at the cardboard boxes. 'This one is labelled *Dolphin*,' she said. 'And the one next to it says Incomplete Otter. This one says Assorted Whale Vertebrae. They're all labelled. I guess she had a system.' Selena peered closer. 'The one that's labelled Dolphin says Kallin Harbour on it – that's where the Grimsay fishermen moor their boats, sir. The Otter one says Green Point. That must be where she found the skeletons of the dolphin and otter.'

Treading carefully, Rachel picked up the book lying on the floor. *Vikings and the Western Isles*. The one underneath was *Skellig Michael*. On its cover was a picture of a brown-clothed monk. Her curiosity roused, she flicked through drawings of monks' cells, their clothes and settlements.

She showed it to the DI. 'The Gaelic name for the Monachs means Island of Monks,' she explained. 'More reason, I'd suggest, to believe that whatever Ellen thought she'd found, it had something to do with them.'

'I agree. I'll ask Sergeant MacVicar to get on to the coastguard to arrange a trip out there as a priority. Constable, arrange for the cottage to be secured and stay here until it is. Make sure no one else pays a visit. I'll need to take your vehicle.'

'Stay here?' Selena's voice came out with a squeak. 'For how long? *Thighearna's a Dhia*, you have to be kidding.' She flushed as she realised she'd overstepped professional boundaries. 'Apologies, sir. Of course, I'm happy to stay. I just thought I'd be accompanying you on your investigations.'

Du Toit frowned at her. 'Would you like me to ask Sergeant MacVicar to send someone to relieve you?' It was clear from his tone what the right answer was.

Selena glanced around the room, a look of revulsion passing across her face. 'That won't be necessary, sir.' She squared her shoulders and managed a smile. 'It's not as if the ghost of an otter or a dolphin is going to get me, is it?'

NINETEEN

'She's a good police officer,' Rachel said to Du Toit as they walked back towards the car. 'If it were up to her, she would have secured the house. She likes to do everything by the book – ergo, the PDF of Police Scotland's SOP on her phone.' Now it sounded like she was making fun of Selena. 'But she has flair too. She'll make a great detective.'

'I'm aware Constable MacDonald has applied for a post with CID in Inverness. All the more reason to learn to stick to her guns when she realises procedures aren't being followed. However, securing the premises – the whole investigation – was entirely Sergeant MacVicar's responsibility,' Du Toit replied tetchily.

Rachel almost felt sorry for the sergeant.

'They do things differently here. It's as if the whole island is frozen in time. I don't think the possibility that Ellen had been murdered occurred to anyone,' Rachel said.

If anything, the inspector seemed even more irritated. 'No excuse for not knowing and following correct police procedure. The phone should have been found; the scene secured.' He gave her a hard look. 'No one, not even you, should have been allowed to enter the cottage. I recognise that without you we might never have looked into Ms Hargreaves' death – but from now on, you need to leave the investigating to us.'

'Inspector, I appreciate I made some mistakes – trust me, it won't happen again – but I intend to stay involved,' Rachel said, keeping her voice level. She didn't want him to know how important it was to her that she saw it through to the end.

'No,' he said flatly.

A wave of anger surged through Rachel. If either Douglas or Du Toit thought she was going anywhere until the mystery of Ellen's death had been solved, both were very much mistaken.

'May I remind you, Inspector,' she said stiffly, 'it's not up to you whether I stay or go. If you want to take it up with my office, you are of course, free to do so.' Although she was praying he wouldn't; the last thing she needed was for him to complain to Douglas that she was interfering to the detriment of an investigation, and maybe worse for her boss to point out he'd already called her back to the office. She eased the anger from her voice. 'I might even be able to help, you know.'

He gave her a long, contemplative look. 'Very well. I'm warning you, if you get in the way, I'll have you off the island before you know what's happening. You do nothing, speak to no one, without consulting with me first.'

Without waiting for a reply he strode off, leaving Rachel speechless with fury. Who the hell did he think he was to talk to her like that? But he was the senior investigating officer – and if he complained about her to Douglas... bollocks. She needed to keep him sweet. She took deep, calming breaths before following in his wake.

When they reached the car, Du Toit got into the driving seat. Rachel waited until they were back on the main road before she spoke. 'How long have you been with Inverness's MIT?' she asked, almost certain he wasn't part of the team during her mother's murder investigation. Didn't mean he didn't know all about it, however.

'Around three years,' he replied to her relief. So not there when her mother's death was being investigated. 'I was a Detective Sergeant with Glasgow's MIT before then.'

'How come you're here on your own?' she asked. Normally in Scotland, police officers worked in pairs.

'I usually have a DC with me. However, the Major Investigations Team in Inverness is overwhelmed at the moment. We have a couple of officers off sick and my sergeant has had to take maternity leave early. My boss hopes to second someone from Skye or one of the other islands.'

Sheep strolling across the road caused Du Toit to brake sharply.

'What are your initial thoughts?' Rachel asked, once they were safely past the animals.

'I need to go over everything again before I draw any conclusions.'

'But you have a plan of action?' Rachel persisted.

'I want to speak to Mr Howard. I'll do that and drop you off at the same time.'

Rachel pointed out the turn he needed to take. She'd pick up her car later. The inspector had been booked into one of the hotels in Lochmaddy.

'After that I'll have a word with Sergeant MacVicar. Make sure he's on top of things. If everyone knows one another on this island as the constable suggested, then someone is bound to know more than they are telling.'

When Du Toit asked Rhoda to let Mike know he wished to speak to him, the man appeared almost at once, accompanied by his wife. Not giving Du Toit a chance to object, Rachel took a seat at the table in the empty conservatory alongside them.

'Did either of you know Ellen Hargreaves?' Du Toit came straight to the point.

The husband and wife exchanged a glance.

'She came in here once for a coffee. After she'd been to the chambered cairn. You know the one on the hill up there that I told you about, Rachel?' Michelle gestured to the blackness outside the conservatory doors. She turned back to Rachel. 'It was her who told me about the crows.'

'When was Ms Hargreaves here?' Du Toit asked Michelle.

'I'm not sure. Two, three weeks before her body was found?' Michelle turned to her husband for confirmation. Mike nodded.

'She wanted to know how she could get out to the Monach Islands. I suggested she ask Mike,' she continued.

'And did she?'

'Yes. I told her no,' Mike said. 'I'm a commercial company. I don't do trips for tourists.'

'Why didn't you tell me this when we talked before?' Rachel demanded.

'I took it for granted you knew.'

'You were seen out there at the same time Ellen was on the island,' Du Toit said to Mike.

'That's bull. I never took her anywhere. Whoever told you that was mistaken.' He narrowed his eyes. 'Who told you?'

'Roddy,' Rachel said. There was no reason for him not to know.

'Then he's lying. If anyone took her out there, it would be him.'

'Why do you say that?'

'When I told her I wouldn't take her, I suggested she ask one of the fishermen instead. I specifically mentioned Roddy – he's the only one who lands there regularly. The tides around those particular islands can be tricky. I saw her talking to him in the bar a few days later. I assumed she asked him then.'

Either Roddy was lying or Mike was.

'She was here at the hotel more than once?' Rachel asked.

Mike shrugged. 'Maybe twice,' he conceded. He took a cigarette out of his pocket and fiddled with it as if longing to light it.

Rachel thought of the cigarette end outside Ellen's house.

'Have you been to Ellen's cottage recently, Mr Howard?' she asked.

'I have never been to Ellen's house. Recently or otherwise.' Mike glanced at his watch. 'Are we finished here? Can we go? My wife and I have a dinner service to prepare for.'

Du Toit nodded. 'I'll need to speak to you about this again.'

As soon as Mike and Michelle were out of earshot, Rachel explained about Roddy smoking outside her room. 'If his cigarette butt is still there, can we send it away to test it for DNA? If I remember correctly we can test for DNA without permission if it's on something that has been discarded.'

Du Toit gave her a long, hard look. 'Your reasoning?'

'The DNA on it might match the DNA on the one we found at Ellen's cottage. We could test Mike's while we're at it. We'll know then if either of them has been to Ellen's cottage. If so, I can't think of any innocent reason why they might deny having been there.'

'OK. I'll collect them, but it's unlikely they'll be tested as a priority.'

After Mike's cigarette end and the one from outside Rachel's room had been bagged, they returned to the bar to find Calum there, pint in hand. He turned to Rachel with a broad smile.

'Hey, I just wanted to apologise again for last night. I don't know what got into Mother. I'm sorry it spoiled our evening.'

Rachel winced internally. Bollocks. Last night's dinner wasn't information she wanted the inspector to have. When he gave her a sharp glance she knew he had clocked it. Of course he had. The inspector didn't strike her as a man who missed much. 'That's all right,' she told Calum, 'I know she gets confused. It must be very distressing for her.'

As she introduced the two men, she knew her cheeks were flushed.

'Ah, the coastguard,' Du Toit said. 'Just the man I wanted to see. I'd like to go to the Monach Islands with some of my colleagues and I'd like you to take us.'

Calum frowned as he gave Du Toit the same spiel he'd given Rachel about tides, channels and bad weather forecasts.

'Nevertheless. I intend to go,' Du Toit said, undeterred. 'When will the tide be right?'

'Around six tomorrow morning. But for fuck's sake, they're forecasting a force eleven – possibly even twelve! Do you have any idea what that means? Waves metres high, flooded roads. Ninety mile per hour winds that will blow your roof off. People die in storms of that magnitude...'

'When do you expect this storm?' Du Toit asked.

'Not for another forty-eight hours.' Calum sighed. He clearly knew when he was beaten. 'But it's not possible to predict exactly. I'm warning you, if the storm comes sooner than expected and it's not safe, I won't risk you or my boat.'

'Fair enough. Unless something changes, we will see you at six.'

When Du Toit left, Calum turned to Rachel.

'Why have they sent a detective inspector from the mainland?' he asked. He narrowed his eyes as he thought it through. 'Because I was right. You do think that woman was murdered,' he answered his own question. 'And they think it has something to do with the Monach Islands. What? What's the connection?'

'I can't tell you anything. That will be up to the inspector.' Rachel really didn't want to get into it. 'I'm sorry, but given it's going to be an early start tomorrow and I have stuff I need to do, I should get to bed.'

Before she could turn away, Calum took her hand and gave

her a crooked smile. 'I could drive you to the harbour in the morning.'

Rachel hesitated, torn. He was attractive, and spending the night with him would help the time pass. But it would be impossible to hide his presence in her room and bed and she suspected the islanders knew enough of her business already. Making up her mind, she gave a small shake of her head. 'Sorry. Another time perhaps.'

She saw the regret in his eyes, but he smiled again, shrugged and released her hand. 'In that case, sleep well and I'll see you tomorrow.'

TWENTY

SATURDAY – DAWN

The Rigid Inflatable Boat, or RIB as Calum referred to it, bounced across the sea, threatening to dislodge Rachel with every bump.

He'd remained reluctant to make the trip, muttering about the weather. Which, Rachel had to agree, was pretty lousy. Relentless driving rain and wind and, out to sea, a definite swell.

Calum handed out life jackets while reiterating that landing on the Monachs was tricky at the best of times and they might not be able to land at all. If his attitude irritated Du Toit, the detective inspector didn't show it.

Apart from Rachel, there were four others in the boat. Calum, DI Du Toit, Sergeant MacVicar and Selena. Constable Campbell had been left behind to police the rest of the island.

They'd gathered at Kallin harbour just as dawn was break-ing. Selena had emerged from the police car with the inspector, looking pleased as punch to be included with the expedition.

According to Selena, Sergeant MacVicar had come close to exploding when Inspector Du Toit told him that he wanted Selena and Fergus to go and not him.

'He was having none of it,' she whispered to Rachel. 'Said he was in charge of the police force on the island and that he was coming along. He kept muttering about interference, people not knowing their arses from their elbows. Can you believe he said "police force" when there's only two of us under his command!' Selena widened her eyes at Rachel. 'I get the feeling he got a bit of a bollocking from the inspector yesterday.' She looked over at her immediate boss. 'I can't believe I'm saying this, but I actually feel sorry for him. However, he did get his way.'

Du Toit, informal in a fisherman's jersey and jeans under a waterproof police jacket, stood facing forward, legs slightly apart for balance, seemingly unaffected by the movement of the boat. Rachel, on the other hand, felt nauseous.

'Hang over the side,' Sergeant MacVicar advised her, not unkindly. 'But make sure you stay downwind from the rest of us.'

Rachel nodded, the movement bringing another cramping wave of nausea. *Don't let me be sick*, she prayed. Not in front of everyone.

Just when Rachel thought she couldn't swallow her nausea any longer, Calum throttled the engine of the RIB back and the boat stopped its vomit-inducing bouncing.

It was fully light by the time they reached the Monach Islands. As they coasted in, Calum pointed to a nearby rock where hundreds of seals, clumped together in a heaving breathing lump, were eyeing them dozily. 'Biggest colony of grey seals in Europe,' he informed them.

Holding the rope attached to the front of the boat, Calum jumped into the sea and pulled the RIB towards the shore. Following Selena's example, Rachel tugged off her trainers and socks and rolled her jeans to above her knees. She slipped into the water, gasping as the cold took her breath away. Tentatively, lest she step on a crab or a fish, she followed the rest of the group onto the shore. The sand squirming between her toes brought back a memory of her and her mother running along the beach, laughing as their bare feet sunk into the wet sand. They'd been so happy that day. Her throat tightened and she shook the image away. Remembering hurt too much.

Immediately in front of her were the ruins of what had once been several houses, only one of which still had its roof. This must be where Duncan Mór and his family had lived; the rest once housing the families who had settled and abandoned the island before Duncan had arrived.

The breeze had dispersed the clouds and the sun sparked off the sea. To the left, on the smaller island of Shillay, separated from the one they were standing on by a strip of sea, a lighthouse dominated the skyline.

Rachel had finally managed to access the internet long enough to find some information on the Monachs and a better map than Ellen's hand-drawn one. According to legend, the lighthouse had been built on top of where the monks had once lit beacons to warn passing ships away from the rocks. It had been decommissioned in the sixties.

'Where do we start looking?' Selena asked Du Toit.

'We'll divide the area into grids. We each take one. Start from there,' Du Toit said.

'What exactly are we looking for?' Calum asked.

'Any sign that the ground has been disturbed. Evidence of a grave or digging. It shouldn't be too difficult to find.'

Selena looked around doubtfully. 'There's a helluva lot of ground for us to cover.'

'Then we'd better get started,' Du Toit said. 'Remember if you find anything that looks like it might be a possibility, don't touch; just call me over. OK?'

Everyone nodded and, in a line, shuffled forward, eyes trained on the ground. Calum managed to position himself next to Rachel.

'I always wanted to be part of search and rescue on the ground,' he said wryly, 'but never imagined I'd end up as a volunteer member of the police force. I can't help but feel this is a major waste of time.' The words were said lightly but there was tension in his voice. Something was off with him. He seemed on edge, constantly scanning the horizon and frowning. Perhaps it was the responsibility for getting everyone back to Uist safely? Or maybe the macho male in him had resented the way Du Toit had ordered him to take them here. Or was he secretly annoyed by her rejection? Whatever. Too bad if he was.

Rachel was getting a crick in her neck from staring at her feet when at midday Du Toit called a break.

It had begun to drizzle so they made for the only ruin that still had a roof. The interior of the house smelled of wood smoke and damp. The main room had a concrete floor, an open fireplace with the remnants of a wood fire, and beside it a worn armchair that looked as if it had provided supper for rats on more than one occasion. Off to one side was a room with two sets of bunk beds. Rumpled sheets were still on one and a sleeping bag hung haphazardly over the side of the other. Judging by the state of the room and the damp towel draped over a chair it had been occupied fairly recently. By whom? There was also a small kitchen and a table with a couple of rickety dining chairs. The table was missing a leg and some enterprising person had used a piece of driftwood to balance it. The new leg wasn't an exact fit and the table listed precariously to one side. Leaning against the wall, looking as if they'd been salvaged from someone's house, were a number of kitchen units. On top of one was a single-ring gas stove, a couple of jars, tea bags and several grubby mugs. There was also a sink with an old-fashioned brass tap.

'Someone's stayed here recently. I smell body odour.' Selena said out loud what Rachel had been thinking, sniffing ostentatiously. The smell of worn socks and unwashed skin was unmistakable.

'Probably a passing fisherman caught in a storm,' Calum replied. The tension was back in his voice.

Roddy? Rachel wondered, turning on the sink tap. But Calum had been adamant no one stayed overnight. The tap spat brackish water into the sink.

Rachel turned to Calum. 'I thought you said there was no running water?'

'Someone must have laid a pipe to the well.' Calum shrugged. 'It's been a while since I was here.'

'The water's fine, in case you're wondering,' MacVicar said. 'It's only that colour because of the peat. It'll not do you any harm.'

Despite his assurances, Rachel was glad she had the flasks of coffee Michelle had given her that morning, along with several rounds of sandwiches and bags of crisps.

After dishing out the picnic, she took her coffee outside. The rain had petered out and she found it preferable to the stuffy interior of the old house. All she could see was ocean. She knew there was nothing between the west of the island and America. It was beautiful but so remote. Truly an island on the edge of the world. What would it have been like for Duncan Mór and his family? No shops, no company except sheep and rabbits. How had they entertained themselves? Being so cut off would have driven most people stir-crazy.

Du Toit came to stand beside her, and they looked out to the horizon in companionable silence, chewing their sandwiches.

'Do you get this involved with all your cases?' Du Toit asked. 'Or was there something in particular about Miss Hargreaves?'

Rachel considered her reply. Du Toit was astute. He'd already guessed there was more to Rachel being here than it being her right as a member of the procurator fiscal service. Any detective inspector worth his salt would have googled her. However, she had no intention of being the one to raise her past.

'Something about this one just didn't feel right. I couldn't believe that any woman would walk off and leave her bag and shopping on the doorstep. Women don't do that. What about you, Inspector?' she asked, turning the conversation back to him. 'Do you enjoy your job with the MIT?'

Du Toit wiped his mouth with the back of his hand. 'Call me Kirk,' he said. 'Yes. On the whole. Most of the murders we deal with are the result of drink and drugs – stabbings, drunken brawls, husbands killing wives, girlfriends and vice versa. The case where the perpetrator and motive are more obscure... those are rare, but more interesting.'

'Why do people kill? I'll never understand it. How does anyone plunge a knife, or a machete or whatever, into another human? Again and again? As for killing your spouse... if you stop loving someone, why not simply walk away?' She dug the nails of one hand into the palm of the other. Why the fuck had she gone and said that?

Du Toit gave her a piercing look. 'Naturally it is better to prevent crime rather than have to solve it. We are making some progress.' He looked out to sea, appearing to give her words some thought. 'Scotland has halved knife crimes just by making it an offence to carry a blade. With the help of criminologists, we might find other ways to stop people killing each other. Until then, we must do our best to catch them and lock them away.'

He might have said more if Calum hadn't come to join them. Until now, he'd kept his distance from Kirk.

'Where are you from?' Calum asked the inspector. 'You're not from Scotland, are you? I'm guessing Holland, or South Africa.'

Kirk half smiled. 'You guessed right. My parents are South African; my father's Afrikaans. He didn't like the way things were going in Africa – he's die-hard right wing – so he arranged for me to go to university in Glasgow. My mother's family were from there and she made sure I had a UK passport growing up. After I graduated I joined the police force, and here I am.'

'Do you go back?'

'Sometimes. To see my mother. My father... well, he and I don't get on. Different beliefs,' he said with a flicker of distaste. He drained his cup. 'Let's get back to it.'

'We have another couple of hours max and then we have to leave with the tide,' Calum said. 'Otherwise we'll have to stay the night. I don't know about you, but I'd rather sleep in a proper bed.'

As he was speaking, Rachel's attention was caught by a fishing boat that had been drawing closer. It had stopped several hundred metres from the shore. She could vaguely make out a figure standing on deck, but it was too far away for her to see whether the shape was male or female. A flash of light on glass suggested they were being watched through a pair of binoculars.

'Looks like we've got company,' Rachel nodded in the direction of the boat.

'Probably one of the fishermen preparing to lift his creels and wondering what the hell we're doing out here,' Calum said.

'Do you recognise the boat?' Rachel asked him.

'It's too far away for me to be sure but I think it belongs to one of the Grimsay fishermen – Roddy. He drops his creels this way.'

Rachel's skin prickled. Was Roddy spying on them? On her?

As they prepared to resume their search, Rachel glanced towards the smaller island with the lighthouse on it. The tide had receded to reveal a thin strip of sand connecting it to the one they were on. If they wanted they could walk across.

She recalled that the lighthouse had been built on the rumoured site of the monks' beacon. If Ellen had been searching for evidence of a medieval site, would she not have looked there?

She was about to say as much to Calum when there was a shout followed by a frantic wave from Selena. Everyone hurried to where she was standing – very close to the edge of the island, where it rose up around a metre from the sea floor. It looked as if the coastline had eroded, revealing what appeared to be part of a burial cairn like the one near Tioran Lodge, only smaller.

Selena pointed. 'There,' she said. 'Something's been disturbed recently.'

Sure enough there was freshly turned earth and next to it a stick had been planted. This had to be where Ellen had found the bone.

Rachel was about to step forward to have a closer look when Du Toit grabbed her by the elbow. 'Stay back. If there is something here we need to be very careful not to destroy any evidence.'

Selena took several photos with an expensive camera and Rachel took some on her phone.

While Selena was snapping away, Du Toit slipped on a pair of gloves and gently scraped away at the sandy soil.

The sand came away easily, as if it had been previously removed and then replaced to reveal a narrow entrance. His careful excavation revealed a number of coins, a piece of cloth, and a small bone that looked like a finger. Rachel's stomach churned as her mind flashed. By the time her mother had been found little had remained of her but her skeleton and soft tissue. She pushed the nauseating memory away and forced herself to concentrate on the here and now.

Du Toit turned the coins over in his hand. One was a penny, the other she recognised as an old ten pence.

MacVicar was the first to speak. 'If those coins belonged to our John Doe then we don't need an archaeologist to tell us they don't belong to a long dead monk, or a druid or a bronze age dweller. Whoever this is couldn't have died before 1972, because they're post decimalisation new pennies. And that happened in 1970 or 1971 – I'm not sure which.' MacVicar rocked back on his heels, looking pleased with himself. 'Therefore, if he died before then he couldn't possibly have had those coins on him.'

They already knew the bone belonged to someone who had been alive after 1955. This helped narrow the window.

'After Chrissie and Duncan had left here then,' Rachel said, relieved that it seemed the elderly siblings couldn't have been involved. 'They told me they left in the winter of 1969.'

She looked at MacVicar for confirmation.

'That sounds about right.'

'Can you double check, Sergeant?' Du Toit asked.

'I'll ask my father,' MacVicar said. 'He was the policeman back then. He has a very good memory.'

'Maybe somebody else dropped them?' Selena suggested. 'The person who buried the remains?'

'Same difference,' the sergeant continued. 'That would have had to have been post-seventies too. And if, for argument's sake, we consider that someone who had nothing to do with the death stumbled across some bones, why didn't they report it?' He paused as if something had just occurred to him.

'Unless, like Ellen, they weren't sure that the bone belonged to a human,' Rachel suggested.

'It couldn't have been Miss Hargreaves who dropped the coins,' Du Toit said. 'There's an old ten pence piece amongst them. If I remember right they were withdrawn in 1993.'

'Maybe whoever the poor sod whose grave it is got stuck out here. Perhaps his boat sank or something and he took shelter and the ruin collapsed in on him,' Calum suggested.

'What? And he just happened to stab himself in the ribs

while he was at it!' Selena made no attempt to hide her incredulity. 'The bone Ellen found showed clear evidence of a clean break, most likely from a sharp blade.'

'I didn't know we'd been looking for someone who had been stabbed.' Calum shot back. 'But if someone killed him and buried him, where is the rest of him, Sherlock?'

'Animals,' Selena said, glaring at him.

'No animals here apart from rabbits,' MacVicar interjected, with a bob of his head. 'And as far as I'm aware they have no interest in scavenging.'

'What if whoever killed our John Doe knew that Ellen had found the bones?' Rachel said. 'What if they killed her to stop her telling anyone? Perhaps they moved the rest of the bones after she was dead?'

'In which case they didn't do a very thorough job,' Calum said.

Finally, Du Toit intervened. 'It is far too early to speculate. However, I'm going to assume this is the site where Ellen found the bone. The rest of the skeleton must be somewhere but I'm going to get advice from the forensic anthropologist before any more digging takes place. Until then, we'll protect the site as best we can. Someone will have to stay here until we can get SOCO out. Sergeant MacVicar? We can't take the chance that one of the fishermen, or someone else – because people *have* been here – stumble across it.'

The sergeant looked none too pleased at the thought of being left on the island. 'I need to get back. There's something I—'

'I'll arrange for someone to relieve you as soon as possible,' Du Toit interrupted. 'But meanwhile, I'm afraid there's nothing else for it. OK. Let's get what we found bagged and labelled and cover the burial site with a tarpaulin. Sergeant, could you start a log? Mr Stuart, Rachel, could you step away please? The fewer people contaminating the scene the better.'

'I'll brew us some tea,' Calum said, and headed back to the house.

Rachel needed a pee. Somewhere she couldn't be seen. Which wasn't as easy as she thought it'd be. There were no convenient trees, and the land was above sea level so wherever she looked she was in sight of someone. There was no way her bladder would relax if she thought that her bottom was in view. The obvious place was on the other side of the island, on the opposite side to the fishing boat which was *still* hanging about. If she went down to the shore the slope would hide her from all eyes except those of the birds.

Slipping away, she trudged across the machair. As she scrambled down towards the shore, she spotted a cluster of large rocks and decided that would be as good a place as any.

She slithered across them until she found a suitable hollow where she'd be protected from the casual observer. Tugging her jeans and pants down to her ankles, she hunkered down, careful not to lose her balance. Who *was* John Doe? How had he got here? Who had he been with?

Retrieving a wad of tissues from her pocket, she wiped herself and pulled her knickers and jeans back up. As she was making the final adjustments to her clothing, her eyes fixed on a clump of rocks to her left. There was definitely something not right about them – something that didn't belong there. Slowly she edged closer, her heart knocking against her ribs.

At first, her brain refused to believe what she was seeing.

Draped across the rock, in a macabre embrace, was a body in a black wetsuit. The head, encased in a neoprene hood, was turned to the side, a huge seagull perched possessively on top. A diving cylinder was still attached to the body's back.

The seagull pecked at the blood-drained face and stared at Rachel with black eyes.

Sickened, Rachel swung around, hoping to see one of the others so she could call for help, but there was no one in sight. It was possible that the person was still alive and she couldn't afford to waste any time. The seagull gave a harsh cry and aggressive flap of its wings as she shooed it away. Dread drying her mouth, she forced herself to walk around to the other side of the body. A pale face washed white stared up at her. Nausea roiled in her stomach. She hadn't seen a dead body except in photographs before, but she didn't have to feel for a pulse to know she was seeing one now. It was very different. More real. Much more visceral. But what was worse, what she already knew she'd never be able to get out of her head, was that something had eaten away at the face, leaving half of the jawbone and an eye socket exposed, the eye nestling like a chick in a ravaged nest.

Bile flooded her throat. She took deep, shuddering breaths until the nausea passed and she was able to breathe normally. Then she turned and, moving as fast as she could without losing her footing, scrambled back across the rocks, barely registering the jagged texture of the stone tearing at the skin on her hands. In the distance she could see the figures of Kirk and the others, and she waved her hands in the universal sign for help, shouting Kirk's name. The wind whipped her words away. Still struggling to stay upright she staggered closer, calling, trying to get their attention.

Eventually Kirk turned in her direction. He paused and she yelled harder, gesticulating behind her.

'Over here!'

The police officers started running towards her. Relief drained the last bit of strength from her legs and she hunkered on her heels to wait for them. Kirk and Selena arrived first, a red-faced MacVicar close behind.

'What is it?' Du Toit crouched beside her. 'What's happened?'

The sergeant had his hands on his knees as he gasped for breath.

'Back there,' Rachel pointed towards the crop of rocks, before realising they were hidden by the rise of the land. 'On rocks. A body. Dead.'

Kirk pulled her up, none too gently, by the arm.

'Show me.'

With Sergeant MacVicar and Selena following close behind, Rachel led them across to the edge and pointed to the body.

'C'mon, MacVicar,' Kirk said. 'Constable MacDonald. Let's have a look.'

Rachel sat down on a tussock of grass and hugged her knees, trying to stop her body shaking. The image of the pale, bloodless face, the empty socket and the opaque film over the remaining eye wouldn't go away. How long had the body been there? And who the hell was it? She couldn't even be certain if it were a man or woman.

Now they had three suspicious deaths. Whoever their John Doe was, however he'd died, it was too much of a coincidence that another body had washed up in the same place.

Something horrifying was going on. The sense of menace was pervasive, wrapping around her like tendrils of fog. She had no idea where the threat was coming from, but it felt close.

She jumped as a hand pressed her shoulder. She looked up to find Calum standing behind her. 'What's happened?'

'I found a body. I think he's a diver.' She shuddered. 'The birds have been at his face.'

Calum tugged her to her feet and put his arms around her. For a brief moment she leaned into him, allowing herself the comforting warmth of another human being. Then, remembering where she was, she pulled away. They stood in silence, waiting for the others to return.

It seemed like forever before they did. Kirk was trying his mobile.

'It's no use.' He looked as if he was tempted to fling the

phone in the sea. 'Someone will have to go back to the boat and use the radio to call for assistance.'

'I'll go,' Calum volunteered. He looked at Rachel. 'Are you all right?'

Of course she fucking wasn't. She nodded. 'Does anyone have any idea who it could be?' Rachel asked.

'I didn't recognise him,' Selena said. The blood had drained from her face. 'But then it's not as if there's much of a face left to make a positive ID. From his physique I think he's male. He could be a tourist who came up to do some diving, or he could be one of the divers from the Uist Diving Company. Oh my God, for one awful moment I thought it was Johnny before I remembered I passed him on the road this morning.'

'Johnny? The diver with Mike's company? You know him?' Rachel asked.

'Yes. He goes out with Rhoda. My cousin?'

Rachel didn't know and felt she should have.

'Has anyone been reported missing in the last few days?' Du Toit asked.

MacVicar shook his head. 'No, but we should speak to Mike Howard. He'll know if there are visitors on the island who are diving – they often get him to fill their cylinders. I can't see it being one of his team; he would have noticed he had a diver missing. That body looks like it's been in the water for at least a couple of days.'

Du Toit turned back to Selena. 'I need you to take photographs of the body. Do you think you can do that?'

Selena nodded. She appeared to have recovered her composure.

'In that case, Sergeant, you go out to the boat with Mr Stuart. Call it in to Inverness. Alert them that we'll need a scene of crime officer and reinforcements. In the short term, another police officer from Stornoway. Mr Stuart, could you take the others back and get the coastguard to send another boat to retrieve the body? In the interim we have to do what we can to secure the scene.'

Wrapping her arms around her chilled body, Rachel watched as Calum and the sergeant waded out to the RIB. Du Toit had gone with Selena to photograph the body. The tantalising image of a hot bath and a glass of wine – at *least* a glass – swam in front of her. However, slinking back to the sanctuary of her hotel room was not an option. Douglas expected her at her desk by Monday, so she only had a day and a half to discover what all this had to do with the death of Ellen Hargreaves, and that needed a clear head.

By the time Du Toit and Selena returned, Calum, accompanied by MacVicar, who was carrying something heavy cradled in his arms, were wading back towards them.

'The Stornoway coastguard will get a boat out as soon as they can,' Calum told them.

'Inverness reckons it'll take time to get a forensic archaeologist and a SOCO out here,' MacVicar said, dumping what he was carrying on the ground. 'They'll need to track them down and organise a helicopter first. They're worried the storm might beat them to it. For the time being, here's a couple of tarpaulins.'

Du Toit nodded. 'Right, Sergeant, you and I can rig these over the body and the burial site. Everyone else needs to get going before the tide goes out much further. Selena, when you get back to the station, I'd like you and Constable Campbell to try and find out who our body might be.'

He brushed his hand over his head and looked at each one of them in turn. 'We need to get to the bottom of what is going on here before someone else ends up dead.'

TWENTY-ONE

The boat trip back was even worse than the one out. The wind had picked up by several knots and the boat bucked and yawed, sea spray from the waves crashing over the side, soaking anyone unfortunate enough to be in the wrong place. Rachel clung to the side of the RIB, almost thankful it took all her concentration to stay upright.

By the time they reached Lochmaddy, Rachel felt as if the life had been sucked out of her – mentally and physically.

The police station was damp and cold. Rachel put the kettle on while Selena fiddled with the Rayburn, trying to coax a flame from it. When it was burning to her satisfaction, she took Rachel's jacket, shook the rain off, and hung it beside hers on a washing line above the stove. Rain hurtled against windows and wind howled around the walls. The predicted storm was on its way. Calum had been right to be anxious. Selena eased off her boots and rubbed her feet. The aroma of peat and damp wool filled the room.

Selena fizzed with excitement. 'Two bodies within the space of a couple of weeks. Isn't it gre— I mean, ghastly?' Realising what she'd nearly said she flushed and shot Rachel an embarrassed look. 'Sorry. That was a stupid and terribly ignorant thing to think, let alone say.'

Maybe. Many would say so. Rachel got Selena's reaction, the excitement of the chase, the drive to solve a puzzle. She also knew that on the other side was terrible, crushing pain. Whoever the diver was, there was a mother, a wife, a sister or brother, a child perhaps, whose life was about to be shattered.

Images spooled through Rachel's head as she was catapulted back to her worst day; six years ago, when the police had knocked on her door. There had been two of them, both women.

'Miss McKenzie?' the older cop had asked.

'Yes.'

'I'm Constable Fletcher and this is Constable Whyte.' She nodded in the direction of her colleague, who gave Rachel a wan smile. The police officers held up identity cards. 'May we come in?'

Oh shit. There was only one reason police made house calls. Had something happened to her father? A heart attack? A traffic accident? Was he seriously injured – or worse? She hadn't seen him for at least a month. Not since the last time they'd gone fishing together.

Every instinct had her wanting to pretend Miss McKenzie was out and wouldn't be back until later.

Instead, she stepped inside and led the way into the sitting room. Books and coffee mugs covered almost every surface. She and her flatmate weren't tidy at the best of times and with exams looming... She picked up a couple of mugs, glanced around for somewhere else to put them and failed.

'Please sit down, Rachel. May I call you Rachel?' Constable Fletcher said.

'Is it my father?' she asked.

The two police officers exchanged a glance, 'No. Your father is...,' the smallest hesitation, a shared glance, '... fine.'

'Then what is it?'

'Is there anyone you can call? A friend?'

'No. My flatmate's out. Please just tell me what you've come to say.'

'When did you last see or hear from your mother?' PC Fletcher asked.

'Mum? Why are you asking?' The feeling of impending doom was getting stronger.

'Please, Rachel, just answer the question.'

'About four years ago. When she left Dad and me. Is she hurt?' Rachel's heart was racing so fast she could barely breathe.

Constable Fletcher leaned forward, her eyes filled with sympathy. 'I am very sorry to have to tell you that we have identified a body found in a forest near Aviemore as that of your mother, Mary Ann McKenzie.'

'Her body? You mean... as in dead?'

Constable Fletcher nodded. 'I'm so very sorry.'

Rachel slumped into an armchair, still clutching the mugs to her chest like a shield. A wail threatened to erupt from somewhere deep inside. No! It was impossible. Mum couldn't be dead.

'Where? How? What happened?'

'She was found in the park by a dog walker.'

Rachel struggled to compute what the policewoman was saying. Mum had been living in Aviemore. So close! Yet Mum had never taken the time to come and see Rachel. And now the reunion she'd been dreaming of for years would never take place.

'How did she die?' She still couldn't believe she was saying those words.

The two police officers exchanged another look.

'I'm very sorry to have to tell you, Rachel, that your mother was murdered.'

. . .

'It could be an accident,' Fergus said from behind his desk, pulling Rachel back to the present. She took a deep breath. She needed to focus. There was work to be done. Whatever was going on here required her full attention.

'Someone who was stupid enough to go out on his own and have no one to help when he got into difficulty?' he continued. Selena could have been talking about a TV programme for all the excitement he'd shown when she'd told him about the dead diver.

Selena flopped back in the armchair, a mix of incredulity and amusement on her face. 'What happened to his boat then? Do you think it might have drifted off and sunk itself and nobody noticed? And why hasn't anyone reported him missing?' She jiggled her leg up and down. 'It's just about possible that this death is an accident, but given the fact there are two other bodies, one of which was definitely murdered, I think it's unlikely, don't you?'

'But we can't be sure, can we?' Fergus persisted.

'At this stage we can't be sure of anything,' Selena agreed. 'Hopefully the post mortem will tell us more.' She got to her feet. 'God, Fergus, I don't even know why you became a police officer. You don't have a suspicious bone in your body.'

Rachel took a seat at the desk opposite Selena's and dialled her boss's number.

'D e a th' – each syllable drawn out – 'Mainwaring.' It was her boss's unconventional way of identifying their department. Her boss sounded so mournful Rachel could well believe the rumour that, once, an elderly relative had rung looking for an update on his wife and been convinced he'd spoken to death himself.

She explained about the dead diver and that it looked like they had another suspicious death on their hands and that Du Toit had sent to Stornoway and Inverness for reinforcements. She went on to tell him that they'd located what they believed to be the burial site and that the coins they'd found further confirmed the rib belonged to someone who'd been killed post-seventies.

'You found a body? And you think it might be another murder? Christ's sake, I didn't send you up there to stir up a hornet's nest. In fact, I thought I told you to get your arse back here. Leave investigating to people who know what they're doing.'

She just stopped herself in time from telling him that *she* hadn't been responsible for any of the deaths, unless – her chest tightened – inadvertently she had been. What if the diver, whoever it was, had been killed because of something Rachel had said or done? Because she'd rattled someone's cage?

'I can't come back to Inverness, sir.' When had she started calling him sir? 'All flights in the next couple of days are fully booked. The ferries are a bit hit and miss at this time of year too. Apparently there's a major storm on its way...'

'I don't care how you do it. Swim if you have to, but I expect to see you in the office on Monday.' As usual he disconnected without saying goodbye.

While Rachel had been speaking, Selena had downloaded the photos she'd taken of the dead diver onto her computer. Fergus had come to stand behind her. Rachel joined him.

'Any chance you recognise the poor sod, Fergus?' Selena asked.

The police constable shook his head. 'Nope. Not that there is much left of his face to go on.'

Selena put her stab vest back on. 'Come on, Fergus. Get a shifty on. I've managed to get hold of Mike. He's down at the pier at Kallin. I said we'd see him there. Hopefully he'll know who our dead diver is. You coming, Rachel?'

Rachel thought longingly of a hot bath and a large glass of wine. 'Absolutely.' She struggled into her own still-damp jacket.

Fergus picked up the keys to his vehicle. 'I'll meet you there,' he said.

They found Mike tidying up his boat. Dark clouds skidded across a pigeon-coloured sky. Empty crisp packets danced in the wind before blowing away.

Kallin harbour was similar to the one in Griminish where Rachel had met Calum, but smaller. A number of boats varying in size, mostly well maintained, were crammed between the U-shaped walls. On land, dozens if not hundreds of the ubiquitous creels were neatly stacked along with other fishing boat para-phernalia. There was a distinct sharp smell of rotting fish and the ever-present discordant screech of seagulls circling in the hope of some scraps. Despite its generally prosperous feel, this was clearly a working harbour. A few moments after they arrived, Constable Campbell's police vehicle pulled in behind Selena's.

Mike jumped out of his boat and came towards them. In front of him, on the pier, a number of air cylinders of the type divers used were lined up in a neat row. A coil of rope sat to one side next to a shed-sized metal container. Mike was wearing a thick fisherman's jersey with holes in the sleeves, and faded jeans tucked into wellington boots. He smelled of engine oil and fish.

'Constables. Miss McKenzie. What's this all about then?' His eyes were alive with curiosity. If he was guilty of murder, if he had anything at all to fear, it didn't show in his manner or expression.

Fergus took out his notebook.

'Are you missing any divers?' Rachel asked. She had to raise her voice to be heard above the wind.

'Missing divers? Why?' Mike frowned.

'Please leave the questions to us, Mike,' Selena said.

'I have three divers working for me at the moment and, as far as I can tell, none of them are missing.'

'That would be Shark, Seal and Johnny?' Rachel said, thrusting her hands in her pockets to keep them warm. Part of a broken creel rolled across the ground.

Mike nodded, still looking baffled. 'Why? What's going on?'

Rachel ignored his question. 'You said you have three at the moment. How many do you usually have?'

'It varies. Anywhere between three and six. I take what I can get.'

'Have any of your divers left recently?' They'd agreed not to show Mike the photographs of the dead diver. It was unlikely he'd be able to identify anyone from the ravaged face alone.

He looked puzzled. 'Two. One a few days ago, the other last month.'

Rachel and Selena shared a glance.

'Where did they go?' Rachel asked.

Mike's frown deepened. 'No idea. Australia, Spain, back home. Who knows?'

'Don't they tell you?'

'Sometimes. Other times they just up and leave.' As he spoke, Mike removed some diving cylinders from his boat, lining them up with the others. 'It's a nuisance, but what can I do? I can't make them stay.'

He checked the dial on each of the cylinders before putting three in the back of a van. 'You have to understand something about divers. Many are young and they can make a lot of money in a short space of time. It burns a hole in their pocket. There's only so much they can spend on the islands so as soon as they make enough, they're off. They're notorious for their nomadic lifestyle.'

'The two divers who left recently – we'll need names and contact numbers for them, and I'll need to speak to the divers still working for you,' Selena said.

Mike slammed the back doors of his van shut. 'Not a problem. But can't you tell me what this is about? Have my divers been getting into mischief? Has someone been making complaints about them?'

'Why do you ask? Are there often complaints?' Rachel asked.

Mike cupped his hands and lit a cigarette. 'You know what young men are like when they have too much money in their pocket and nothing much to occupy them. They tend to go drinking and sometimes there's trouble. Particularly with the locals.'

'A month or two back, a couple of the divers ended up in a fight with the locals,' Selena told Rachel. 'Nothing too serious. Just a few bruises and split lips. Most of them were too drunk to do much damage. A night in the cells sorted them out.'

'Do you know what the fight was about?' Rachel asked Mike.

'Not really.'

'But you have your suspicions?'

'One of my divers claimed his boat – my boat, if we're being precise – had been cut loose from its moorings. He had to swim out to retrieve it. He thought one of the locals did it.'

'You didn't report it?' Selena asked with a glance at Fergus, who shook his head.

'There was no harm done. The boat didn't drift very far. It was easily recovered. It wasn't worth the bother of reporting the incident to you lot. What were you going to do about it? Anyway, it was far more likely that one of the divers didn't secure the boat properly and was just looking to pass the blame.'

Mike flicked his half-smoked cigarette into the sea, folded his arms and leaned back against his van.

Was he really as laid back as he was letting on, Rachel wondered. Surely he must have been a teensy-weensy bit annoyed. Something niggled in the back of her mind, something someone had said that could be important, but she couldn't think what it might be.

'You still haven't told me why you're asking all these questions,' Mike said, glancing at his watch. 'Don't you think I have the right to know if one of my divers is in trouble?' Rachel saw dawning realisation in his narrowed eyes. 'Does this have something to do with the woman my team fished out of the blowhole?'

Rachel thought it interesting that it had taken him so long to come to that conclusion. It would have been her first question had she been Mike.

'It might,' Selena said. 'Earlier today, while we were on the Monach Islands, we found the body of a man wearing a diving suit. We need to identify him.'

The colour washed out of Mike's face. 'Fuck. Why didn't you tell me this straight away?' He pulled a mobile from his jacket pocket. 'I'll speak to Seal. He's my most experienced diver. He'll know where Shark and Johnny are, or if any tourists have come over to do some diving. There's been a lot of talk about a wreck off the coast of North Uist. Amateur divers love trying to find wrecks and when they're here they often come to us to get their tanks filled with compressed air. They usually check in with the coastguard as well in case there's a problem and they need help.' He looked as if he were at the point of adding something, but then with a shake of his head, started to punch the keys of his phone.

Rachel reached out a hand and stopped him before he could finish.

'Don't say anything to Seal about the body. Not yet. Just check where he is, if he's seen Shark recently and whether he knows if there are, or have been, any visiting divers and if so, what he knows about them. Their names, or where they were staying.'

A thought struck her. Perhaps Sophie would be able to

help? As the owner of the only car hire company on the island, she might know if there had been recent visitors. That is if they hadn't brought their own transport and come on the ferry. She'd suggest it to Selena.

'Before you ring him, give Selena the mobile numbers of the divers who recently left your company. I'm assuming you still have contact numbers for them on your phone?'

'Blogger left first.' As he scrolled through his phone, Mike gave a slight shake of his head. 'All the divers have nicknames. Blogger was a travelling Aussie who liked to blog. If you can't get him on his mobile, all you'll have to do is go online to find what he's been up to. His real name is Andrew Morton.'

Selena wrote the name and number Mike reeled off on her pad.

'The other diver was Pinocchio. You know, because of his nose.' He made a hooking gesture in front of his face. 'His real name is Rufus... Dawson, if I remember right. He's from some-where down south. I have both their home addresses in my office if you can't reach them on their mobiles.' He read another number out to Selena. 'That's Rufus's number. Now, can I phone Seal?'

Frustratingly, he stepped away from them to make his call. Rachel would have loved to have been able to hear what was said.

So Rufus had been the third diver with Seal and Shark when they'd retrieved Ellen's body. She thought back to what Katherine had said at Polochar Inn that there had been a third diver. It hadn't occurred to her to ask Seal or Shark his name. Was it significant?

Everything led back to the Monach Islands. Ellen, the dead diver, their John Doe, Roddy. They had to be linked. But how? As Du Toit had said, they needed to find out before someone else ended up dead. She turned to Fergus and Selena. 'Time to have a word with Roddy and his family.'

TWENTY-TWO

Chrissie answered the door and led them into the sitting room. In front of the fire a table was set with teacups and side plates. Rachel and the two constables all declined a cup.

'Out. Why?' was the short reply they got when Selena asked where Roddy was. Speaking in English for Rachel's benefit, Selena explained they'd been to the Monach Islands that morning and had found a burial site where they believed Ellen had discovered a human bone. They'd agreed to hold back the information about the dead diver for the time being.

'Do you know who might be buried there?' Selena asked.

The elderly siblings exchanged a startled look.

'No,' Duncan replied. 'We haven't been there for years.'

'Is there anything you can tell us that might be helpful?' Selena continued.

Duncan glowered, 'I don't know why you persist in thinking Ellen's death or her interest in the Monachs has anything to do with us. Never mind that bone she found! We told you: we left in the winter of 1969 and haven't been back.' He made no attempt to hide his exasperation.

'We don't want to upset you,' Rachel said gently. 'But we now know for certain that Ms Hargreaves was murdered and we believe it has to do with the bone she found.'

The colour drained from Chrissie's face. Her hand slid towards Duncan, who covered it with his own. 'We don't know of anyone buried on the island. But it's not impossible that there is more than one body buried there. A number of families lived on the Monachs before us. Presumably some of them might have died and been laid to rest there.'

'We believe this person died sometime between 1971 and 1993.'

'We haven't been back since we left.' There was an edge to Duncan's voice that Rachel hadn't heard before.

'But Roddy has.' Rachel took a punt. 'It looks like he even sleeps out there sometimes.'

Chrissie, who appeared to have recovered from what must have been a shock, frowned. 'Well, yes, he does. Very occasionally. When the weather turns bad unexpectedly – or sometimes when it's really good and he wants to stay out fishing. It's not a crime, is it?'

It took everything Rachel had not to look at Selena.

Selena leaned forward. 'When was the last time he was out there? Was he out fishing the Monachs today?'

Chrissie shrugged. 'I have no idea. He's a grown man. He does what he likes.'

'We'd like to speak to him. Where is he now?'

'On the croft somewhere. But he has nothing to do with anything. He's a good, churchgoing man – a decent man, given who his father—' Chrissie broke off. Duncan gave her hand a squeeze before getting shakily to his feet.

'Do you have anything else you'd like to ask?' His eyes were dark with anger.

When Selena shook her head, he crossed over to the door

and opened it. 'In that case, although it pains me to be so rude, I will have to ask you to leave.'

'When you see Roddy, could you ask him to either phone the police station or call in?' Selena said as they got to their feet. 'Whatever he knows, or doesn't know, we need to hear it from him.'

TWENTY-THREE

On the way back to Lochmaddy they stopped at the small village shop in Clachan and Selena ran inside. When she reappeared, she was laden with packs of sandwiches, a couple of litres of Diet Coke and one of Irn Bru. She chucked her purchases onto the back seat, before turning to Rachel with a wide smile. 'Don't know when we'll get a chance for proper food, so best be prepared.'

Back at the station, while Selena tried to get hold of Andrew and Rufus, Rachel telephoned Kevin, the archaeologist at GUARD. After some preliminary small talk, she told him about the stones where they believed Ellen had found the bone. She kept the info about the coins and the dead diver to herself. While they were talking, she emailed him the photos she'd taken of the burial site.

'From what I can see it could very well be a monk's cell, possibly part of a larger settlement. If so, it would be quite a find. A similar settlement in Ireland, Skellig Michael' – Rachel immediately recalled the name of the library book in Ellen's cottage – 'gets hundreds of thousands of visitors and pilgrims every year. Ellen would have made a name for herself. No wonder she was so keen to have my opinion on the bone and so secretive about it. She probably wanted to keep her discovery to herself until she was sure. Of course, it will need experts to do more excavating and to confirm the find.'

Did Roddy kill Ellen? Rachel wondered again. But for what possible reason? Roddy resented her excavating the wheel-house, but that was a pretty flimsy motive for murder. Did someone else kill Ellen to protect the site? Was she focusing too hard on Roddy? Nevertheless, he should be interviewed – sooner rather than later.

'Although the site itself might be significant, the bone Ellen sent is not old enough to belong to that time,' Kevin reminded her.

Across from Rachel, Selena was still punching numbers into her phone. The police constable had a hole in her sock through which a varnished toe wriggled.

'What has this to do with Ellen's death?' Kevin continued.

'We're still not sure. Maybe nothing.'

After promising to keep him posted, Rachel disconnected, leaned back in her chair and stretched. The heat radiating from the stove was making her sleepy. It was getting dark, and the wind was blowing hard enough to sway a lamppost on the road outside, causing it to cast a flickering light on the drizzle. Sporadic bursts of rain rattled the windowpanes.

'Bugger,' Selena swore. 'Andrew's phone keeps diverting to voicemail and Rufus's is either switched off or has run out of battery.' She dropped the receiver back on its cradle and hooked her hands behind her head. 'Storm's getting worse. Better batten down the hatches.'

'How bad will it get?'

'Not sure. The Met Office is predicting a force ten, possibly eleven or even twelve. I was a child at the time of the bad storm in 2005, but I still remember it.' She shook her head. 'The tide was exceptionally high that night, the wind gusts over a hundred miles per hour. The combination pushed the waves over the roads, submerging the causeways and making them impassable. The electricity was out across the whole island, so people lost connection to landlines or mobiles. There was no access to the internet, no TV, no way of finding out what was happening. There was no way of getting off the island – many couldn't even leave the house. You forget how dependent we've become on knowing what's going on all the time. Most of us on the island didn't sleep a wink that night. Some of us thought we were going to die. And the next day...' She puffed out her cheeks. 'It was as if a hurricane had hit us. Roofs were missing, power lines lay across the road, carcasses of dead sheep lay all over.' She sighed deeply. 'We were complacent about our ability to ride anything out until that night. We'll never be complacent again. People who don't live on an island have no idea what a real storm can be like. How terrifying the wind can be. And when you combine gale force winds with spring tides....' She gave Rachel a tight smile. 'I just hope the one that's coming isn't as bad as the one in 2005.' Selena ripped open a packet of crisps with her teeth and crammed a handful in her mouth. She waited until she'd swallowed before continuing. 'The last storm we had in January was pretty rough, and probably the one that blew all the sand off the barp or cell or whatever it is where the body was buried on the Monachs.'

The kettle screeched as it came to the boil and Selena padded to the stove in her stocking feet. 'Cup of tea. Then I'll try those numbers again.'

'Why didn't you mention that Johnny was dating your cousin?' Rachel asked, suppressing a yawn. It had been a long day.

'I didn't think to.' It was Selena's turn to sound exasperated. 'As I said, everyone has some connection with everyone on this island. Some go back as far as people can remember – some are more recent – but the connections are there. If so

and so doesn't know x or y he or she will almost certainly
know someone who does. Assume from now on that I either
know, or know somebody who knows, every resident on this
island. Even the incomers like Michelle.' Selena paused,
frowned, sipped her tea and then as if having made up her
mind said, 'There's a rumour she's having an affair with one of
the divers.'

Rachel groaned inwardly. 'Which one?'

'Don't know. Depends on who you speak to.'

'Why on earth didn't you mention this sooner?'

'Because I don't know that it's true! It could be a load of
cobblers. Rhoda told me. Remember, I'm also part of this
community. It's hard enough being a police officer here without
gobbing off about everyone's secrets at the drop of a hat.' She
paused for a beat. 'Everyone has secrets – something they'd
prefer people not to know.' She looked Rachel directly in the
eye when she said this. 'Everyone has a right to some privacy,
wouldn't you agree?'

Rachel knew then without a shadow of doubt that Selena
had found out about her past. Fuckity fuck. But she wasn't
about to get into a conversation about it. She shook her head.

'In a potential murder investigation no one has the right to
privacy – not even the victim.' Her skin crawled as she remembered how every detail of her mother's life had been picked over
in public. Things had been revealed in court that Mum –
anyone, probably – would have hated being exposed to the
public. But that was the way justice worked. Had to work.

'You need to tell Inspector Du Toit about Michelle, Selena.
If you won't, I will. And I think it would be much better coming
from you.'

Selena, her neck splashed with colour, glared at Rachel.
Rachel held her gaze.

'Can I use your computer?' Rachel asked. 'I'm going to
google Andrew Morton and see whether he's been blogging in

the last day or two. With a bit of luck, we might even find out where he is right now.'

'Knock yourself out.' Selena waved to a door leading off the kitchen. 'There's a couple in there. I was using one of them to play Patience earlier.'

Before Rachel could help herself she raised an eyebrow and Selena, catching the look, pushed out her lower lip, mimicking a little girl caught with her hand in the sweetie jar, then laughed. 'Up until recently there wasn't much else to do during a shift.'

Rachel grinned back. They were going to be all right. It mattered more than she thought it would.

Selena put her mug down with a thump. 'I'm going to give the other diver a try again. After that I'll phone the car hire company and ask if they know of any tourist who might have come to dive.'

Seating herself at Selena's desk, Rachel typed Andrew Morton into Google and immediately the computer responded with a number of hits. Second from the top was the address https://andrewmorton.blogspot.com and Rachel clicked on it. It seemed she had scored first time. The most recent blog was dated two days previously and gave a lurid account of the diver's weekend in Tasmania. He'd clearly spent it in a haze of drinking and partying and he made no attempt to hide his glee that he had spent the night with a woman (unnamed) who he'd met at one of the parties. Whatever else Andrew was up to, it hadn't been him lying dead on the rocks. Unless of course someone else had logged on and pretended to be him. Unlikely though it was, they would still need to speak to him to make sure.

Selena came to stand behind her. 'Still no reply from that other number. And Sophie says she's not aware of any divers on the island, apart from those working with Mike. She also agreed that didn't necessarily mean there weren't any. They could have come with their own cars or hired one from her and not said anything about diving.' She leaned over Rachel's shoulder and read for a few moments.

'God, he doesn't half fancy himself, does he? Anyone would think he was a bit of all right if they read that. Couldn't be further from the truth. He's no oil painting.'

'You know him too?' Rachel suppressed a sigh. Selena just didn't get it.

'Not really. Only by sight. He was one of the men involved in the fight I told you about. He was out of his tree at the time. So was his pal, Rufus Dawson. And I don't think it was just alcohol.'

'Go on.'

'You know how Rufus's nickname is Pinocchio? Well, some folk thought it was because of the size of his nose. Others thought it was because he was always spinning tales – you know, about how much money he was making, that sort of thing. I think it might have more to do with the fact that he was always sniffing, like coke addicts do.'

'You didn't say anything to Inspector Du Toit about that either,' Rachel said.

Selena pulled a face. 'I have no proof. It was just a gut feeling. Drugs used to be unheard of on the islands. Now they're rife. A few months ago we had our first fatal overdose. Some think it's worse here than on the mainland, but that's not true. It's more in your face, that's all. We know every kid who has a serious problem and usually their families too. Most of the time we pick them up and take them home. We tell the parents to keep an eye out. Some do, some don't.'

'Where do the drugs come from?'

'They could come from anywhere. Stornoway, the mainland. Most likely South America via Spain or Morocco.'

'You must have an idea who's dealing them.'

'We know some of the dealers but none of them are big time. They sell mainly to their pals. And as for the supplier?

Your guess is as good as mine. If I ever do find out, I'll make sure they get what they deserve.' Selena's ready smile had disappeared. 'If I could, I'd personally beat the crap out of them.' She held up her hands, palms facing Rachel. 'And before you ask why I didn't say anything before – because I didn't, and still don't, see what drugs have to do with Ellen being murdered.'

Rachel couldn't see a connection either. But if someone on the island was dealing drugs it could be a dangerous game – all sorts of shit going on.

A gust of wind blew through the office as the outer door banged and a few moments later Du Toit walked in, his dark hair slick with rain. He shook his head as if he were a dog and Selena silently handed him a towel.

'What news, sir?' she asked, as he rubbed his hair dry.

'The body has been transported to the hospital mortuary. The local police surgeon has arranged to have it transported by air ambulance to Inverness in the morning. I'll accompany the body and attend the PM. Sergeant MacVicar is still on the Monach Islands. Constable Campbell will need to relieve him in the morning. He was outside having a smoke. I told him to take the night off. I'm afraid that means you'll have to stay on duty until the officer they're sending over from Stornoway arrives. Is that all right?'

Selena nodded. 'I can always catch some kip on the chair if it's quiet,' she said.

Du Toit nodded curtly.

'Have you had any luck identifying our dead diver?' He threw his wet jacket onto the chair. Selena picked it up. 'I'll just dry this for you, sir.' She gave it a shake and hung it over a line above the Rayburn.

'We spoke to Mike, the diving company owner,' Rachel said, pouring boiling water into mugs. 'He's had two divers leave in the last month. Both without giving notice, apparently.'

Du Toit accepted the tea from Rachel and helped himself to a pack of cheese and tomato on brown from the table. 'Go on.'

Selena brought him up to speed with what they'd learned from Mike.

Du Toit ripped open the pack and took a large bite of his sandwich.

'Mike gave us the numbers of the two divers who left,' Selena continued. 'We can't reach either on their phone, but one of them, Andrew Morton, has been blogging recently. Apparently, he does it regularly from wherever he is, which is currently Australia, so I think we can rule him out.'

'And the other man?' Du Toit chucked his empty sandwich carton in the bin and helped himself to another one.

'Rufus Dawson, known here as Pinocchio,' Rachel said, with a swift glance at Selena. 'Potentially because of his drug taking. Cocaine in particular, so rumour has it. He was one of the divers who helped retrieve Ellen's body. We can't get hold of him at all. His mobile seems to be switched off. I called Mike to ask for a home number for him. He'll call with it when he gets back to his office.'

'Don't wait for me to tell you what to do,' Du Toit growled. 'Get onto him again. We need to identify that body.'

Selena, looking gutted to be on the receiving end of Du Toit's disapproval, picked up the phone and started to dial.

Du Toit scrutinised the constable through narrowed eyes. He shook his head and a smile transformed his face. 'Ach, man. Ignore me. I'm tired.' He rubbed a hand across his chin. 'We have three unexplained deaths. We don't know anything about two of them and very little about the third. My team will return with me tomorrow afternoon, hopefully with a SOCO, and I'd like to have more to tell them. Soon there will be dozens of people crawling all over this place, including, I imagine, the press – and they are going to want to know what we're doing to find out who is responsible for these deaths. I suspect the locals won't be too happy either.' He stood and stretched. 'Right, time to ask Mr Howard a few more questions.'

'One more thing, sir, before you go.' Selena took a deep breath and squared her shoulders. 'I should tell you that some people think that Mike's wife was having an affair with one of the divers – at least, that's the gossip.'

'Why didn't you tell me this before?' Du Toit demanded, clearly exasperated.

Selena flushed. 'Because it's gossip, sir. If I had to pass on every bit of tittle-tattle about everyone here on the island, you'd have a list of suspects as long as your arm. What you need to understand is that in a small community like this, people often say things that might have a grain of truth but have been distorted every time they get passed on. On the other hand, sometimes the locals know stuff they know they should tell us – the police I mean, sir – but out of some misguided sense of loyalty, they keep to themselves.'

'I appreciate, Constable, that it must be difficult to work as a police officer in a small community, but in any investigation, all information, rumour or otherwise is relevant. Now is there anything else I should know?'

Selena repeated what she'd told Rachel about the drug-related death.

'Definitely time to up the ante with Mr Howard and his crew.'

'I'll carry on trying to contact Rufus then,' Selena said, as Du Toit reached for his still-wet jacket and slipped it on. He'd already wolfed down the second sandwich.

The DI nodded. 'I have the feeling Miss McKenzie is intending to accompany me.'

Rachel grabbed her jacket. 'And you'd be right.'

TWENTY-FOUR

At Tioran Lodge a number of drinkers stood at the hotel bar and a couple huddled close to the open fire, but the conservatory was completely deserted. When Du Toit and Rachel walked in, it was evident from the low murmurs and curious glances that news of the dead diver had already reached the locals.

Rhoda hurried over, clutching a couple of menus.

'The diver who was found – do you know who he is?' she blurted, her dark eyes anxious.

Rachel had ceased to be surprised at the speed news travelled on the island. 'No. Not yet,' she replied. 'Does Johnny have any idea who it could be?'

'I don't think so.'

'Where is Johnny now?' Du Toit asked.

'At home. As far as I know.'

'And Mr and Mrs Howard? Where are they?'

'He's in the kitchen. She's in bed. Not feeling well.'

'Thank you, Rhoda.' He glanced at the menus she held. 'We won't be eating.'

As Rhoda scurried away, Du Toit's phone rang. He held up a finger. 'Excuse me,' he said.

While he took the call, Rachel slipped to the ladies.

'That was Selena,' he said, when Rachel returned. 'She's managed to get hold of Andrew Morton, who is alive and well in Australia as his blog suggested. She also managed to get a number for Rufus Dawson's parents from him. She's been on the phone to them. Apparently they haven't seen their son since he left for the islands. The last time they heard from him he was still here and didn't say anything about leaving. They've also been trying his mobile but he hasn't been answering their calls. They're worried. So am I. Let's find Mike.'

They found Mike in the hotel kitchen wiping down the cooker. A young lad with pimply skin and a morose expression was mopping the floor without much conviction. Probably someone's son or nephew, forced to earn a bit of pocket money.

'Could we have a word, Mr Howard?' Kirk asked.

'What now?' Mike growled.

'I think this conversation should be private,' Du Toit replied.

Mike dismissed his employee. The boy, clearly delighted to be relieved from his duties early, hurried away with a mumbled goodnight.

Kirk didn't bother making small talk. 'I know my colleague has told you about the body we found on the Monach Islands today.'

Mike looked up, and then carried on with his attack on the oversized stainless-steel cooker.

'I understand two of your divers left recently. Without warning.'

Mike kept his back to them.

'As I explained to Miss McKenzie, it's not uncommon for the divers to up sticks and leave without saying anything. I gave

Constable MacDonald their phone numbers as she asked. I don't see what else I can do.'

'Our enquiries have given us reason to believe the dead man could be Rufus Dawson,' Kirk said abruptly. Mike stopped what he was doing and leaned heavily, palms down, on the cooker.

After a moment he turned to face them. His eyes were troubled. 'I thought it might be Pinocchio – I mean, Rufus. Seal said he hadn't heard from him since he left. Not even a phone call to ask for his last pay to be forwarded.'

'When did you last see him?'

'Three, maybe four days ago.'

'Didn't you think it was unusual that he left without the money he was due?'

Mike was flushed and perspiring slightly. He still wore his chef's apron and he used it to dab his face, hiding his expression from them in the process.

'I didn't think anything of it. It's only been a few days. I can't follow up on every one of the men who leave suddenly. It's none of my business if they don't have the courtesy to tell me they're leaving. Sometimes they disappear for a few days and return hungover, knowing I've no option but to give them their job back. If he didn't come back I imagined he'd get in touch about his pay eventually. To be honest, I hadn't decided whether I was going to forward Rufus's pay or not.'

'Why was that?' the DI asked.

'I didn't see why I should. I had to cancel two days' work at short notice. Work I had promised to do. It doesn't do my reputation much good when I fail to meet my obligations. It's difficult enough keeping the business going without idiots like him dropping me in it.'

Rachel wondered if that was the real reason he hadn't wanted to contact Rufus. Her conviction that he had heard the gossip about his wife was growing. Maybe he suspected Rufus of being the diver in question? She thought again about what Michelle had said about a crow's parliament. Perhaps he had decided to take matters into his own hands? It wouldn't be impossible for a professional diver to stage an accident at sea.

'The body is at the hospital morgue in Benbecula,' Kirk said. 'How would you feel about coming with us to see whether you can identify it?'

A flicker of revulsion crossed his face. 'I can't say I fancy it at all, but I guess I don't have much choice. Just give me a minute while I tell Michelle where I'm going. I'll meet you outside in five.'

'You don't have to come,' Du Toit told Rachel as they walked to the door. 'I can ask Selena to meet me there. It couldn't have been very pleasant for you seeing the body first time round. Why don't you stay here? Have some supper, an early night?'

The tone of his voice, the sympathy in his eyes, made her throat tighten.

'I'm coming,' Rachel said flatly. It had shaken her, seeing the devastated face, but this time she knew what she'd be facing and would be prepared.

As soon as Mike appeared they set off towards Benbecula. Rachel sat up front with Kirk while Mike huddled in the back.

'How long have you lived here?' Kirk asked Mike.

'Almost all my life. Apart from the time I spent in Glasgow when I was at uni.'

'Is that where you met Michelle?' Rachel swivelled in her seat so she could see Mike's face.

'Yes. She was studying English Lit there.' He stared out of the window, although there was nothing to see in the pitch darkness but a curtain of rain.

'What brought you back to the islands?' Rachel asked.

Mike gave no indication he'd heard her. The headlights of the car picked out the road markings and the empty moor running alongside. 'It was never my intention to leave for good,' he said, just when she thought he wasn't going to respond. 'I always knew I wanted to start up my own business. I took a B Comm and then, when Michelle finished her degree, we got married and came back here.'

'Does she like living on the island?'

Another shrug. 'It suits us both. We're a team. She runs the business side of the hotel and the diving company. I do most of the cooking in the evening. We work hard but we make a good living.'

It wasn't exactly a ringing endorsement, but then again how many people were ecstatically happy with the lives they had chosen for themselves? However, the image of Michelle and her disappointed mouth wouldn't go away. Did they make a good enough living to keep Michelle happy? Recalling Michelle's comments about how tough it was to make ends meet, and the cut-price rooms, on the whole Rachel thought not.

'Do you ever manage to get time off together?'

'What is this?' Mike leaned forward, grasping the back of Rachel's seat, his voice hard. 'Is this part of your investigation or are you just being nosey? How would you like to have your personal life interrogated?'

Did he know too? Did everyone?

Before she could reply, Mike flopped back in his seat. 'Sorry. It's been one helluva a day. If this body you found does turn out to be Rufus, what on earth am I going to tell his parents?'

'If it does turn out to be him, one of my colleagues will go and see them. We'll have further questions for them anyway,' Du Toit said.

At the T junction, Kirk took the road towards Benbecula. After a short distance the single-track road widened into two lanes. They had to slow down to navigate a flock of sheep but, apart from the animals, it was almost eerily deserted. Rachel glanced at her watch. It wasn't much after nine but could have been the middle of the night for all the activity. She peered into the darkness. Rain lashed the windscreen, the wipers struggling to keep it clear long enough to see. On the other hand, who would be out on a night like this unless they had to?

Mike leaned forward again. 'What about you?' he asked Rachel. 'Where do you come from? If I'm not mistaken, there's a hint of an island accent in your voice.'

Rachel shifted in her seat. She much preferred it when she was the one asking the questions. She was conscious of Kirk looking at her, as if he too were interested in her reply.

'It's complicated.'

'Isn't everything?' Mike said. There was no mistaking the bitterness in his voice.

They drew up outside the hospital. The mortuary was set adjacent to the main building and could, from the outside, have been a house or a small shop. There was nothing to tell the casual passer-by that this was where bodies were kept before being flown to the mainland. Nevertheless, Rachel suspected most of the islanders would know exactly what it was used for.

A tired and worried-looking Dr Logan came to the door to meet them. She nodded to them all, including Mike.

'We think Mr Howard might know who the victim is,' DI Du Toit said, in response to her raised eyebrow. 'Initial thoughts?' he asked her, as they trooped inside.

'The cause of death in diving accidents is very difficult to pinpoint even with a PM, which I'm not qualified to do. All I can tell you is that fish have been at him, suggesting he's been in the water for at least a day or two. Apart from that,' she pursed her lips, 'nothing. Only that he's a young man and I would put my reputation on the line and say it was unlikely that he suffered a cardiac arrest and then drowned. But it's not impossible. Really, only the forensic pathologist will be able to say what he died from after opening him up to have a good look.'

They followed the doctor down a corridor and into a room the size of a small classroom. There was nothing in it except a desk and what looked like an oversized filing cabinet. In the centre of the room was a table not unlike one found in an operating room. On the table was a sheet-covered body.

Mike glanced behind him as if he wanted to be anywhere except this room. Then he breathed deeply and straightened.

Dr Logan looked at him. 'It's not very pleasant I'm afraid. You should prepare yourself. Birds and fish have had a good go at the face. It might make it more difficult for you to recognise him, so take as long as you need.'

Nausea rose in Rachel's throat as an image of her mother – or what had been left of her – laid out on a trolley not dissimilar to this one flashed into her head. Mum had been so badly decomposed she had to be identified by her dental records. Imagining how she must have looked by the time her body was found was what gave Rachel her worst nightmares.

When Mike nodded, Dr Logan carefully lifted the sheet. Rachel had to force herself not to look away. The face, or what was left of it, was blanched of all colour, except for the lips which were a deep blue. Part of the cheek and the flesh on the left side of the face had been eaten away, exposing the teeth in a crazy macabre grin. The flesh around the left eye was gone as well, the eyeball in the cusp of the socket, appearing to stare directly at her. Vomit swirled in her mouth and she swallowed hard.

Mike's left eye was twitching.

'Do you recognise him?' Kirk asked him, clearly unaffected by the sight of the dead man. No doubt he'd seen dozens, if not hundreds, before and in worse condition.

Mike covered his face with a hanky before leaning forward slightly. 'I'm not sure. It's hard to tell. But yes, I think it's Pinocchio. I mean, Rufus. If you want to be certain, he has a Gunners tattoo on his right wrist.'

The body was still dressed in the diving suit which was zipped up to the neck.

'Can we have a look?' Kirk asked Dr Logan.

The doctor rolled back the sleeve on the diver's arm.

Despite the mottled flesh, the tattoo was clearly visible.

'It's him,' Mike said. 'It's Rufus. Christ, what the hell happened?' If Mike was putting on his shock and dismay, he was doing a damn good job.

'Are you absolutely sure?' Kirk asked. He was studying Mike intently. 'Because if you're not, you must say so.'

'It is him. I was almost sure to begin with. It's just that he's so bloated and white and he has no expression, and with his face half gone... But yes, I am now a hundred per cent sure. It's definitely Rufus Dawson.'

'Where are Rufus's tanks and the rest of the equipment that were found with his body?' Mike asked as they walked along the hospital corridor.

'Bagged and at the police station,' Du Toit said. 'It will all be checked in Inverness.'

'Make sure the cylinders are tested.'

'I'll make certain of it. In the interim, I want to speak to your divers. Where do they live?' Du Toit continued.

'Seal has his own house in Peter's Port, at the road end. The other divers share one in Iochdar. I'll tell Seal to meet you there. Take the causeway from Benbecula into South Uist and swing a right at the first main road you come to. Their house is on the corner, overlooking the loch. You can't miss it. There's an old bus outside the house opposite that has been decorated with shells. No idea why, but it acts as a landmark. I'd show you myself but I need to get back to the hotel.' Mike stood. 'Don't worry about giving me a lift. I'll find my own way back.' He pulled his mobile from his pocket as he walked towards the exit.

'I'll need to speak to Michelle,' Kirk called after his retreating back, 'As soon as I've spoken to the other divers.'

Mike whirled around and swore in Gaelic. 'Speak to Michelle? What for? None of this has anything to do with her. Look, I've done everything you asked. Answered all your questions. Identified Pinocchio's body. There is nothing Michelle can tell you, trust me.'

'She must know, or have met your divers,' Du Toit persisted.

'Well, yes. They come into the hotel bar sometimes, but—'

'Then I need to speak to her. Tonight.'

'Surely it can wait until morning?' Mike wasn't giving up.

'*God in hemel,* Mr Howard. I have three unexplained deaths, including two people who have died recently in suspicious circumstances. So, no. It can't wait.'

It seemed it *was* possible to get underneath Du Toit's skin.

Mike's eyes flashed with annoyance. It looked as if he were about to argue further but then he shook his head and turned on his heel. 'I'll let Michelle know you want to speak to her,' he flung over his shoulder as he disappeared into the night.

TWENTY-FIVE

Despite the darkness, they found the divers' house easily. Even without the unusual bus squatting on its deflated tyres, the outside of the bungalow, cluttered as it was with more diving cylinders and a washing line of flapping T-shirts and wetsuits, would have given it away. Rachel fully expected the sodden clothes to fly away at any moment. Du Toit climbed out of the car and Rachel was about to follow suit when her mobile rang.

Recognising the number, she sucked in a breath before answering. Didn't her boss have better things to do with his weekends?

'Why haven't you been in touch?' Typically, no greeting, no pleasantries such as 'how are you'. 'I didn't send you up there to gad about and have a holiday, you know.'

'I tried to phone you, Douglas, but either you weren't available or I couldn't get a signal. I was going to try again later.'

'What the hell is going on up there?'

She gave him a brief, but detailed, summary of everything that had happened. 'I'm with the inspector at the moment and we're about to interview the dead diver's colleagues.'

Du Toit, lit by a pool of light from an outside lamp, was crouching down outside the house, examining the cylinders.

'For God's sake, tell me something I don't know,' Douglas's voice continued in her ear. 'I've had the Highlands and Islands chief superintendent on the phone as well as the goddamn press. I would have preferred to have heard it from you. You're making this office – making me – look like an organ grinder who doesn't know what his monkeys are up to. Did I not say that I was fed up with this office being made to look like it doesn't know its arse from its elbow? Which part about being part of a team did you not understand? No! I do not want to speak to the effing press!' he shouted. 'Tell them I'll get back to them. Now where was I?' Rachel realised that his last comments had been directed to someone in the room with him and not to her. She felt sorry for those who would be stuck in the office with Douglas over the next few days.

'I'm sorry, Douglas, I have to go. The inspector is waiting for me. I'll get back to you as soon as I know anything more.' She could still hear her boss's voice shouting as she thumbed the red off button.

All three divers were already assembled. Du Toit showed his ID and Johnny let them in, taking them through to a sitting room, furnished with a faux leather sofa, a couple of armchairs and a TV. Empty beer cans and fast-food cartons littered the coffee table and a major part of the floor. Rachel was happy to remain standing, which was just as well as no one invited them to sit.

Johnny looked anxious and upset, Seal and Shark grim-faced. Seal must have already been there or nearby. They acknowledged they'd heard about the dead diver.

'I should tell you that he has been positively identified by Mr Howard. It's Rufus Dawson. You knew him as Pinocchio, I believe,' Du Toit said.

None of the men seemed particularly surprised. 'We thought it might be,' Seal said. 'Pinocchio sometimes took one of Mike's boats to do some diving for himself. There's rumoured to be a wreck off the west coast of the Monachs and he liked searching for it.' Seal shook his head. 'He was a professional. He should have known better than to dive on his own.'

'Why didn't you tell the police this before?' Rachel said.

'Mike would have given him the boot,' Shark chimed in. 'Pinocchio nearly got caught once. Mike came down to the harbour and noticed one of his boats wasn't there. We told him someone must have cut it loose. We lied. Pinocchio had taken it. Mike was none the wiser.'

'Wait,' Rachel said. 'How many boats does Mike have?'

'Three, when they're all working.'

She winced internally. She should have realised a commercial company would have more than one.

'He took the blowhole woman to the Monachs with it,' Johnny said. 'Seal gave him a right bollocking when he found out.'

Roddy had been telling the truth. Only it hadn't been Mike he'd seen that day, but Rufus in one of Mike's boats.

'When was this?' Du Toit asked.

'Two, maybe three weeks ago.' Seal lifted a can of lager and took a long gulp. They were no longer smirking and joking. At last, they appeared to have grasped the seriousness of the situation. Seal, Shark and Johnny must have recognised Ellen when they'd helped retrieve her body. Yet none of them had said.

'She asked Pinocchio again a few days later, but he told her no chance. I'd warned him if he took one of Mike's boats again, I was going to drop him in it. He wasn't going to risk trouble for the few quid she offered. He told her to ask one of the fishermen.'

They were back to Roddy again. Had there been a second trip?

'How do you think Mr Dawson got back out there? Did he "borrow" one of Mike's boats again?'

Seal shifted uneasily. 'None of Mike's boats are missing.'

'Has anyone reported an unmanned boat adrift at sea?' Du Toit asked, his expression inscrutable.

'Not as far as I'm aware,' Seal said. 'Possible it's washed up somewhere and nobody has noticed it yet.'

'Why didn't you tell someone when Rufus didn't return? It must have occurred to you he'd got into difficulty?' Rachel asked.

'Nope. Would have eventually, I suppose.' Shark swigged from his can of ale, wiping the froth from his mouth with the back of his hand. 'We didn't know he was missing. After the row with Seal, he said he'd had enough. He fancied going somewhere with better weather. He knew he could walk into a job anywhere. We thought he'd gone to the mainland to talk to someone about one. He'd left his stuff. We expected him to come back eventually.'

'Does he have a car?'

'No. We assumed he took a taxi to the airport.'

'What do you think happened?' Du Toit asked the men.

Seal folded his arms across his chest. 'He must have been looking for the wreck when he got into trouble. Because he was on his own, there was no one to help him get out of it.'

'After Rufus took Ellen out, did he say anything about her finding something?' Rachel asked.

Seal looked at Du Toit as if the inspector had asked the question. 'Not a word.'

'What now?' Rachel asked Kirk when they were outside again.

Du Toit rubbed a hand across a stubbled chin. They had been up and working since six and it was almost midnight. 'I'll need to accompany the body to Inverness in the morning.'

'Are we going to speak to Michelle tonight? Find out if she was having an affair with Rufus.'

'Yes. But first, Rufus's parents need to be informed.'

Sadness washed over Rachel. Another unsuspecting family about to have their world torn apart.

Kirk phoned Selena and asked her to speak to the police from the area Rufus's parents lived. When he'd finished, they drove back to Tioran Lodge in silence.

They found Mike behind the bar washing the last of the glasses. He looked as if he was carrying the weight of the world on his shoulders.

'I told Michelle you wanted to speak to her. I'll let her know you're here,' he said. 'Give us a few minutes and we'll meet you in the conservatory. Help yourselves to a drink.'

'You go to bed if you want,' Du Toit told Rachel after Mike had left. 'It's been a long day.'

'No. I'd like to hear what Michelle has to say.' Like hell was she going anywhere. She found the light switch by the door, flicked it on, and the conservatory flooded with light. The heating had been turned off and Rachel shivered in the chilled air. She longed for a hot bath and bed.

Du Toit paced the small room, picking up ornaments from above the fireplace and examining them absent-mindedly before replacing them.

Eventually Mike appeared with Michelle. Her puffy face was scrubbed of make-up, her eyes rimmed with red. She had tied her hair into a plait and wore a dressing gown over bare legs. Rachel couldn't help but look at her in a new light. Had she been having an affair? If so, when did she find the time? As far as Rachel could tell she was always working. Moreover, if she had been, or still was, having an affair with Rufus or someone else, it hadn't made her happy.

'Apologies for getting you out of bed, Mrs Howard, but we need to ask you some questions.'

'Michelle, you can call me Michelle.'

Mike went behind the bar and poured a large whisky. He went back to his wife and, crouching down, pressed the glass into her trembling hands. 'Drink this, love.'

Rachel sat next to Michelle, resisting the impulse to put her arm around her. Mike's wife looked terrible.

'If you don't mind, I think I'll have one too,' Mike said, returning behind the bar.

'Would you like Mike to stay?' Du Toit asked Michelle. 'Or would you prefer to be on your own?'

Her eyes were blank. She ran a tongue across her lips and took a sip of whisky. 'Why shouldn't Mike stay? I have nothing to hide from him.'

Du Toit placed his phone on the table and pressed the record button. 'You're not under arrest but I need to record this conversation, if that's OK?'

Michelle shot a look at her husband. When he lifted a shoulder as if to say it was up to her, she nodded her agreement.

'Did you know Rufus Dawson, Michelle?' Du Toit asked.

She took another sip of whisky before nodding. 'Mike told me it was Rufus you found.'

'How did you know him?'

'He works... I mean, worked for Mike. He's one of the divers.'

'How well did you know him?'

Michelle pulled the edges of her dressing gown tighter. 'Not very well. I don't have much to do with the day-to-day running of Mike's business. But the divers come in here sometimes for a drink or something to eat. I chat to them if it's quiet, same as I would to any customer.'

'How about the other divers? How well do you know them?'

There was no mistaking the look of alarm on Michelle's face. 'Why are you asking me that? I have nothing to do with

Mike's diving company. I mean, I help with the accounts, but that's all.'

It could have been a fever that was making her cheeks redden, but Rachel doubted it.

Du Toit changed tack. 'Is there anything you can tell us about Rufus in particular that might help us?'

Michelle slid a glance at her husband, who was leaning against the bar, watching her carefully.

'He was funny. He made me laugh.'

There was a snort of disbelief from Mike.

'It gets boring here,' Michelle burst out. 'Always the same old faces, the same bloody routine night after night. Day after day.'

Mike's face tightened.

'Did you ever see Rufus outside work, Michelle?' Kirk continued calmly.

Once again, Michelle looked at her husband before answering. 'No,' she said. 'Why would I? Just because I liked his stories.' She caught her breath, 'Oh. I see what you're getting at. You want to know if there was anything between me and Rufus.' She stretched her lips into an unsuccessful attempt at a smile. 'I see. The jungle drums again. No. There was nothing between Rufus and me. He was at least ten years younger than me. But I liked him. I thought he was fun. I was disappointed, but not surprised, when he left, but that's all.'

'Why weren't you surprised when he left, Michelle?' Rachel asked. 'I gather it was a sudden thing.'

Michelle shot quick, desperate glances at the door. 'I... I don't know. The divers leave all the time. They all get bored sooner or later.' She paused and again there was that surreptitious glance at her husband. 'But...'

At the bar, Mike stiffened.

'Please continue, Mrs Howard. What were you going to say?' Kirk leaned forward and smiled encouragingly.

'Oh, I don't know. I can't think it's important, but a couple of weeks ago the divers were all in for a bar supper. They were having a heated discussion about something. At one point, Rufus got up to leave. He seemed angry but the others made him sit down again. After that they ordered a few more drinks and then they carried on as usual as though nothing was wrong.'

Rachel glanced at Du Toit, wondering whether he was thinking the same as she was. That this was the argument the divers had told them about – when he'd taken Mike's boat without permission. Or had it been about something else entirely?

'It's not uncommon for people who work together to fall out, is it?' Mike interjected.

Michelle hesitated again. She looked as if she were about to say something but, catching her husband's eye, appeared to change her mind. 'No, I guess not.' She picked at a nail before folding her hands in her lap. 'You can't think it was anything but an accident. Divers can get into trouble. Especially if they dive on their own.'

Du Toit's gaze sharpened. 'Did you know that Rufus was in the habit of diving on his own, Mrs Howard?'

She shook her head so hard her hair swung against her cheeks. 'No. How could I? I just assumed... He was found on his own. No one reported him missing.'

Du Toit studied her for a while in silence. 'OK, Mrs Howard, Mr Howard, I'll let you get some sleep. You've been very helpful. Thank you.'

Michelle looked bewildered and relieved. 'Is that it? You mean I can go?'

'Yes. I may have more questions later, but that's all for now. It was good of you to take the time to speak to us.' Du Toit smiled as if he were taking his leave from a dinner party.

Michelle hurried off.

Mike looked after her, a frown on his face. 'I'll be back in a minute to let you out, Inspector,' he said. 'I need to lock the door behind you.' He followed his wife out of the room.

Rachel stood too. Couldn't Du Toit see? If Michelle wasn't lying outright, she was, at the very least, hiding something.

'Why didn't you ask her if she was having an affair with one of the other divers?' she asked.

'Because the time wasn't right. I want to keep my powder dry until I know more.'

She had to assume he knew what he was doing. 'If you'll excuse me, Inspector Du Toit,' she said. 'It's been a long day.' She pushed her hair behind her ears. 'Is there anything you'd like me to do while you're in Inverness?'

'I'll be away less than a day. Out with the air ambulance in the morning, back on the late ferry.' His brown eyes darkened with concern, 'Try to keep out of harm's way until I get back. Don't forget, even for a moment, there might well be a murderer on this island.'

TWENTY-SIX

SUNDAY MORNING

Katherine stepped into the roaring wind. Her eyes were gritty from exhaustion. She'd barely slept last night – not just because of the wind rattling the windowpanes, but because she'd been too excited and, if she were honest, worried that she wouldn't get past her mother. In the end it had been easier than she could have possibly hoped. God, Mum was so easy to fool. Imagine believing that Katherine wanted to go for a walk. Didn't she know anything about her after sixteen years? She never walked anywhere if she could help it, unless it was to the shops or to meet up with friends. Ensconced in the residents' lounge next to a blazing fire, her mother had glanced outside, seen the weather – which, to be fair, was even more crap than usual – and had reluctantly offered to go with her. When Katherine had smiled and shaken her head, Olivia had happily gone back to her book.

Katherine pulled the collar of her jacket up to stop the rain blowing down her neck. She had left her waterproof on the peg by the front door. It was so not cool, the bright pink colour more appropriate to a child. He would tease her if he saw her in it. Part of her regretted it now. Its enormous hood would have helped keep the rain off her hair. If this continued, it wouldn't be long before it would be in rats' tails, a frizzy nest.

Mum had bought the waterproof for her last birthday. She'd secretly loved it, but of course she couldn't admit that to Mum, especially when she'd been such a pain.

A sliver of guilt threatened to spoil her good mood. Why should she feel bad? Mum only had herself to blame. Katherine wouldn't be meeting him if Mum hadn't dragged her away from her friends. And Olivia should know you could get stuff anywhere as long as you knew how. Katherine had slipped out of the hotel a few nights ago to go to a dance with Pinocchio. He'd picked her up outside, given her some dope. He'd offered her something stronger but she'd pushed his hand away and the tiny white pills had spilled on the ground. He'd laughed. Said there was more where that had come from. Enough to make him rich. She thought he'd fancied her, but she hadn't seen him since. Last night was the first time he'd been in touch.

It had taken several texts and a veiled threat about telling someone about his little gifts to make him meet her. She felt bad about that, but she would show him that she wasn't a kid, even if it meant going with him to his house.

They'd arranged to meet out of sight of the hotel on the road leading towards Eriskay. He promised he'd something to cheer her up. A delicious scary thrill ran up her spine. There was nothing good about being a virgin at her age. Most of her friends had done it. Several times with different boys. She'd joined in their conversation and pretended she knew what they were talking about. But she didn't. Not yet. Maybe after today, she wouldn't have to lie about it.

She squinted at her phone, using her sleeve to wipe the screen. She'd ten minutes to get to their meeting place. She walked faster. The last thing she wanted was for him to get fed up waiting for her and leave.

TWENTY-SEVEN

Rachel stood in front of the two-storey croft house she remembered from her childhood. It still had the picket fence on which she'd sat when the photograph of her and Mum had been taken, the byre to the back and the peat stack to the side and even what looked like the same tractor her grandfather had driven over the croft, Rachel on his lap.

Now lichen clung to the stone, the paint had peeled away and several roof tiles lay shattered on the ground. Threadbare curtains were half drawn across windows sitting uneasily in warped frames. The byre door hung from its hinges and the peat stack was down to the last broken pieces normally kept for banking the fire. She felt a pang of concern and quickly repressed it.

Although it had started to rain again and the wind dashed the drops into Rachel's eyes, it wasn't the weather that made her shiver. Her whole body ached with fatigue. She'd slept badly last night, her dreams filled with bodies in various stages of decay, of pieces of flesh stuck to eyeless skulls. She'd woken before it was light and been unable to get back to sleep, thinking about who killed Ellen and very likely Pinocchio too. She'd tried to read, given up, done a few press-ups and, still restless, debated going for a run. The howl of the wind had convinced her it was a bad idea. Not in the mood to face Michelle, she'd foregone breakfast, making do with several cups of instant coffee. She changed out of her workout gear and sat on the bed. It was no use. She knew she was only putting off the inevitable. She'd be leaving the islands soon. If she was to see her grandfather it had to be today. Still, it had taken a long walk and a visit to the cemetery before she'd been able to bring herself to come to his house.

Her mind drifted back to the day the police came to tell her about her mother's death. If learning her mother had been murdered hadn't been bad enough there had been worse to come.

'Murdered?' Rachel had echoed when the police officer had told her.

One of the mugs she'd been holding fell to the ground with a crash. 'Are you sure?' They had to have made a mistake. She felt numb. It was as if she were watching herself from a distance.

'There's no doubt.'

'It can't be her.'

'She's been positively identified by her dental records.'

'Then there's been a mix-up.'

'We need to ask you some questions if that's all right? We can do it now or you can come down to the station later this week.'

She had too many questions of her own to let them leave. Like who had identified the body? Where had they got the so-called dental records from? What was her father saying about it?

'Let's do it now.' She wrapped her arms around her body in a futile attempt to stop the shaking.

'Your mother was never reported missing, was she?'

'No, she left of her own volition.'

'When was this?'

'About four years ago.'

'Did she write? Telephone? Visit?'

'No. At least *I* didn't speak to her. She remained in touch with my father. At least to begin with.'

'Didn't you think that was strange?'

'Well, no. Mum and I hadn't been getting on. I was a terrible fifteen-year-old, a real pain. We were barely speaking. She once said she wished she could run away – live a life with no responsibilities like me.' The words gushed out of her. Something horrible was building up inside her. Threatening to erupt. 'Wait a minute – does my father know?'

Constable Whyte nodded. 'Yes.'

Then why hadn't he been the one to break the news? Although they were no longer close, he must have known how much of a shock it would be.

'How do you know your mother was in contact with your father after she left?'

'Because he told me.'

The two officers exchanged a glance. 'And why did you believe your mother left of her own volition?'

Despite her racing thoughts, Rachel noticed immediately the way the question was framed. 'Dad told me. He said Mum had a boyfriend and was going to live with him.'

'Without telling you herself?'

'He said Mum knew I'd just try to argue her out of it and that would lead to another pointless fight. She said she'd get back in touch with me when I'd grown up and could be more rational.' She wasn't sure they believed her. It sounded weak even to her own ears. But not for a second had she imagined her mother wasn't alive and living happily with her lover, maybe even with a whole new family. 'Look, speak to my father. He'll tell you.'

The two police officers shared another look. Constable Fletcher clasped Rachel's hand.

'Rachel, I'm afraid there is more. Your father was arrested earlier and is being questioned in relation to your mother's murder.'

Rachel dashed the tears from her rain-soaked face. Bollocks. Would the memories ever stop knocking her sideways? She knocked on her grandfather's front door and, without waiting for a reply, pushed it open and walked inside. The odour of damp and decay made her heart contract. The last time she'd stepped into this house it had been to the smell of peat and baking.

'Hello,' she called out into the silence. 'Anyone at home?'

'*Thig a'staigh!*' Come inside. The voice summoned her from behind a doorway halfway up a narrow hall. Rachel tapped the door and walked into the kitchen.

The interior was as neglected as the outside. The small north-facing windows prevented what meagre light there was outside from coming in. Most of the illumination came from an old-fashioned fluorescent ceiling strip light.

The linoleum, in a pattern that had been popular in the seventies, was worn through in places, the brown swirls failing to disguise the grubbiness. The kitchen table took up most of the floor in the centre of the room. Rachel blinked as an image of her perched at that same table, listening as her mother and grandmother, up to their elbows in flour, talked in Gaelic too fast for Rachel to follow, swigging tea and giggling. This room, this house, had once smelled and tasted of happiness.

Now on the same table a teapot jostled for space with a pile of newspapers that, judging by their number, must have dated back to the millennium. Against the wall, the ubiquitous Rayburn pulsed thin heat into the room. Next to the stove in a high, straight-backed armchair that almost engulfed him, was her grandfather.

Time had not been kind to Ailean Dubh. Bone disease had curved his spine into the shape of a new moon, his thin frame almost submerged by a large moth-eaten pullover. His lower half, apart from two large feet shod in a pair of wellington boots, was mostly hidden by a throw. What was left of his white hair clung to his scalp in sparse tufts, his pallid colour emphasising his blue lips. Rheumy eyes blinked at Rachel through thick lenses. In front of his chair, pulled close, was a foldaway table, the kind people ate TV dinners from. On it was a paperback and a mug.

Something she preferred not to identify shifted behind her ribs.

In her memory he'd been tall and upright, always neatly dressed even when working the croft, and while he didn't have the joy Rachel associated with her mother and grandmother, he had seemed content, his eyes resting on his family often and with quiet pleasure.

They faced each other in silence, each taking stock of the other. She couldn't tell from his expression whether what he saw pleased or offended him.

'Suidh sios,' he said, indicating a kitchen chair with a wave of his hand.

After shooing a cat who stalked away with an annoyed swish of its tail, Rachel sat.

'You look just like your mother did at your age,' Ailean Dubh said in Gaelic. His voice shook a little.

'I'm surprised you remember,' she replied in English. She wasn't going to make it easy for him, by playing the part of the prodigal granddaughter. 'How did you know I was here?'

'I heard a smart young lawyer had come to look into the death of a woman and that lawyer was called Rachel McKenzie,' he said, reverting to English. 'I also heard that she was making a pest of herself, but that she was clever and like a dog with a bone.' The ghost of a smile crossed his face. 'You were always a stubborn wee thing.' He swallowed hard, removed his glasses and rubbed damp eyes with an arthritic finger.

Rachel forced down the pity. Just because he was old and her grandfather didn't mean he had an automatic right to either her sympathy or forgiveness. 'Your mother would have been proud of you,' he said, replacing his glasses.

When he smiled she saw a glimpse of her mother and the pressure in her chest increased.

'Perhaps. If she'd had the chance.'

'Aye well.' He cleared his throat. 'You have a right to be angry.'

'We're agreed on that.'

'I'm so glad you've come. I wanted to see you before I died.'

Years of anger, hurt and betrayal simmered through her. 'You could have seen me before. Sixteen years it's taken for you to get in touch. One phone call, or a letter, is all it would have taken. You didn't even call me when Mum went missing! I was only fifteen. Apart from my father, you and Gran were my only relatives. Mum was your daughter. You were supposed to be there for her.'

'I spend every day regretting I wasn't.' His voice quavered.

'I thought you loved us.' Rachel swallowed hard. She didn't want him to see how much it still hurt. The strip light flickered, casting shadows over her grandfather's face, making it appear skeletal. She took a steadying breath. 'At least I thought you loved Mum.'

'We did love her!'

'Not enough!' Rachel snapped. The room seemed to

shudder as the wind forced its way in through the gaps in the windows and doors, wrapping cool tendrils around Rachel.

Ailean leaned forward. 'Mary Ann was my daughter. My only child. That's what I wanted to tell you. I'm sorry for it all. So sorry I wasn't there for her in life and so sorry I wasn't there for her in death.'

'Why weren't you?' Rachel demanded. If he thought an apology could make everything right, he was mistaken. 'For years I thought Mum left because I made her unhappy. I wasn't an easy teenager, so it wasn't hard to believe she'd got fed up with me and left – although I always believed she'd come back for me one day. Of course, she never did. And then when you and Grandma abandoned me too...'

She'd known she was impossible to love, she finished silently. She wasn't going to bare her soul, she'd revealed enough – more than she'd revealed to anyone. But she'd harboured, even nurtured, that fury. She'd used it to change into the daughter her mother deserved – believing if she was the right sort of daughter, Mum might come back. With the help of her father, she'd persuaded her school to take her back. She'd stopped mixing with her previous friends and instead had spent every free moment studying. It hadn't been easy turning around her abysmal school record, but she'd done it, driving herself on by picturing her mother's astonishment and pride when she returned to find Rachel was now top of the class when she was once at the bottom.

'When Mum's body was found it broke me into a thousand pieces. And then to discover who had murdered her! If it hadn't been for Dad's best friend who took me under his wing... I don't know where I would have ended up. Nowhere good, that's for sure.'

Ailean Dubh shook his head, looking bewildered. 'Your gran and I never stopped thinking of you. Your gran wrote you at least once a week. We wanted you to come and stay with us that summer your mother left, but your father said you wanted nothing to do with us. Gran kept writing. Up until she had her stroke when she heard Mary Ann was dead – I took over the writing after that. You never replied. We tried phoning too, but according to your father you refused to speak to us.'

The ache in Rachel's chest deepened as a new realisation hit.

'Dad must have kept the letters and phone calls from me.' She dug her nails into her palm in a futile attempt to transfer the pain. She hadn't thought it was possible for her father to hurt her more. 'He knew how wounded I was when you didn't get in touch – especially when they found Mum.'

It fitted with everything she now knew about her father. It had taken his trial for her to realise he'd wanted to control Rachel in the same way he'd tried to control his wife. All those years when she'd believed that her mother had left her behind because she preferred a life without her difficult daughter, her father had reinforced that belief, telling her Mary Ann hadn't really wanted to be tied down by a child, that she wanted to be free of responsibility and that included her job. He'd told Rachel her mother had abandoned them for another man, and that she'd been planning it for years.

It had all been lies.

But she'd believed every word. It was why Rachel had left home to live on the streets the day she'd turned sixteen, thinking her mother might return if Rachel wasn't there to burden her.

How little Rachel's happiness had mattered to him. But the hurt and disbelief of those years had been nothing compared to the shock and horror when her mother's body had been found. Months and years of mixed emotions had followed. On one hand blistering grief that her mother was dead, on the other overwhelming guilt that she hadn't trusted her mother's love and that part of her had preferred knowing that her mother had been murdered and not left Rachel of her own free will.

Finally, excruciatingly, the gradual realisation that it was her father who had killed her mother. No wonder she was screwed up inside.

His defence – that he knew bad people who would not think twice of hurting him by hurting his family – was easily picked apart by the prosecution.

He'd been sentenced to life. She'd decided to become a lawyer.

Rachel hadn't seen him since.

She became aware her grandfather was waiting for her to respond. Although she believed him about the letters and calls, she wasn't ready to let him off the hook.

'What about the years before Mum went missing? When you cut her off. What happened on that holiday? You and Gran must have suspected something wasn't right with my parents' marriage.'

'Your mother talked more to your grandmother than to me.' He sighed. 'But yes, we'd suspected for some time that she wasn't happy with your father. We were even more certain when she came on holiday without him.'

Rachel had always assumed her father had been too busy to join them that summer. She hadn't been aware of any chinks in her parents' relationship then. It had been a shock to learn at the trial her mother had wanted to leave her father years before he'd killed her.

Regret crumpled her grandfather's face. 'Mary Ann talked about leaving David. Divorcing him. As practising Catholics, we couldn't support her decision.'

Rachel's laugh was hollow. 'What? You can't be serious!' She'd never given her mother's religion any thought. Her mother had attended chapel, but irregularly, and had never forced Rachel to go. She leaned forward. 'Tell me you helped her anyway?'

He gave a shame-faced shake of his head. 'She asked. She

needed money if she was going to leave your father. She had none of her own. But our conscience wouldn't let us.'

Rachel stared at her grandfather in disbelief.

The money issues had been another thing to come out during the trial. Although Mary Ann had worked full-time, Rachel's father had insisted all her salary be paid into his bank account, out of which he gave his wife an allowance for housekeeping and the odd treat. It wasn't the only way David had controlled his wife, but it was the one that had stopped her getting away from him in time. The lack of money – and support – explained why she hadn't left when she had the chance. Poor, trapped Mum.

Rage burned in Rachel's chest like acid. 'He was abusing her! Mum must have told you that! If you'd helped Mum – even offered her a place to stay – she'd probably still be alive.'

Tears welled in his eyes. 'Don't you think I don't know we could have saved her? I've had to live with that knowledge every day of my life. The day Mary Ann's body was discovered was the day your grandmother died. Not physically, it took a few more months for that to happen, but inside.' His voice caught on a sob. 'Her heart quite literally broke. She never stopped blaming herself. She never stopped blaming me.'

His obvious distress was enough to soften the edges of Rachel's anger. Her father was the one to blame for her mother's death, not her grandparents.

'But I have to tell you this,' he continued. 'Your grandmother never believed your father did it.'

Oh, no. She was not going down that rabbit hole. She'd been there before. 'Then she was mistaken. There's no doubt he murdered Mum. If Gran had been at the trial, she would have known just how much evidence there was against Dad. Nobody wants to believe their loved one has been killed by the person supposed to love them. I should know. I didn't – couldn't – believe it either, but all the evidence was there. I attended the trial every day. I was left in no doubt.' She squeezed her eyes shut, remembering the slow sweeping horror of realising her father was guilty. Each irrefutable fact laid out by the prosecution like a trail of crumbs.

The memories of those weeks made her insides churn. She paused to collect herself. The wind shook the house, sneaking through the doors and windows with mournful shrieks.

'My father,' Rachel continued, when she felt in control again, 'was a very bad man who used his legal – and criminal – knowledge to plan and then cover up Mum's murder. And when he was charged he tried to pin it on someone else. Dad tried to make everyone – including me – believe Mum was having an affair, claiming it was her fictional lover who had killed her. I believed him at first. Because I wanted to.' Her voice caught. 'But there wasn't the tiniest shred of evidence of another man in Mum's life despite Dad trying to point a finger in that direction. It turned out it was him who was having an affair and Mum who threatened to divorce *him.*' Apparently, her Mum had been planning to use evidence of the affair to divorce her Dad and get a decent settlement.

'Dad had motive, means and opportunity. He killed her when I was staying overnight with a friend. He claimed to have returned home late from work to find Mum gone. He said she'd taken a small suitcase and her passport. Everyone, including the police, many of whom knew my dad from the years he'd worked as a criminal solicitor, believed him. Over the years, Mum had apparently used her debit card on a regular basis – just a hundred here and there. Proof she was alive, but just didn't want to be found. Of course, when they found her body and it was clear she'd been dead for years they knew it hadn't been Mum using the card.'

Rachel sighed. 'Dad wasn't as smart as he'd like everyone to believe. When Mum's debit card, the one that had been used to draw money, was found in the safe in our house, even he couldn't explain it away.'

There had been no other logical verdict for the jury to arrive at but murder. Planned, committed and concealed by David McKenzie. Rachel's grandmother had died a week after the trial concluded.

The overhead strip light flickered again before finally going out completely, casting the room into semi-darkness.

'I have no doubt as to your father's guilt, but Marion was never convinced.'

'Perhaps guilt prevented her,' Rachel said baldly. 'No mother would want to think she sent her daughter back to the arms of her killer.'

He winced, as if Rachel had physically struck him. 'I deserve that. And it's what I used to think. After that last holiday, Marion and I agreed to cut off relations with Mary Ann until she came to her senses. But, as I learned later, Marion and Mary Ann kept in touch. Not very often, only now and again because...' His eyes filled again. 'Because they didn't want me to find out.'

The ache in Rachel's chest eased a little. Gran hadn't entirely forsaken her daughter.

'Gran didn't think it strange when the phone calls stopped?'

'No, because I came in one day when they were on the phone and made Marion promise she wouldn't ever go behind my back again.'

His mouth trembled and he sank back in his chair, seeming to shrink into himself. This, Rachel thought, is what guilt and regret looked like. The wind gave another other-worldly moan as if it were a live presence demanding to be let in. After a moment he sat up again and took a deep breath like a soldier preparing to fling himself into battle one last time.

'Storm's here,' her grandfather said. 'The electric will likely stay out for the duration. Hope you have a good torch handy.'

'Why wasn't Gran convinced about Dad's guilt?' She had to ask.

'Marion insisted your mother was very frightened about something that had nothing to do with your father,' he said. 'Marion only told me this when it was clear your father was going to be found guilty.'

'Why wait until then?'

'Because Marion hated David – blamed him for making Mary Ann unhappy; maybe she even wanted him to suffer the way we'd suffered – but in the end she said she couldn't go to God with a lie on her conscience.'

'What was Mum worried about?'

'Mary Ann didn't say. Only that she thought her life was in danger. Marion thought it was to do with your mother's work.'

Rachel struggled to make sense of what he was saying. No one had mentioned anything like this in all the years since Rachel's father had been arrested. It had to be wishful thinking on Gran's behalf.

'What danger could Mum have been in because of her job? I know social workers can be threatened, but everyone loved Mum.'

Apart from Dad.

'I'm only telling you what Marion told me. She said she tried to ask Mary Ann more, but she heard my car and finished the call. Mary Ann never mentioned it again. She disappeared a couple of weeks later.'

'Did Gran share this with the police?'

'At first she didn't think too much about it. But when months passed and we didn't hear from Mary Ann, Marion began to worry. She phoned Police Scotland and reported Mary Ann missing. They didn't seem very interested. Said they would look into it. They phoned back to say there was no evidence she hadn't left of her own volition. What else could we do? Your mother had reason to be angry with us.' His eyes welled again. 'We chose to believe she was happy.'

'Why are you telling me this now? Why not before?'

'I wondered whether to tell you at all. You've been through enough. I believe your father's guilty verdict is the right one. But I'm going to die soon. When I heard you were here, I knew I had to tell you. Leave it to you to decide what to do with it.'

Sadness pulsed from Ailean in waves.

Rachel lurched to her feet. She shouldn't have come. She didn't want to feel his fucking pain. She had enough of her own to deal with. 'My father murdered my mother. There's no doubt.' She had to get out of there before she lost it. 'I have to go.'

Wind and rain battered at the doors and windows, and the house shook as if it was about to be plucked from the earth like the house in *The Wizard of Oz*. It was going to be a hell of a day. Huddled in his chair, her grandfather looked as if a gust of wind would whip him away.

'Will you be all right?' she asked, torn between pity and desperation to leave.

He gave a small smile. '*Mo graigh*, I've weathered worse storms than this.'

From somewhere deep in the house a telephone rang.

TWENTY-EIGHT

Rachel's grandfather heaved himself to his feet, holding up an arthritic finger when Rachel moved to help him, and shuffled away to answer the phone. Rachel couldn't leave until he returned. While she waited, she thought about what he'd said. Gran had been mistaken. She must have desperately wanted for it not to have been Rachel's father who had killed her daughter. Grief and guilt had made her believe someone else meant her daughter harm.

'It's Constable MacDonald for you,' her grandfather said, coming back into the room.

Why was she surprised that Selena knew exactly where she was? She should have learned by now she couldn't move on this island without being observed.

'Could you tell her I'll call her right back?' Rachel asked and slipped outside. She waited until she was inside her car before taking out her mobile. There were several missed calls from Selena. Her vehicle rocked in the wind as Rachel waited for Selena to pick up.

'Hey,' Rachel said, when she did. 'My phone was on silent. What's up?'

'Katherine Mowbury – the girl who found the body... well, she's missing,' Selena said.

'Missing? When?'

'Her mother says she went out for a walk over three hours ago. She's not returned to the hotel.'

'Three hours hardly counts as missing. She could be anywhere. Perhaps her walk took her further than she thought. She might have lost track of the time.'

'I agree but someone should go and see the mother. Sergeant MacVicar is on his way back from the Monachs – the coming storm makes it too dangerous for anyone to stay out there without proper gear and provisions. The coastguard went to collect him and until he arrives, I'm stuck manning the phones here. I can't get hold of Fergus – he's not answering his phone or his radio. Probably thinks that because he's supposed to be off duty he doesn't have to. Sweet though he is, no one could accuse him of being a workaholic. So could you go speak to Olivia? Find out if she's right to be worried?'

Investigating missing teenagers wasn't part of Rachel's remit. But a killer could be on the island. Until they'd been identified, they couldn't be sure anyone was safe.

'Of course,' Rachel said slowly. 'I'm not far from Polochar Inn, as it happens. I'll go there right now.' She waited a beat. 'How did you know I was here?'

'I phoned the inn. Rhoda told me someone had left a message asking you to call them back.' Selena paused. 'Aw crap. I can't lie to you. The day you arrived I googled you. I know everything, including that Ailean Dubh is your grandfather. I took a punt I'd find you there.'

'I see,' Rachel said, her heart giving a sickening thud. 'Who else knows?'

'I haven't told anyone, if that's what you mean. Not even Inspector Du Toit. I meant it when I said before that everyone is entitled to their privacy. But I wouldn't be surprised if he knows. I'm not sure about MacVicar. I doubt it. He's not the type to think of googling people.'

'I'll call you after I've spoken to Katherine's mother,' Rachel said, and disconnected. She could have done without this added complication. She rested her forehead against the steering wheel, taking deep breaths to calm her fluttering heart.

It was inevitable her past would come out. She'd accepted that a long time ago. There was nothing she could do about it. Except not let it get in the way of her doing her job.

Was there any truth in what her grandmother had believed? Was it possible her father was innocent? She instantly dismissed the thought. No matter how much she wished it could be different, as she'd told her grandfather, there wasn't the slightest shred of doubt. Rachel's father had killed her mother.

Rachel said goodbye to her grandfather, asking again if he'd be OK on his own, and when he reassured her he'd lived here all his life without depending on anyone, promised she'd visit again before she left. If she could.

When Rachel pulled up at the inn, despite the wind and rain, Olivia was pacing outside. 'Where is the inspector?' she demanded, looking over her shoulder as if she could make him materialise. 'I want a full search. I want every bloody policeman on this island out looking for my daughter.' Her hair was plastered to her forehead, her skin waxy, lips drained of colour.

Rachel touched her elbow. 'Let's go inside and you can tell me exactly what happened. Inspector Du Toit is not available right now, but Constable MacDonald will be here as soon as she can.'

Olivia shook off Rachel's hand. 'I don't want to go back inside and I'm not bloody well waiting around for a constable. I need to speak to someone more senior. Kat has to be found. It's hellish out there. What if she's fallen into the sea like the woman we found? What if she's lying out there somewhere, hurt and frightened? We *have* to find her.' The last sentence ended in a wail.

'Olivia, I know you're frantic, but she's only been gone a few hours. If she *is* lost or hurt –and there could be other reasons why she's not made it back yet – we have to plan where we're going to look for her. You have to trust that the police will do everything they can to find her. Come on. Come inside.'

Olivia sagged against Rachel, who patted her shoulder awkwardly. 'Something's happened. I know it has!' the older woman murmured.

'Let's go up to your room,' Rachel coaxed, guiding Olivia towards the hotel. 'We can talk there. I'll let reception know where we are so they can tell Constable MacDonald when she arrives.'

Upstairs, Olivia's room was more than large enough for the two single beds it contained. Housekeeping had been in, the beds neatly made, the sachets of coffee and tea refreshed. Over the arm of an armchair was a neatly folded pile of clothes – although the legs of the jeans were inside out and a sock hung from one. The dressing table was covered in make-up, many of the little pots with their lids off.

If it hadn't been bucketing down, Rachel would have been able to see over to Skye from the bedroom window. As it was, she could see almost nothing. Rain slammed against the panes like grit. Rachel hoped Katherine was safe indoors.

Rachel eased Olivia into a chair. 'Now, tell me when you last saw her.'

'She said she was going out for a walk. Just before lunch. Four damn hours ago! I asked her if she wanted me to come too, but she said she wanted some time on her own. I should have gone. God, why didn't I? But the weather was so awful and I was so warm and comfortable. I decided to stay behind and finish reading my book. Besides...' She jumped up from the bed and crossed over to the window. 'It's so bloody difficult being with her all the time. She's not exactly easy to be around at the moment.'

'Why is that?'

Olivia turned to face Rachel. 'Have you children, Miss McKenzie?' When Rachel shook her head, Olivia continued. 'Even though you don't always like them, you love them. Despite what they like to believe – that all you want to do is ruin their lives – you'd do anything for them. When they're small you can't wait for them to grow up so they can be more independent and you can get on with your life. Then they do grow up and all of a sudden all they want is to get away from you and all *you* want is to keep them close so you can keep them safe.'

Every word was a stake in Rachel's heart.

Olivia peered out of the window, every sinew in her body tense as she watched for her daughter. 'I told you that my husband and I had split up. It wasn't my fault, but Katherine blamed me. She started getting into trouble at school. Recently there's been talk of drugs. The school wanted to suspend her.' Olivia pulled a hand through her hair. 'My husband – ex-husband – is a lawyer. He threatened to sue the school if they did suspend Kat – said they didn't have enough evidence. The school backed down. I thought if I brought her here, away from her friends and any temptation, she'd be fine. I thought if we were alone, without distractions, she might start to talk to me again.'

'And did she?'

Olivia looked over at Rachel and grimaced. 'If anything, it made things worse. She hated being here. In the end I was forced to give her back her mobile so she could phone her friends.'

'Could she have run away?' Rachel asked. 'Maybe to her father?'

Olivia sank into the armchair. 'How? We're in the middle of nowhere. She has no car, no money, no way of getting off the island.'

She could have hitched a lift and if she had her phone – and which teenager didn't have it surgically attached? – a way of getting money transferred.

There was a tap on the door and, without waiting to be invited, Selena came into the room. Her police overcoat shimmered with rain.

'They told me you were up here.' She slipped out of her coat and hung it on the peg at the back of the door. 'Is she back? Been in touch?'

Rachel shook her head. 'We should check the ferries and flights just in case she's trying to leave the island.'

'Already done. There was a ferry due to sail out of Lochboisdale tonight at eleven, but I very much doubt it will be going anywhere in this storm. Just to be on the safe side I've been on the phone to tell them to look out for Katherine.'

'What about the airport?'

'Closed. All flights cancelled until further notice. The airport is locked up until then.'

Katherine wouldn't have known that. Perhaps even now she was making her way back. But if no flights were coming in or out, it meant Du Toit and his team wouldn't be coming back today. Possibly not even tomorrow. Neither would Rachel be getting back to Inverness in the immediate future. Rachel's heart gave a sickening lurch. No way off, no way on. If their murderer was still on the island, they were all trapped here together.

Judging by the flash of anxiety on Selena's face, the same thought had occurred to her.

Selena crossed over to where Olivia had sat back down. 'Mrs Mowbury, I promise you, she won't get off this island. I've asked my colleague to pop into all the bars and pubs on the island and check if anyone's seen her. Don't worry, we'll find her.' Selena half smiled. 'This is where the Uist bush telegraph comes into its own. If anyone's seen her, we'll know sooner rather than later.'

Olivia seemed to sink into herself. 'I don't think she's run away. I know she's in trouble. I can feel it. She's out there somewhere, all alone and needing her mother. Please, you must help us.'

Selena crouched down next to the stricken woman. 'We'll do everything we can to find her, Mrs Mowbury, although I suspect she'll be back soon.'

Olivia stood abruptly. 'Coffee anyone?'

Rachel had been examining the make-up strewn dressing table. Curling tongs lay in a tangled heap on the floor. Room service would have tidied it when they'd come in that morning. 'Did Katherine always style her hair and put make-up on before going for a walk?' she asked.

Olivia shook her head. 'Not here – no point, she said.'

'Are you sure there's no one she might have gone off with?'

Olivia's hands trembled as she emptied a sachet of coffee into a cup. 'She doesn't know anyone here. I've told you that a hundred times.'

Rachel took the cup from her and poured boiling water onto the granules. Olivia accepted the cup back with a small upward jerk of her mouth.

'What about the divers?' Rachel said. 'She seemed friendly with them the day I came to see you. Could she be with them?'

'Do you think she might be?' The hope in Olivia's eyes was almost painful to see. 'Could you speak to them? I don't know where they live. But the constable could find out, couldn't you?'

Selena nodded. 'I have their address. And a phone number – although I don't think there's any point in calling ahead. If Katherine is with them, she might persuade them to lie for her.

Much better if I go there and put the frighteners on them myself. It's worth a try at any rate.'

Rachel suppressed a smile. Selena clearly watched too many American cop shows.

'I'll go with you,' Rachel said. 'Olivia, you should stay here. Katherine might come back, or if her mobile isn't getting a signal, phone the room from a call box, if any are still working. Call us straight away if you hear anything.'

With final, hopefully reassuring, smiles they stepped into the corridor.

'We're in deep shit,' Selena said in a hushed voice.

'What do you mean?'

'Look, please don't share this with anyone, but I think Sergeant MacVicar is on a bender.' She gave an irritated shake of her head. 'What a time to choose!'

'As in drink bender?'

Selena nodded. 'It happens periodically. Between me, Fergus and Dr Logan, we usually manage to keep it under wraps. If Du Toit finds out, the sergeant is going to be in a world of pain – probably lose his job and his pension along with it.'

Selena's mobile buzzed. 'Bugger. Speak of the devil. It's Du Toit.'

She put him on speakerphone.

'The PM result has come back on Rufus. He died from oxygen toxicity. His cylinders had been filled with oxygen instead of air. Someone must have messed around with the gas in his cylinders. It looks like we have three murders on our hands.'

Rachel's insides churned.

And at least one murderer. Who could be aware of their every move, watching them, deciding when they were too much of a threat. There was just the two of them, if you excluded missing in action MacVicar, and waste of space Campbell. And they were cut off from outside help, unsure who to trust.

In the backlight from her mobile Selena's face was ghostly. A gust of wind wailed under a door.

'I'm bringing my team from MIT but I'm not sure when we'll get there.' Du Toit's disembodied voice came across the line. 'I'm told all ferries and flights are currently suspended. That means I can't get you reinforcements from anywhere either.'

'I understand, sir,' Selena responded.

'I can't get hold of MacVicar or the constable. Any ideas?'

Selena glanced over at Rachel. 'The network gets very patchy when we get a storm like this – even some of the land-lines are down. And our radios are practically useless even at the best of times.'

Damn. To make matters worse, Selena was making Rachel complicit.

'Bring them up to speed on my behalf. The three of you will need to hold the fort until I get back.'

'We'll do our best, sir, but there is something you should know.' She explained the situation with Katherine. 'She knows the divers,' Selena finished. 'Her mother thinks she might be with them. Rachel and I are going to check it out.'

'Knows the divers! Why didn't you tell me before?' There was no mistaking the irritation in Du Toit's voice. 'Why is everyone apparently incapable of giving me all the facts?'

'It never came up. I don't think she knows them well. Possibly had an orange juice with them in the bar one evening.'

'Find out if she's seen them since. Or if she's been in touch with anyone else on the island.'

'Sir.'

'And Constable, Rachel...' There was a pause on the other end of the line. 'I don't have to remind you that our murderer might still be on the island. And if he, or she, is then they are trapped by the storm too and trapped people get reckless. You guys take care, OK?'

TWENTY-NINE

Katherine was on her side, all scrunched up, her feet and head jammed against something hard and slimy. Her head was really, really sore, she was freezing and soaked to the skin.

What had happened? Where was she? He must have put her here – wherever here was. It was too dark to see.

Slowly memory trickled back. Pinocchio texting her, suggesting they meet. A car drawing up alongside the place the text had said, the driver winding down his window – her surprise that it was him and not Pinocchio. Him saying Pinocchio had asked him to fetch her, the fishy smell in the car, his reply when she asked where they were going – *somewhere out of sight of nosy folk*. She hadn't been frightened then – not at all. She'd been too excited.

Eventually they'd pulled up at the end of a long narrow road. He was right. There were no nearby houses, no chance of anyone walking their dog in this shitty weather or a passing car coming along. She'd felt the first stirring of disquiet.

He'd seen she was nervous and pulled out a small plastic bag from his pocket. 'A small hit first – to relax you?' he'd said, offering her some white pills. 'While we wait for Pinocchio.'

Although she'd liked it that he thought she was cool, she'd shaken her head. What he was offering wasn't a joint or some E. This was serious stuff. The type of stuff that turned you into an addict faster than the speed of light. It was one thing pretending she took hard drugs, another actually taking them. She wasn't nearly as daft as her mother thought.

He'd been annoyed when she'd refused; she remembered that.

The rest was blurry. He'd grabbed her phone out of her hands, clamped his hand over her mouth, and something had stung her leg. He'd dragged her out of the car and tied a cloth over her mouth. Then he'd bound her ankles and taped her hands behind her back. She'd a vague impression of being half carried, half dragged, forever. Then he'd lowered her into this hole, letting go of her when her feet were still dangling. She'd banged her head when she'd fallen. She must have knocked herself out – that's why her head was so sore. How long had she been here? She'd no idea. It could be days.

Panic clawed at her throat. Why had he done this? Had he meant to kill her? Or keep her prisoner? Was he planning to come back? However much she dreaded his return, the thought of him not coming was worse.

She struggled into a sitting position, crying out as her stiff limbs protested with every tiny movement, and leaned against the slimy stone wall. She was in a small space, a hole of some sort. It smelled dank and earthy. *She was in the ground.* Her breath began to quicken again, making it even more difficult to breathe. Sometimes she had an asthma attack. What if she had one now? And died?

Above her rain poured in through some sort of gap. The water was already an inch high. What if it continued to rise? What if it got so deep it covered her head and she drowned?

Overtaken by panic again, she flailed around trying to loosen her bonds, shaking her head from side to side, her heart beating so hard she thought it would explode. Within seconds she was exhausted. She slumped back against the wall and forced herself to take long, slow breaths through her nose, imagining her mother talking to her, telling her everything would be all right. She always said if you stayed calm you could think yourself out of almost any situation. She had to keep calm until help arrived. And it would. Mum would have told the police she was missing. They'd be out looking for her. Tears streamed down her cheeks. *Mummy. Please find me, Mummy. I'm so sorry for everything. I'll never do anything bad again, I promise.*

THIRTY

'I think you should have told Du Toit about MacVicar,' Rachel said as they clambered into Selena's police vehicle. They'd decided to go to Seal's house first. He was clearly the leader of the divers, the one most likely to know where the other divers were and what they were up to.

'It wouldn't have made any difference. Even if the inspector knew it was just me and Fergus, he still can't send officers to help.'

Selena had a point. Nevertheless, Rachel worried what would happen to the officer's career if Du Toit found out. She might not have been overly impressed with him as a police officer, but he was one, and without him their little team was severely depleted.

Seal lived in a renovated black house in Peter's Port on the east coast of Benbecula. Although it wasn't yet four, the thick dark clouds made it feel much later. Weak light spilled from a window at the back.

Selena parked the car in a lay-by and they both had to put their shoulders to the car doors to get out. The wind tossed icy rain into Rachel's face, down the collar and up the sleeves of her jacket.

Selena knocked and, as they waited for an answer, Rachel looked around. Unlike the house where the other divers lived, the outside of Seal's home was neat and tidy – no diving cylinders or wetsuits left to take their chances in the weather.

The door was flung open by Seal, who was clearly none too pleased to see them. Selena made to push through but he blocked her way with his arm.

'What do you want?' he asked.

'*Thighearna's a Dhia*,' Selena protested. 'Let us in! We're in danger of being blown away out here.'

Seal considered them for a long moment before reluctantly stepping aside. Selena scooted past him, Rachel following in her wake. The door led into a small sitting room, from which another door led off, presumably to a bedroom. To one side was a two-seater sofa and, across from it, a table on top of which were a couple of dirty plates and a casserole dish. The remnants of a peat fire glowed in the grate and Selena held out her hands to warm them. Off to the left of the open-plan space was a tiny kitchen with a two-ring cooker, a couple of kitchen cabinets and a sink. Vying with the aroma of the peat was the faint but distinctive scent of perfume, and draped over the arm of the sofa a jewel-coloured scarf that Rachel was certain she'd seen before, although definitely not on Katherine. It wasn't the sort of thing the teen she'd met would dream of wearing. So unless Seal was a metro male...

'How well do you know Katherine Mowbury?' Rachel came straight to the point.

Seal glanced behind him. From what Rachel knew about the construction of the black house, there would be a bedroom in the other half. Originally this would have been open to the rest of the house. In this one, a partition had been erected, dividing the room in two. There was another door in the middle of the room, probably leading to an extension.

The wind wailed under the front door as if a hundred demons were begging to be allowed in.

'I don't know her. First time I set eyes on her was at the blowhole the day we fished that woman out.'

'When did you see her last?' Selena asked.

'In the bar at Polochar.' He jutted his chin in Rachel's direction. 'You were there.'

Rachel moved towards the kitchen table and felt the casserole dish. As she suspected, it was still warm. There were two dirty plates next to it.

Seal was watching her, tracking her movements. He looked ready to pounce.

'Why do you want to know?'

'She's gone missing. She went out for a walk this afternoon and hasn't returned,' Selena continued.

'What does that have to do with me?' Seal demanded. Something shifted in his expression. 'Unless you're wanting us to go and search for her. Is that it? Do you think she could have come to harm? Fallen? Got lost?' He shook his head. 'There's not much point in taking a boat to look for her. Not until this wind dies down and it gets light.'

When he glanced at the front door, Rachel followed his gaze. On the floor was a holdall that looked as if it were packed and ready to go.

'Going away for a few days?' Rachel asked.

Seal smiled tightly. 'Dirty laundry, if you must know. There's no washing machine here so I have to take my clothes to the laundromat. I plan to drop it off on my way to work tomorrow morning. If it's any business of yours – which it isn't.'

Rachel picked up the scarf from the sofa. 'Who does this belong to?'

Seal grabbed it out of her hand. 'Not Katherine Mowbury, if

that's what you're thinking. It's not an offence to have a woman's scarf in your house is it, Constable?'

'Nope.'

'Can you think of any place Katherine might be? Could she be with Shark or...' Rachel glanced at Selena, 'Johnny?'

'Why don't you ask them?'

'We intend to.'

As silence stretched, Rachel searched for the right question to ask. Seal knew something. She was sure of it. 'I must advise you, Mr Ferguson, if you or your mates have anything to do with the death of Ellen Hargreaves or Rufus Dawson, or the disappearance of Katherine Mowbury, you are going to be in deep trouble.'

Seal strode towards the door and opened it. The wind rushed in, sending papers flying. 'Unless you're going to charge me with something, I'd like you to leave.'

Rachel caught Selena's eye and shook her head. There was nothing else they could do. They had no grounds to search his house, even if Rachel strongly suspected there was someone in the bedroom. Someone Seal didn't want them to see. Either Katherine – or Michelle. Suddenly she remembered where she'd seen the scarf before. Michelle had been wearing it as a bandana the day Rachel had checked in. Seal was the diver Michelle was having an affair with! Rachel glanced at the holdall again. Were they intending to run away together?

'Thank you for your time,' Selena said. 'If by any chance you do hear anything about Katherine, perhaps you'd let us know. If she hasn't turned up by first light we're going to have to ask you to help us search for her. Would you be prepared to do that?'

Seal seemed to relax a little. He even managed a half-smile. 'You'd have to check with Mike. It's his boat and his diving gear, after all. You may also want to get the coastguard involved.' He looked pointedly at Rachel and she felt her cheeks warm. She should have guessed that someone would have seen her car at Calum's house.

Selena moved towards the door, but Rachel hesitated. She picked up the scarf and ran the silky fabric through her fingers. They had to know one way or another that Katherine wasn't here.

Before she knew it, Rachel was brushing past a slack-jawed Seal and flinging open the door to the extension.

A white-faced Michelle stood next to a rumpled bed.

'Who gave you the right to barge in?' Seal snarled, coming into the room behind Rachel. 'I told you the girl wasn't here.' He put his arm around Michelle and pulled her in to his side.

'What girl?' Michelle asked Rachel, moving away from Seal.

'Katherine Mowbury. The lassie who found the body. She's missing,' Selena replied. 'Has been for hours. Her mother – we – are very worried about her.'

'Do you have any idea where she is, Michelle?' Rachel asked.

'No. Of course not. I've never even met her.' She grabbed the scarf out of Rachel's hands and shoved it in her pocket.

Rachel stepped towards her. 'Michelle, we think Katherine has got caught up in whatever is going on here. I beg you, if you know anything, anything at all, that might help us find her...'

Michelle darted a look at Seal, running the tip of her tongue across her upper lip. She looked as if she were about to say something but then, to Rachel's disappointment, she shook her head. 'I'm sorry. There isn't anything I can tell you. Now if you'll excuse me, I need to go.'

THIRTY-ONE

Rachel and Selena stepped back into the screaming wind. While they'd been at Seal's house the storm had worsened, and walking to the police vehicle was like struggling in the arms of a giant.'

'Damn!' Selena swore when, once inside the car, she tried to get a signal on her phone and couldn't. 'I think the networks have gone down.' She reached for her radio instead. 'For the first time I'm glad MacVicar insisted on keeping the old technology.'

Selena switched on the police vehicle's blue flashing light and sidelights, driving slowly so they could each scan a side of the road for Katherine. The car bucked and swayed and Selena gripped the steering wheel as if by doing so she could keep the car anchored to the ground.

Keeping one eye on the road, Selena tried to get MacVicar on the radio. To her obvious frustration he didn't answer. Fergus came on instead.

'Hello. What's up?'

'Where the hell have you been? I've been trying to get hold of you. Where are you?'

'Just approaching the South Uist causeway from the North.

Why?'

Succinctly, Selena explained about Katherine and the possibility she might be with Johnny and Shark. 'Could you check? We've just left Seal's house. She's not there.'

'Will do.'

'What about Roddy? Has he called?' Selena asked.

'No. I tried his mobile a couple of times – no answer. Won't be able to get hold of him now.'

'If you do hear, let us know.'

'Very well. Over and out.'

A sheet of rain smashed against the front windscreen, obscuring their vision. Neither Rachel nor Selena needed to say out loud what the other was thinking. If Katherine was outside in this, if she hadn't managed to take shelter, she'd be cold and wet and hypothermia would be setting in.

Fergus radioed them back fifteen minutes later. His visit to Shark and Johnny's house had been as fruitless as theirs to Seal's had been. Both men had vehemently denied having anything to do with Katherine's disappearance.

By the time they returned to Polochar Inn it was completely dark outside – as was the hotel.

'*Thighearna's a Dhia*,' Selena cursed, slamming her hand on the dashboard. 'That's all we need. The power going down.'

The barmaid met them at the door, wearing her coat and holding a battery-powered lamp.

'Oh, hello. Any luck finding that wee lass?' she asked, her eyes creased in concern.

'She's not back then?' Rachel's heart sank.

'No. We've searched the hotel just in case. She's definitely not here. Her mother is in her room, poor soul. She keeps trying to get her daughter on the phone but of course all the networks are down. I'm glad I'm not in her shoes. I'm praying her daughter has had the sense to take shelter in someone's house or a byre. With the phones and networks being down, maybe they can't get through. I've told all the customers in the bar to go home. I don't want them holed up here because they can't get away. I also want to get home before the storm reaches its peak. I'd advise you to do the same.'

'We'll check the hotel grounds first,' Selena said. 'But off you go.'

Rachel and Selena plunged back into the storm and searched the area surrounding the inn, including the outbuildings. Rachel had forgotten how intense the darkness in Uist was. If you didn't have a powerful torch like the one Selena carried, the night was impenetrable – impossible to see your hand in front of your face, let alone the road, or a lochan. And Katherine only had the torch on her phone – supposing it hadn't run out of battery.

As much as Rachel and Selena wanted to, there was no way they could search the moors. They were too vast, too dangerous in current conditions. It was easy to get disorientated on a terrain like Uist where there were few features to get your bearings even in broad daylight, never mind under current conditions.

'It's no use,' Selena shouted into Rachel's ear, when part of a sheet of corrugated iron cartwheeled across the road, narrowly missing them. 'Let's hope that she's holed up somewhere. We'll give it another go as soon as it's light.'

'No. We've got to find her!' Rachel protested.

'Look, Rachel. We all want to find her, but it's not happening tonight. Believe me. Us staying out in this fucking weather isn't going to help Katherine one bit.'

As the wind swirled around them Rachel was forced to concede defeat. The police officer was right. The chance of them finding Katherine in this was zero.

'OK. You win. I'll stay with Olivia. Let you know if Katherine turns up.'

Selena squeezed her shoulder. 'I hope to God she does.'

THIRTY-TWO

MONDAY MORNING

Rachel woke with a jerk as the first rays of light poked through the curtains of the bedroom. At first she couldn't think where she was. Then she remembered. She'd spent the night in a chair in Olivia's bedroom.

Olivia was sitting by the window, her face as grey as the cement-coloured sky. It appeared Katherine hadn't returned.

'How are you doing?' Rachel asked softly, easing the kinks from her muscles and uncoiling herself from the chair.

'She's out there. On her own. Needing me,' Olivia whispered. 'What if she thinks I'm not coming for her? What if she's...' She didn't finish the sentence.

Rachel knelt in front of Olivia and took her cold hands in hers. 'She's young and she's strong. Perhaps she got lost – it's so dark out there – and she's taken shelter or is with someone and can't let you know. She'll be back. You just have to hold on.'

Olivia stood, shaking Rachel's hand away impatiently. 'I'm going to look for her. I can't just do nothing.'

'It would be better if you stayed here,' Rachel said. Although she knew if she were in Olivia's shoes she'd want to be out there too.

Olivia shoved her arms into the sleeves of her coat. 'Do what you want, but I'm going to find her.'

'Listen,' Rachel said, becoming aware something had changed. 'What can you hear?'

Olivia stood still. 'Not much.'

'That's just it. The wind's died down – the storm is retreating. Listen again. What else can you hear?'

Raised voices drifted up to them. Rachel crossed to the window and looked out. There were cars parked outside the hotel as far as the eye could see and more were arriving. People milled about in groups. Amongst them Rachel recognised Calum and Mike.

'I think we've got help. Come and see.'

Olivia hurried over. Rachel shot her a smile. 'Looks like the cavalry has arrived. C'mon. Let's join them.'

Everyone stopped talking as Rachel and Olivia came down the stairs. As they moved through the crowd, people reached across to Olivia and patted her on the arm, offering awkward words of sympathy and encouragement.

Mike and Calum came through the door, deep in conversation.

Calum strode towards them and Rachel waited for her heart to give a little blip. But all she felt was a pang of regret.

'Mrs Mowbury,' Calum said, all quiet assurance. 'These people are here to find your daughter. They've come from all over to help. They know this island like the backs of their hands. If anyone can find her, they can.'

Olivia clutched his sleeve. 'You should be out there, right now, looking. You're wasting time.'

'I promise you every person on this island is going to do whatever it takes to get your daughter back to you,' Mike said, holding Olivia's gaze. 'I'm going to use every resource I have at my disposal to help find her.'

'The people here are going to organise themselves into groups and search every inch of land,' Calum added.

'What about helicopters?' Rachel asked him. 'Won't they be able to see better?'

Calum looked uncomfortable. 'The search and rescue helicopter won't come out just yet. They want us to search the land first. As soon as the ferries can sail again the police will come with tracker dogs. If we still haven't found her after that, then they'll bring the 'copter.'

'Then let's just get started,' Olivia pleaded. 'The longer she's out there...'

The inn's barmaid brought a tray laden with sandwiches which she placed on the reception counter. 'Help yourself, folks. I'm doing flasks of tea and coffee too. I'll keep it coming as long as you need it.'

A strange, unfamiliar sensation tightened Rachel's throat and her eyes stung. She hoped she wouldn't start crying. The islanders might be a contrary bunch, but they cared enough to turn out en masse to help a woman they didn't know.

She touched Calum on the arm to get his attention. 'What would you like me to do?' she asked. He looked at her as if he couldn't quite place her, before giving her a distracted smile. 'You and Olivia must leave the search to the locals. They know the terrain much better and are far less likely to get into trouble. Plus, they'll know where and what to look for. I know Olivia wants to help, but she can do that best by staying here to coordinate the search.'

Olivia's lack of familiarity with the area wasn't the only reason for her to be discouraged from participating in the search. In the worst-case scenario, no one wanted the mother to be the one to find her daughter's body.

'We'll give her a map to mark off the areas we're going to

search. That way when more help arrives they won't have to go over the same ground,' Calum continued. He nodded in the direction of the barmaid. 'Maggie will keep an eye on her.'

What he said made sense. The search for Katherine was in the best hands possible, the experts and the locals. Rachel would only get in the way. It was time for her to turn her attention back to Ellen.

THIRTY-THREE

Despite everything, Katherine must have fallen asleep and while she was out of it the wind had died down a bit and the rain had slowed to a drizzle. But – her heart shuddered – the water was still rising. Now up to her hips. It had to be coming in from somewhere. The sea! That's why it tasted salty. Realising she was starting to hyperventilate again, she slowed her breath. She mustn't lose it. Not now when help was bound to be on its way. There was a glimmer of light coming in from above and daylight meant people would be searching for her. But she wasn't going to wait to be rescued.

She wriggled her feet, trying to force blood into them. To her surprise she could move them much more easily than before. The water must have loosened the tape binding her ankles. A few more minutes of wriggling and her feet were free from their binds. *See*, she told herself, *small steps. You can do this.* By digging her heels into the ground and a sort of shuffle against the wall with her back, she managed to raise herself onto her feet. She peered upwards. Her heart sank. Way above her head, the hole was covered by some sort of grid. There was no way she could haul herself up high enough to lift it, let alone squeeze her body through the opening. However, standing, the air was sweeter and she could breathe better. Perhaps if he came back for her she could... what? Pull him into the hole with her then crush him with the weight of her body?

The hopelessness of it all made her cry again. She allowed herself a few minutes before she forced the tears away. Crying blocked her nose, making it even more difficult to breathe; besides, it did nothing to help. Once her breathing was under control she took stock of her situation. She was sure the tape over her wrists was slacker.

At that moment she heard something over the sound of the wind. She held her breath, straining to hear. Was it him coming back for her? To make sure she was dead? Her heart jerked sickeningly.

'It has to be here somewhere,' a male voice she didn't recognise shouted. The wind had dropped just enough for her to make out the words.

'Did you check the bloody map?' a woman's voice responded.

Katherine tried to cry out but all that came out from behind her gag was a muffled sound.

She tried again, summoning every atom of energy she could muster, but it still wasn't enough.

'I think it's that way,' the woman called. 'I'm sure that's what we were told.' Her voice sounded louder. Could they be looking for her? Was this nightmare finally coming to an end?

'Don't be daft, woman. There's bugger all in that direction. And since when have you had a clue where you were going? You even get lost in Edinburgh.'

'We should have come to it by now. I don't get lost in Edinburgh, by the way. You're more likely to get lost than me. I have no problem asking for directions.'

'Then can't remember what the person said.'

Katherine stamped her legs on the ground, but the earth was too soft for her to make any noise. A dog barked. It sounded close.

'Come here, Buster,' the woman's voice called out. 'Damn it, Keith, we should put him on the lead. There are lambs about.'

The dog appeared at the opening above her. He started whining while scraping at the ground. Hope flared again. Surely the owners would come and see what he was up to? They would find her and everything would be OK. They would get her out of here, take her back to Mum and she would tell them what happened and they would arrest the bastard. Mum would be mad about the drugs, but when Katherine promised that she would never so much as smoke a cigarette as long as she lived, she would forgive her. From now on, she'd be a good girl, the perfect daughter.

'Buster!' the man's voice was impatient. 'Back here! Now!'

Katherine mewed behind her gag. No! They had to come after the dog.

'What's he doing?' the woman asked.

'He's probably seen a rabbit,' Keith said. 'C'mon, Buster.'

Buster looked Katherine in the eye. Then he turned his head towards the voices as if trying to make up his mind whether he should ignore his masters.

Stay here. Make them come for you. Don't listen to them, Katherine begged silently. After one more look over his shoulder, Buster barked and ran back to join his owners.

It wasn't over yet. Perhaps he was going to fetch them to show them his strange find. Lead them to her. She had to believe that.

'Put his collar on. If he goes after the sheep there'll be hell to pay,' Keith said. Their voices were moving further away.

And then Katherine couldn't hear anymore. Her only chance, and it had been snatched away. If there were people looking for her – and she knew her mother would make them – and they came across the couple with the dog, they would tell them that there was no one out here.

She was going to die here and there was nothing she could do about it.

THIRTY-FOUR

Once everyone, including Olivia, had been assigned a task, Rachel decided it was time for her to leave. As she was about to get in her car, Selena and Fergus pulled up in front of the inn.

Selena took Rachel aside. 'Fergus and I went to MacVicar's house this morning. Found him pissed as a fart. He hasn't been on a bender this bad for years! Dr Logan's going to look in on him. Hopefully he'll sober up by the time DI Du Toit gets back. Pray we've found Katherine by then too. Still no word from Roddy either. Fergus tried calling him several times.'

The two police constables and Rachel conferred briefly. They agreed that Fergus should help with the search while Selena returned to MacVicar's house to check on him and to make sure he was sobering up and looking as if he were in charge. According to Fergus, engineers would be out soon to start repairing the landlines, although they and the mobile networks were likely to remain down for some time yet.

Rachel badly needed to get out of her wrinkled clothes. 'I'm going back to the hotel for a quick shower and change. I'll go and see Chrissie and Duncan after that. See if they know why Roddy hasn't been in touch. Or where he is.'

Selena frowned. 'I don't like the thought of you challenging Roddy on your own. If he has anything to do with what's going on he could turn nasty. Go have your shower. After I've checked on MacVicar, Fergus and I will meet you at Tioran. We'll all go.'

It appeared they had a plan.

Having showered and changed in ten minutes flat, Rachel was just leaving her room when she came face to face with Rhoda. The younger woman was flushed, her eyes anxious.

'I need to talk to you. I've been trying to get hold of Selena but I can't get through to her phone,' she said.

'I'm in a bit of a hurry. Can it wait?'

Rhoda chewed her lower lip. 'Selena likes you, so I think we can trust you. I told Johnny he has to tell *someone*. He's worried he's going to get into trouble, but I told him he'll be in much, much worse trouble if he doesn't tell.'

'Where is Johnny now?' Rachel asked, finishing tucking her blouse into her jeans.

'In the bar.'

'Then let's go and hear what he has to say.'

Johnny was pacing the bar, as if ready to make a run for it. Rachel suggested they sit down at one of the tables.

'OK, Johnny,' she said, with what she hoped was a reassuring smile. 'What did you want to tell Selena?'

When he didn't reply, Rhoda nudged him. 'Go on! Tell her.'

'The other divers have been dealing drugs,' he blurted. 'I didn't think it had anything to do with anything, thought it was just dope, but now that girl Katherine has gone missing and they've gone...'

'Gone? What do you mean gone?'

'Left. Taken their stuff and one of Mike's boats.'

'Are you sure they're not out searching for Katherine?'

Johnny glanced helplessly at Rhoda, who nodded for him to continue.

'I overheard them talking. Seal was telling Shark that it was all over and they had to leave, but they had one more pickup to do before they could clear off for good.'

Rachel's heart thumped. 'When was this?'

'Last night. After you lot had been to see them.'

'Last night!' she echoed disbelievingly. 'And you waited until now to tell someone?' She levelled her voice, needing Johnny's cooperation. 'Does Mike know about the drugs?'

'I don't think so, else we wouldn't have had to pretend we were diving when they were picking up the drugs.'

'You were with them?'

Johnny was looking more miserable by the minute. 'Just once. After Pinocchio left, Mike wouldn't let them go out without a third diver so they had to take me. They had to tell me what was going on then.'

'And what was that?' Rachel asked.

When he continued to stare at his feet, Rhoda elbowed him in the ribs. 'Go on,' she ordered. 'You have to tell her everything.'

'Seal said the drugs were dropped at sea and marked by a buoy. Someone sent them the GPS coordinates. We went out there and dived for them. After we got them we'd do our regular work so Mike wouldn't suspect.'

'Did he say who this someone was?'

Johnny shook his head.

'What did the divers do with the drugs once they'd retrieved them?'

'I don't know. Honest! They didn't want me to know. Said it was bad enough having one blabbermouth in the team.'

'Pinocchio?'

Johnny nodded.

Were drugs the reason Rufus was murdered? Nothing to do

with Ellen. Was it possible there were two murderers on the island? At least one of whom wouldn't baulk at murdering again. Who and where were they?

'Do they have Katherine?'

'I don't know. Maybe. Seal was pissed off. He didn't want Pinocchio to have anything to do with her.'

Rachel frowned. 'What do you mean?'

He shuffled his feet. 'She came to a dance with him. Slipped out of the hotel when her mother was sleeping. Pinocchio picked her up at the side of the road. I was with him – driving. He was high on drugs. He boasted to her he could get her anything she wanted. He fancied her like mad and wanted her to think he was cool.'

Rachel's heart knocked against her ribs – instinct telling her they were getting close to the truth. 'Why didn't you tell us all this before?'

His expression turned belligerent. 'I wasn't going to drop Pinocchio in it when I didn't think it had anything to do with the woman who died, was I? And 'sides, I did tell you Pinocchio took that old lady to the Monachs, didn't I?'

Rachel fought the urge to shake him. 'Is there anything else you need to tell me?' she asked.

Johnny gave another forlorn shake of the head.

'You're going to have to repeat all this to Constables MacDonald and Campbell when they arrive. You must promise me you won't leave the hotel until then. Will you do that?'

Johnny nodded. Rachel believed him. His ties to the island were stronger than his loyalty to his fellow divers. Especially now they'd left.

'The constables shouldn't be long.' She turned to Rhoda. 'Do you know where I can find Michelle?' She might know where Seal was headed.

'Dunno. I haven't seen anyone today! It's like the Marie Celeste around here! You could try her room. Number three in the annexe.' She hooked her arm into Johnny's and led him away.

Rachel stood where she was, watching their retreating backs, trying to decide what to do first. She didn't know what was worse: Katherine injured and exposed to the elements, or the captive of a drug-smuggling gang who might have killed more than once and might well kill again.

She felt ill. Was all this her fault? Had her coming here, stumbling around, asking questions – as Mainwaring had so aptly put it, like some inept Miss Marple – led to Rufus's death? Was Katherine's life in danger because of her? She'd been so certain she'd been doing the right thing, seeking the truth for Ellen, but had it all been arrogance on her part? A pathetic, misguided attempt to assuage her guilt for not saving Mum?

She pushed the thoughts away. Beating herself up wasn't going to solve anything. She'd made a mess and it was up to her to put things right. Starting with finding Katherine.

As she reached Michelle and Mike's room, Rachel heard shouting. She knocked and, without waiting for a reply, walked straight in.

Michelle was sitting on the double bed, her face streaked with tears. Mike stood in front of his wife, fists clenched by his sides. He spun around to face Rachel. Michelle moaned softly and collapsed in on herself, wrapping her arms around her body and rocking.

'Do you know that Seal and Shark have buggered off with my bloody boat?' Mike demanded. 'I went looking for them to get them to help me search the sea, only to discover they'd gone.' He jabbed a finger in his wife's direction. 'She knew Seal was planning to go.' He turned back to Michelle. 'Why the fuck didn't you go with him?'

Michelle raised her tear-stained face. 'I wanted to, but he wouldn't let me. He said he'd come back for me.'

'You cow,' Mike said, taking a step towards her. 'You swore

to me there was nothing going on. And I was stupid enough to believe you.'

Michelle reached out a beseeching hand. 'It isn't what you think!'

Mike ignored his wife's hand. A terrible sadness crossed his features. 'They've been trafficking drugs,' he told Rachel softly. 'They've been using my boats, my gear, my bloody business to traffic drugs. Christ! And she knew about it.' He turned back to his wife. 'How could you, Michelle?'

'We needed the money. You know we did! We're in danger of losing everything we worked so hard for. I never meant for anyone to get hurt. Seal said it was only cannabis...' Michelle reached for her husband again but he backed away. She turned an imploring face to Rachel. 'I didn't know the girl was missing until you pitched up at Seal's house. I realised then she must have got caught up in what's going on.' She started crying again, wrenching sobs that shook her too-thin frame. Her husband made no move to comfort her.

'Tell me everything, Michelle,' Rachel said. 'Katherine's life might depend on it. Do they have her?'

'I don't know! But why would they take her? Seal said they had one more pickup to do as soon as the storm had passed and then they were going to disappear. He didn't say anything about the girl.' She took a shuddering breath. 'Even if he does have her, she'll be all right. He wouldn't hurt anyone.'

Rachel bit down the retort that rose to her lips. Now wasn't the time to remind Michelle that they were hurting thousands by dealing in drugs.

'They've been using the company's boats to retrieve the drugs off the coast, that's all I know,' Michelle rushed on. 'Seal said he can't believe no one has done it before.'

Maybe because on the whole people were good and decent.

'This pickup. Do you know where it's happening?'

Michelle shook her head. 'Just that it was out at sea.'

Rachel wasn't sure whether she believed her. 'What happens after they have the drugs?'

'They arrange for them to be transported to the mainland on the lorries that take the scallops. He said someone else does all that – the Main Man, he calls him. All Seal gets is a message about where to dive for the drugs, what time and where to leave them again until it's time for them to be transported to the mainland. That's all I know. I promise.'

Mike sat down on the bed and buried his head in his hands.

'Where does he store them?' Rachel continued.

'On the Monachs, or when they can't land there, the disused well at Ellen's house. At least I think that's where. I don't know for sure!'

Rachel groaned inwardly as pieces slotted into place. There was her connection. Ellen had been a customs officer before she'd been a librarian. That was the nugget of information that had been niggling away at the back of her mind. Ellen must have found the drugs or come across the divers either storing them on her property or retrieving them. She would have recognised instantly what she was seeing. Perhaps she'd challenged them and they'd killed her, dumping her body out at sea. It all fitted.

'The person in charge – the Main Man – do you know who he is?'

Michelle shook her head. 'Seal doesn't even know. Said he'd never met him. All his instructions came by text from a disposable phone.'

The Main Man could be anywhere – not necessarily even in the UK. But Rachel would put money on him knowing the Western Isles. In which case he was probably on the island. Or very close.

'OK, Michelle. When the police officers get here you're going to have to repeat that all over again, understand?'

Michelle nodded. 'What will happen to me?' she asked in a small voice.

'I don't know,' Rachel said. No point in lying. 'But it will help that you've told us everything. In the meantime, give me your mobile and don't go anywhere. Just pray that we find Katherine and that she's OK.'

Another thought struck her. 'Mike, could I have a word? In private.'

Like her room, theirs had patio doors leading into the garden. Outside, the force of the wind almost picked her off her feet. Mike took her by the elbow to ground her and pulled her around a corner where there was some shelter from the wind. Even so, she had to lean into Mike in order to make herself heard.

'Do you think the divers will risk a pickup tonight?'

'No, they're either long gone or anchored in a sheltered spot.'

'Any idea where?'

Mike gave a despairing shake of his head. 'There are hundreds of small bays and inlets along this coastline.'

'Maybe the coastguard could pick them up with heat-seeking equipment? I'll call Calum and find out.' She looked at her phone. 'Crap. Still no signal.'

'Doesn't matter. Calum's not the right person to ask. Your detective inspector will need to ask the RAF for help. Although they won't fly until the wind dies down.'

'When will that be?'

'Can't say for sure.'

'Best guess?'

'Sometime between now and sunrise.'

Rachel bit her lip in frustration. 'Can Seal and Shark dive in the dark?' she asked.

'They usually wouldn't. But they must know that as soon as the weather allows every vessel and 'copter available will be out looking for them. I suspect they'd rather take a chance and dive in the dark than risk being spotted, but if I were them, I'd be putting as much distance as possible between me and the islands.'

'They won't know for sure that we're on to them so they might risk hanging about until the storm blows itself out. Someone will need to keep an eye on Michelle. She might try and warn Seal.' She looked him in the eyes. 'Did you really know nothing about Michelle and Seal?'

Mike took a ragged breath. 'I suspected Michelle was seeing someone else, but when I challenged her, she got angry and denied it. Said I was just being paranoid. How could I have been so stupid? As for the fucking divers... If I get my hands on them, I'll throw them into the Minch myself.'

Almost as soon as they stepped back into the room there was a knock on the door and an exhausted looking Selena came in, looking as if she'd slept in her uniform.

She looked at Michelle and Mike in disgust. 'I'm not sure what the hell is going on, but at some point we are going to have to take a statement from you both.' Rhoda had clearly brought her up to speed. 'Please don't leave the hotel until we can arrange to do that.'

Rachel indicated to Selena that they should step into the corridor. They could see Mike and Michelle through a crack in the door. Michelle was crying; Mike was slumped in a chair.

'This doesn't look good for Katherine,' Selena said. 'The divers' disappearance and hers must be connected. Maybe they took her as some sort of insurance?'

'That's my suspicion – in which case hopefully they'll be motivated to look after her. It's also possible they're responsible for Ellen's and Rufus's deaths, so we shouldn't count on it.'

'How the hell are we going to find them?' Selena asked. Rachel had rarely seen her so downcast. 'What a cock-up. I guess there goes my transfer to the CID.'

'It's not your fault. You couldn't arrest them last night. Nor watch their house. But someone needs to get hold of the coast-guard. Get them out looking for the divers as soon as possible.'

Selena checked her phone. 'Still not working. Shit... I'll radio Fergus. Get him on to it.'

'It's still possible Katherine's disappearance has nothing to do with the divers,' Rachel said.

'Don't worry. The locals will keep looking for her until she's found.'

Neither said what they were both thinking. *Until she's found, dead or alive.*

'Any news re Sergeant MacVicar? I thought you were on your way to his house?'

'I was. Then I heard about the divers pissing off. My aunt, Rhoda's mum, waved me down to tell me.'

'The modern version of sending messages by smoke signal,' Rachel mused.

The two women grinned at each other, enjoying a moment's relief.

'Anyway, I thought I should come here,' Selena said, losing the smile. 'Check it out for myself.'

'How long before the inspector gets back?'

'No bloody idea. Christ! If I'm in trouble it's nothing compared to what Du Toit is going to do to MacSticker.' Selena eased the kinks from her shoulders. 'I'm so bloody knackered I could sleep standing up,' she said. 'Who would have thought that we had a drug-smuggling ring here and none of us knew a dicky bird about it. And that doesn't even include three murders. Un-fucking-believable.'

'Somebody should check the well at Ellen's place. In case the divers left any drugs there. Ditto the Monach Islands as soon as the weather permits.'

Selena smiled wryly. 'Pity there aren't half a dozen of us.'

Rachel thought for a moment. 'Look, no one is going

anywhere until the storm passes over. Why don't you ask Fergus to let Calum know what's happening, ask him to speak to the RAF search and rescue while you check out the well? Better do that before it gets dark. I'll go and see Duncan and Chrissie. There's always a chance Roddy might be back there.'

'Do you think that's wise? I thought we agreed to go together?'

'That was before we knew about the divers. I was wrong about Roddy. It doesn't look as if he has anything to do with the murders. Maybe he knows where the divers are. Perhaps he'll even help us find them.'

By the time Rachel arrived at Duncan's home, although it was still blowing a hooley, the wind and rain were definitely less vicious. However, driving along the rain and wind-lashed roads was still tortuously slow. It was different for Selena in her four by four with its flashing blue light helping to illuminate the way. Rachel had lost sight of the police vehicle before she'd even reached the main road. How long before the storm died down sufficiently to allow the ferries to sail with Du Toit and the cavalry on board? If Mike was right, that could be hours away. On the other hand, if the storm was on its way out, the divers – if they were hanging around – might seize the opportunity to retrieve their drugs and disappear. Nothing Rachel could do about either scenario. She had to accept that some things were out of her control.

She tapped on the door of Duncan and Chrissie's house and walked straight in. Chrissie was kneading dough at the kitchen table by the light of an oil lamp. She flipped her dough over and smiled sadly at Rachel.

'I was wondering when you'd come,' she said, in her soft island accent. 'I didn't think it would take so long.' She shaped the dough into a ball and, taking a rolling pin, set about flattening it.

The room was like a sauna compared to outside. A wave of exhaustion washed over Rachel. Right at that moment, she would have given anything to close her eyes. But then Chrissie's words sunk in.

'Why did you think I'd be back to see you?'

'Because when we told Sergeant MacVicar our story, we knew someone would come.'

Rachel was confused. She recalled the sergeant saying he'd speak to Chrissie and Duncan, but he'd never, as far as she knew, reported back that he had. Otherwise, Selena would have told Rachel.

'Would you mind telling it again? To me?' Rachel asked.

Chrissie placed the scones onto a skillet and set it on top of the stove. 'Why don't we go through to the sitting room? There's a fire on and Duncan is there. I think it's better if we both tell you.' She wiped her hands on a tea towel and indicated to Rachel to go in front of her.

Duncan was in the same chair he'd sat in when Rachel first met him, half-hidden in the flickering light from a couple of candles. His eyes were closed. There was no sign of Roddy.

From a tape recorder (Rachel had had no idea they still existed) a male voice was intoning the first line of a hymn, and then the congregation repeated the line in a soaring voice. Rachel had heard presenting before and it never failed to move her.

Chrissie took Rachel's jacket from her and hung it on the rail above the Rayburn.

'Suidh sios, a'ghaoil,' Duncan said. 'I'd get up but my bones ache so much it would take me a good five minutes.'

'Please don't.'

'What have you learned?' Chrissie asked, lowering herself into an armchair. 'What do you know?'

Rachel had no idea what Chrissie was talking about. 'I think it's better if you tell me whatever you think is most important,' Rachel replied. 'Quicker too.'

Chrissie turned a pleading face towards her brother. 'We have to tell her, Duncan,' she said. 'Things have gone too far.'

Duncan switched the tape recorder off. 'You have to realise what it was like here when we were young,' he began. 'One policeman covered the whole island at that time and he was one of the locals.'

'Sergeant MacVicar's father?'

'Yes. Sergeant Peter. Most of the time he'd be in the bar with the rest of us men. If he wasn't there, he'd be snoozing at the police station. Who could blame him? The most crime that ever happened here was the odd brawl. So, we got used to sorting things out ourselves. It was better that way.'

'A crow's parliament,' Rachel said, remembering what Michelle had told her. Registering their blank looks, she explained. 'It's when a flock of crows pass judgement on one of their own. If they decide it's guilty, they peck it to death.'

'Well, well, well,' Duncan said. 'Imagine that. I didn't know it myself.'

Chrissie folded her hands in her lap. 'I suppose you could say it was a bit like that here.'

'Anyway, our sister, Peggy, was born when our mother was getting on a bit. When I was twenty and Chrissie fifteen,' Duncan continued. 'Although Peggy was as pretty a girl as anyone had ever seen, she was never quite right in the head. Simple, we called it.'

Chrissie smiled. 'My mother knew there wasn't much point in sending her to school, so she let her stay at home. Peggy liked to run wild. She'd spend hours on the croft searching for rabbits or swimming or digging for cockles. Ach, no one really knew what she was doing, but she was happy and she was safe. Everyone would watch out for her. Or so we thought.'

The smile left her face and her eyes filled with pain. She looked at Duncan, who picked up the story. 'She didn't have boyfriends – didn't matter, either. She was fine at home with our mother. And when Mother died, we looked after her. Neither Chrissie nor I got married either, as it turned out, so it worked quite well.'

Chrissie sniffed the air and creaked to her feet. 'I'll just check my scones. I won't be long.'

Duncan waited until she'd left the room before continuing, 'I didn't get married because I never found a woman I wanted to settle down with, but my sister gave up her only chance because he didn't want the bother of Peggy. Chrissie never complained, never resented. She couldn't have loved Peggy more supposing she was her mother. She just got on with looking after her. She's a good woman, a decent woman. You should know that.'

'Please go on, Duncan,' Rachel said, her skin prickling. What the hell had Chrissie done?

'He was a powerful man in these parts – a man who thought he was above everyone, even the law. He liked young girls, there was always talk about that. Everyone knew he couldn't be trusted around children. Peggy looked younger than her years, almost like a child. She was only fourteen – a young, trusting fourteen – and was only beginning to develop up top. Why shouldn't she trust? She knew everyone on the island and everyone knew her and watched out for her. He was watching too. He saw Peggy running wild and he thought he could do what he liked with her. He thought she didn't matter. He thought none of us mattered. May God forgive him.' Duncan's eyes blazed with disgust. 'We found out later for certain that she wasn't his first. There had been other girls. Younger even than Peggy.'

'Who was the man?'

'Colin Stuart, Dr Stuart's husband. The Factor as we called him, he managed the North Uist Estate.'

Calum's father! A chill ran up her spine. She had a strong suspicion where this was leading. 'Peggy fell pregnant?'

Chrissie came back into the room in time to catch Duncan's last words. 'Aye. With Roddy. Poor girl didn't know what was happening to her body. She had no understanding that having sex could give you babies. He'd made her promise not to tell anyone what they'd been doing. To make sure she didn't, he warned her if she told anyone she would be damned forever in the sight of the church. That she would rot in hell. He was like a god to her. Of course, she believed him. When she realised she was going to have a child she assumed he would marry her – even though he was married already! But my Peggy didn't know that. He lied.' Chrissie's pale eyes glistened. 'She thought he'd be happy she was going to have a baby.' Her voice cracked. 'Peggy was out shearing the sheep when he came to see her. He always knew where to find her. Perhaps he saw she was pregnant, or maybe she told him. He laughed in her face. Told her she was mad thinking a man like him would marry someone like her. And if she knew what was good for her she'd keep her mouth shut. Told her if anyone found out she was going to have a baby they would send her away to a mental asylum and take the baby from her. He was a cruel, cruel man.'

Chrissie drew a shuddering breath. 'He came towards her. Maybe he wanted sex one last time, maybe he wanted to make sure she could never tell anyone. She had the sheep shears in her hand. It was an accident. I swear on my life, she didn't mean to kill him.'

Rachel knew she shouldn't be hearing this – not without someone with her to corroborate. But she needed to know the rest of the story. She leaned forward. 'What happened next?'

'Peggy came running down to the house, covered in blood,' Chrissie continued. 'She was incoherent. Kept babbling about how she'd killed him. I thought she was dreaming or mad. Duncan and I – we were much younger then, of course – we ran all the way up to the fank – the sheep pen. He was lying there. Dead. She must have got him in the heart with those shears.'

'Why didn't you go to the police?'

'We did. We telephoned the police station. Sergeant Peter and Dr Stuart came to the house. There was nothing the doctor could do for her husband. Didn't even seem to be all that surprised he'd been killed. Turned out she knew the kind of man her husband was – both she and Sergeant Peter.' She looked across at her brother. 'We didn't know it until that day, but Sergeant Peter was in love with the doctor and she was pregnant with his child.'

Rachel's mind raced as she struggled to connect the pieces. 'What happened to Peggy?'

Chrissie wiped her eyes with her sleeve. 'She died a couple of weeks after Roddy was born.'

'And the child Dr Stuart was pregnant with?'

'The coastguard,' Duncan said. 'Calum Stuart.'

Christ. It was like a punch to her solar plexus. That would make Calum and Sergeant MacVicar half-brothers. Did either of them know? Selena hadn't been kidding when she said everyone on the island was linked. The place had more than its share of secrets. But which ones were relevant?

'We agreed between us there was nothing to be gained in taking matters further,' Chrissie's voice broke into Rachel's thoughts.

'You decided to take the law into your own hands.'

'It was a way out for us all. What was the point of Peggy going to gaol? When she was about to deliver a child? All of us would have suffered. And for that devil? The world was a better place without him.'

Not only a way out for Chrissie and Duncan, but surely an answer to Dr Stuart's and Sergeant Peter's predicament. They had conspired to conceal a murder. Was *that* the secret Dr

Stuart had begged Rachel not to tell Calum? Had she intuited that Rachel would somehow discover it? As for Sergeant Peter... what had he been thinking?

'Then what happened?' Rachel asked.

'Between the four of us we got him in the boat, then Chrissie and I sailed for the Monachs. There was very little chance of anyone looking for him there. If anyone looked for him at all. It was a full moon that night and we could see perfectly. It meant we could be seen too, but we had to take that chance.'

'You buried Colin Stuart's body on the Monachs?'

'In one of the funny buildings that were there. We used to use it as a byre when we lived there but it kept filling up with sand. We thought it was the best place to bury him. We knew one day it would be completely covered with sand and machair. We didn't know very much about erosion then and never imagined a storm would come along and expose it again.'

So, the bone Ellen had found had belonged to a local – a well-connected local. Was her discovery of the body the real reason she'd been murdered? Nothing to do with the divers and drugs at all. Had Rachel's first theory, her first suspect, been right all along? In that case, had Roddy murdered Ellen? To protect Chrissie and Duncan. Her head ached as she tried to put the pieces together.

'Does Roddy know about this?' she asked.

Duncan glanced at Chrissie, who nodded to let him know she was happy for him to continue.

'He always thought of Chrissie as his mother. We told him when he was small that his father was dead and that we never knew much about him. When he was older he asked a few more questions but he never seemed that interested. But he knows everything now. When she came to see us, Ellen asked particularly about grave sites and whether we knew of anyone who had been buried on the Monachs. We realised straight away she had

most likely found a part of Colin Stuart. We also knew it
wouldn't be long before Ellen or someone else went out there
and found the rest of the remains.'

Duncan reached into his pocket for his pipe. 'The poor
woman was all excited. Thought she might have found a cemetery, maybe even a settlement of medieval monks' cells. She told
us if she was right, the Monach Islands would become as
famous as Scara Brae in Orkney – or Skellig Michael in
Ireland.' He tapped his pipe on the side of the stove to remove
the old tobacco. 'That would mean that there would be people
digging up the island and the whole sorry story would come
out.' He closed his eyes as he sucked on his unlit pipe. 'We
knew we had to tell Roddy the truth.'

'Did Roddy kill Ellen?' Rachel asked bluntly.

Chrissie threw up her arms in horror. 'No! No, indeed he
did not! He wouldn't do a thing like that. He only did what we
asked him to.' It was clear she believed what she said. 'We
needed him to move the remains before Ellen went back and
dug up the rest.' Chrissie sank back in her seat and sighed. 'But
before he could, Ellen's body washed up and you arrived with
all your questions.'

'At first we just asked Roddy to keep an eye on what you
and the police were doing.' Duncan took over from Chrissie.
'We're more isolated here, don't get the news the way we
used to.'

So she'd been right to feel herself watched. 'He killed that
crow and left it for me to find, didn't he?'

'It was only a bird,' Chrissie protested. 'Just a pest.
Everyone shoots them here. He only put it outside your door as
a warning because he wanted to frighten you into leaving. He
would never hurt another human being.'

Rachel wasn't so sure. 'If he wanted me to leave, why did he
offer to take me out to the Monachs?'

'Because when you didn't leave, didn't stop with your questions, he knew you'd persuade someone to take you there eventually. If anyone took you, he wanted it to be him.'

'To stop me finding the burial site?' Find a way of shutting her up if she did? When neither sibling replied, Rachel continued, 'What happened to the rest of the remains?'

Chrissie looked down at her hands. 'Roddy was in the process of lifting the bones when he saw a boat coming in. He panicked and chucked them into a sack. There's an old lighthouse out there on the smallest island – Shillay. The lighthouse has a small storage area in its base. He put them there as a temporary measure.' Ending up in a sack seemed a fitting end for the Factor.

'Where is Roddy now?'

'Now that's the thing. When he moved the remains to the lighthouse he found drugs in the store. Piles and piles of them wrapped in plastic. He didn't know what to do. If he told the police about the drugs before he got rid of the bones, then everything would come out – and he didn't want that to happen.'

Rachel struggled to work out what it all meant. Had Rufus been on the boat Roddy had seen approaching? Had Roddy killed the young diver because he'd seen what Roddy was up to? Was this how it was all linked? Ellen to the bones, the bones to Roddy, Roddy to Rufus?

Everything kept coming back to Roddy. Did he have something to do with Katherine's disappearance too?

'Did Roddy kill Rufus – the diver?' Rachel asked.

'I keep telling you he didn't kill anyone! He isn't capable,' Chrissie cried.

They were bound to think that.

'The worst thing he did was to go into that dead woman's house and look for her notebook,' Chrissie continued. 'He didn't know what she'd written about us, about that bone she'd found. He didn't find a notebook. It must have gone into the water with her.' Chrissie shook her head. 'He knows you think he killed Ellen. He also knows who really did. And he can prove it.'

'Who?'

'He wouldn't tell us. He said it would be dangerous, said it was safer for everyone if he talked to the inspector. Then the inspector left the island before he could.'

'Has he got Katherine?'

'The missing girl? No!' Chrissie said. 'Why in God's name would he have her?'

For the same reason Rachel had thought the divers might have her – as insurance. 'I need to know where Roddy is. You must tell me.'

Duncan glanced at the grandfather clock. 'He's down at Kallin harbour, waiting for the storm to die down and the tide to be right. Then he's going to the Monachs to get the proof of the drug trafficking. At the same time, he'll dispose of the rest of the bones in the sea. He knows that it won't be long before the police are all over the Monachs.'

Rachel got to her feet and grabbed her jacket from above the Rayburn.

'You told all this to Sergeant MacVicar? Everything? Including his father colluding in covering up the Factor's murder?'

'Yes! When he came to see us!'

Yet he hadn't said. He'd chosen to get pissed instead – most likely because of his father's involvement. Selena had said he'd worshipped him and Rachel knew only too well how the stench of someone else's disgrace could cling to those close to them. However, it in no way excused his behaviour.

'We told him everything – including how his father had helped. It was all a terrible shock, as you can imagine. Anyway, he promised he would deal with it, but he hasn't been near us since.'

Duncan shook his head. 'We can't wait around for him to do

something. When we heard about that diver being found, we knew things were getting out of hand. Someone else might get hurt. Ellen and the lad who died must have found out about the drugs or have been involved in some way. And we're frightened for Roddy. If he's caught getting rid of the remains he'll get into trouble. Maybe even worse trouble if the police catch him there with the drugs. They might think they belong to him. Or blame him for Ellen's death, or the diver's. Even if they catch the person really responsible, they might charge Roddy with helping to cover up the Factor's murder. It doesn't matter about us, we're old, but he still has his whole future ahead of him. We told him to leave things well alone. That it was up to God now whether the remains of the Factor were found, and up to the police to punish the people involved with the drugs, but he wouldn't listen.'

'Never mind all that now,' Chrissie interrupted. 'Someone has to watch out for Roddy! We can't get hold of Selena, or MacVicar. Constable Campbell is worse than useless. You're the only one left who can stop Roddy. Tell him we've told you everything so there's no use him going out there.'

Rachel thought rapidly. Did they really expect her to single-handedly take on drug smugglers and a potential murderer or murderers? She still wasn't convinced there wasn't more than one. But she had to do something. What if the last pickup the divers were referring to was from the lighthouse in Shillay? If so, it would probably be too late to intercept them by the time Du Toit and his team arrived. They needed the divers to get the name of the Main Man and without evidence of drug smuggling it would be difficult to get convictions for any of them – let alone tie them to the deaths of Ellen and Rufus.

Furthermore, if Roddy arrived there at the same time as the divers and tried to prevent them taking the drugs, it was bound to end badly. Worse still, Katherine could somehow be caught up in all of this. Acutely conscious of two pairs of eyes on her,

she checked her phone. Still no signal. No way to call Selena or
Fergus, no way to reach Du Toit, and Sergeant MacVicar was
out of action. She allowed herself a wry inward smile. It
appeared she was on her tod.

'Roddy will almost be there by now.'

Duncan shook his head. 'No. He won't be planning to leave
until the tide's right. It needs to be high enough to fill the channels...' He looked over to the grandfather clock on his left.
'Which is anytime now. His boat is at Kallin harbour.' He sat
upright. 'Look, maybe you can still catch him. Persuade him it's
pointless to go.'

Rachel put on her jacket. 'I'll try and stop him, but I'm
going to ring the police and the coastguard and get them to help
me.' The elderly siblings looked at her calmly, but even in the
dim light from the lamp Rachel could see the hope in their eyes.
She put as much reassurance as she could into her smile. 'I
won't let him get hurt, I promise.'

Rachel reversed out of the driveway, tyres spinning on the
gravel. Perhaps she'd get some reception on her phone further
along the road. Duncan had been right. The wind, although still
gusting, was nothing like it had been, and the rain was definitely
lighter. The storm was passing.

Jabbing fruitlessly at the phone, she flung it on the seat and
took the right turn towards the harbour. When she arrived, she
jumped out of the car.

At last! A piece of luck. Calum was there, in his RIB.
Calum could call in the Stornoway coastguard. If they all
worked together they might be able to find Katherine, stop the
divers retrieving their drugs and bring Roddy back safely. With
his height and muscled build Calum was more than a match for
the other man. Unless Roddy had his rifle with him. She hoped
to God not.

She clambered down the ladder and jumped into the RIB.

'What the hell?' Calum spun round. 'Where did you come from?'

'Have you seen Roddy? The fisherman? He lives on Grimsay?' She wondered if he knew that Sergeant MacVicar was his real father and the man he believed his father, actually Roddy's.

'Roddy? He was just here. I saw his boat leaving as I arrived. Why?'

'Fuck. We need to stop him. Is the RIB ready to go?'

'Yes. But, Rachel, it's still pretty rough out there. The storm is moving westwards. I'm not risking our lives. Unless,' he smiled grimly, 'you give me a good enough reason.'

She explained as succinctly as she could: what they'd learned about the divers and how she thought they might be on their way to the Monachs to retrieve drugs they'd stored there. That Roddy was going there too, and she was scared of what would happen if he and the divers clashed. She didn't tell Calum about the Factor's murder. There would be time for that when this was all over.

'Roddy also told Chrissie and Duncan he knows why Ellen was killed and where to find the evidence to prove it,' she continued. 'I also think there's a chance he – or the divers – have Katherine.'

Calum looked pale and drawn in the grey light, as if he couldn't believe what he was hearing.

'You can tell me the rest on the way.' He threw her a life jacket from the front of the boat. 'Put this on and hold tight. It's going to be bumpy.'

As he manoeuvred the boat away from the harbour, Rachel tried her mobile again. Damn. Still no signal. She wrote a text to Selena. *With Calum. Going after R who is trying to get to Monachs. Says he has evidence who killed Ellen. Divers might be going there too. I think either R or the divers might have Katherine. Send help as soon as you can.* Rachel pressed send. Hopefully the policewoman would get it at some point. And it wouldn't be too late.

Calum throttled the engine and manoeuvred the RIB out of the harbour, deftly avoiding the shifting fishing boats straining against their anchors. Rachel moved forward to stand next to him. The wind blasted her hair into her eyes and roared in her ears.

Calum kept glancing at a screen next to his steering wheel.

'This shows the depth,' he yelled across to her. 'And if there are any submerged rocks. But if the storm blows up again we might have to anchor somewhere and wait it out.'

'Do you have a radio? I still can't get a signal on my phone. We need to tell the police what's happening and get hold of Stornoway coastguard so they can liaise with the RAF.'

'Radio isn't working,' Calum said. 'I was trying to fix it when you arrived.'

Fuckity fuck.

'We might be able to get a signal on your phone when we get further out.' He held out his hand. 'Let me have it. I'll keep a watch on the bars. You concentrate on holding on.'

'How long until we get there?'

'Twenty to thirty minutes. Roddy can't be too far ahead of us. Those fishing boats only do about eight knots an hour. This RIB can do three to four times that. Do you know what proof he has about the drugs?'

'Apparently he found them when he moved the rest of the skeleton Ellen found. Don't ask – it's a story for another time.' And possibly for someone else to tell him. 'He moved the bones to the lighthouse. That's where he found the drugs. Says he knows who put them there.'

Calum shot her a look from over his shoulder. 'The lighthouse on Shillay? Fuck! Of course it has to be. There's only one.'

'Why? What's the matter?'

Calum concentrated on steering the RIB over a particularly high wave. He waited until they'd crashed down on the other side before answering her question. 'They build lighthouses where there's rocks, so we'll have to land a bit away and walk to Shillay.'

'In that case, so will Roddy.'

Calum muttered something Rachel couldn't catch. He gunned the boat forward, the upward surge almost causing Rachel to lose her footing. She stumbled and grabbed onto one of the rope handles on the side of the boat, but not quick enough to stop herself from falling on her backside. Something hard underneath her bottom made her cry out in pain. Calum didn't even glance her way. Perhaps he hadn't heard her yelp above the roar of the engine? Maybe she would be better off staying on the floor of the boat. It was less windy and more comfortable. If she could get rid of whatever was jabbing into her bum.

Lifting her bottom, she felt underneath her. Whatever it was, was covered by some sort of sacking. She tugged and, as she did, a piece of the cloth came away. Curious, she peeled a little more until she revealed something hard and made of metal. She recognised it at once. It was the barrel of a shotgun. She glanced at Calum's back but he was too intent on steering the boat. Quickly she wrapped the cloth back around the gun. What was Calum doing with it on his boat? It was one thing him carrying it around the estate when he was working; quite another having it on board and concealing it.

She should ask him. She would ask him.

Perhaps he went out in his boat to shoot cormorants? Angus John had said they were considered a delicacy on the island. That had to be it. She was just overexcited. All the same, she wished the gun wasn't on the boat.

Using the handles on the side of the RIB, she hauled herself to her feet.

Now they were further out the sea was rougher, the waves higher. Her stomach rose and dipped every time they crested a wave and came banging down the other side. Seawater and spume shot over the side of the boat. For the second time in twenty-four hours she was soaked to her skin.

'How much further?' she yelled into the wind. The clouds were clearing but sunset wasn't far away.

Calum pointed a finger and in the gathering dusk Rachel could just make out the silhouette of land.

'Another five minutes. I'm going to reduce our speed and go in quietly. He's unlikely to hear the engine of our boat over the storm but I don't want to take any chances.'

He pulled back on the throttle and the boat slowed. As they drew closer, Rachel caught sight of Roddy's boat, anchored a little way out from the shore where they had landed the last time they'd been here. There was no sign of anyone on board. Or of another boat. She wasn't sure if she was relieved or disappointed. Either Seal and Shark had been and gone or were waiting for the weather to improve. She wished she had a pair of binoculars.

Seemingly reading her mind, Calum stooped and fumbled around in a bag by his feet. 'Here,' he said, handing her a pair. 'See if you can spot Roddy. I suspect he's already waded ashore. If he wants to get back on his boat before the tide comes in, he'll have to be quick. So will we. We have no more than an hour at the most.'

'Try my mobile again,' Rachel said, raising the binoculars and squinting.

There was definitely no one on the fishing boat. And as far as she could tell, no one wading to the shore. He must be on the island already and further in.

'Still no signal,' Calum told her, dropping anchor. 'You stay here. I'll go and see what he's up to.'

'No way. I'm coming too.'

Calum frowned. 'That's not a good idea. It could be dangerous.'

She almost smiled. He hadn't a clue. 'This is my gig, so to speak, Calum. Where I come from women don't sit by the hearth waiting for the menfolk to do battle.'

'Don't say I didn't warn you,' he replied, although he still looked unhappy. 'Just don't do anything crazy.'

THIRTY-SIX

MONDAY 6.50 P.M.

Selena tripped over a rock and swore out loud. Although the wind had died down there were still sporadic breath-stealing, body-rocking gusts and the thick black clouds made it seem later than it was. Even so, it'd be dark soon enough.

She crested the hill and Ellen's cottage came into view. A line of crows sat on the telegraph wire watching her progress. They'd better not try and fly at her. She wasn't in the mood. She was too damn exhausted and furious.

She'd been torn between going to get Sergeant MacVicar and keeping an eye on Michelle, Mike and Johnny. In the end, she'd decided to leave both jobs to Fergus while she searched the well on Ellen's croft. The locals were perfectly able to continue searching for Katherine on their own. On the off-chance there were still drugs stored in the well – and she hoped to hell there would be, something had to go right in this whole sorry mess – they'd need to be secured, photographed and logged as soon as possible. Thank God, Du Toit and his team had finally left port on the ferry and would be back on Uist in a couple of hours. If, by the time he arrived, Fergus had located Sergeant MacVicar and between them they'd actual evidence of the drug-smuggling ring, it might go some way to alleviate Du Toit's ire.

The bones were still outside Ellen's house when she reached it. God knew what else behind the now padlocked door. Feeling as if she were being watched she whirled around. Jesus, someone could be right behind her and she'd never hear them over this damned wind. She was suddenly conscious that she was alone – a long way from help. If the divers hadn't already removed the drugs they might be on their way to do so, and she had no desire to come face to face with men who were very likely guilty of murder. Perhaps she should have waited until another police officer could have accompanied her? But damn it! This was her chance to impress after all the fuck-ups and she wasn't going to waste it. The support of Inspector Du Toit might be her only chance of transferring to CID.

She searched the croft for the well, spotting it halfway between the house and the shore. She hurried over. The sooner she got out here the better. A grid had been placed over the well. She crouched down and examined it more closely. A faint moan came from the gloom and she spun around, her heart lodged in her throat. The moan came again but now it seemed to be coming from the well.

Her heart pounding against her ribs, she shone her torch between the bars of the grid and yelped as enormous eyes in a mud-streaked face stared up at her.

'Katherine? What the f...! Is that you?' The girl shook her head from side to side then up and down. Her mouth was covered by what looked like duct tape.

She was alive! For now at least. She was bound to be cold and wet. Maybe hypothermic. Possibly injured too. Selena shot another glance over her shoulder. Whoever had put her there could come back to check on her at any moment. But Selena had to stay calm for the teenager's sake.

'It's all right, Katherine. I'm a police officer,' Selena called down, keeping her voice level. 'You're safe now. I'll have you out in a sec.'

She straddled the iron grid, squatted and braced before tugging hard. When it shifted she sent a silent prayer of thanks for all the hours she put in at the gym. Another huge effort and she had it off. Dumping it to one side, she directed the beam of her torch into the darkness.

'Are you OK? Are you hurt?' she asked.

Katherine looked up at her helplessly.

Twat, Selena scolded herself. *Clearly the poor girl couldn't answer.*

The hair on the back of Selena's neck prickled. She glanced behind her. No one there – only a single, enormous crow on the cottage roof. It flapped its wings and cawed as if acknowledging her presence – or warning her off. Harbinger of death or not, it gave her the effing creeps.

Selena turned her attention back to Katherine. The bottom of the well was at least three metres down. There was no way the girl could climb out unaided, and no way Selena could get her out. Not by herself.

'Look,' she told the girl. 'I'm going to need to fetch help to get you out.'

But she couldn't get a signal on her phone, nor anyone on her radio. What the fuck were MacSticker and Fergus up to? Fergus had nothing to do but keep an eye on a couple of people while Sergeant MacVicar should have sobered up by now.

She blew out her cheeks in exasperation. She wasn't going to park her backside here until either man deigned to answer. Neither could she leave Katherine alone while she went for help. There was always a chance whoever had put her here would come back.

She shot a quick glance over her shoulder. If they were coming, she had no chance of hearing them over the sound of wind and rain, almost no chance of seeing them in the gathering gloom. Every instinct in her body screamed to get away. But she couldn't bolt. She was a police officer, sworn to help and protect.

Neither could she keep a lookout and deal with Katherine at the same time.

She rearranged her features into her best 'I know what I'm doing' look and turned her attention back to Katherine.

Shit. The water was definitely getting higher. Probably seawater from the higher than usual tide, pushed even higher by the gale. She didn't know if it was still coming in. She had to act as if it was.

'I can't lift you out, Katherine. Any chance you could climb?'

Katherine shook her head, holding out her bound hands.

Of course she couldn't climb out!

'Katherine, I'm going to find something to make a rope. I'll be back as soon as I can, OK?'

Katherine stared up at her for a long moment before nodding.

Selena ran back to Ellen's house. There was bound to be a sheet or blanket she could fashion into a rope. But as she approached, she spotted the enormous padlock along with steel panels that had been used to seal the cottage door until forensics had a look. The windows were boarded up too. She groaned. Whoever had done the work had made damn sure no one was getting inside. There was almost always a byre with this age of house. She found what remained of it in a dip nearby. It was doorless and only partially roofed but in her experience lengths of rope were often retrieved by the older islanders and stored where they might yet be of use to someone.

She gave a whoop of triumph when she realised she'd been right. Inside the ruined byre, amongst old creels, a car bumper, an old sink and even a discarded Rayburn protected from the elements by a sheet of corrugated iron, Selena unearthed a coil of blue rope. It was heavy but, filled with adrenaline, Selena found herself back at the lip of the well, rope over her shoulder, with almost no recollection of how she got there.

'It's all good, Katherine,' she shouted down to the waiting girl. Crap, the tide was definitely coming in. The water was now up to Katherine's waist. 'You're going to be out of there in a jiffy. I'm going to throw you down a rope.' *Bugger.* That wasn't going to work. How was Katherine going to tie it around herself when her hands were taped? Selena would have to take it down to her. A quick look around only told her what she already knew. There were almost no trees on the island, and certainly none on Ellen's croft where she could anchor the rope.

'Get me out of here! Please! Hurry! I don't want to drown.' The voice came from the well.

'How the hell...?' Selena shone her torch at Katherine. Somehow she'd managed to loosen the tape binding her wrists as well as the gag covering her mouth.

'The water loosened the bindings on my feet, so it came to me I could do the same if I submerged my wrists. It worked! I should have thought of it hours ago! I'm so stupid.'

'You are so not stupid. You are brave and resourceful, you hear me? Now I'm going to throw down the rope. Tie it under your arms. But you're still going to have to help me, OK?'

Katherine nodded. As the girl struggled to tie the rope, Selena dashed the rain from her eyes and looked around. Daylight was failing – and that was exactly the right word – the roof of the cottage melting into the gloom. She couldn't hear or see anyone but that didn't mean they weren't there.

It took several long minutes before Katherine was able to tie the rope and give Selena a thumbs up. Selena's own fingers were so numb it took her almost as long to secure the other end of the rope around her own waist.

If Katherine's weight pulled her into the well God knew

what would happen to them both. She took a steadying breath and braced.

'OK, let's do this,' she called down.

Determined eyes latched onto Selena's. Katherine pushed her back into the wall before lifting one foot and then another on to the wall on the opposite side. Painfully slowly, grunting with the effort, using her elbows as well as her feet, she inched upwards.

'That's it, Katherine,' Selena encouraged. 'You're doing great. Come on, not too far now.'

As soon as she was near to the top Selena reached in and caught her under the armpits. With one final heave and with Katherine helping, Selena hauled the teenager out and onto the ground where they sprawled, arms wrapped around each other, catching their breath.

'I did it!' Katherine cried. 'I didn't think I could but I did. I'm alive! He thought he'd won but he was wrong. Dead wrong.'

Selena desperately wanted to know who *he* was. But first she needed to make sure Katherine was OK. She helped the teenager to her feet and took her jacket off to wrap it around the blue-lipped girl. They couldn't afford to relax. The divers, or whoever had put Katherine in the well, could appear at any time.

'We need to get you somewhere warm,' Selena said urgently. 'Do you think you can walk? It's nearly two kilometres to my car.'

'I think so. I'm not staying here, that's for sure.' Katherine's voice shook. Her bravado had disappeared. 'Where's my Mum?'

'I'll call her. She'll be hugely relieved to know we've found you. She's been out of her mind with worry.'

Knowing messages would send as soon as her phone logged on to a network, she sent a group text to Olivia, Du Toit, Fergus and Rachel, letting them know she'd found Katherine safe and unharmed.

'Was there anything in the well?' Selena asked. 'Packages, blocks wrapped in polythene? Anything?'

'Not that I saw.'

Using the beam of her torch, Selena checked the well. To her disappointment, if there had been any drugs there they were long gone. When she was done, she looped Katherine's arm across her shoulders and placed her arm around Katherine's waist, taking most of the exhausted teenager's weight.

'Any idea who did this to you?' Selena asked.

'No. I've never seen him before. He said he was taking me to Pinocchio. Then he stabbed me in the leg with a needle.' Katherine's voice was filled with indignation. She paused to suck in a breath. 'When I came round, I didn't know where I was, only that it was dark and wet and I could hardly move.' A shudder ran through her slender frame.

'What did he look like?'

'He was tall. His hair was blond. He spoke in a posh English accent.'

Selena's heart stood still. It couldn't be who she thought it was, could it?

Rachel rolled up her trousers and slipped off her shoes and socks before following Calum over the side of the RIB. The freezing water, black and swirling, made her gasp. Night had fallen in the time it had taken to anchor the boat and the rain fell in relentless sheets, the wind slapping it into Rachel's face. On the plus side the wind kept the clouds skidding across a full moon, periodically illuminating a path of silver in front of them. They only had one torch between them and Calum was holding it.

Rachel kept her eyes fixed on his back until finally they were on the shore.

'How do we get to the lighthouse?' she panted through chattering teeth. 'And what the hell are we going to do when we get there?'

Calum raised his rifle, broke the stock and peered down the barrel. Rachel backed away, holding up her hands, palms out in front of her. 'Whoa there, cowboy! Careful with that.' She hadn't realised he'd brought it with him.

'I'm not going to use it,' he said. 'But he won't know that.'

This was so not the scenario Rachel had anticipated. In this dark and desolate place, she was beginning to think she'd made a mistake. She was out of her depth in more ways than one. She should have waited until either Selena or Fergus could have come with her. She shivered again, and this time it wasn't from the cold. Fuck it. She was here now. Nothing else for it but to follow through.

Her legs were heavy in her saturated jeans as she clambered after Calum up a small rise and onto land. When she'd last been here the narrow strip of land separating the larger island from the smaller one had been exposed for a short time. If Calum was correct about the tide, they only had a brief window in which to cross and get back again.

The ruins of the houses were silhouetted against the sky and Rachel had the uneasy sensation of the ghosts of the people who had lived and died here watching them. On her previous visit the remoteness of the island had seemed romantic, until she'd found the body of the diver. Now she was acutely aware of how cut off from the rest of the world it was. She, Calum and Roddy could be the last people on earth.

It took her and Calum five minutes to cross the moor to the narrow fjord. As Calum had predicted, it was uncovered. Rachel hoped the sand would be solid underfoot.

Calum turned to her. 'Why don't you stay on this side, shelter in the house?' He swept his hand in the direction of the house they had drunk their coffee in – could it really only be two days ago?

Rachel shook her head. A: she was so not going to cower somewhere like a damsel in distress and B: there should be two people to witness whatever it was that Roddy was up to. Still carrying her shoes, she stepped onto the sand. It seemed solid enough. Calum strode beside her, keeping the rifle across his chest as if he were in the bloody SAS. She wished like hell he'd left it on the boat.

The lighthouse was a giant, solitary sentinel in the darkness.

The moon broke through the clouds and for a second she saw a figure dragging a box out of the door of the lighthouse.

She grabbed at Calum's arm and he stooped so that his ear was close to her mouth.

'I think I see Roddy,' she said. 'Over there.'

Calum's gaze followed the direction of her pointing finger. 'Christ!' he shouted, starting to run towards Roddy, leaving Rachel to follow as best she could. He had the torch, his legs were longer and he was more used to the terrain; as the moon dipped behind the clouds again, she lost sight of him.

The wind was blowing so hard, it was as if she had to push against a wall in order to take a single step. The clouds cleared once more. Roddy – it was definitely him – was by the shore edge. He had opened the box, his arm making throwing movements into the wind. Calum continued running towards him, shouting words that were impossible for Rachel to make out.

She kept going towards them, crying out when she stepped on something sharp. She should have stopped to put her shoes back on. There was no time now.

Within seconds she was close enough to make out two shadowy shapes in the shifting light. Calum was shoving Roddy away from the opened box.

'For God's sake! Stop!' Calum bellowed. The rest of his words were lost in the wind.

'You're the devil,' Roddy shouted back in Gaelic. 'Bringing this stuff here. Killing the young folk. Well, you won't be having this.' His hand swept into an arc and a trail of dust was swept away with the wind.

Rachel froze. What did Roddy mean? Had she understood correctly?

Before she could move, Calum raised his rifle to his shoulder.

'Stop, or I'll fucking shoot.'

'Jesus, Calum! What the hell! Put the gun down,' Rachel

yelled, still trying to process what was happening. It struck her in a flash of blinding clarity. Calum knew about the drugs. And there was only one way that was possible. Her throat dried. She remembered the CCTV; the telescope pointing out to sea; Calum's reluctance to take them here. How could she have been such a fool?

'You,' Rachel cried. 'You were behind it all.' There was no point pretending she hadn't grasped the truth. 'God, Calum. Why?'

Calum turned to face her, keeping the gun pointing at Roddy. 'Money, of course.' He stretched his lips, baring his teeth like a wild animal. 'Do you think I live on this godforsaken place for fun? Just one more run and I was going to get out of here.' His eyes seemed to glitter in the shifting light. 'Hey! You could come too. I've a place in the Caribbean. All ready and waiting. No one will ever know.'

'Roddy knows.'

'Roddy isn't going to tell anyone.'

'He's part of your family, Calum,' Rachel said, taking a step forward.

Calum lowered his gun, a nasty smile on his face. 'No he's not. Mother confessed her sordid secrets earlier. She wanted me to know it all before it became public knowledge.' His lip curled. 'Old Sergeant Peter went to see her. His son had discovered the truth – the whole shooting match. Who could have imagined what folk got up to here back then? Naughty, naughty, devils. I wonder how many other dirty secrets there are?'

Roddy had stood, unmoving, while Calum spoke. Then in one swift movement he bent and upended the box.

Calum raised his rifle to his shoulder and pointed it at Roddy. 'For God's sake. Will you stop?' The other man didn't so much as glance his way.

'Don't hurt him, Calum,' Rachel pleaded.

Calum's answer was to click off the safety catch.

Rachel flung herself at him, but she wasn't quick enough to stop him pulling the trigger. The bullet hit Roddy and spun him around. Almost in slow motion, he crumpled to the ground.

Time froze as she absorbed the scene: the rain-lashed land; Roddy face down and motionless, his wispy hair blowing in the wind; Calum lowering his rifle...

Then energy surged through her, catapulting her forward. She ran to Roddy and crouched at his side. Blood soaked the back of his shirt, mixing with the rain, running in rivulets into the sand. She couldn't feel a pulse.

'You've killed him,' she screamed into the wind.

Calum swung his gun in her direction.

Without conscious thought, Rachel was on her feet, bolting back towards the boat. She had to get help. But how? She'd given Calum her mobile. Played into his hands.

Her breath came in short, painful rasps as she negotiated the uneven terrain, straining to see in the shifting light. The moon, appearing in bursts, was both her friend and her enemy, helpfully lighting her path but at the same time making her visible to Calum. She had no option but to plunge on. How long did she have? Minutes? Seconds?

She risked a quick look behind her. She couldn't see him. Perhaps he was checking to see if Roddy had destroyed all the drugs? After all, time was on Calum's side. She increased her pace. If she could get to the RIB maybe she could lift the anchor, call for help on the radio. She had to believe it wasn't broken, that Calum had lied, that it was another ruse to stop her contacting the police.

'Come back, Rachel.' Her breath caught on a sob as his voice came behind her. 'I won't hurt you. I promise. We can work this out.'

Rachel kept running. Did he think she was stupid? He was

never going to let her go when she'd witnessed him kill Roddy as coldly and clinically as he'd shoot a rabbit.

She reached the edge of Shillay. The tide was coming in fast, almost covering the strip of sand between the two islands. If it rose before Calum reached it, it would delay him and she might have a chance. Moving as fast as the sucking sand and swirling water allowed, she crossed to the other side.

Clouds covered the moon again, plunging her into darkness. She forced herself on. Every extra minute gained might make the difference between living and dying.

An unseen rock brought her headlong flight to an abrupt end. She landed face down on the machair, winded. She rolled over and felt her ankle. It was already swelling under her fingers. It was hopeless. Maybe Calum *would* let her go? She closed her eyes, feeling the tears squeeze between her lids. She thought of her mother, Ellen, Rufus... all dead because it suited someone else's purpose, as if they didn't matter. Hot, red anger surged through her.

Fuck that. Fuck Calum. No way was she giving up now. No way she was giving up ever. Not as long as she had breath in her body. She hauled herself to her feet, gritting her teeth as pain shot through her ankle as she put weight on it. She needed to buy time. Selena would have got her text. The police would come looking. If she could find somewhere to hide until they did, she might have a chance. Gritting her teeth, she forced herself on.

But where to hide? The ruins of the houses were too obvious – the first place he'd look.

It came to her. The monk's cell! Calum knew about it, but it might not occur to him to look for her there – at least not until he'd searched everywhere else. It was a faint chance but the only one she had. She veered towards it, sending a prayer of thanks upwards as the clouds covered the moon again.

The darkness disoriented her. Where was the cell? She

pictured its position in her head. It had been about fifty metres from the restored house, around forty-five degrees west and close to the shore.

Ignoring the pain in her ankle, she sprinted in the direction where she hoped it was. Suddenly she was upon it. Fuck. She'd forgotten it was covered with a tarpaulin. Perhaps that was a blessing in disguise. She lifted the edge of the heavy cloth.

'Rachel! This is nuts! Please, let's talk.' She froze in horror as his voice came from behind her. He couldn't be more than a few metres away. She prayed that the moon would stay hidden for a few seconds longer.

She dropped to her stomach and slithered under the tarpaulin, working her way towards where she prayed the entrance to the cell was.

To her relief she found it first go. She squeezed through the gap, gagging as the smell of rotten vegetation and decomposing flesh hit her. Wriggling as far away from the mouth of the cell as she could get, she brought her knees to her chest and clutched them hard against her to stop them shaking. Slowly, her breath steadied. She had a chance. Maybe Calum would give up searching for her and head off, taking his drugs with him. Eventually someone would come. All she could do now was wait.

After Selena had delivered Katherine to the care of her very relieved mother, she radioed Fergus and explained briefly what she suspected: that Calum was the Main Man involved in the drug-trafficking ring, and that she was on her way to his house and needed Fergus to meet her there.

She hadn't been able to get a hold of Rachel or Du Toit. Neither was answering their phone.

With the help of her siren and blue light, she made the trip in under forty minutes. Once more, she had to hoof it across the moors to reach her destination. She'd never been inside Calum's house, but had walked past it several times. There was a single light coming from one of the rooms on the top floor, but no sign of Calum's car. He was probably long gone. Nevertheless, she had to make sure.

Selena knocked at the door and rang the bell, but no one answered. She didn't have a warrant to enter uninvited. Glancing up, she noted the CCTV cameras. How come she'd never noticed them before? Suddenly, the door was flung open by Sergeant MacVicar. His hair looked as if it hadn't been brushed in a while, his shirt collar was unbuttoned, and there was a splodge of what looked like tomato sauce on the knee of his trousers. But it was the wild look in his red-rimmed eyes that worried Selena most.

'You're too late,' he said, rocking on his feet and reeking of stale booze. 'Dr Stuart and her son are gone. Him to hell, I hope.'

Selena squeezed past him, ran up the stairs and into the room from which the light had been shining. Her phone pinged with an incoming message, but she ignored it.

Dr Stuart was slumped in an armchair, a small brown bottle nestled in her upturned half-open hand. Loach's chin was on her feet, his sad, brown eyes fixed on her face.

'No need to feel for a pulse,' MacVicar slurred from behind Selena. Fuck's sake. He was obviously still as pissed as a wasp in a can of lager.

Ignoring him, she placed her fingertips on the side of the old lady's neck. Nothing. She checked Dr Stuart's pupils. Fixed and dilated. Several white pills lay scattered on the side table and floor.

'Did Calum give them to her?'

MacVicar shrugged. 'I don't know. She was dead when I got here.' He looked scared and bewildered in equal measure. She suppressed a pang of sympathy. He'd totally fucked up. Lost all right to her respect.

'Why are you here? Where is Calum? Do you know?'

He stared back at her with unfocused eyes. 'She had an affair with my father. Did you know that?'

Selena said nothing. She'd heard rumours to that effect.

'The DNA result came back on the bone.' He hiccupped. 'It matched the DNA on Roddy's cigarette end. Father and son. How do you like that? The Factor fathered Roddy. I went to see Chrissie and Duncan. They told me everything. My father – the great policeman.' He opened his arms wide as if addressing an audience. 'My hero, screwing around with the upright doctor, and helping Chrissie and Duncan cover up a murder!' His arms dropped to his side and he swayed on his feet. 'How the hell is that going to make me look?'

Selena didn't give a toss. Not her problem. And certainly not a priority at this moment. She yanked her phone from her pocket. 'We need to let Du Toit know what's going on.' Before she could dial the number, she noticed that the message that had pinged earlier was from Rachel.

It had been sent an hour ago: *With Calum. Going after R who is trying to get to Monachs... Send help as soon as you can.*

Dear God.

Selena looked at MacVicar. He was worse than useless. No help at all.

She called Fergus on the radio. To her relief, he answered straight away.

'Fergus. Where the hell are you?' she demanded. He should have been here a while ago.

Wind muffled his reply.

'Look, never mind. You're going to have to get your boat and go to the Monachs. Rachel is out there with Calum Stuart. If I'm right about him being the head of the drug ring then she's in danger. I'll explain later. I'll get in touch with Stornoway Coastguard and alert them too, but we can't afford to wait for them. You have to go after them. Now!'

This time, Fergus didn't argue about using his boat for police business. Selena only hoped he wouldn't be too late. First, she had to phone Dr Logan. She dragged her hand through her hair. When she'd told Rachel she wanted something exciting to happen, she hadn't meant this.

Rachel sensed him before she heard him; the impact of his boots vibrating the soft, boggy ground.

'I'm not going anywhere without you, Rachel,' he shouted. 'Why don't you talk to me? I can explain everything.'

He was crazy if he thought he could explain himself out of any of this. He'd murdered Roddy with as little compunction as he'd shoot a bird. Most likely Ellen and Rufus too. In one respect Rachel had been right. Ellen coming here and finding the bones had led to her death. But not at the hands of Roddy. Calum had more reason than anyone to keep people away from the island.

Rain pattered on the tarpaulin.

She thrust her shaking hands into her pockets. As she did, her fingertips brushed against a familiar shape. Her gutting knife. She curled her fingers around the smooth, comforting hardness of its handle. She wasn't totally defenceless.

Her heart leapt to her throat when she heard the sound of the tarpaulin being ripped away.

He shone his torch into her eyes, blinding her. 'I never told you I knew this place like the back of my hand, did I? Mea culpa. This is where I would have hidden. There's nowhere else.' He lowered the beam of the torch, held out his hand and beckoned with his finger. 'Why don't you come out? We can be comfortable while we talk.'

Rachel knew she was beaten. If she didn't do what he asked, she wouldn't put it past him to shoot her right where she was. If she were going to die, it wouldn't be without a fight, cowering like a trapped animal. She unkinked her limbs, forcing blood back to her extremities.

'OK,' she said. 'But only if I can ask you some things.'

'Sure. Anything you like. Can't promise to answer though.'

She emerged to find him in front of her, squatting on his heels, his gun resting in the crook of his arm, the torch on the ground, its beam angled slightly away. As the rain stopped and the clouds scudded away she saw his face lit by the moonlight, the steel in his eyes, the rigidity to his jaw. What she didn't see was regret – or mercy.

'We can talk,' he said evenly. 'For a little while. I don't think anyone will miss you or Roddy for a couple of hours – maybe not until morning. All the same, I'd rather not take any chances.' He grinned. 'Lady Luck hasn't exactly smiled on me lately.'

Calum stood. Behind him, out at sea, Rachel saw a flicker of light. A boat. Coming in this direction. The Stornoway coast-guard or the police? Seal and Shark? There was no way of knowing. In the meantime, she needed to keep his attention on her. Keep him talking.

'Why did you do it? Why take the risk? You have a life here.'

He gave her a rueful smile.

'When I worked for the Stock Exchange, every day was different. God, the thrill of playing with other people's money! Excitement is hard to give up when you thrive on it – so is wealth – and I was making a small fortune. You can't imagine how easy it is to spend. I needed more. So, I took risks

I shouldn't have – and lost a shitload of clients' money. My employers let me go; kind of embarrassing all round. And a problem when it came to getting another job. Then I thought of here. Mother was ill, needed help. No one, not even Mother – *particularly* not Mother – had to know I'd been fired.'

He was a cold, calculating bastard.

'If you knew how boring it gets here, you'd understand.' He tipped his head to the side. 'Or maybe not.'

'How do you think your mother will feel when she learns the truth about you?'

'That's not something I need to worry about.'

'What is that supposed to mean?'

She risked another glance over his shoulder. The boat had tied up and a figure was wading towards them. She needed to keep Calum's attention focused on her.

'She's dead.'

Rachel thought herself incapable of being more shocked. She was wrong. 'How did she die?'

'Let's just say I helped her on her way. It's what she wanted. You saw her; she was in so much pain. I can't stay here anymore and without me there would be no one to care for her.'

Rachel felt sick. 'You killed Ellen and Rufus, didn't you?'

'Is that the conclusion you've come to?' He sounded almost amused.

'It's the only one.'

She risked another quick glance over his shoulder. The figure had come ashore. Relief washed over her. It was a uniformed police officer – too tall for Selena, too slim for MacVicar. Fergus! She kept her face expressionless.

'I had to get rid of Rufus,' Calum said. 'The idiot was keeping some of the product to give to his friends. He gave some to that silly girl at a dance. He was going to lead the police – proper police – directly to us. It would have taken them no time to work out it was me behind it all. Much easier to fuck with the gas in his tank.'

'But killing him! He was barely more than a kid himself.'

Calum shrugged. 'Them's the chances you take when you get involved in this caper. He was being paid well enough to set him up for life if he'd stuck to the plan.'

'Did he know you were the boss? Did Seal? Shark?'

'Of course not. How long do you think my identity would have stayed a secret if they had?'

Fergus was creeping closer. She had to keep Calum focused on her. 'How did you communicate with them?'

'Texts to Seal from a burner phone, would you believe? I bought twenty of them the last time I was on the mainland. I use them once, then get rid of them. In case the police ever get hold of Seal's phone.'

'And Mike had nothing to do with any of this?'

Calum smiled again, but his eyes were as dark as the Wolf Sea he had told her about. 'Mike?' He snorted with laughter. 'You've got to be kidding. Mike hasn't the balls for this type of work. Unlike his wife. Michelle was happy to help. For a cut. I find most people will do pretty much anything for money.'

As he'd killed for money. Oh, the sheer banality of evil.

'Not most decent people. What about Ellen? Why kill her?' She raised her voice so Constable Campbell could hear.

'I didn't kill Ellen, as it happens.'

'I don't believe you,' Rachel said. But why would he lie, given he'd already admitted to Rufus and his mother?

'What about Katherine?' she pressed on. 'Did you kill her too?'

'God no! What kind of monster do you take me for? She's fine. I needed a distraction. I knew it was only a matter of time before you lot found your way to the Monachs again. We had one more drop arranged for tonight. It was going to be the last for a while, at least until things calmed down a bit. Seal and

Shark were to lift the stuff out at sea while I collected what we'd stored here. Between the police being on the island and the storm, I couldn't get it earlier. I wasn't going to abandon it either. It is – was – worth hundreds of thousands. Taking the girl and hiding her was the best way to keep the police occupied until I recovered my merchandise. She's in the well on Ellen's croft, where we hid the drugs some of the time. She'll be all right. A bit wet and sorry for herself, that's all.'

'Why put the drugs in a well on Ellen's croft?' Rachel continued, still playing for time. 'You must have known that was risky.'

'We only used the well to hide the drugs when we couldn't get on to the Monachs. That croft had been empty for years! We'd no idea the bloody woman had gone and bought it. Most of the merchandise we hide here. In the lighthouse in Shillay, as that idiot Roddy clearly discovered. I was on my way to fetch it when you called. Everyone was running around like headless chickens – looking for the girl, chasing the drop. It was my best chance. But then I saw Roddy heading out. I was just about to follow him when you arrived and insisted I had to take you. If only you'd missed me. You'd have been safely tucked up in bed. Everything would have been over by the time you woke.'

Fergus was no more than a few metres away, the wind disguising the sound of his movement. She had to continue to distract Calum long enough for the policeman to overpower him.

'You don't know everything,' she said.

Calum raised an eyebrow.

'Roddy's aunt and uncle know he was coming here and why. They also knew I was coming after him. If neither of us return they'll guess something's up and send someone. Plus I sent a text to Selena. Told her I was coming here with you. She'll come looking too.'

'But they think help is already on its way.'

'What do you mean?'

Fergus had stopped moving.

'My God, you think you have it all worked out.' Calum stepped forward and grabbed Rachel by the shoulders. 'Do you want to know who really killed Ellen?'

He spun her around.

Rachel used the movement to pull the knife from her pocket, while letting herself fall against him as if she had lost her footing. As he instinctively reached out to steady her, she raised her fist and, with all the strength she could muster, plunged the knife into the arm holding the gun.

He released her and the gun and staggered, staring at the blood running down his fingers in astonishment.

'Not quite the pushover I thought you'd be,' he spat.

Her diversion had worked. Fergus had scooped up Calum's gun and was aiming it at him. If he could keep Calum covered until the others arrived, it would all be over.

'Be careful, Fergus,' she called out. 'He's dangerous. He killed Roddy. And Rufus! Probably Ellen too.'

The police officer kept his rifle trained on Calum.

'What the hell do you think you're doing, Fergus?' Calum demanded. 'There's no time for arsing around. What took you so long anyway? We need to get the stuff and clear off.'

Rachel's stomach clenched as realisation hit.

'If you want to know who killed Ellen, ask him,' Calum continued, nodding in Fergus's direction. She watched in slack-jawed disbelief as Fergus took a stride towards Calum.

'Do you really think they'll believe I acted alone, Campbell?'

'Shut up!' Fergus shouted.

'Ellen wanted to come back here,' Calum continued. 'Fergus was unloading merch near her house and she came down to the shore to ask him if he'd take her. As soon as she saw what he was unloading, she knew. I don't know how.'

'She used to be a customs officer,' Rachel said, still trying to make sense of this latest turn of events.

'Why did you tell her about me?' Fergus said, indicating Rachel with a nod of his head. 'She didn't need to know. Now you've left me no choice.'

He fired twice and Calum fell backwards onto the ground. Before Rachel could move, Fergus swung the gun in her direction.

Rachel's head spun. Meek, mild Fergus: a murderer and a drug trafficker?

'I had no choice. As soon as she saw me, I realised the game was over. Thankfully, there was no one around. I did what I had to do, shoved her body in my boat and dumped her out at sea. It was bad luck she got dragged into the blow-hole. I'd assumed it would be much longer before her body washed up – if at all. Even then everything would have worked out fine if you hadn't come here with your damn questions.'

Rachel's skin crawled.

'What's going to happen now?'

'I'm truly sorry, Miss McKenzie, but they're going to find your body next to Roddy, and Calum's gun with Roddy's finger-prints on it. They're also going to find my boat wrecked with no sign of my body. I don't know what they'll think exactly, but hopefully they'll believe I came to grief while on the way to rescue you. If not...' He shrugged again. 'Too bad. I'll just have to make sure they never find me.'

Rachel squeezed her eyes shut. An image of her mother came into her head and she focused on it as she waited for the bullet to hit her. When nothing happened, she opened her eyes again. Maybe he couldn't bring himself to kill her in cold blood? But when she saw the darkness in his eyes, she knew he abso-lutely could.

'I'm not going to shoot you here, silly cow,' he said gently. 'I need everyone in the right place.' He prodded her with the barrel of his gun. 'Come on, we've wasted enough time.'

Fuck him! She stood her ground, tasting the salt of her tears. She refused to make it easy for him.

He studied her thoughtfully for a moment. 'OK, have it your own way.'

As he raised the gun again, from behind him, a figure stumbled from the darkness. It took all Rachel's willpower not to react. Roddy! She'd thought he was dead. He must have only been unconscious. She felt a surge of hope. Maybe now they had a chance. Roddy swayed on his feet before agonisingly slowly, he lifted his gun and steadied it against his shoulder. He and Rachel locked gazes for one, long moment. Then Roddy gestured with his free hand that she drop to the ground. Rachel threw herself down as a shot rang out. Then... silence. Tentatively, she raised her head. The police officer's face had all but disappeared. Rachel's stomach heaved and she was violently sick.

'Come on,' Roddy laid a hand on her shoulder. 'We have to get to my boat and radio for help.'

His shirt was covered in blood, his eyes glassy. She doubted he had the strength to make the boat. She crawled over to Calum and checked his pulse. Nothing.

Rachel staggered to her feet and put her arm around Roddy's waist, her fingers immediately becoming sticky with blood. 'Where are you hit?'

'My shoulder. It hurts like hell.'

Lean on me,' she told him. She had to find something to stop the bleeding. 'Do you have a first aid box on your boat?'

'In the wheelhouse.'

Helping Roddy to sit, Rachel stripped to her T-shirt and then took that off too, uncaring that the wind was like ice against her skin. She ripped her T-shirt into shreds and bandaged Roddy's shoulder as best she could. When she was done, Rachel inserted her shoulder under his again and, carrying her jumper and jacket in one hand, helped him hobble towards the boat. How long had they been here? The best part of an hour anyway. Would the tide be too high to allow them to wade back to the boat? Rachel sobbed with frustration when she saw that she was right. Far from shore, both boats bobbed in the path of the moon. Despair washed over her. There was no way she could swim and hold on to Roddy at the same time.

Roddy understood the situation at once. 'You can make it if you go now. Leave me here. You can come back for me when help comes.'

Rachel hesitated. She didn't know if she could make the boat even without the extra burden of Roddy. But if she didn't get help, Roddy would die. Of that she was certain. She was his only hope.

She led him over to a rock and propped him against it. She covered him with her jumper and jacket. 'Stay here and don't move. I don't want your wound to bleed any more than it has. As soon as I've radioed for help, I'll be back. I just need you to tell me...'

But Roddy was out cold. Rachel removed her sodden jeans and turned towards the sea.

FORTY

Selena phoned Dr Logan, explained that she'd found Dr Stuart dead and needed the GP to come. Sergeant MacVicar was in a chair in the sitting room, snoring gently. Selena's phone beeped and vibrated as emails and text messages flooded in. The telephone network must be functioning again.

She tried Rachel's number again, without success. The signal was rubbish. The networks didn't always go up at the same time. What was happening out there on the Monachs? Had Fergus got there in time? She had to hang on to that faint hope.

She turned to the emails. The one nearest the top was from Ellen's phone company with a copy of her records. She flicked through the most recent emails and texts. Nothing of interest. Acting on impulse, she checked the photos from Ellen's phone. At first her brain couldn't compute what she was seeing. Date-marked on the day Ellen had died, and clearly taken outside her house, was a photo of Fergus in plain clothes loading or unloading what looked like bricks wrapped in polythene. Selena realised what they were immediately. She'd seen similar photographs during her training.

It took only moments for it all to fall into place.

Thighearna's a Dhia! She'd sent him after Rachel. On his own.

Her fingers were trembling so much it took her several attempts to unlock her mobile. Du Toit's number was near the top of her recent calls. He answered immediately. The ferry had just docked in Lochmaddy. Selena took a deep breath, knowing she needed to explain the situation as quickly and as succinctly as she could.

'Rachel's in danger, sir. We need to get the hell out to the Monach Islands. Like now.'

As Dr Logan stepped into the room, Selena only paused to give MacVicar a sharp kick on the shins. Hopefully that would be enough to rouse him. The sergeant had to handle things here. She was needed elsewhere.

FORTY-ONE

TUESDAY

Rachel opened her eyes to find herself in a hospital bed with Selena by her side, watching her anxiously. Du Toit paced up and down near the door.

'Hey, you're awake,' Selena said softly. '*Thighearna's a Dhia*, girl, what have you been up to? Don't you know you could have been killed?'

'How did I get here?'

'We brought you back, don't you remember?'

Rachel shook her head, wincing as a wave of dizziness washed over her. She closed her eyes. Fragments came back like disjointed clips from a movie. Bodies on the ground. Calum chasing her. Fergus. Shots. Plunging into water – the black, swirling waves sucking her down. It had been so cold. Her desperation to get to the boat. Why...? Roddy! He'd needed her help.

'Roddy! Is he OK?'

'He will be. Thanks to you.'

She'd reached the boat, she remembered that now, but she'd been exhausted, tried to haul herself over the side and into the boat time after time but failing, thinking she was going to drown

– let everyone down. Until with a final effort – somehow – she'd managed. She'd lain there exhausted, catching her breath, knowing every minute counted.

'How did you know where to find us? I couldn't get anyone on the radio.' God, the despair when she couldn't get a response – realising she had to get back in the water with its treacherous current and to Roddy. She'd taken the first aid kit from the boat, jumped into the freezing water again, made it back to shore and Roddy. He'd been unconscious. She'd patched him up as best she could then put her arms around him, talked to him, telling him to hang on. After that... nothing.

'We picked you up on the radio,' Selena was saying. 'We could hear you, but you couldn't hear us. By the time we got to you, you were back on land, next to Roddy and pretty much out of it. You were hypothermic. You bloody well nearly died.'

'Fergus!' Rachel said. 'He shot Calum.' She clutched Selena's arm, using it to lever herself into a sitting position. It was as if her whole body was weighed down. 'I think they're both dead.'

Selena met Du Toit's eyes. He gave her a brief nod. She turned back to Rachel. 'I am sorry. There was nothing anyone could do. Are you up to telling us what happened?'

Rachel's head felt like it was going to explode. Two more dead. One by Roddy's hand. To protect her. It was her fault. She should have worked it all out sooner.

There was another urgent matter. 'Katherine! I know where she is! Calum put her in the well on Ellen's croft. He told me. He wanted to distract us so he had time to get away.'

'It's OK,' Selena soothed. 'We found her. She's shaken up, but fine.'

Relief flooded through Rachel. At least the girl was OK.

The blind on her window looking on to the corridor was partially open and she saw Chrissie, with a frail-looking Duncan, walk past.

What would happen to the old couple? It was ironic that now when, for the first time in as long as she could remember, she'd begun to feel she belonged somewhere, she might be about to destroy the lives of people who should be allowed to spend the time left to them in peace.

A nurse came into the room and lifted Rachel's wrist to take her pulse.

But getting to the truth was her job. One she had sworn to do to the best of her ability. She had a responsibility to the dead, no matter how much the living were hurt in the process. Everyone deserved the truth, regardless of how much pain it caused. Every victim, every death, had to be treated the same. That much she owed her mother. She glanced over to Du Toit. He was leaning against the wall, his arms folded.

Once the nurse had left, Du Toit pushed himself away from the wall and came to stand next to Rachel's bed. 'We know Fergus and Calum were running the drug ring together, but you still haven't explained what you were doing on the Monachs.'

Rachel took a few moments to sort her jumbled thoughts. 'Roddy was going there to dispose of his father's body. To get proof of the drugs being stashed there too. He found them in the lighthouse when he was hiding the bones. I thought the other divers might be heading there and that they might have Katherine. I couldn't get hold of Selena, so I drove to Kallin harbour to try and stop him. Calum was there in his boat. I was such a fool...'

When Du Toit still looked puzzled she realised they couldn't know about the Factor's murder. 'Roddy's mother – Chrissie and Duncan's sister – killed our John Doe: Dr Stuart's husband and the man Calum believed to be his father. He was Roddy's biological father, he raped Roddy's mother.' Because that's essentially what it was. Peggy couldn't have given consent. 'Roddy didn't know until Ellen found the bone and Chrissie and Duncan told him everything. By moving the bones, he was trying to protect the two people who cared for him all his life.' Rachel took another shuddering breath before continuing. 'I thought Roddy was our murderer, but he saved my life. Fergus was going to kill me.' She squeezed her eyes shut against the memory of cold, dark eyes. 'If Roddy hadn't shot him, I'd be dead. No doubt about it.' If needed, she'd hire the best defence lawyer in Scotland to prove it. Luckily, she knew just the man.

'Fergus killed Ellen because she saw him unloading drugs. Calum killed Rufus because he was stealing drugs for his personal use and had given some to Katherine. Calum thought Rufus was going to attract the attention of the police.'

She felt hollowed out. Her eyes were heavy. She couldn't keep them open any longer.

'You'll be happy to know we managed to waylay the crew that was making the drop, as well as Seal and Shark. But now, you need to rest.' Du Toit's voice was gentle. 'We can go over it all again later.' He squeezed her shoulder. 'You did a good job, McKenzie. You should be proud of yourself.'

As she gave in to the urge to close her eyes, Rachel wondered if her boss would share this view. She had a sinking feeling he would not.

EPILOGUE

TWO DAYS LATER

Rachel followed the narrow, rutted road as far as she could and climbed out of her car. There were no other vehicles in the small parking area, which was little more than moor trampled flat by hundreds of cars before her. Apart from a couple of red-suited scarecrows whose plastic jackets flapped in the afternoon breeze, and the twittering of a flock of sparrows, it was perfectly quiet.

Spread out in front of her was the sandy land she knew was machair. When she'd been to Uist as a child in the summer, it had been covered in wildflowers, a brilliant carpet of red, orange and yellow swaying in the wind. This time, apart from the odd buttercup, the land was bare.

She opened the passenger door and helped her grandfather out of the car. She was leaving on the afternoon plane, but knew she'd be back.

The cemetery was on a hill overlooking the sea and Rachel tucked her arm into her grandfather's, supporting him as they climbed to the highest point. It was hard to imagine the storm of a few days ago, bathed as the land was in golden light. A crow on a telegraph pole watched as they picked their way across the mounds of the recent, and not so recent, dead, pausing now and again to read the name and inscription on the stones.

Douglas was furious with her but was taking a no pro – no further proceedings – view on the historical murder. The most Chrissie and Duncan could have been charged with was helping to conceal a murder, and there was little appetite to take octogenarians to trial. Sergeant MacVicar had been suspended. The best he could hope for was to be retired on medical grounds. Seal and Shark would go to prison, hopefully for a very long time. Selena's exam results had come through. She'd passed, so she'd immediately applied to CID in Inverness.

'Here she is,' Ailean murmured, pointing to the grave of her grandmother.

Rachel had told him how, long after the memorial service, when her mother's body had been finally released, she'd had it cremated. How early one morning she'd hiked up the Cairngorm plateau and scattered her mother's ashes to the wind.

Rachel and her grandfather had agreed to buy a bench in Mary Ann's memory and to place it in the cemetery next to the low wall looking towards the sea. Maybe others would find comfort there. Rachel thought her mother would have approved.

In many ways she was sorry to leave, but she needed to get back to the office. And she wanted to check out this rumour her grandmother had mentioned about her mother being scared by something at work. Just out of curiosity.

The crow flapped its wings and soared into the air, circling and swooping above their heads, chattering and scolding – or maybe, Rachel thought wryly, expressing its approval. Justice – of sorts – had been done.

Rachel placed her fresh flowers next to Ailean Dubh's. She straightened, and together she and her grandfather looked out to sea. Then, without speaking, they turned. It was time to leave the dead behind and focus on the living.

A LETTER FROM THE AUTHOR

Huge thanks for reading *The Liar's Bones*, I hope you were hooked on Rachel's journey back to the Outer Hebrides and her quest to solve Ellen's murder. If you want to join other readers in hearing all about my new releases and bonus content, you can sign up for my newsletter!

www.stormpublishing.co/morag-pringle

If you enjoyed this book and could spare a few moments to leave a review that would be hugely appreciated. Even a short review can make all the difference in encouraging a reader to discover my book for the first time. Thank you so much!

As soon as I heard about the Death Unit – or the Scottish Fatalities Investigation Unit as it is more correctly known - I knew it would be the perfect setting for my heroine, Rachel McKenzie, a lawyer with a troubled past.

Although Rachel lives and works in Inverness, most of the book is set on the Uists, part of the Scottish Outer Hebrides, where my parents were born and raised. I spent many happy summer holidays there as a child.

In 1945 my grandfather had the somewhat madcap idea of resettling the Monachs, islands off the coast of North Uist. The family of six lived there for four years, with only the occasional visiting fishermen for company. Sometimes when my grandfather and two uncles would sail over to North Uist for provisions, bad weather would prevent them from returning and my mother, my aunt and my grandmother would be left to ride out the storm. This once again uninhabited island seemed an appropriate place for the book's finale.

My first job as an adult was in Uist, creating signposts and paths to some of its best known historic sites scattered across the islands. My victim is an amateur archaeologist with a passion for uncovering new sites.

Tragically several years ago, a visiting tourist disappeared without trace, leaving her shopping on the doorstep of her rental cottage. It begged the question; what happened to her? Why did she leave her shopping by the door? Her body was eventually found on the west coast of South Uist. Her disappearance and the questions it provoked were the main inspiration for this story.

The Western Isles are beautiful, but they are remote. Storms can lash the coast, and with few trees to act as a barrier, winds can reach speeds rarely seen on the mainland. The storm of 2005 was particularly terrifying. Five members of a local, well-loved family lost their lives and I'd like to dedicate this book to them.

Thanks again for being part of this amazing journey with me and I hope you'll stay in touch – I have many more stories and ideas to entertain you with!

Morag Pringle

ACKNOWLEDGEMENTS

I am blown away at how generous (and patient) people are with their time.

In particular, I would like to thank my first readers and all round support team: Sigi Goolden, Lisa Clifford, Karen Reynolds, Kathryn Hadley-Mackenzie, Orna O'Reilly Webber, Stewart Pringle and Flora Van Kleef.

Those who gave generously of their time and knowledge: Eric Hunter, Katy Hunter, Paul Duffy and Duncan Maclauchlan. (All errors are mine!)

To Sasha Green for directing me to Storm Publishing.

And to my brilliant editor, Emily Gowers, and the rest of the fantastic team at Storm.

Printed in Great Britain
by Amazon

54284935R00192